THE LAST GUNFIGHTER:
SAVAGE COUNTRY

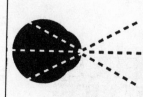

WILLIAM W. JOHNSTONE

THE LAST GUNFIGHTER: SAVAGE COUNTRY

WHEELER
PUBLISHING

Published in 2006 by arrangement with Pinnacle Books, an imprint of Kensington Publishing Corp.

Wheeler Large Print Western.

The text of this Large Print edition is unabridged.
Other aspects of the book may vary from the original edition.

Set in 16 pt. Plantin.

Printed in the United States on permanent paper.

Library of Congress Cataloging-in-Publication Data

Johnstone, William W.
    The last gunfighter. Savage country / by William W. Johnstone.
        p.   cm. — (Wheeler Publishing large print western)
    ISBN 1-59722-273-9 (lg. print : sc : alk. paper)
    1. Morgan, Frank (Fictitious character) — Fiction.   2. Outlaws
— Fiction.   3. Fathers and sons — Fiction.   4. Large type books.
I. Title.   II. Title: Savage country.   III. Series: Wheeler large print
western series.
PS3560.O415L35545 2006
    813'.54—dc22   2006009827

THE LAST GUNFIGHTER
SAVAGE COUNTRY

Chapter 1

Frank Morgan heard laughter as he strode into the lobby of the Grand Central Hotel in El Paso, Texas. Ugly laughter, the sort that made the hair on the back of his neck stand up. It came from the barroom to his right.

Frank ignored the sound as best he could, and continued on across the lobby toward the desk. Whatever was going on in the hotel bar, it was none of his affair. He had come to El Paso on business of his own.

The clerk at the desk greeted Frank by saying, "Yes, sir, may I help you?" His manner was polite, even though Frank was dressed in worn range clothes that still carried the dust of the trail and had a pair of saddlebags slung over his left shoulder. In a bustling frontier city like El Paso, a man who looked like that might be a saddle tramp with barely a penny to his name — or he might be an important businessman with

7

millions of dollars in the bank.

As a matter of fact, Frank came closer to fitting the second description, although he wasn't sure if his business interests were actually worth a million dollars or not. He left such details to his lawyers in Denver and San Francisco. But he wasn't hurting for money, that much was certain.

He rested his left hand on the desk and said, "You should have a reservation for me. Name's Frank Morgan."

The clerk's eyes widened a little as they went to the Colt .45 Peacemaker with walnut grips holstered on Frank's right hip. He knew the name, all right. More than likely, he had seen it in some of the dime novels that had been written about the man known as The Drifter. Most of them were unmitigated trash made up by Eastern scribblers, but they contained enough kernels of truth so that Frank's reputation as a gunfighter had spread far and wide.

"Yes, sir, Mr. Morgan," the clerk said hastily. "We have your room all ready for you, one of the finest in the hotel. If you'll just sign in . . ."

Another burst of laughter came from the nearby barroom as the clerk turned the book around for Frank to sign. Frank glanced in that direction, then picked up the pen from

8

the inkwell and signed his name. He left the space for his home address blank. It had been a long time since he'd had one of those that meant anything.

He had spent the past few months in South Texas, far down the valley of the Rio Grande, waiting there for winter to be over and enjoying the company of an intelligent, attractive woman at the same time. As pleasant as that interval had been, with the coming of spring he had begun to grow restless, and the arrival of a telegram from Conrad Browning asking Frank to meet him in El Paso had been all he needed to prompt him to move on. He had put some supplies on a packhorse, kissed a regretful Roanne Williamson good-bye, and ridden northwest on Stormy, the big Appaloosa, trailed by the big cur known only as Dog.

"Thank you, Mr. Morgan," the clerk said. "If you have a buggy or some other vehicle you'd like to put in our barn . . . ."

"Nope, just a saddle mount and a packhorse, and I already left them at a livery stable down the street, along with my dog. Fella named Gomez runs it, I think."

"Oh, yes," the clerk said. "Pablo Gomez. A good man. He'll take good care of your animals."

"That's what I thought from the looks of

9

the place," Frank said. He frowned as laughter exploded again in the bar. "What's going on in there?"

The clerk shook his head. "I'm afraid I wouldn't know, sir."

Frank shrugged, telling himself again that it was none of his business. The clerk plucked a key off a rack on the wall behind the desk and started to give it to Frank. Another moment and Frank would have taken the key, gone up to his room, and forgotten all about the hyenas in the barroom.

If only a voice hadn't suddenly called out desperately, painfully, "No! Please, don't! Please . . ."

Frank's face hardened. Somebody was in trouble in there, and whether it was any of his business or not, he wasn't the sort of man to turn his back on folks who needed help.

"Hang onto that key," he said to the clerk. "I'll be back in a minute or two."

A couple of lithe steps brought him to the arched entrance of the barroom. Although it was the afternoon of a bright spring day outside, the windowless barroom was shadowy, lit only by a couple of oil lamps in the form of chandeliers. The L-shaped bar was to Frank's left, with tables in front of him and booths along the wall to his right. A nervous-looking bartender stood behind the bar.

10

There were only three other men in the place. Two of them had the third man bent backward over the table in one of the booths. One of them had a hand planted in the middle of the third man's chest, holding him down, while a bowie knife glinted in the other hand.

"I'll hold him while you take his pants off," the knife-wielder said to his companion. "I bet he'll sing real pretty once we carve on him some."

Frank glanced at the bartender. "Aren't you going to do something about this?"

Beads of sweat glistened on the man's high forehead. "Reckon I ought to go for the law?"

"Likely it'll be too late by the time they got here," Frank said.

"You don't know those Callahan b-boys," the bartender stammered in a half whisper. "They're c-crazy!"

Frank might not know the Callahans, but he had a feeling he was about to make their acquaintance. He stepped closer to the booth where the two men were tormenting the third one and said sharply, "Hey!"

One of the Callahans had the hapless prisoner's trousers halfway off. He stopped what he was doing and straightened, turning toward Frank. The one with the knife kept the

11

man pinned down, but he turned to look over his shoulder at Frank.

"Move on, mister," he growled. "This ain't got nothin' to do with you."

"Yeah!" the other one said. "Get the hell outta here, if you know what's good for you!"

They were cut from the same cloth, with coarse, beard-stubbled, ratlike features. More than that, there was a family resemblance, and Frank felt confident they were brothers. The one with the knife appeared to be a little older.

A faint smile touched the grim line that was Frank's mouth. "That's the problem," he said. "I've always had a hard time doing what was good for me."

"Well, you better do it now," the one with the knife threatened, "or we'll slice off your *cojones* too!"

"What about him?" Frank asked in a deceptively mild tone as he nodded toward the man bent over the table. "What did he do to make you want to mutilate him?"

"Do? He didn't *do* anything! He was just here."

"So you decided to torture and probably kill a man simply for the fun of it?"

"Why the hell not?" the younger Callahan brother demanded. "If you're mean enough and strong enough, you can do anything you want in this world, and there ain't nobody meaner and stronger than us!"

"That's where you're wrong," Frank said.

"You bastard! I'll learn you—" The younger brother's hand dived toward the gun on his hip.

Frank waited until the man's hand had closed around the butt of the revolver before he drew and fired in one smooth motion that was almost too fast for the eye to see. The Peacemaker bucked against his palm as it drove its leaden messenger of death deep into the man's chest. The impact threw him back against the partition between booths. He bounced off and let go of his half-drawn gun. It slipped out of the holster and thudded to the floor. The mortally wounded man pressed a hand to his chest. Blood welled between his fingers, but not much. His heart had already been stilled by Frank's bullet.

"Simon!" the man croaked. Then he fell to his knees and pitched forward on his face. His legs kicked a couple of times before he lay still.

The man with the knife hadn't moved. His name was Simon, Frank guessed. He stared at Frank, who still held the Colt level and steady, for a few seconds before he asked,

"Who in blazes are you, mister? I never saw a draw like that before."

"Name's Frank Morgan."

"The Drifter?"

"Some call me that," Frank admitted.

Simon Callahan swallowed hard. "I ain't gonna draw on you, Morgan. I wouldn't have a chance. No more than my brother Jud did."

"Put the knife away and let that man up, and there won't be a need for any more shooting."

"Yeah. Yeah, sure." Callahan took a step back away from the table. He slid the bowie into a beaded sheath on his left hip. "You didn't have to kill him. He wasn't near as fast as you."

"Fast enough so that there was no time to get fancy," Frank said. He motioned with the barrel of the Peacemaker. "Take his body and get out."

Callahan bent to hoist his brother's limp form. He got his arms under his brother's arms from behind and began dragging the corpse toward the lobby of the hotel. Jud's boot heels made scraping sounds on the floor.

"This ain't over," Simon Callahan said. "I ain't about to forget this, Morgan."

"Your choice," Frank said. "But the smart

thing to do would be to bury your brother and ride on out of El Paso."

Simon's face contorted in a grimace of hatred. "Reckon I have a hard time doin' what's good for me too."

With that, he dragged his brother's body out of the Grand Central Hotel, past the horrified gaze of the desk clerk and a couple of other people who had come into the lobby.

Frank holstered his gun and turned toward the man who had been the object of the Callahan brothers' cruelty. He had straightened up and was trying to pull his clothes back into a semblance of order. He was thin and well dressed, from the look of him a gambler maybe. El Paso had plenty of them.

"Thank you," the man said as he picked up a black hat that had fallen off and settled it on his sleek black hair. "I . . . I think those lunatics would have killed me if you hadn't come along to stop them, Mr. . . . Morgan, was it?"

"That's right."

The man held out a hand with long, slender fingers, another sign of a man who made his living with the pasteboards. "Jonas Wade."

Frank shook with him. "Was that really all

15

there was to it, just sheer meanness on their part?"

"I assure you it was. I was just sitting there, playing solitaire" — Jonas motioned to a nearby table where a deck of cards was already laid out in a hand of solitaire — "when they came in and looked around and then set upon me, taunting me and trying to goad me into fighting with them. When I refused, they . . . they said I was a coward and that I didn't have any need for my . . . for my . . ." A shudder ran through him as he contemplated what the Callahan brothers had been planning to do to him.

"Well, it's over now," Frank said. "I don't reckon the one that's left will bother you again."

"Maybe not, but I don't intend to give him a chance." Jonas smiled ruefully. "I believe I'll fold my tent and steal away like an Arab in the night. My stay in El Paso has been profitable, but let's face it — there are other places where a man can play cards."

Frank couldn't argue with that. He gave Jonas a nod as the gambler gathered up his cards and left the barroom. Frank couldn't quite comprehend just yelling for help and not fighting back when threatened with trouble, but he supposed some folks were like that. He was glad he had stepped in to help

Jonas, whether the gambler had really deserved it or not.

His contempt was reserved more for the bartender who had stood by, apparently intending to do nothing while the Callahans had their sadistic fun. He turned toward the man and asked scathingly, "What the hell's wrong with you, mister? Don't you have a shotgun or at least a bung-starter under the bar in case of trouble?"

The bartender took out a bandanna and mopped his damp forehead. "We don't have trouble in here," he said defensively. "This is a civilized place."

"Better stop letting folks come in then. Human beings aren't naturally civilized. Sometimes they have to have it forced on them."

The clerk had come out from behind his desk and now stood in the arched opening between the lobby and the barroom. He said, "I'm sorry for the disturbance, Mr. Morgan. Thank you for stepping in when you did. Otherwise, things might have gotten, well, awful."

Frank nodded. "Sorry about the blood on the floor."

"It could have been a lot worse."

"I reckon I'll take that key now."

"Of course. If you'll come with me . . ."

Frank followed the clerk to the desk. Once again the clerk took a key from the rack, and once again he was about to hand it to Frank when he was interrupted, this time by one of the men who had come into the lobby while Simon Callahan was dragging out the body of his brother.

"Well, I see that some things never change," the man said from behind Frank.

The voice was familiar. Frank turned slowly and found himself looking into the eyes of Conrad Browning, the man who had asked him to come here to El Paso.

Conrad Browning . . . who was also Frank Morgan's son.

Chapter 2

A smile spread slowly across Frank's face. "Conrad," he said. "It's been a while. You've changed."

"You haven't," Conrad snapped.

Frank shrugged. "I reckon I'm a little older, a little grayer. But you . . . you're a grown man now."

It had been several years since Frank had seen the son he hadn't even known that he had for most of Conrad's life. He had missed out on so much, just as he hadn't been able to be a part of Victoria Monfore's life while she was growing up. At least he knew for sure that Conrad was his son, while there was still a little uncertainty as to whether or not Victoria was his daughter.

The last time Frank had seen Conrad hadn't been under the best of circumstances. Conrad had been a youngster then, with one year of college behind him. He had been kidnapped, not once but twice, by a gang of vicious outlaws led by Ned Pine and Victor Vanbergen. The same bunch of desperadoes had been responsible for the death of Vivian Browning, Frank's former wife and Conrad's mother. Frank had been able to rescue Conrad and wipe out most of the gang. Pine and Vanbergen were both dead, although ironically not by Frank's hand. Conrad had gone east to finish his education at Harvard and to tend to the wide-ranging business interests inherited from his mother, the same business interests that had made Frank Morgan a rich man because Vivian had left a percentage to him too.

Frank hadn't seen Conrad since that time, and they had been in touch only sporadically. Nearly everything was handled by Frank's lawyers and the attorneys who worked for Conrad. To put it bluntly, Conrad didn't like Frank and a part of him still blamed The Drifter for his mother's death. Conrad regarded as his real father the man Vivian married after her short-lived marriage to Frank had been annulled by her father.

Frank wished that things were different between him and Conrad, but wishing never brought a man much. Conrad had chosen to go his own way, and Frank had had no choice but to let him.

Now they were face-to-face again, and it was Conrad's doing. That had to give Frank at least a little hope for a reconciliation.

Conrad had filled out some. He wasn't a college boy anymore, but rather a young man in the prime of life, wearing an expensive suit and a fine hat. He had even cultivated a closely clipped mustache. He wore his sandy hair long, over his ears. Frank supposed that was not only to be fashionable, but also to cover up Conrad's disfigured left ear, the top of which had been cruelly sliced off by one of the outlaws while he was their prisoner.

"I need to talk to you," he said coolly to Frank. He gestured toward the barroom and went on. "Why don't we go in there? I'm sure the smell of freshly burned gunpowder won't bother you."

Frank's jaw tightened a little. That last comment hadn't been necessary. It was starting to look as if Conrad wasn't interested in being friends, let alone having a real father-and-son relationship with Frank after all.

If that was the case, then so be it. Frank said, "Sure. I'll buy you a drink."

They went into the barroom and sat down at a table well away from the spot where Jud Callahan had died. Without asking what

21

Conrad wanted, Frank called over to the bartender to bring them each a beer.

"Excuse me," Conrad said. "I'd rather have a cognac. With water on the side."

Frank shrugged. He didn't care what Conrad drank. "Your letter caught up to me while I was down in South Texas," he said. "I'm glad I was able to get out here to El Paso while you're still here."

"I would have waited for you as long as I possibly could. It's very important that we talk."

Frank nodded. "I agree."

"A lot of money is riding on it."

Money . . . but Conrad's impersonal tone made it clear that nothing else was involved here. This meeting was just business. That was all.

The bartender brought over their drinks. He still looked a little pale and shaken. Frank picked up the mug, sipped the beer, and said to Conrad, "Tell me about it. What brings you to El Paso?"

"I came to talk to you, of course." Conrad took an appreciative sip of his cognac. "This is the closest large city to Ophir . . . although compared to Boston, it's hardly a city at all, of course."

Frank's eyes narrowed. "What's Ophir?"

"I'm getting ahead of myself," Conrad

said with a little shake of his head. "Perhaps I'd better start at the beginning."

"That's always a good place," Frank murmured.

"Since my graduation from Harvard I've taken a more active hand in the running of our businesses. I trust you've been getting regular reports from your attorneys?"

Frank nodded. "When I stay in one place long enough for them to catch up to me."

"Then you've seen for yourself that the various companies are doing quite well and turning a healthy profit."

"You've done a good job. I'm sure your mother would be very proud of you."

Frank saw Conrad's fingers tighten on the glass and supposed he shouldn't have mentioned Vivian. That just dredged up bad memories and piled them on the table between them.

"Yes, well, you may not be aware that we've recently purchased a railroad."

Frank's eyebrows went up. "No, I don't recollect seeing anything about that."

"The New Mexico, Rio Grande, and Oriental line. We're building a spur route from Lordsburg up to Ophir, in southwestern New Mexico Territory."

"So Ophir is a town. I hadn't heard of it."

"A boomtown actually. It hasn't been

there very long. It sprang up because of the gold and copper and silver deposits in the area. There are quite a few lucrative mines near there in the Mogollon and Mimbres Mountains."

Frank nodded. He was familiar with the area, although it had been a long time since he'd passed through those parts.

"Browning Mines and Manufacturing owns several of those mines," Conrad went on with a note of pride in his voice. "I expect that they will make us richer than we already are. As will the railroad too, of course . . . if it gets built."

That last bit sounded a little ominous to Frank. "Having trouble with the railroad?" he asked.

Conrad got a pained look on his face. "The railroad has been nothing but trouble, right from the start. We've run into numerous delays. Some trouble is to be expected, of course, in an undertaking as major as the construction of a rail line, but I'm not just talking about bad weather and construction difficulties. According to the superintendent, there have been numerous instances of deliberate destruction. On top of that, one of our payroll shipments was stolen, and the workers threatened to quit unless they received a bonus to compensate them for their pay being late. To make matters worse, they've also been threatened by some of the local savages."

"Indian trouble?" Frank asked with a frown. "It's been a while since I've heard about any of that. Old Victorio was killed more than ten years ago down in Mexico, and Geronimo and his warriors are on the White Mountain Reservation, living in peace for a change."

"Not all of them evidently. From what I've been told, the marauders are definitely Apaches."

Frank drank some more of his beer and mulled that over. While supposedly all the young men had surrendered to the U.S. Army along with Geronimo several years earlier, it was possible that a few bands of renegades were still hiding out in the mountains. There had always been rumors of such things, and they were aggravated every time any horses went missing from some isolated rancho.

"It sounds like you have trouble, all right," Frank said after a moment.

"*We* have trouble," Conrad corrected him. "Although your percentage is relatively small, you own part of these businesses too."

"I let other folks handle that," Frank said with a shrug. "Folks who know what they're doing when it comes to that sort of thing."

"Who knows more than the famous Drifter about handling trouble?"

There was a slight sneer in Conrad's voice as he asked the rhetorical question. Frank felt anger flare inside him. From the sound of things, Conrad was getting around to asking for his help, but yet the young man couldn't keep from expressing, at least a little, his disapproval of his father. Maybe what Frank ought to do, he thought, was tell Conrad to stomp his own snakes.

But before Frank could do or say anything, a heavy footstep sounded in the entrance to the barroom. Frank glanced in that direction and saw a bulky man in a dusty black suit coming into the room. Light from the oil lamps reflected on the tin star pinned to his lapel. He spotted Frank and Conrad sitting at the table and came toward them with a determined look on his dark-complected face.

"Frank Morgan?" he said as he came up to the table.

Frank nodded. "That's me."

"I hear tell you killed a man in here a while ago."

"That's right. He drew first, or at least he tried to."

The lawman snorted. "Hell, you're The Drifter! Anytime you draw against anybody, it's the same thing as murder in my book."

"Then it's a good thing for me your book isn't the same as the law," Frank said.

The man glared at him. "I'm the constable hereabouts, name of John Selman. I'd arrest you if I could, Morgan, but since I can't, I'll just say I want you out of El Paso."

"A warning like that usually comes from the sheriff or the city marshal," Frank pointed out. "I don't see them here."

"My say-so's good enough," Selman blustered. "Better get on your horse and ride."

Frank had heard of John Selman, although their trails had never crossed before. The man had a long reputation as a shootist and a shady character operating on both sides of the law. Frank considered it a minor miracle that someone like Selman had evidently been legally elected to a law enforcement position, but he supposed that was the prerogative of the citizens of El Paso.

"I won't be in town for long," Frank said. "I have business elsewhere."

"Well, see that you don't linger. The law can't guarantee your safety from Simon Callahan. You killed his brother, and he's liable to come after you to settle the score."

"And you wouldn't lose any sleep over it if Callahan was successful in that, would you, Constable?"

"Not a damn bit," Selman growled. "I hate all you famous gun-throwers. Somebody ought to shoot the whole lot of you."

"But it won't be you, will it, Selman? Not unless they all turn their backs on you."

Frank knew it was a harsh thing to say, but he felt a deep, abiding, instinctive dislike for John Selman. The man just had the look of a backshooter about him.

Selman's face turned pale with rage, but he was able to contain his anger. "I've had my say," he snapped. "If you stay in El Paso, then whatever happens is on your head, Morgan."

Frank didn't say anything. After a minute, the fuming Selman turned and stalked out of the barroom. His boot heels rang on the lobby floor as he crossed to the hotel entrance and slammed out.

"I see you make friends just as easily as ever," Conrad commented dryly.

"I'm not interested in being friends with a polecat like Selman." Frank drained the last of his beer and set the empty mug aside. "Now, Conrad, you were talking about all the trouble you're having getting this railroad spur to Ophir built."

"Yes, and I was wondering. . . ." Conrad paused and drank the last of his cognac, chasing it with water from the glass at his side. He took a deep breath, obviously struggling with what he was trying to say. Finally, he blurted out, "I was wondering if you'd help."

"Help get that spur line through?" Frank asked, wanting to make sure there was no misunderstanding.

"That's right."

"I don't know a damn thing about building a railroad."

"I do," Conrad said confidently, "and so does my construction superintendent. What we need you to do is to find out who's responsible for all the problems plaguing us and put a stop to them."

"In whatever way is necessary?"

"In whatever way is necessary," Conrad said flatly. "The company has sunk a great deal of money into this project already. Not only that, but to make the most from our mining interests that we can, that railroad needs to go through. I wouldn't go so far as to say that our financial survival depends on this, but it *is* important, Frank. Very important."

Although he hated to admit it even to himself, there was a part of Frank that wanted to tell Conrad to go straddle a stump. The boy had made it plain, not only today but in all their previous encounters, that he didn't like

Frank, didn't think of him as a father, and just flat didn't have much use for him.

But that had changed now, at least the part about not having any use for him. *Now* Conrad needed him. But not as a father. No, not that.

He needed Frank Morgan's skill as a gunfighter.

Walk away, Frank told himself. Stand up, walk out of here, and don't look back. The boy had wanted to stand on his own two feet. Now let him.

And yet, Conrad didn't know how to handle a situation like this. He had no idea what he was facing. If Frank refused him, he would have to hire some other troubleshooter, somebody who might not be as honest or as capable as Frank was.

"All right," Frank said, "I'll do it. . . ."

A look of relief began to appear on Conrad's face.

"For a hundred dollars a month and expenses," Frank finished.

"What?" Conrad asked, a startled frown on his face.

"A hundred a month and expenses," Frank repeated. "Those are fighting wages. At least, they used to be the last time I took a job like this."

Conrad stared across the table at him.

"Let me get this straight. . . . You want me to hire you?"

"Seems fair," Frank said with a shrug. "Since we're just talking business and all."

"But . . . you own part of the company!"

"You'll be paying me with company funds, so I reckon I'll be footing part of the bill for my own wages. You don't hear me complaining about that."

"This is insane! You're my—" Conrad stopped short. Understanding dawned in his eyes. "Oh. This is your way of getting back at me for not calling you Daddy."

"I've told you my terms," Frank said. "Take 'em or leave 'em."

Conrad glared at him for a moment before a resigned look came over his face. "I'll take them," he said.

Frank held out his hand. Conrad hesitated for a second, and then the two men shook on it.

Chapter 3

Since it was too late in the afternoon to get very far, they made arrangements to leave El Paso the next day. That would give Frank a chance to stock up on supplies too.

"You have a saddle horse?" he asked his son.

Conrad shook his head. "No, I arrived here on the train, and I haven't had need of a horse."

"You need one now," Frank said. "I'll see about getting you a good mount."

"We could take the train to Lordsburg," Conrad suggested.

"No, I'd rather ride. Stormy doesn't cotton much to being cooped up in a train car, and neither does Dog."

For that matter, Frank didn't care much for it either. He preferred being out in the open air. It would take several days longer that way, of course, but the ride would be a pleasant one in the mild spring weather.

And maybe he was just being a little contrary, he told himself, as well as curious. He wanted to get Conrad on the back of a horse and see how the boy handled himself.

Conrad was also staying at the Grand Central Hotel. Built by former Army officer and El Paso businessman Anson Mills, it was the finest hotel in the city, quite possibly the finest between San Antonio and Los Angeles. Frank thought they might have dinner together in the Grand Central's dining room, but Conrad begged off.

"If we're going to be traveling all the way to Ophir on horseback, I need my rest," he said. "I believe I'll take dinner in my room and retire early."

"Suit yourself," Frank said with a shrug. "Just be ready to ride first thing in the morning."

"If you insist."

Frank's lips tightened, but he didn't say anything. He went up to his own room, dropped off his saddlebags, and then walked down the street to Gomez's Livery, where he had left Stormy and Dog.

Pablo Gomez was a wiry little Mexican with sweeping white mustaches and a knowing way with a horse. Even Stormy seemed to like him, and the Appaloosa was pretty much a one-man horse. Frank saw that Stormy had been placed in a roomy stall with clean straw and had been curried and combed as well. Dog appeared content too, lying in the entrance of the livery barn with his tongue lolling out.

Frank rubbed the thick fur around the big wolflike creature's neck, then said to Gomez, "I need to buy another saddle horse."

"Why, Señor?" the little stableman asked. "You will not find one anywhere that is better than the horse you rode in here."

"I know, but this is for somebody else. A . . . business associate."

Frank didn't know if Conrad had mentioned their relationship to anyone in El Paso. It might be better to keep that quiet. More than once in the past, trouble had descended on Conrad's head simply because he was the son of Frank Morgan. It wasn't fair, but it was a fact and had to be dealt with.

"This man, is he a good rider?" asked Gomez.

Frank remembered seeing Conrad dressed up in a fancy English riding outfit, sitting an odd-looking little saddle that didn't even have a horn on it. He had wondered at the time how in the hell a fella was supposed to take a dally with a saddle like that, in case he needed to dab a loop on something. He supposed that gents who used such saddles didn't do much lasso work.

Despite those trappings, though, Conrad had stayed on the back of his horse just fine. He'd had plenty of practice back in Boston. So Frank nodded and said to Gomez, "He can ride."

The Mexican crooked a finger and led Frank out to the corral behind the barn. "That one," he said, pointing to a fine-looking black horse mingling with the other horses in the corral.

Frank let out a little whistle of admiration.

"His name is El Diablo," Gomez went on. "He has plenty of speed and stamina, what you Texans call sand. You can ride him all day and he will not tire."

Frank sensed that something wasn't quite right, despite what Gomez said. A horse that impressive, with all the good qualities Gomez listed, ought to cost a pretty penny. "How much?" he asked.

"For you, Señor . . . with saddle and tack thrown in . . . two hundred American dollars."

"I expected you to say at least five hundred," Frank said with a frown.

Gomez shrugged eloquently. "El Diablo was born and bred to be a racehorse. He is fast enough. But when you put him on a track with other horses . . . they run away from him. He is happy to run behind them, no matter how hard his rider whips him. He has not the . . . the fire in the belly, Señor. So his owner, in disgust, brings him to me and says, 'Gomez, sell this horse for me. I do not care how much you get for him, just sell him fast, so I can forget about what a disappointment he is to me, what a dagger in my heart it is to see him running behind horses he could easily defeat.'"

The little stable man sighed and shook his head dramatically.

"So that's the story, is it?" Frank asked.

"*Sí, Señor.* As a horse to ride, El Diablo will do very well for your friend. It is only as a racehorse that he is unsuited."

"Let me take a closer look at him."

"Of course, Señor."

Gomez opened the gate and let Frank into the corral. For the next few minutes, Frank checked over the animal with an experienced horseman's eye. Everything about El Diablo indicated that he was indeed a fine horse. The fact that he didn't have a competitive nature couldn't be held against him.

"All right," Frank said with a nod. "I'll take him."

"Your associate will not be disappointed, Señor."

Frank thought that he wouldn't count on that. Conrad didn't like much of anything about the West. Frank wouldn't be surprised if he didn't care for El Diablo either.

From the livery stable, he went to Holtzmann's Mercantile and gave the clerk an order for enough food, supplies, and ammunition to last him and Conrad until they got to Lordsburg. They could resupply there for the rest of the journey to Ophir. The clerk promised that everything would be delivered to Gomez's early the next morning.

With that taken care of, there was nothing left for Frank to do except return to the Grand Central, eat dinner alone in the dining room, and make an early evening of it. El Paso had plenty of saloons, of course, and he could have gone out for a drink, but while he enjoyed an occasional beer or glass of whiskey, booze didn't hold much appeal for him, and neither did sitting around a smoky saloon.

So after his dinner he went up to his room, took a book from his saddlebags — a volume of stories by Bret Harte — and stretched out on the bed to read by the light of the lamp on the night table. A smile touched his mouth as he opened the book.

He wondered what all those folks who had thrilled to his dime-novel exploits would think if they could see him now, leading the dangerous, glamorous life of a gunfighter . . . reading a book in a hotel room.

Frank was up before dawn the next morning. Despite the fact that spring had come, at this hour there was a lingering chill in the air from the night before as he walked to the livery stable. Pablo Gomez and his sons, who worked for him as hostlers, were already up and about, of course. The supplies from Holtzmann's store had been delivered, and Gomez was lashing them to the packhorse when Frank came in.

"*Buenos dias,* Señor Morgan," the liveryman greeted him. "We will have your Stormy and El Diablo saddled soon and ready for you and your friend."

"*Gracias,* Señor Gomez," Frank said. "It was a quiet night?"

"Very much so," Gomez replied with a smile.

"I'll be back in a while, after my associate and I have had breakfast."

"All will be in readiness, Señor. On this you have the word of Pablo Gomez."

"Good enough for me," Frank assured him with a grin.

When he got back to the hotel, Frank looked in the dining room but didn't see

Conrad. He knew the young man's room number; Conrad's room, in fact, was just down the hall from Frank's. So he went upstairs and banged a fist on the door.

"Wha . . . who the hell . . . ?" Conrad's voice came sleepily from the other side of the panel.

"Time to get up," Frank said cheerfully. "We've got a long way to go, so we need to get ridin'."

Conrad's only answer was a groan. Then, after a moment, he said, "I'll be downstairs. Just give me a few minutes."

"Don't take too long. We're burning daylight."

"Daylight?" Conrad muttered, the word barely audible through the door. "The damn sun's not even up yet!"

Smiling, Frank went downstairs to the dining room and ordered breakfast for both of them. The food was on the table and Frank was halfway through his first cup of coffee by the time Conrad entered the dining room. The young man's eyes were bleary with sleepiness.

"This is an ungodly hour for anyone to be up," Conrad complained as he sat down across from Frank.

"Drink some coffee and get yourself on the outside of some flapjacks and bacon and eggs," Frank suggested. "You'll feel a lot better then."

"I wouldn't count on it."

Despite what he said, Conrad seemed to have a hearty appetite. He dug into the food and almost matched the amount that Frank put away. The coffee was strong and black, and that helped too. By the time they were finished, Conrad looked like he felt halfway human again.

Frank leaned back in his chair to sip the last of the coffee in his cup. "You'd better go back upstairs and change clothes," he said.

Conrad glanced down at the suit and vest and tie he had on. "What's wrong with what I'm wearing?"

"I suppose it's fine if you're going to be talking to a banker or a politician, but it's not very good for riding." Frank leaned a little to the side so he could look down at Conrad's feet. "You'll want to put on some boots too, instead of those shoes."

"What if I don't have any?"

"Then we'll go over to Holtzmann's and buy you whatever you need."

"I have boots," Conrad said with a sigh. "I'm just not accustomed to dressing like a . . . a ranch hand."

"Better get used to it." He paused. "Do you have a gun?"

"Do I need one?"

"You might," Frank said. "Out here, it's better to be ready for trouble."

"Yes, I recall how it seems to follow you around."

Frank suppressed the urge to point out that Conrad's trouble was the reason they were going to Ophir. Those sarcastic comments were liable to get mighty tiresome before they got there, though.

"You didn't answer me about the gun," Frank reminded his son.

"I have one," Conrad admitted.

"How about a holster?"

Conrad nodded. "I remember what it's like here on the frontier. I thought it prudent to be prepared."

"Good. After you've changed clothes, strap on that gun belt too. I reckon you didn't bring a long gun?"

"You mean a rifle?" Conrad shook his head. "That didn't occur to me."

"That's all right, I bought a Winchester for you at Holtzmann's. It'll be at the livery with the rest of our gear."

"So I'm to be decked out as a gunfighter as well."

Frank smiled grimly. No matter what sort of clothes Conrad wore, or how many guns he carried, Frank doubted that anybody

41

would ever take him for a gunfighter.

"Let's get started. I reckon you've got some luggage."

"Of course."

"Make arrangements to leave it here at the hotel until you get back from Ophir. You won't need anything except the clothes on your back and your gun."

"Not even a change of clothes?" Conrad looked like he could barely comprehend that idea.

"All right, one change of clothes," Frank said. "Everything else we'll need is already on the packhorse." He stood up. "I'll head back over to the stable. Join me there as soon as you can."

Conrad nodded. Frank stopped at the desk in the lobby to tell the clerk to add what he owed onto Conrad's bill — that was one of those expenses Conrad was supposed to take care of — and then left the Grand Central.

The sun was up now, but it was still low on the horizon to the east. El Paso was starting to come alive for another day. Already there were quite a few people on the streets.

Frank had a long-standing habit of being cautious, of course. That was the only way he had stayed alive so long. His eyes were always moving, checking his surroundings. He saw a loaded freight wagon pull around a corner and start slowly toward him, its cargo piled high in the bed behind the driver.

What he didn't see until only about a dozen feet separated him from the wagon was that Simon Callahan was walking behind the vehicle, a shotgun clutched in his hands. Frank didn't know Callahan was there until the man suddenly stepped out into the open and jerked up the Greener.

Flame erupted from both barrels as Callahan pulled the triggers, slamming a deadly double charge of buckshot at The Drifter.

Chapter 4

Callahan was too close. Years of living on the edge of danger had honed Frank Morgan's senses and instincts to a razor sharpness. Even before he was consciously aware of it, before the sight of Simon Callahan pointing a scattergun at him had fully registered on his brain, Frank's muscles were moving. He threw himself forward in a rolling dive that brought him even closer to Callahan.

The buckshot was just beginning to spread out as it passed over Frank's head and through the space where he had been an instant earlier. One pellet stung Frank's shoulder, but that was all. Behind him, though, the man driving the freight wagon cried out in pain as some of the flying buckshot struck him in the back.

Frank somersaulted and came up in a crouch, the Colt Peacemaker already in his hand. Frantically, Callahan threw the empty

Greener aside and grabbed for the pistol on his hip, but he was too slow by a mile. His hand had barely touched the butt of the gun when Frank's Colt boomed twice.

The bullets struck Callahan at a rising angle. The first one tore through his groin and on up into his belly before it shattered his spine. The second slug took him in the middle of his torso and punched a hole through his left lung, barely missing his heart. Even without hitting his heart, the two bullets did more than enough damage. Blood filled Callahan's mouth as his suddenly nerveless legs folded up underneath him. He hit the ground hard. A crimson pool quickly formed under his body, too much for even the thirsty dust of the street to soak up.

Frank straightened from his crouch and strode toward Callahan as the echoes of the shots died away. Callahan gasped for breath, unable to draw any air into his body. All he managed to do was to produce a grotesque whistling and bubbling. Gun still in hand, Frank looked down at him and said, "You had to try to even the score, didn't you, Callahan? And all it got you was killed."

"Y-you . . . bastard!" Callahan managed to grate, the words thick and garbled because of the blood in his mouth. "You ain't . . . heard the last—"

His head fell to the side, and more blood spilled from his mouth.

"I've heard the last of *you*," Frank said, even though Callahan was dead and couldn't hear him.

He holstered his gun and turned toward the freight wagon, hurrying forward to check on the wounded driver. The man had dropped the reins when he was hit, and the team of mules pulling the wagon had come to a stop in the middle of the street. The driver was hunched forward. Blood dotted the back of his vest.

"How bad are you hit, mister?" Frank asked as he came up and put a hand on the man's shoulder.

"Don't know," the driver replied. "All I know is it hurts like hell!"

Several townspeople were approaching, drawn by the shots. "Somebody fetch a doctor," Frank snapped at them, and one of the men turned and ran in the other direction. Frank didn't think the driver was seriously wounded, but the man definitely needed some medical attention.

It was damned lucky that no one else had been close enough to be hit by the shotgun blast. The rest of the buckshot had harmlessly peppered the street and a nearby water trough. If Callahan had made his move a few seconds earlier, enough distance would have separated him from his target so that Frank wouldn't have been able to get out of the way. As it was, it had been a mighty close thing.

Pablo Gomez came up to Frank. "Señor Morgan, you are all right?" the liveryman asked anxiously.

Frank nodded. There was a little blood-stain on the left shoulder of his shirt. He pulled the garment back and saw that the piece of buckshot had scraped the skin, leaving a little gash. The wound stung, but wasn't serious at all.

"Come to my stable," Gomez urged him. "I have some medicine I can put on that scratch."

"Something you use on your horses?" Frank asked with a smile.

"It is better than anything you will get from a regular doctor," Gomez insisted.

"All right. Let's go."

They had taken only a couple of steps, however, when an angry voice demanded, "Stop right there, Morgan!"

Frank recognized the voice, so he wasn't surprised when he turned slowly and saw John Selman standing there. The constable glared at him, looked at Callahan's body, and then glared some more at Frank.

"You just couldn't keep from killin' somebody else, could you?"

"Seemed like the thing to do at the time, since Callahan had just let loose at me with both barrels of a Greener and was reaching for his pistol."

"*Sí,* Señor Selman," Gomez put in. "*Es verdad.* I saw it happen. So did my sons, and there must have been twenty or thirty more people along the street who saw Señor Callahan attack Señor Morgan."

"If I want your opinion, greaser, I'll ask for it," Selman growled. "Didn't I tell you to get out of town, Morgan?"

"That's what I was trying to do. I was on my way to the livery stable to get my horse."

"How come you didn't ride out yesterday?"

"Because I had things to do," Frank said curtly. "I still do. Now either arrest me, Selman, in which case I'll hire the best lawyer in town and get any charges thrown out as soon as a judge hears what happened, or stay out of my way."

Selman looked like he was just itching to hook and draw, but he had the sense not to try it. He was a gunman, but not a fast draw. The craven shot from ambush was more his style.

"You say you're leavin'?" he asked.

48

"As soon as I can."

"Reckon I could make you stay for the inquest on this fella, and on his brother too."

"Again, try it," Frank said. "I'll put the best lawyer in El Paso to work right away."

Selman glowered for a moment longer, but then he jerked his shoulders in an angry shrug and said, "All right, as long as you're leavin', I don't reckon it matters all that much. There were enough witnesses to both shootin's so that the coroner's jury won't have no trouble comin' back with a verdict."

"I'm obliged," Frank said with a nod.

"Just don't let the sun go down on you again in El Paso."

"Don't worry . . . it won't."

Selman turned and barked at the crowd, "Ain't nobody sent for the damn undertaker yet?"

Frank saw that one of the local doctors had arrived and was tending to the wounded wagoneer. Satisfied that the man was going to be taken care of, Frank walked on down the street to the stable with Pablo Gomez.

"Never have I seen a man move so quickly, Señor Morgan," Gomez said. "I stepped out of my barn and saw that man Callahan with a shotgun, walking along behind the wagon. Then I saw you coming toward us, and I remembered what I had heard about you

49

shooting that Jud Callahan yesterday. But before I could call a warning, everything began to happen at once. . . . My apologies, Señor Morgan."

"There's nothing for you to apologize for, amigo," Frank assured him. "There was nothing you could have done. Anyway, you helped me out with Selman, and I'm grateful for that."

"Selman!" Gomez repeated. He made the sign of the cross. "*Dios mio,* that one is a bad hombre. If he is your enemy, it is wise to have eyes in the back of your head, I am thinking."

Frank couldn't argue with that.

Dog bounded out of the stable with plenty of canine enthusiasm to greet Frank. The big cur was getting on in years, but he still acted like a puppy at times. Stormy tossed his head, also obviously glad to see Frank. The three of them, man, horse, and dog, were trail partners and would be as long as they all lived.

El Diablo and the packhorse were ready to travel also. Gomez dabbed some of the medicinal ointment on Frank's wounded shoulder, and Frank put on a clean, faded blue shirt from his saddlebags. Once that was done, all the party was waiting on was Conrad.

He showed up about ten minutes later, wearing boots, jeans, a flannel shirt, a canvas jacket, and a brown Stetson. A gun belt was buckled around his hips, and in the holster was a pistol that Frank recognized as a .38 caliber Colt Lightning. It was a good gun, even though he preferred the added stopping action of a .44 or .45.

Before Frank could say anything, Conrad said, "I noticed the undertaker's wagon down the street, and it came as no surprise when I heard some of the bystanders talking about how Frank Morgan had killed another man."

"He didn't give me much choice," Frank said.

"Who was he, the brother of the man you killed yesterday?"

"As a matter of fact . . . yes."

Conrad regarded him coolly. "What if they had other brothers?"

"I reckon I'll deal with that when and if the time comes. Wouldn't be the first time such a thing has happened."

"No, I imagine not."

Frank's jaw tightened in anger at Conrad's obvious disapproval. "You know," he said pointedly, "if I wasn't good with a gun, you never would have come to me for help with your railroad problems, now would you?"

"No, I suppose not." Conrad looked

51

around, unperturbed by what Frank had said. "You mentioned something about having a horse for me?"

Pablo Gomez led El Diablo forward. "Here you are, Señor. A finer mount you will not find in El Paso . . . except, of course, for Señor Morgan's Appaloosa."

Conrad eyed the big black horse dubiously. "He's an evil-looking brute. I'm not sure I trust him."

Despite El Diablo's name — which had probably been wishful thinking on the part of the horse's previous owner, Frank had decided — the animal appeared placid, not the least bit skittish or troublesome. Frank took the reins and handed them to Conrad. "Give him a try."

Conrad was still suspicious. "Is this one of those tricks you Westerners play on greenhorns? As soon as I mount up, is this animal going to go wild and start bucking and trying to throw me off?"

"This horse has never bucked anyone off, to my knowledge, Señor," Gomez said. "El Diablo is a friendly horse."

Conrad grunted, obviously still not convinced. But he put his foot in the stirrup and swung up into the saddle, every muscle tense as he awaited some sort of explosion underneath him.

The explosion didn't come. El Diablo simply sat there, waiting.

"All right, maybe the horse isn't wild," Conrad said after a moment. "That still doesn't mean I trust it."

"You will learn to trust him, Señor. He will not disappoint you."

Frank mounted up as well and took the reins of the packhorse from Gomez. "I reckon we're ready to ride." He had already settled accounts with the stable keeper. "So long, amigo."

"*Vaya con Dios,* Señor Morgan. Be sure to bring Señor Stormy and Señor Dog back here when you return to El Paso."

Frank wasn't sure he would be returning to El Paso once he had dealt with the troubles plaguing Conrad's rail line, but he didn't say as much. He just smiled and waved to the little liveryman as he heeled Stormy into motion.

Beside him, Conrad banged his heels harder than necessary against El Diablo's sides, but the horse just took it stolidly and walked down the street next to Stormy.

As they rode along, Frank realized that he kept thinking of the railroad as belonging to Conrad, when in reality he owned part of it too. But Frank had never really cared that much about owning anything except his guns. He supposed that in the eyes of the world, he owned Stormy and Dog, but to him they were more like friends and traveling companions. A bunch of other possessions would just weigh a man down.

There had been a time in his life when he had dreamed of starting a little ranch somewhere, of raising cattle or maybe some fine horses. Of being married and having a family.

He had been married twice. The first union had been annulled by Vivian's father. The second one, to a beautiful woman named Dixie, had ended in tragedy when she was cut down by outlaw bullets. Vivian too had died senselessly at the hands of owlhoots. Since then, Frank had vowed to himself that never again would he place a woman in the dangerous position of being married to him. His romances, such as the one with Roanne Williamson, were sweet but not the sort that lasted, and he made sure that the women involved knew that from the beginning. The dreams of permanence he'd once dreamed had now receded. Now he truly lived up to the name he had been given so long ago.

The Drifter.

The scenery was beautiful as they left El Paso. The early morning sun washed over the Franklin Mountains to the north, the twisting Rio Grande to the south, and the rugged hills that rose in Mexico on the other side of the border river. The Mexican city of Juarez, originally known as El Paso del Norte, sprawled along the southern bank of the Rio Grande, an older and even larger settlement than the American city to the north. People had lived here for hundreds of years. It was the most important border crossing along the entire boundary between the United States and Mexico.

Frank had spent considerable time in Mexico the previous autumn, and he had found the inhabitants to be a warm, friendly people — the ones who weren't trying to kill him, that is. He wasn't going to miss it, though. As always, his eyes were turned to the future, to the next hill, the next sight that he hadn't seen before.

He and Conrad angled northwest, following the course of the river for a short distance, then crossed the Rio Grande on a long wooden bridge that paralleled a railroad trestle. That put them in New Mexico Territory, because the river had turned north. They had left Texas behind. Now they followed the railroad instead of the river.

The terrain flattened out some. There was another range of small mountains ahead of them, but they wouldn't reach those for another day or so, and then would loop around them to the north. Around mid-morning, a locomotive went past on the tracks a couple of hundred yards to their left, billowing smoke from its stack and heading westbound with a long line of passenger cars and freight cars behind it.

Conrad gazed wistfully at the train and said, "We could have been on there, you know, riding in comfort in a club car."

"Breathing smoke and cinders, you mean," Frank said. "It's better to be out here in the fresh air."

"That's a matter of opinion," Conrad muttered.

"Besides, a train goes too fast," Frank went on. "You don't have a chance to see anything. For example, you'd never see that from the train." He pointed to the ground at the base of a bush that Conrad was riding past.

El Diablo suddenly shied as a buzzing sound filled the air. Conrad looked down where Frank had pointed, saw the huge rattlesnake coiled there, and cried, "Oh, my God!" He grabbed the saddle horn with one hand and tightened his grip on the reins with the other to bring his spooked mount under control. Looking over at Frank, he demanded, "Aren't you going to kill it?"

"Why?" Frank asked with a shrug. "Snake hasn't done anything to me. If we ride on and leave him alone, he'll leave us alone."

"But . . . but it's poisonous!"

"Venomous," Frank corrected. "The poison only comes into play if he bites you. You can eat rattlesnake meat. I have, and it's not too bad. Tastes a little like chicken."

Conrad looked aghast. "Eat snake? I don't think so!"

"You'd change your tune if you were hungry enough. Then you'd eat snake and be glad to get it."

Conrad shook his head and said, "I'd never get that hungry."

"Just because you never have doesn't mean you never will."

"Well, if you're not going to kill that vile creature, I am." Conrad drew his Colt Lightning. "Even if it doesn't harm one of us, someone else might come along and get bitten. You can't just sit by and ignore something dangerous like that. You get rid of it so it can't threaten anybody else."

He steadied El Diablo, then drew a bead and squeezed off two fast shots from the double-action revolver. The rattlesnake's head blew apart as the bullets struck it. The thick, headless body writhed furiously for a moment before setting into the stillness of death.

"Sure you don't want me to take it along and cook it up for supper tonight?" Frank asked.

Conrad took a couple of fresh cartridges from the loops on his gun belt and replaced the empties in the chambers he had fired. "No, that's perfectly all right," he said coolly. "Leave it for the buzzards."

Frank shrugged. "Your kill. Your choice."

They rode on. Frank didn't let Conrad see the smile on his face. It wasn't because Conrad had demonstrated his marksmanship, although Frank was pleased by that too. He was glad that Conrad had risen to the veiled challenge and recognized the danger of leaving a rattler alone just because it wasn't about to strike you. The real danger was to the innocent, unsuspecting folks who might come along later.

The boy was learning, all right. Yes, sir, he sure was.

Chapter 5

They rode all day, stopping only to rest the horses and to eat a cold lunch of biscuits and salt pork. When they made camp that evening at dusk, Conrad said, "I don't think those mountains up ahead are any closer than they were when we left El Paso this morning."

"It sort of looks like that," Frank agreed, "but the truth is that we covered a nice piece of ground today."

"How long will it take us to get to Lordsburg?"

Frank did some quick calculations in his head, based on what he remembered from maps he had seen of the territory. "Five days, maybe six," he estimated.

Conrad sighed. "We could have been there on the train in less than a day."

"If wishes were horses, beggars would ride," Frank quoted.

"I *have* a horse already. What I'm wishing

for right now is a nice comfortable Pullman berth." Conrad pressed his fists into the small of his back and groaned as he stretched sore muscles.

Frank built a small fire in a ring of stones he put together, fried up some bacon, heated a pot of beans, and brewed some coffee. They still had biscuits too. The fare was simple but good, the sort of food that sticks to a man's ribs. Conrad didn't complain too much as he was eating. Frank let the fire burn down as they spread their bedrolls on either side of the dying flames.

An extra lasso had been included in the supplies he bought at Holtzmann's. Now Frank took his own rope and the extra one and arranged them in a circle on the ground around the bedrolls. Conrad asked, "What's that for?"

"Snakes are cold-blooded critters, so they seek out warmth," Frank explained. "If you don't want to wake up with a rattler sharing your blankets, put a rope around your bed like this. A snake won't crawl over a lasso."

Conrad shuddered. "We wouldn't have to worry about such things if we had—"

"Taken the train, I know," Frank finished for him. "But there's something else you'll never see from inside a train car." He pointed up.

60

Conrad tilted his head back to peer at the now-dark sky. "What are you talking about? I don't see anything."

"The light of Western stars," Frank said. "If you can't see that, I reckon I feel sorry for you."

Conrad sat there in silence for a few seconds, and then he said quietly, "Oh. I suppose I see what you mean. There *are* rather a lot of them, aren't there?"

"Millions," Frank said.

They stretched out on their bedrolls, using their saddles as pillows. Conrad complained a little about how uncomfortable it was, but Frank wasn't surprised when he heard soft snores coming from his son only a few minutes later. A long day in the saddle wore a man out when he wasn't used to it. If you were tired enough, a bedroll and a saddle weren't that bad.

Frank stayed awake for a while longer, looking up at the stars and listening to Stormy and El Diablo crop at the sparse grass around the campsite. Dog lay nearby, his head on his paws. The night was mighty peaceful.

Then Frank heard the clink of metal against rock.

The sound was so faint that at first he thought he had imagined it. Then it came again and he knew he hadn't. It could have been almost anything, but Frank knew it for what it was: the sound of a horseshoe striking a rock. It hadn't come from Stormy or El Diablo. The distance was too great for that. Out here in the still, thin, dry air, sound could travel for a long way. The horse responsible for those two clinks — which hadn't been repeated — might be a quarter of a mile away.

That was still too close for comfort. Frank reached over and scooped up a handful of sand. He tossed it on the embers of the fire, covering up some of them. Two more handfuls of sand put out the rest of the embers. Only when the faint red glow had been completely extinguished did Frank sit up and reach for his Winchester, which he had placed beside his bedroll before he lay down.

He didn't say anything to Conrad, didn't try to wake him. Conrad would start talking, asking questions and such, and his voice would carry too, just like the sounds Frank had heard. Instead, he sat there with every sense alert, being utterly still and quiet.

The moon hadn't risen yet, so there was only the light of the stars to illuminate the semidesert around them. The ground was rocky and sandy, with scattered clumps of hardy grass and stubby mesquite trees and some other bushes here and there. It was going to be difficult for anybody to sneak up on them. He listened intently, putting as much faith in his ears as he did in his eyes.

Somewhere out there in the darkness, a horse blew air through its nose, a sound that was cut off abruptly. Dog lifted his head and growled. Frank knew that someone had clamped a hand over the horse's nose to silence it, but the damage was already done. A man yelled, "Get 'em!" and suddenly orange flashes of muzzle flame bloomed in the night.

Frank was ready, though. The Winchester came to his shoulder in a swift motion. His hand worked the rifle's lever as he lifted it, throwing a cartridge into the chamber. He fired as soon as the barrel was level, aiming for the muzzle flashes that had just started to split the darkness.

Frank cranked off five rounds in a little more than three seconds. The firing from the lurkers in the darkness stopped, and as Conrad came thrashing up out of his blankets, yelling in alarm, Frank heard the rataplan of hurried hoofbeats a couple of hundred yards away. He barked at Conrad, "Get down! Stay down!"

Conrad flattened back out on the tangled blankets. He was on his belly now, and he had his revolver in his hand. "What are we shooting at?" he hissed at Frank.

"*We're* not shooting at anything," Frank replied in a whisper. "Somebody tried to bushwhack us, but I think they're gone now. Stay down, though, until we're sure."

"All right."

A couple of minutes went by. Frank asked, "Were you hit by any of those bullets?"

"No, I'm fine. I was just startled by the shots." Conrad paused. "What about you?"

Frank was a little touched that the youngster would ask. He said, "I didn't get elected. Thought I heard one of those slugs come close enough to almost nominate me, though."

"Can't you just say that you weren't hit?"

Frank chuckled. "Reckon I could. But it wouldn't be as colorful."

Conrad muttered something. Frank couldn't make out the words, but he figured it was something about Westerners and their way of talking, or maybe something about how Frank could make light of the situation when somebody had just tried to kill them.

After a moment, Conrad asked, "Who do you think it was?"

"No way of knowing. I didn't get a look at them, didn't really see anything except their muzzle flashes. But if I had to guess, I'd say they were friends or relatives of those Callahan boys, back in El Paso. They're the only ones I've had trouble with lately."

"Of course, it could have been someone looking to avenge one of the other hundreds of men you've killed," Conrad said scathingly.

"I wouldn't say hundreds. . . ."

"Scores then."

Frank didn't argue with that.

He hadn't heard or seen any signs of the drygulchers since those hoofbeats. It seemed likely they were gone, but he wanted to be sure. He leaned over, put an arm around the big cur's neck, and felt him quivering with eagerness. Frank said, "Go take a look around, Dog." When he let go, Dog bounded off into the darkness.

"You trust an animal to do your reconnoitering for you?" Conrad asked.

"There's not a better scout around than Dog."

Frank waited tensely for the quarter of an hour or so that went by before Dog came loping back into camp. He carried a dead jackrabbit in his strong jaws.

"What's that?" Conrad asked in disgust. "Some sort of animal?"

"A jackrabbit," Frank said. "Fresh meat for breakfast in the morning."

"You mean the dog just went out and ran down a rabbit instead of doing what you told him?"

"No, that rabbit tells me there's nobody else around now. If there had been, Dog wouldn't have taken the time and trouble to do a little hunting. He would have come right back."

"You're placing an awful lot of faith in the judgment of an animal."

"You've got to trust a few folks in this life," Frank said. "Dog hasn't let me down yet." He came to his feet. "Pull your boots on and get up. We're getting out of here."

"What?"

"We're moving our camp, just in case those hombres decide to come back. And it'll be a cold camp this time, with no embers or smell of wood smoke to lead them to us."

"I thought you said they were gone," Conrad said as he sat up and reached for his boots.

"Shake those out before you put them on, just in case any scorpions crawled in there while you were asleep."

"My God," Conrad muttered as he shook out the boots. "How many menaces are there out here?"

"More than you can count," Frank told him. "And like I said, just because those bushwhackers are gone now, that doesn't mean they can't come back."

"That's not *exactly* what you said. But I suppose you implied it."

They saddled up. The darkness didn't bother Frank. He had saddled so many horses he could have done it if he was blind. Conrad struggled with the heavy Western saddle, though. Finally, he got the cinches tightened and everything ready to ride.

Frank led the way. The moon rose, adding its light to that of the stars, so they had no trouble being able to see where they were going.

When they passed a dry wash, Conrad pointed at it and said, "What about there? That looks like a good place to camp."

"Nope. You never make camp in an arroyo like that. Too much danger of flash floods."

"Floods?" Conrad repeated. "Out here in this dry country?"

"It can come a cloud, even out here. And when it does rain, it rains hard. The water runs off fast, and the dry washes fill up in a hurry. Then they're not dry anymore. They're nasty little rivers that can sweep a camp away in seconds."

"Yes, perhaps, but there's not a cloud in the sky tonight. All those stars you pointed out are proof of that."

"It doesn't have to storm here. A heavy rain up in the hills will do it too."

"All right," Conrad said wearily. "I bow to your superior expertise, Frank."

As they rode on, Frank thought about Conrad calling him by his given name. He didn't expect the young man to call him Pa or Dad or anything like that. After all, Frank hadn't raised him. He and Conrad had been complete strangers, unaware of each other's very existence, until Conrad was eighteen. It was no surprise that Conrad didn't really regard him as a father. Faced with the trouble Conrad had encountered with his rail line, he had turned to Frank more as a business partner than a member of the family.

Still, that didn't mean Frank couldn't try to teach him a few things. . . .

They made another camp about two miles from the spot of the previous one, and the rest of the night passed quietly. Frank slept lightly, waking up often to look and listen and make sure no one was trying to sneak up on them again. He relied on Dog's senses too. The big cur would smell men or horses if they were upwind. Dog didn't growl in warning the rest of the night.

The next morning, after the sun had risen, Frank built another fire and roasted the jackrabbit Dog had caught the night before. As the smell of the cooking meat filled the air, Conrad asked, "Why didn't those men press their attack last night? There must have been several of them, judging by all the shooting that was going on. I'm sure they outnumbered us."

"I was ready for them and put up a fight," Frank said simply. "They didn't like that."

"But if they wanted to avenge the men you killed, surely they were prepared to face some danger in doing so."

"Some fellas want more than just to have the odds on their side," Frank explained. "They don't want the other fella to have a chance at all. From the way those hombres lit a shuck out of there, I'd say that's the sort they were. If we hadn't fought back, yeah, they would have killed us. But once they heard a few slugs whistling around their own heads, they decided it wasn't such a good idea." He gazed off into the distance. "Man like that, though, will usually hang back and bide his time, wait for another chance to get what he wants. That's why we have to keep our eyes open."

Conrad frowned. "Are you saying that we'll have this threat hanging over our heads until you manage to kill all the men who are after us?"

"Or until they get tired of it and give up, whichever comes first."

"A veritable Sword of Damocles," Conrad muttered, "hanging by a thread."

"I wouldn't worry too much."

"And why not?"

"It takes a damned good shot to hit a thread," Frank said.

Chapter 6

By mid-morning, even Conrad's inexperienced eyes could tell that the mountains were getting closer. By noon, the two riders, the packhorse, and the dog that padded along with them had swung farther to the north and west, still following the railroad tracks, and the mountains were to their south. To the north was a long range of even taller peaks, most of them with white mantles of snow on their crowns. That snow would remain even in the middle of summer, when the temperature climbed to well over a hundred degrees down here on the flats.

Straight ahead of Frank and Conrad was an easy pass between the two mountain ranges. As they rode through it, Frank said, "Those mountains to the south of us are the Floridas. The ones to the north are the Mimbres."

"I'm aware of the Mimbres Mountains,"

Conrad said. "We have a mine there. I believe it produces silver ore."

"I'm not surprised. There's ore of various kinds all over this part of the territory. In the old days prospectors sunk little one-man shafts in quite a few places, but it was too hard to get the ore out and there wasn't enough of it to make the effort worth their while. With modern mining methods, though, I reckon it's easier to make a mine pay."

"How much do you know about modern mining methods?"

Frank shrugged. "I'm no expert, if that's what you're asking. Most of what I know comes from listening to men talk who do know something about it. But I've heard enough to know that mining isn't a game for a lone man anymore. Hasn't been, really, since the big companies went into the Comstock Lode up in Nevada and showed the way to get really rich. One man operations just won't do anymore. Last place they did was probably in the Black Hills, around Deadwood. And that boom was over more than ten years ago."

"Browning Mines and Manufacturing is quite successful." There was a note of pride in Conrad's voice.

"I'm sure it is. All the reports I've gotten

from my lawyers have been positive."

"Now that we've started branching out into railroads, it's only a matter of time until the Browning holdings represent one of the largest, most lucrative business enterprises in the country."

"I reckon you'll have your hands full just keeping up with everything."

"Yes, I'm sure I'll need a great many competent men working with me."

Frank's eyes narrowed as he looked over at Conrad. "You're not talking about *me* doing something like that, are you?"

"You? Good Lord, no! What do you know about business? Except, of course, the killing business."

Frank stared straight ahead again and didn't say anything.

After a few minutes of strained silence, Conrad said, "I didn't mean for that to sound so offensive, Frank. Honestly, I didn't. It's just that the thought of you in a suit . . . with a tie around your neck . . . shut up in some stuffy office . . . Well, I just can't imagine it. I truly can't."

"That's all right, kid," Frank said gruffly. "Neither can I."

Another train passed them, eastbound this time. Frank wondered briefly if any of the passengers looked out their windows and

73

saw the two men riding in the distance. At the fast clip those trains moved, he and Conrad wouldn't be visible for long. There and gone, dwindling into the distance and then vanishing, almost as if they had never been there, at least from the perspective of those rail travelers, speeding east into a newer, modern, more civilized world.

A few minutes after the train had passed out of sight behind them, Frank got a vivid reminder that there were still vestiges of the older, more untamed West. He reined in sharply and looked toward one of the foothills of the Mimbres Mountains. The rise was a good half mile away, but The Drifter's eyesight was still as keen as that of a much younger man.

"What is it?" Conrad asked as he hauled back on the reins and brought El Diablo to a stop. "You look like something's wrong."

Frank rested his hands on the saddle horn and leaned forward. "Don't know if it's wrong or not. Could be they don't mean us any harm."

"Who?"

"Look yonder, at the top of that hill." Frank didn't point, but the direction of his steady gaze was enough for Conrad to follow.

"Good Lord!" Conrad exclaimed after

squinting at the distant hilltop for a few seconds. "Are those Indians?"

"That they are," Frank said quietly.

Three men sat on ponies atop the hill, motionless. Frank knew they were looking at him and Conrad, just like he was looking at them. He saw a flash of red and another of blue. The riders wore blue shirts, more than likely, and had red headbands holding back their long black hair. That was the standard getup for Apache warriors, along with buckskin leggings and high-topped moccasins.

Apaches weren't really horse Indians, like the Comanche or the Sioux. Often, they thought of horses more as a source of food than as something to ride. An Apache warrior could trot along at a fairly fast pace all day, even in the burning sun. He could keep going when a horse had to stop to rest. That was why an Apache could often chase down someone who was trying to get away from him on horseback. It was a matter of perseverance and dogged determination.

At times, though, the Apaches used horses, especially if they were moving their families. Frank hoped the fact that those men on the hill were mounted meant that they weren't looking for trouble. Maybe they were just curious.

He remembered, though, that Conrad had

said something about the Apaches threatening the construction of the railroad spur line between Lordsburg and Ophir.

Conrad swallowed and asked, "Are they going to attack us?"

"Maybe not. My hope is that they're not part of a war party. But there are three of them and only two of us, so they might be tempted."

"What can we do? Should we just sit here and . . . and try to outstare them?"

"I can't see that it's hurting anything. Keep an eye on them while I look around to make sure they're not just trying to distract us while some of their friends sneak up on us."

"How could anybody sneak up on someone in this arid wasteland? There's no place to hide!"

"You'd be surprised how little cover it takes to hide an Apache warrior," Frank said.

He checked their surroundings and was confident that no one was skulking toward them. While he was doing that, Conrad suddenly said, "Frank, one of them is doing something."

Frank looked up at the hilltop and saw that one of the warriors had raised his arm above his head. Clutched in his hand was a rifle. Frank reached for his own Winchester and slid it out of its saddle sheath. One-handed, he thrust the rifle into the air above his head.

The Apaches wheeled their ponies and disappeared in the blink of an eye.

"What the hell was that all about?" Conrad burst out.

Frank replaced the Winchester in its sheath. "Just their way of saying howdy, I reckon. A sort of acknowledgment that we each knew the other was there."

"They're going back to get the rest of their tribe, or whatever you call it, and then they're going to attack us."

"I hope not. We might could handle two or three of them, but a whole war party . . ." Frank shook his head and smiled. "I imagine we'd lose our hair."

A shudder ran through Conrad. "Snakes and scorpions and now Apaches."

"That's right. There's something interesting everywhere you look."

Conrad didn't seem to think any of those threats were particularly interesting.

By late afternoon, they were clear of the pass. Open plains stretched to the south, and Frank knew they ran all the way down across the border. The line of mountains loomed to the north as far as the eye could see, though.

The Mimbres, the Mogollons, and the other small but rugged ranges were the tail end of the Rockies, at least as far as the United States was concerned. More mountains reached down through Mexico and all the way to South America. Down there they were called the Andes, and Frank wondered suddenly if he would ever see them. He doubted it. But wouldn't it be something if he did?

They made a cold camp again that night. Frank thought about suggesting that they take turns standing guard, but when he saw how eagerly Conrad crawled into the blankets and fell asleep, he knew there wouldn't be any point in it. Conrad would never be able to stay awake during his turn. Frank couldn't stay awake all night either, so he knew he would have to rely on Dog and Stormy to alert him if anybody came too close. And he would sleep lightly too, he was sure of that.

When trouble arrived, it didn't come creeping. Dog lifted his head and growled, and Frank sat up and reached for the Winchester as hoofbeats sounded somewhere close by in the darkness. The unseen horse wasn't galloping. It moved at a steady walk.

Frank waited until the large, dark, bulky shape of horse and rider came into view before saying sharply, "Hold it, mister! That's far enough."

Someone gasped, and surprise went through Frank as a woman's voice called out, "My God! Is someone there? Oh, help me, please help me!"

She sounded exhausted and scared and who knows what else. Frank didn't fully trust her, though, simply because she was a woman. He kept the rifle trained on her as he stood up.

The talking had roused Conrad from sleep. He sat up, reaching for his gun, and said, "Who's there? Frank? What's going on?"

"Stay where you are," Frank told him. He took a step toward the woman and her horse. "Get down off of there, ma'am, slow and easy."

Instead of doing as he said, she suddenly let out a groan, swayed in the saddle, and then slumped to the side, falling off the horse as she appeared to pass out. Frank sprang forward and grabbed the animal's reins. The woman's foot might be caught in the stirrup, and he didn't want the horse to bolt and drag her.

He saw a moment later that wasn't the case. Both of her feet had slipped out of the stirrups when she fell. While Frank held the horse, he said, "Conrad, get over here and drag her over by the bedrolls."

"Who is she?" the young man asked as he scrambled to do as Frank said.

"I don't have any idea. She just rode up out of the night and said that she needed help."

Frank tethered the woman's horse to a mesquite and then joined Conrad in kneeling next to her. She was stirring a little and making small noises, so Frank knew she was regaining consciousness.

"We're going to have to have some light," Conrad said. "Otherwise, we won't be able to tell how badly she's hurt, or even if she's hurt."

"You're right. Gather up some of those dead mesquite branches, and I'll build a fire."

"Why don't you gather the branches? I thought I might loosen her clothes a bit, so that she can breathe easier."

Frank chuckled. "It sounds to me like she's breathing just fine. And if there's any clothes-loosening to be done, it might be better for somebody older and more settled to do it."

"Like you?"

"Well, I do fit the description more than you do," Frank said dryly.

Muttering as usual, Conrad went to gather the wood.

Frank checked the pulse in the young woman's neck. It beat strong and steadily against his fingers. She seemed to be in no real danger. Likely, she had passed out from exhaustion.

He could see well enough in the starlight to tell that she was dressed in men's clothing: a shirt, a pair of denim trousers, and boots. She'd had a hat on when she rode up, but it had fallen off when she took her tumble from the horse. Thick waves of fair hair fanned out around her head. She had sounded young when she spoke, and nothing about her appearance belied that impression.

Conrad came back with the wood and dumped it beside the bedrolls. Frank arranged some of the mesquite branches into a pile and poked dry grass among them for tinder. He took a lucifer from the little tin case in his pocket and struck it, setting fire to the tinder. It caught and flared up, and a moment later the mesquite branches began to burn as well. Soon the little fire was going strong, casting a reddish-yellow glow over the ground where the still-unconscious woman lay.

Frank looked her over for bloodstains, but

didn't find any. Conrad stared at her face and said, "My God, she's beautiful!"

Frank couldn't argue with that assessment. The young woman looked to be about twenty years old, and she was undeniably lovely. Her eyes were closed, of course, but Frank found himself wondering if they were blue or brown.

A wry smile tugged at his mouth. He was too old to be thinking such things, especially about a girl young enough to be his daughter. She would have to settle for being mooned over by Conrad, who seemed perfectly willing to take care of that chore.

In the meantime, they had to find out who she was and what she was doing out here in the middle of nowhere. From the sound of what she had said, she was in some sort of trouble. That meant that someone could be dogging her trail, and they might show up at any minute, looking for a fight.

Frank picked up one of her hands and chafed it between his hands. "Miss?" he said as he leaned over her. "Miss, you'd better wake up. Can you hear me?"

She moaned and stirred again, and this time her eyelids flickered open. As her eyes focused on Frank and Conrad, she gasped and tried to sit up. Frank's hand on her shoulder stopped her.

"Take it easy," he advised her. "You passed out and fell off your horse. I don't think you're hurt, but we can't be sure of that just yet."

She said, "I . . . I . . . Who are y-you?"

"I'm Frank Morgan." He nodded to Conrad. "This is Conrad Browning."

The girl closed her eyes again, and a sigh came from her. "So I found you," she said. "I didn't expect to be so lucky."

A frown creased Frank's forehead. "You were looking for us?" he asked.

She opened her eyes and peered up at him. "For *you,* Mr. Morgan."

"Why?"

A shudder went through her. "Because they want to kill you."

Chapter 7

"Maybe you'd better sit up after all," Frank said, his voice becoming grim. "You'll have to explain that."

"Yes. Help me up."

He was going to put an arm around her shoulders and lift her into a sitting position, but Conrad beat him to it. When the girl was upright, Conrad asked, "Are you all right? Do you feel dizzy or anything?"

She managed to smile weakly. "I'm all right. Thank you."

"Let's hear what you've got to say," Frank put in curtly. "Start with your name."

She looked at him. "It's Rebel . . . Rebel Callahan."

"What an unusual name," Conrad said. "But quite lovely. It suits—" He stopped short as the full import of what she had said sunk in on him. "Did you say . . . Callahan?"

"That's right. The name means something to you, doesn't it?"

"It does," Frank said. "Are you related to Simon and Jud?"

Rebel Callahan nodded. "They were my cousins."

"Until I killed them," Frank said in a stony voice.

"Yes. You did. And because of that, their brother Ed and my brothers Tom and Bob want to kill you."

"They're the ones who ambushed us last night," Frank guessed.

Again the girl nodded. "That's right. They thought they could finish you off without any trouble, but it didn't work out that way."

"It usually doesn't," Frank said. "One thing I've learned over the years is that killing a man can be simple sometimes, but usually it's a complicated affair. You never know what's going to come of it."

"Like tossing a pebble into a pond and watching the ripples from it," Rebel said.

"That's right." Frank paused. "What's your part in all this?"

Conrad spoke up, saying, "They must have forced her to come along with them. Isn't that right, Miss Callahan?"

Rebel smiled at him and nodded again.

85

"That's right. Tom and Bob said it . . . it was my duty as a member of the family to help avenge Simon and Jud. My brothers and my cousin and I, we're the only ones left in our family. They said you had to die because of what you'd done, Mr. Morgan."

"But you didn't agree with that."

"Of course not! I don't agree with cold-blooded murder. I waited for my chance, and then I got away from them as soon as I could. I rode after you, hoping I could find you and warn you."

"You did that out of the goodness of your heart?" Frank asked coldly.

Conrad glared at him. "Blast it, Frank, you sound like you're suspicious of this poor girl! She risked her own life to help us, and you cast aspersions on her motives!"

Rebel lifted a hand to forestall Conrad's protest. "No, he's right, Mr. . . . Browning, was it? Mr. Morgan is right to be suspicious of me. After all, I belong to the same family that wants to kill him, and to kill you too, since you're traveling with him."

Conrad didn't say anything about him and Frank actually being related, not just traveling companions or business associates, and Frank didn't mention it either. Instead, he said, "It's a mite unusual to find a young woman wearing pants and gallivanting around the countryside like you're doing, Miss Callahan."

She gave a defiant toss of her head that made her blond hair swirl a little. Frank suspected the gesture was a habit of hers.

"I've always been a tomboy, I guess you could say. I can ride and shoot as well as either of my brothers. I had to learn, because we all worked hard running a ranch down in the Davis Mountains. That is, until . . . until we lost it."

"Outfit went under, did it?"

"Rustlers drove us into bankruptcy," Rebel explained. "We couldn't keep the place going. It was a blow losing it. Our father started it when he came out to West Texas after the war."

"I reckon he must have fought for the Confederate side."

"Of course he did, but how did you know . . . Oh. Because of my name."

Frank shrugged. "Seemed like a reasonable guess."

"And you're right. My father was from Georgia, and he was a staunch Confederate. My brothers were named after Stonewall Jackson and Robert E. Lee. When I came along, my father couldn't think of any famous Confederate women, so he just called me Rebel."

"Guess he never heard of Belle Boyd. She was a spy for the South." Frank steered the conversation back to a more important subject. "What about those cousins of yours? Did they work the ranch with you?"

"No, not at all. Simon and Jud and Ed were older. Ed even fought in the war. But they've always been drifters. Grub-line riders, I guess you'd call them, if they ever did any actual work. I've thought for a long time they were probably outlaws and hired gunmen."

Conrad started to say something, probably about hired gunmen, but Frank silenced him with a look.

"Tom and Bob heard that they were in El Paso," Rebel went on, "so we came out to see if we could join up with them for a while, since we didn't have anywhere else to go. I thought I might be able to get a job working in a store or something like that. But then you killed Jud, and Simon didn't tell us about it because he wanted to settle the score with you himself, and then you killed him too, and when Ed and my brothers heard about it . . ." She paused and shook her head. "They went crazy mad, Mr. Morgan. They won't stop until they've killed you."

"Or until I've killed them."

"You wouldn't! They're all the family I have left."

Conrad said, "Frank, we've got to do something about this. Miss Callahan can't be left alone in the world. You've got to make it right somehow with her brothers and her cousin."

"How would you suggest doing that, Conrad?" Frank asked quietly. "Some debts have to be paid in blood."

"Hogwash! Anything can be negotiated. There's always a way to reach an equitable settlement—"

"Money, you mean?" Frank cut in.

"Well, yes."

Frank laughed humorlessly. "You've spent too much time back East. Folks there always think that the best way to solve a problem is to throw money at it, but in most cases that doesn't accomplish a thing except to make the problem worse."

"All right, what solution do *you* propose?"

"To keep those Callahan boys from killing us, whatever it takes. If we can do it without killing them, so much the better."

Rebel said, "But if you can't?"

"No offense, ma'am," Frank told her, "but I'm not going to let your family gun me down out of revenge and not try to do something about it."

"I . . . I understand." Rebel took a deep breath. "And I know you're right. That's why I broke away from them and came to warn you, because I think they're doing the wrong thing. From what I heard, Simon and Jud tried to kill you first. You were just defending yourself."

Frank nodded. "That's the way it happened, all right."

"Maybe if you explained that to Ed and Tom and Bob . . ."

"You really think that would work?"

"Well . . . no," Rebel said. "I doubt that it would." She looked up. "But maybe I could talk to them. Maybe they would listen to me."

"I got the feeling you already tried to talk to them, and it didn't do any good."

"That's true. But it might be different now. I've actually spoken to you now, and I know you acted in self-defense."

Frank didn't think that would make a damned bit of difference to the Callahan boys. He supposed he could understand why Rebel wanted to try, though. Though she didn't seem to care that much about her remaining cousin, her brothers were the only close family she had left, and she didn't want to lose them. If they continued their vendetta, there was a good chance they would wind up dead.

"There's a water stop up ahead where the railroad crosses the Mimbres River," Rebel went on. "You could leave me there, and when the boys catch up, I'll talk to them. I'll do my best to convince them to abandon the whole idea of vengeance and go back to El Paso. If it doesn't work . . . well, you haven't lost anything by letting me try."

Conrad said, "You shouldn't go back to them, Miss Callahan. It sounds as if they treat you terribly. From the sound of it, they seem to regard you as . . . as one of the boys, rather than as the lovely young woman you are."

Frank couldn't tell because of the firelight, but he thought Rebel blushed. Conrad was the one who ought to be blushing, the way he was so blatantly trying to flatter her.

"I suppose it wouldn't hurt anything for you to try to talk sense to them," Frank said after mulling it over for a moment. "I've heard of that water stop. Called Mimbres Tank, isn't it?"

"That's right," Rebel said. "You can reach it by noon tomorrow."

"How far back of us are the others?"

"They camped back the other side of the pass. They're at least an hour behind you."

"Aren't they liable to come right on after you when they discover that you're gone?"

Rebel smiled. "They're all sound sleepers, and I left my bedroll made up to look like I was in it in case one of them wakes up. They probably won't know I'm gone until morning."

"You must have ridden hard after you slipped away, to catch up to us like you did."

"I knew it was important, so I didn't mind pushing my horse — or myself."

Conrad said suddenly, "What were we thinking? Would you like something to eat or drink, Miss Callahan? We have some beans and salt pork, and we can put on a pot of coffee if you want some."

"Thank you, Mr. Browning, but I'm fine. I ate with the boys before we all turned in."

"You're sure? It wouldn't be any bother—"

"The lady said she wasn't hungry, Conrad," Frank drawled.

"Well, I'm just trying to be a good host. This may be the frontier, but there's no excuse for poor manners."

Frank tried not to smile. The next time he ran into a kill-crazy gun-thrower who wanted to ventilate him or a bloodthirsty Apache who wanted to lift his hair, he'd be sure to tell them that their actions didn't conform to the accepted notions of proper etiquette.

Right after he shot them, that is.

★ ★ ★

Frank wasn't willing to gamble that Rebel was right about her brothers and cousin not discovering her absence until the next morning. He and Conrad took turns standing guard during the night, and Rebel's presence had the hoped-for effect on Conrad: He stayed awake and alert during his stint on watch.

Rebel seemed to sleep well. Frank and Conrad each gave up a blanket, and she was able to improvise a bedroll from them. The next morning Frank kindled the fire back to life and cooked a hot breakfast. The food and coffee, as well as the cool morning air, put a definite glow in Rebel's cheeks and made her more lovely than ever.

She was beautiful, there was no question about that. The light of day confirmed the fact, as well as revealing that her eyes were a deep, rich brown. Conrad's eyes seldom left her as they got ready to break camp.

While Rebel had gone off a short distance into the brush to tend to her private needs, Frank said quietly to Conrad, "You're acting a mite like you've never seen a pretty girl before."

He flushed in a combination of anger and embarrassment. "That's not true. I've had many lady friends, including some back in

Boston who would put this . . . this frontier hoyden to shame."

"Somehow I doubt that."

"That I've had lady friends?"

"That any of them could put Miss Rebel to shame. She's as pretty a girl as I've seen in a long time."

"You don't seem to mind admitting that," Conrad pointed out.

"I'm just stating a fact," Frank said. "You're the one mooning over her."

"Hardly! I'm just trying to be polite—"

Conrad stopped short as they heard Rebel returning. He went to saddle her horse, having taken it upon himself to care for the chestnut gelding she had ridden up to their camp the night before.

Frank scanned their back trail once he had swung up into Stormy's saddle. He didn't see any signs of pursuit, but that didn't mean the Callahan boys weren't back there. "Let's go," he said as he heeled the big Appaloosa into a ground-eating trot. Dog ran ahead, eagerly sniffing the ground and looking for something interesting.

They followed the railroad tracks during the morning, moving closer to the right-of-way than Frank and Conrad had been traveling previously. Although there were plenty of mountains visible jutting up in the distance, the area alongside the tracks was flat and the railroad ran in a straight line for the most part, with only an occasional long, gentle curve. Because of that, they were able to see the elevated water tank beside the tracks for several miles before they reached it.

As they drew closer, Frank saw that the water stop consisted of the tank itself on the north side of the tracks, a siding next to it where cattle cars could be sidetracked and loaded or unloaded, and a small building and platform on the other side of the tracks. This wasn't a manned station, but while trains were stopped to take on water from the tank, passengers could get out and stretch their legs on the platform if they were of a mind to. Likewise, folks from the ranches hereabouts who wanted to board the train could wait in the building or on the platform, depending on the weather.

No train was stopped there now, of course, although there might be a westbound later in the day. Frank, Conrad, and Rebel rode up to the station, letting their horses pick their way across the tracks to the south side of the line. They dismounted and went up the steps onto the platform, stopping in the shade of the awning that overhung it.

Conrad looked around and said, "This has to be the most godforsaken place I've ever seen. Are you sure you want us to leave you here, Miss Callahan?"

"I'll be fine—" Rebel began.

The hair on Dog's neck lifted, and he began to growl. That was enough warning for Frank. He whipped around toward the building, his hand going to the butt of his Colt.

He was too late. The door of the building was already open, and three men stood there with leveled guns in their hands. One of them laughed harshly and said, "Don't worry, boy. You won't be leavin' Rebel here. Fact is, you won't be leavin' at all."

Chapter 8

Frank was fast with a gun, faster perhaps than anyone in the history of the West except for Ben Thompson, Smoke Jensen, and John Wesley Hardin. But not even he could out-draw guns that were already drawn. He froze with his hand on the butt of his Colt as he looked down the barrels of the revolvers pointed at him and Conrad and Rebel.

The man who had spoken was the oldest of the trio. He had a rugged, weathered face and a shock of white hair under a pushed-back black Stetson. The other two had a distinct family resemblance, despite the fact that one was tall and lanky with black hair and the other was built short and stocky and had sandy hair. Frank knew he was looking at Ed Callahan and Rebel's brothers Tom and Bob.

Conrad said, "See here, you can't just—"

"They've got the drop on us," Frank cut

in. "I reckon they can do just about anything they damned well please."

"You're right about that, Morgan," Ed Callahan said. "And it's gonna please us a whole heap to put some bullets in you and this dandified friend o' yours." Ed motioned slightly with the barrel of his gun. "Take your hand away from that Colt, gunfighter. You're makin' me nervous."

"Why should I worry about that?" Frank asked coolly. "You're going to kill us anyway, nervous or not, aren't you?"

"Damn right. I wouldn't mind seein' you squirm a little bit first, though."

Frank laughed. "That's not going to happen."

Ed regarded him intently for a moment and then said, "No, I reckon it's not. Might as well get this over with."

Frank's eyes flicked for an instant to Conrad. The young man was pale with fear, but his face was composed. He wasn't going to panic and start crying or pleading for his life. Instead, Conrad said, "At least have the decency not to make Miss Rebel witness this atrocity."

She stepped behind him and plucked the Colt Lightning from its holster on Conrad's hip. Pointing the gun at him, she moved quickly to the side and said, "They're not making me do anything. It was my idea to fool you and lead you right into this trap."

Conrad stared at her, obviously unable to believe what he was hearing. "Rebel!" he exclaimed. "You . . . you can't mean that!"

"You make an enemy of one Callahan, you make enemies of 'em all," she said.

Frank was surprised, but not completely. He had never fully trusted Rebel and had thought she might try to pull some sort of trick. He had been hoping that he was wrong about her, though.

Clearly, he wasn't wrong. She was after revenge just like her cousin and her brothers. If it came down to brass tacks, he would have to remember that. But it was going to be difficult for him to pull the trigger on a woman, no matter what he knew about her.

"Listen," he said, "you boys haven't thought this through."

"The hell we haven't," Ed said. "We're gonna kill you, and that's all we got to think about."

Frank smiled faintly. "You don't think I'm going to go down right away, do you? Even with lead in me, I'll stay on my feet long enough to get my gun out and get off a shot or two. I'll kill at least one of you before I die."

Ed sneered. "That's big talk."

"Then there's my dog," Frank went on. "In case you haven't noticed from the way he's looking at you and raising his lip, he hates all three of you and can't wait to get his teeth in you. Again, you can shoot him, but he'll live long enough to tear out somebody's throat."

The shorter of the two brothers said worriedly, "Ed, I don't like dogs. Never have cottoned to them."

"Shut up, Bob," Ed snapped. "Morgan's just tryin' to run a bluff. He thinks he's gonna scare us so bad we'll tuck our tails between our legs and slink off like some sort o' coyotes."

Frank shook his head. "No bluff, Ed. Just telling you the way it is. If I can manage to whistle just right before I cash in my chips — and I'm betting I can — that big Palouse of mine will charge right up here on this platform and go to kicking. So between me and my horse and my dog, you'll all die. All three of you. No doubt about it in my mind."

Both of Rebel's brothers looked nervous enough to jump out of their skin. They had been roped into this affair by their cousin, and now they weren't so sure about it.

Rebel wasn't so easily spooked. She said, "Don't listen to him, boys. Let's do what we came here to do."

"I've told you what's going to happen," Frank said quietly. "If you want to pull those triggers and start the ball . . . well, you've got it to do."

Tom Callahan, the taller of the two brothers, turned and took a step toward his cousin, saying, "Ed, I don't—"

Something hummed through the air on the platform. Tom cried out in pain as an arrow thudded into his shoulder and knocked him back. He stared down in shock and horror at the shaft protruding from his flesh.

Frank pivoted as more arrows sang around him. He palmed out the Colt and snapped a shot at the figures that had appeared seemingly by magic on the other side of the railroad tracks. He had told Conrad that it didn't take much cover to hide an Apache warrior, and this attack was proof of that. The Apaches had gotten to within fifty feet of the station before emerging from the scrubby brush to launch their assault on the whites.

The Callahans' vendetta against Frank was forgotten now. In self-preservation, they opened fire on the Apaches. There were about eight of the warriors, but only a couple of them were armed with rifles. The others had bows and arrows.

Frank dropped to a knee and fired again. One of the Apaches who had a rifle spun around, blood spurting from his arm where Frank's bullet had holed it. To Frank's left, Conrad tackled Rebel Callahan, knocking her to the platform as a couple of arrows passed closely above her. The impact jarred the Lightning loose from her grip. Conrad yelled, "Stay down!" and practically crawled on top of her, shielding her with his body as he snatched up the double-action Colt and began firing at the Apaches. It looked like he had forgotten that a few minutes earlier Rebel had been ready to gun down him and Frank both.

The rest of the Callahans fell back toward the station building, firing as they went. So far, Tom was the only one who had been wounded. Bob yelled, "Let's get out of here!" and neither of the others argued with him. They slammed through the front door of the station, ran across the single small room, and burst out the back.

Frank didn't know where they were going and didn't care. He supposed they had hidden their horses somewhere nearby, probably in an arroyo. If they made it to their mounts before the Apaches caught up to them, they would have a chance to get away. And since the Apaches were being kept busy at the moment by him and Conrad, Frank realized wryly that they were helping their sworn enemies to escape.

With the exception of Rebel, who was still pinned down under Conrad and seemingly stunned. Conrad emptied the Lightning at the attackers, and while Frank couldn't tell if the shots hit anything or not, they certainly made some of the Apaches jump for cover.

Three of the Indians ran between the legs of the water tank. Frank angled the barrel of his Peacemaker up and squeezed off a shot. The slug struck the cable that held up the tank's spout and severed it neatly. The long spout dropped, slamming into the three Apaches and knocking them off their feet. Water from the tank inundated them.

"Make for the horses!" Frank shouted as he threw another round toward the Apaches. He leaped off the platform, whistling for Stormy.

The Appaloosa lunged forward. Frank grabbed the saddle horn and swung up in a lithe motion. He holstered the Colt and jerked the Winchester from its sheath. As Conrad leaped up from the platform and hauled Rebel with him, Frank laid down covering fire for them.

Meanwhile, Dog had one of the Apaches down and was savaging him. Three more of the warriors were wounded, although Frank didn't know how badly they were hurt. That left only four of them, and they had to hug the dirt as Frank peppered the area around them with rifle slugs. Conrad and Rebel made it to the edge of the platform. Conrad didn't let go of the girl as he jumped to the ground.

Rebel had gotten her wits back enough to grab the reins of her chestnut. She swung up into the saddle while Conrad climbed onto El Diablo. Frank wheeled Stormy around and snatched Rebel's reins out of her hands. Leading the packhorse as well, he kicked the Appaloosa into a gallop. With Frank tugging on the reins, Rebel's chestnut had no choice but to break into a run as well.

Conrad brought up the rear on El Diablo. As he galloped after Frank and Rebel, he took the Winchester Frank had bought at Holtzmann's from its sheath and twisted around in the hull to fling several shots at the Apaches. It would have been pure luck for an inexperienced shot like Conrad to actually hit anything from the hurricane deck of a racing horse, but at least the boy was trying, Frank thought as he glanced back.

They rode west along the railroad tracks, on the south side of the right-of-way. The tracks were raised a little on a shallow embankment. That didn't give the three riders much cover, but anything was better than nothing. All three horses were strong and not worn out by a full day's ride, so within seconds they had pulled away from the water stop.

The Mimbres River loomed in front of them, spanned by a short trestle. Frank, Conrad, and Rebel didn't try to cross on the bridge. That would have just slowed them down and given the Apaches a chance to catch up. Instead, they put their horses down the sloping bank of the streambed and splashed across the shallow river. The horses lunged up the other bank and kept running.

Conrad was still shooting. Frank called to him, "Hold your fire! You're wasting lead!" The Apaches were a couple of hundred yards behind them now, and the warriors weren't going to be able to catch up on foot, at least not anytime soon. Nor would the Indian ponies, if there were any hidden nearby, be able to match the speed of Stormy, El Diablo, and Rebel's chestnut, even with the packhorse slowing them down a little.

Rebel looked confused and angry and a little scared, but there was nothing she could do as long as Frank hung onto her horse's reins. She bent forward over her mount's neck and rode expertly. Evidently, her story about being able to ride and shoot as well as her brothers hadn't been a lie, although most of the rest of her story had been.

Frank wasn't sure why he had brought her along. He didn't want to leave her to the Apaches, of course. They might not have killed her, but life as a white female captive would have been pure hell for Rebel. Also, he thought that having her with him and Conrad might give them some leverage against the rest of the Callahans, although Frank knew that he wouldn't stoop to actually using her as a hostage. It was more a matter of thinking that they might be able to convince her to abandon her quest for vengeance — the same way her brothers and her cousin had abandoned her to the Apaches.

Frank hadn't seen any sign of Ed, Tom, and Bob since they fled from the station. Most likely, they had reached their horses and taken off for the tall and uncut. They would need to put some distance between themselves and those Apaches before they could stop and tend to the arrow in Tom's shoulder. He was in for a lot of pain. Frank knew that from experience, having been skewered by an Indian arrow a time or two himself.

"Where are we going?" Rebel shouted at him.

"Away from those Apaches!" he told her.

"What are you going to do with me?"

That was a damned good question. Unfortunately, Frank didn't have the answer. He supposed it would depend on whether or not after this fight with the Apaches Rebel still wanted to see him and Conrad dead. . . .

Chapter 9

They didn't slow down until they had put several miles between them and the station at Mimbres Tank. Then Frank pulled back on Stormy's reins and slowed the big Appaloosa to a walk. Conrad and Rebel slowed down beside him.

Conrad looked around and asked, "Where's Dog? Did the Apaches get him?"

"Not likely," Frank said. "I imagine he took off from there when we did. We just outdistanced him. But he'll find us, don't you worry about that."

Rebel hadn't said anything since asking what they planned to do with her. She looked straight ahead, a frown on her face. Finally, she said, "They went off and just *left* me there."

Frank nodded. "Yep, they sure did. I reckon they were more interested in saving their own skins, not to mention their hair."

"But they *left* me! I'm not surprised that Ed would do such a thing. We've never been that close. But Tom and Bob are my brothers!"

"Tom already had an arrow in him," Frank pointed out, wondering even as he did so why he was bothering to defend the Callahan brothers. "He was hurt and scared. I'm sure Bob was scared. And Conrad sort of had you pinned down where they couldn't get to you easily. Otherwise, they probably would have grabbed you and taken you with them."

Rebel didn't say anything. She just kept looking stonily ahead of her.

"Where were their horses?" Frank asked after a moment.

"I don't know for sure. They were going to hide them somewhere close to the station, somewhere you wouldn't see them when you rode up."

"I reckon they circled around our camp and rode all night to get to Mimbres Tank first?"

Rebel nodded. "That was the plan. It almost worked too. It would have if those damned Apaches hadn't shown up!"

"Frank," Conrad said, "do you think those were the same Indians we saw yesterday?"

"More than likely."

"So they did go back and get the rest of their war party, just like I said they were going to."

"Chances are that wasn't the whole bunch."

Rebel asked, "Will they come after us?"

Frank turned to look behind them. "It wouldn't surprise me if they were back there somewhere right now," he said. "But it's possible too that they might have decided they've already paid a big enough price without getting what they wanted. They might go back up into the foothills and wait for somebody else to come along."

Conrad said, "They have to be part of the same group that's threatening the spur line."

"What spur line?" Rebel asked.

"I hardly think that's any of your business," Conrad said coldly. "After all, it's only been a short time since you and your brothers and cousin were trying to kill us."

"That didn't stop you from jumping on top of me when the arrows started flying," Rebel pointed out. She laughed. "You pounced on me like I was a saloon girl and you were a cowboy who hadn't seen a woman in a month of Sundays."

"I'm sure you'd know all about such scandalous behavior," Conrad shot back in a stiff voice.

Frank glanced over and saw Rebel blink and flinch a little as if she had been struck. Clearly, Conrad's words had stung her. Frank wasn't sure why Rebel would care what Conrad said, or what he thought of her, for that matter. They were enemies, after all.

But they were also close to the same age, young and vital and full of life's juices. Hostilities were sometimes forgotten, or at least ignored, in the face of such things.

Frank kept an eye on their back trail as they rode. A short time later, he saw something moving through the scrubby brush, and wasn't surprised when Dog came into view, loping steadily after them. He reined in and motioned for Conrad to do likewise. Dog came trotting up to them, tongue lolling out of his mouth. He seemed a little winded, so Frank said, "We'll rest for a few minutes."

They swung down from their saddles and stretched. The horses cropped a little grass while Frank petted Dog and told him what a good job he had done of catching up to them. Conrad and Rebel stood off to one side. Conrad's eyes were narrowed, and he kept a close watch on Rebel.

"You don't have to stare at me like that," she said after a few moments. "I'm not armed. I'm not going to shoot you."

"Thanks for reminding me." Conrad took his Colt Lightning out of its holster, where he had jammed it after emptying it at the Apaches back at Mimbres Tank. He began to reload it. "I suppose you lied about being a good shot," he said, "the same way you lied about everything else."

"Give me that gun and you'll find out what kind of shot I am."

"Oh, ho! I think not."

She glared at him. "Where the hell are you from? You don't talk like you come from around these parts."

"The past few years I've been in Boston. Cambridge actually, attending Harvard."

"That's some sort of fancy school, ain't it?"

"Harvard is the finest university in the country, as well as one of the oldest."

"Well, then, how'd you come to be out here in New Mexico Territory?" Rebel wanted to know. "Shouldn't you be back there at Harvard with your head stuck in a book . . . or up your—"

"I have business interests in this territory," Conrad said hastily, interrupting her. "I've graduated from the university, and I'm now very involved in running the family enterprises."

"Then how'd you get mixed up with a gun-thrower like Morgan?"

Frank smiled to himself as he heard the question, wondering how Conrad was going to answer it. Would the boy claim him as his daddy?

"Frank and I have known each other for several years," Conrad said. "He, ah, owns a small percentage of the business interests that I control."

So they were just business associates, Frank thought wryly. Conrad didn't want to admit, even to this wild West Texas girl, that he was related to the famous — or infamous — Drifter.

It came as a slight surprise to Frank that he experienced a faint pang of disappointment at this realization.

"So where are the two of you headed?" Rebel asked.

"We're on our way to—" Conrad stopped abruptly. "Wait just a minute. Why should I tell you where we're going? If you were to get away from us and join forces again with your brothers and your cousin, you could tell them where to find us."

"They're going to find you anyway," Rebel said. "Ed will get on your trail again, and he won't give it up until there's another showdown. He's bound and determined to even the score for Simon and Jud."

"Then he's a damned fool," Frank said. "He'll just wind up getting himself killed, along with your brothers."

Rebel gave that toss of her head. "You must not know what it's like to be part of a family, Mr. High-and-Mighty Gunfighter! If you did, you'd know there are some things you just don't give up on, not when it has to do with your family."

Frank didn't say anything, but he looked at Conrad. Conrad didn't seem to want to meet his gaze, however. The young man looked away and cleared his throat uncomfortably.

The rest was a short one. If the Apaches were coming after them, Frank didn't want to give those indefatigable warriors time to close the gap too much. As they mounted up again, Frank said, "You take Miss Callahan's reins this time, Conrad."

"I won't try to get away," Rebel said. "Where would I go? There may be Apaches on our trail, and I don't know where Tom and Bob and Ed are. I'd be a fool to run off now."

"Yes, you would," Frank agreed. "But that doesn't mean you wouldn't do it if the notion struck you."

"How about if I gave you my word?"

"Reckon we've got a heap of reasons to believe that," Frank said dryly.

"No, I mean it," Rebel said, flushing angrily. "I swear, I won't try to run off or pull any other tricks."

"How about giving up this grudge you've got against me? You going to do that too?"

Her eyes narrowed. "You know I can't, not unless Ed does. It was his brothers who got killed, so it's up to him how to pay that debt."

"But what you're saying is that we ought to call a truce."

"For now, yes. That's exactly what I'm saying, Mr. Morgan. In fact, if you were smart, you'd give me a gun. I can help you fight off those Indians if they attack us again."

"When and if that time comes, I'll think about it," Frank said. "Until then, I reckon it would be all right for Conrad to give you your reins back — but no gun."

Conrad handed the reins over to Rebel, and the three of them got their horses moving. Frank set the pace, keeping them moving steadily westward at a good clip without pushing their mounts too hard.

"This is the old Butterfield stage route," Frank said after a while, to break the silence as much as anything. "Back in the days before the Union Pacific and the Central Pacific joined up, the only way you could travel from one side of the country to the other was by stagecoach, and this was the major route."

"Did you ever ride the stagecoach?" Conrad asked.

"Many times," Frank replied with a nod. "In those days it was even more dangerous, because Geronimo and his bucks were still out raising hell. I remember hearing about how they jumped one stage to Lordsburg and chased it for a long way. Might have caught it too, and massacred everybody on it, if one of the passengers hadn't been a good shot with a rifle and held them off until a cavalry patrol came along and made the Apaches turn tail and run. Back then, it was unusual to go clear across southern New Mexico and Arizona Territories *without* running into a fight somewhere."

"Thank goodness the area is more civilized now," Conrad said. "Someday, people will be able to travel anywhere they want to without having to worry about being attacked."

That was a nice dream, Frank mused, but that was all it was — a dream. Someday, the Apaches would be either wiped out or tamed, that much was inevitable, but there would be other threats. Human nature would see to that.

They rode on through the afternoon, gnawing on jerky and cold biscuits to ease their hunger pangs, washing down the food with swigs from their canteens, stopping only occasionally to let the horses rest. During one such stop, Frank climbed one of the telegraph poles that were strung out alongside the railroad tracks. He peered to the east, south, and north, and saw no signs of anyone trailing them. Maybe the Apaches had given up. He wasn't going to count on that, however, because he knew what stealthy varmints they could be. But he was fairly confident that the Callahans weren't back there, at least not anywhere close. He would have been able to see three men on horseback.

That evening Frank led them well south of the railroad to a clump of boulders where they made camp. The spot would be fairly easy to defend in case of trouble, because the rocks provided a considerable amount of cover. If they had to fort up here, any attackers would have a hard time rooting them out.

As night fell, while Conrad tended to the horses, Frank faced Rebel and asked, "Do we need to tie you up for the night?"

"I told you I'm not going to try to get away. I gave you my word. I don't know what else I can do."

Frank shrugged. "I guess I'll have to take your word. If you run off, it'll just put you in more danger and won't have any effect on us."

She looked down at the ground and muttered, "I won't run off."

Frank nodded. "How about fixing something to eat then?"

"All right." Rebel's mood seemed to brighten a little. "I can do that."

Using bits of dry brush, she built a small fire that was so well shielded by the rocks that it wouldn't be visible more than a few yards away. It didn't give off much smoke either. Frank looked on in approval. Rebel knew what she was doing.

Frank got a pan, bacon, and flour from the supplies lashed to the packhorse and brought them to Rebel. She got the bacon frying and when it was done, used grease, flour, and water to cook some pan bread. Frank put coffee on to brew.

Finished with the horses, Conrad wandered over and asked, "Is it safe to have a fire? We don't want those Indians to find us."

"If the Apaches are looking for us, they'll find us whether we have a fire or not. And if it's anybody else—" Frank didn't mention Rebel's brothers and cousin, but they all knew that was who he was talking about.

"They probably won't be able to see this fire, as small as it is."

Conrad hunkered on his heels. "I must admit, that food smells wonderful. It'll be nice to have a hot meal."

"That's what I thought," Frank agreed. "It's been a long, hard day, and we need something to keep our strength up."

"You still haven't told me where you're going," Rebel said.

"And you know why," Conrad told her.

She turned the pan bread. "Yes, but I've given my word that I'll go along with you. Don't I have a right to know where?"

"Attempting to trap us and murder us effectively takes away your rights, I believe."

"Look, maybe I was wrong to do that," she snapped.

"Maybe?" Conrad repeated, sarcasm in his tone.

"Ah, go to hell," Rebel said under her breath.

Conrad looked around. "Judging by the desolate nature of our surroundings, I believe we may already be there."

Frank said, "You two don't intend to keep up this wrangling all night, do you? I was planning on getting some sleep sometime."

"I've said all I have to say," Conrad replied.

"So have I," Rebel said.

Frank would believe that when he saw it and heard it for himself.

The two of them seemed to call a truce and ignore each other, though, which was a welcome surprise to Frank. They ate supper in relative peace and quiet, and then he put out the fire while Rebel cleaned the pan with sand. She replaced it in the pack herself.

"How do you feel about standing first watch tonight?" Frank asked Conrad.

"All right. I can do that."

"Not going to doze off?"

"Of course not. I stayed awake during my turn last night, didn't I?"

"As far as I know."

"Don't worry, Mr. Morgan," Rebel put in. "I'll keep an eye on him."

"Hah!" Conrad said. "As if I need an enemy to do watch over me."

"I thought we called a truce."

"You'd still like to see us both dead."

"Well . . ." Rebel hesitated. "I'm not so sure about that anymore."

That took Conrad by surprise. Frank too, but he didn't show it. Conrad said, "Do you mean you're giving up that quest for vengeance after all?"

"I don't know what I mean," Rebel said with a sigh. "I've spent a day with you fellas now, and you don't seem like such bad sorts. A mite prickly maybe . . ." She cast a meaningful glance at Conrad as she said that. "But I believe Mr. Morgan when he says he didn't want to kill Jud or Simon. They forced him into it. And even though I didn't ask you to, Mr. Browning, you *did* try to protect me when those Indians jumped us at Mimbres Tank. I won't say that I'm sorry for anything that I did, but if I could talk to Tom and Bob and Ed now, I think I'd tell them they ought to just forget about it."

"You said they won't do that, especially Ed," Frank pointed out quietly.

"I don't think he will. I don't think he'll ever give up trying to avenge his brothers' deaths. But if it was up to me . . . well, I'd call the whole thing off."

"That's an awfully quick change of heart on your part," Conrad said. "Why should we believe you?"

"Maybe because I don't give a damn if you do or not," she snapped.

Frank spread his bedroll on the ground and looped his lariat around it to keep snakes out. "We'll hash this out some more in the morning," he said. "Right now I'm going to get some shut-eye, and I reckon you ought to as well, Miss Callahan."

"Oh, for goodness sake, call me Rebel.

Miss Callahan sounds like my old maiden aunt, if I had one, which I don't."

"All right." Frank stretched out on his blankets, resting his head on his saddle. He tipped his Stetson down over his eyes. "Wake me up in four hours or so. Night, Rebel. Night, Conrad."

"Good night, Frank," Conrad said.

The boy still didn't want to call him Pa. He could live with that, Frank told himself as he dozed off. Anyway, with Apaches on the warpath and three gun-toting hardcases probably still on his trail too, it was downright foolish worrying about such things.

Might sound nice, though, just for a change.

Chapter 10

The three of them reached Lordsburg two days later, riding into the settlement in the early evening. The town lay at the foot of the Peloncillo Mountains, a small range of rounded peaks that were little more than hills. They formed a black backdrop against which the lights of Lordsburg stood out brightly, however.

There had been no sign of either the Apaches or Rebel's relatives. During the long hours the travelers had spent in the saddle, Conrad and Rebel had begun to talk to each other more often, simply because there was nothing else for them to do, no other way to pass the time. She asked him quite a few questions about Boston and Harvard and life back East. Conrad didn't know if her interest was genuine or not, but he didn't want to be rude, so he answered her as best he could. In return —

and just to be polite, of course — he asked her about the ranch she and her brothers had operated in Texas. Conrad had been unsure whether that part of her story was true, but after listening to her talk about the place, he was convinced that it was. She had loved the ranch, and losing it had hurt her. He supposed he could understand that. If something had happened to cause him to lose all the companies that made up the Browning holdings, he would have been upset too.

From time to time, he caught Rebel looking at him with a speculative expression on her lovely face. Conrad knew what that meant, and it made him uneasy. As a rich, relatively presentable young man, he had been the object of the affections of numerous young ladies during the past few years. Though he was a bit ashamed to admit it even to himself, he had taken his pleasure with some of them, dallying with the ones who appealed to him the most. He had never been involved in a serious relationship, however . . . until recently.

And it was the thought of that one that made him uneasy when he saw the interest in Rebel's deep brown eyes. Rebel's beautiful eyes. Rebel's compelling eyes . . .

He needed to stop allowing such thoughts

to stray into his mind, he told himself firmly as he and Frank and that disturbingly beautiful young woman rode into Lordsburg.

"Now what are you going to do with me?" Rebel asked as they pulled up in front of the town's best hotel. "You can't keep me prisoner anymore."

"Keep your voice down," Conrad told her. "You don't want to give people the wrong idea. My God, we didn't kidnap you or anything! You're the one who attempted to harm us."

"Yes, and I've told you I'm sorry about that," she said. "I wish I'd never done it." With a shrug, she added, "You can believe me or not. It's up to you."

Frank said, "I reckon where you go and what you do is up to you now, Rebel. The main reason we brought you along is so that those Apaches wouldn't get you. Now that we've reached Lordsburg, you'll be safe enough."

"So I'm free to go?"

"Sure."

She sat there on her horse for a long moment, looking back and forth between Conrad and Frank, before she said, "What if I don't want to?"

"Don't want to what?" Conrad asked.

"Go."

"What are you going to do then?" Frank asked.

"Well . . . I could trail along with you fellas for a while, wherever you're headed."

"I'm not sure that's a good idea," Frank said with a frown. "You've got your reputation to consider. A young, unmarried woman traveling with a couple of hombres she's not related to . . . Things like that cause people to talk."

"You think I care about that? People can say whatever they darned well please. It doesn't mean anything to me."

Conrad said, "Propriety is very important. If people just went around doing whatever they pleased, the world would descend into chaos and anarchy."

"I reckon the world wouldn't fall completely apart just because I rode along with you and Frank, Harvard."

Conrad felt himself blushing. That was the first time she had referred to him by that mocking nickname.

"Tell you what," Frank said. "We'll be spending the night here and stocking up on supplies in the morning. We'll sleep on it and talk about it over breakfast. How's that?"

"Sounds fine by me," Rebel answered without hesitation.

126

"Well . . . all right," Conrad said much more dubiously.

They dismounted and went into the hotel. Within a few minutes, they had rented rooms and arranged to stable their horses in the barn behind the hotel. Dog could stay there too, the clerk told Frank.

Frank and Conrad had adjoining rooms on the second floor. Rebel's room was right across the hall. As they opened their doors to go into their respective rooms, she said, "Why don't we get together down in the dining room in a little while and have supper?"

"All right." Frank nodded. "Sounds like a good idea."

Conrad wished that Frank had consulted with him before agreeing to Rebel's suggestion. He wasn't sure it was a good idea for him and Rebel to spend any more time together than necessary. The feelings he had begun to have, the feelings whose existence he didn't want to admit even to himself, might turn out to be a complication that he didn't need.

He had been relatively forthcoming with Frank about the situation in Ophir, but there were a few things Conrad hadn't told him, a few things that Frank didn't know about yet. . . .

Life out here in the West could certainly

be complex, Conrad thought as he closed the door of his room. At times like this, he longed for the simplicity and elegance of Boston, where no Indians had gone on the rampage since the famous Tea Party more than a hundred years earlier, and where grudges were settled the civilized way, with sneers and cold looks and the occasional lawsuit, rather than guns and fists.

Frank was already in the dining room when Conrad went downstairs. Conrad had taken the time to wash up and change clothes, but Frank still looked like he had when they arrived, except for the fact that he had brushed some of the trail dust off his clothes. He lifted a hand at the table where he sat, catching Conrad's attention.

Conrad went over and took one of the empty seats. "Rebel's not down yet?"

"Nope. I reckon it takes a mite longer for a lady to get ready to eat."

"Yes, but I was speaking of Rebel," Conrad said with a smirk.

Frank's voice held a sharp edge as he said, "She's a lady, and you'd do well to remember it."

"Oh, come now," Conrad said defensively. "She's little more than some wild frontier creature. She tried to help murder us, after all."

Frank shrugged. "She made some bad decisions because she was pressured into them by her brothers and her cousin, that's all."

"Then you really believe that a few days of traveling with us has opened her eyes and caused her to change her attitude? Because I don't."

"I don't know," Frank said. "Figuring out what a woman really thinks is one of the hardest jobs on the face of the earth, son. Just when a man thinks he knows what he needs to do, everything up and changes on him."

"Don't be so damned paternalistic," Conrad snapped. "I can do without the fatherly advice."

He saw the hurt flare in Frank's eyes, and for a second wished that he hadn't spoken quite so harshly. Yet he hadn't done anything except speak the truth. The time was long since past when he needed a father around to dispense such pearls of wisdom.

"Suit yourself," Frank said. "Since you're so smart, I reckon you know how to handle this just fine without me." He nodded toward the dining room entrance.

Conrad turned his head and looked in that direction, and his breath seemed to freeze in his throat. His heart slugged heavily in his chest.

Rebel stood there, wearing a dress dotted with little blue flowers that hugged her slim waist and swooped low on her shoulders, leaving them bare for the most part and revealing as well the gently rounded swells of the upper third of her breasts. She had brushed her blond hair until it shone in the lamplight as it caressed her shoulders. She was breathtakingly, heartbreakingly lovely.

Lovelier than any of the women he had known back in Boston, Conrad realized with a shock.

Without him quite knowing how it happened, he found himself on his feet, standing and waiting for her as she swept regally across the floor toward the table. Frank had stood up too, and he gave Rebel a friendly nod as she came up to them. "You sure I don't need to start calling you Miss Callahan again?" he asked with an easy charm and grace that Conrad suddenly envied terribly. "You look too pretty to be calling you Rebel."

"Rebel will do just fine," she said. "That's my name, after all." She turned and looked at Conrad, a cool smile on her face. "Good evening, Conrad."

"G-good evening," he managed to say, hating himself briefly for that stumble. He didn't want her to know how strongly she had affected him.

She was a woman, though, so she probably already knew. Women had a way of being aware of everything that a man didn't want them to know.

"You look surprised," she said. "What's the matter, did you think that I wouldn't clean up this nice?"

"No, not at all. I mean, that's not what I thought. I mean—"

"Sit down, Conrad," Frank said quietly. "Let's just have some dinner."

He held Rebel's chair for her, and Conrad cursed himself for not thinking to do that. When had Frank become such a gentleman? It just wasn't right for a man such as him — a gunfighter, for God's sake! — to be so courtly. Rebel seemed to be eating it up, though, smiling and laughing as she made small talk with Frank. No one watching what was going on at the table would ever dream there was a debt of blood and violence between Frank Morgan and the family of this charming, beautiful young woman.

A waiter came over to take their orders. Conrad asked, "Do you have a wine list?" and immediately felt foolish because of the way the man looked at him.

"Nope, sorry," the waiter said. "We don't have any wine, so it wouldn't do any good to have a list."

"Just bring us three steak dinners with all the trimmings," Frank said. "That'll do fine, won't it, Rebel?"

"Yes, of course," she answered without hesitation. "It sounds good. Wonderful, in fact, after being on the trail for days."

"That's what I thought."

Conrad sat there trying not to seethe as they continued their chitchat. Clearly, neither of them knew — or cared — that he was considered a witty and engaging dinner companion back in Boston. Otherwise, they wouldn't be ignoring him like this.

Although Rebel was undeniably beautiful, she was no lady, despite what Frank said. She made occasional mistakes in grammar that showed her lack of a proper education, and when she laughed she was a little too loud about it, a little too brassy. She was probably the sort who would scratch herself or spit if the mood came upon her. A man would never be able to take her out and show her off in civilized society.

But he might be able to keep her as a mistress. As he sneaked a glance at her breasts, Conrad thought that she was eminently suited for that role.

The waiter arrived with their steak dinners, crude but hearty and filling food. Conrad found that he was hungrier than he had realized. He dug into the meal, and Frank and Rebel did likewise.

They were still eating when a man came into the dining room, looked around, and then came toward their table after spotting them. Conrad noticed the man walking toward them and glanced at his father. Frank had seen the man too, of course, probably before Conrad had. One thing about Frank — he was constantly alert.

The stranger was a blocky man in a black suit. His weathered face was decorated with white handlebar mustaches. The sheriff's badge pinned to his coat lapel shone in the light from the oil lamps that illuminated the dining room.

The lawman came up to the table, nodded to Conrad and Rebel, and then said to Frank, "You'd be Frank Morgan."

"That's right."

"From the looks o' things, you didn't come to Lordsburg to hunt trouble."

"That's right," Frank said. "I'm just enjoying a meal with my young friends here."

"Passin' through, are you?"

"We'll probably leave in the morning, after we've picked up some supplies."

The sheriff nodded. "That's good. Lordsburg's a peaceful place most o' the time. I'd like to keep it that way."

Frank smiled thinly and said, "Don't worry, Sheriff. I won't start any trouble. You have my word on that."

"Won't start any," the sheriff said, "but you'll dang sure finish it if it comes to you."

Frank shrugged. "I wouldn't have much choice in that case, now would I?"

"Do me a favor," the lawman said without answering Frank's question. "Finish your supper and make an early night of it. Buy your supplies, if you're of a mind to, and ride out early tomorrow mornin'. Then we'll all be happy."

"Sounds exactly like what I had in mind."

"In that case . . ." The sheriff nodded to Conrad and Rebel again. "You folks enjoy your dinner, and have a good night."

He turned and walked out of the dining room.

Rebel took a deep breath, looked at Frank, and said, "Thank you."

"For what?"

"You could have told him about what happened at Mimbres Tank."

Casually, Frank waved a hand. "That would have been out of his jurisdiction. Anyway, it's over and done with, and Conrad and I came through it pretty much without a scratch."

"No thanks to me," Rebel said.

"Over and done with," Frank repeated.

Conrad folded his napkin and frowned. "That man was rather heavy-handed, don't you think, Frank? He had no reason to accost you like that. You haven't broken any laws here."

"Almost everywhere I go, some lawman comes up to me and has the same sort of conversation," Frank said. "Somebody saw me and recognized me, or the clerk at the desk recognized my name when I signed the book. One way or another, the sheriff got tipped off that I was in town, and he felt like he had to warn me not to let any grass grow under my feet."

"But that's not fair! You have a perfect right to be here."

"Fella just wants to keep his town safe for the folks who live here. He wouldn't be much of a lawman if he didn't feel that way."

"And this happens everywhere you go."

Frank smiled. "Just about. Often enough that I've gotten used to it anyway."

Rebel said, "It's not an easy life, is it?"

"Having a reputation with a gun, you mean?" Frank shook his head. "No, it's not, but I reckon it's not the worst life in the world either. Whatever a man does, there'll be good things and bad about it. I never set out to be known as a gunfighter, but that was where circumstances took me and it's too late to change now."

"I could almost feel sorry for you."

"Don't," Frank told her. "I've got a good horse, a good dog, and new trails to ride nearly every day. After all this time, I wouldn't ask for anything more than that."

Rebel reached over and rested her hand on Frank's for a moment. "I had you all wrong, Frank. Ed had me convinced that you were some sort of bloodthirsty killer. I can see now that you're nothing of the sort."

Irritation prickled along Conrad's nerves as he looked at the way Rebel was gazing at Frank. If he didn't know better, he'd think that she felt some sort of affection for him, perhaps even a romantic attraction. But that was insane.

"He *has* killed quite a few men, you know," Conrad said. "Hundreds, according to some accounts."

"Folks tend to exaggerate," Frank said.

Rebel squeezed Frank's hand. "No matter how many it was, I'll bet there wasn't a one of them that didn't need killin'."

"I hope not."

Conrad pushed his chair back, the legs scraping on the floor. "I don't believe I'm hungry anymore," he said tightly. "I'm tired. I'm going up to my room and turn in."

Rebel turned a disinterested smile on him. "Good night," she said. Then she looked at Frank again.

"Night, son," Frank said.

Conrad wanted to tell Frank not to call him son, but he bit back the harsh reaction. With all the poise and dignity he could muster, he turned and stalked out of the dining room.

Insane, he told himself again as he thought about the way Rebel was looking at Frank. Positively ludicrous.

But that didn't make him feel a bit better.

Chapter 11

"You ought to be ashamed of yourself, you little minx," Frank said sternly to Rebel as he looked across the table at her.

She batted her eyelashes innocently as she asked, "What are you talking about, Frank?"

He slid his hand out from under hers, but he did it gently so she would know he wasn't really all that upset with her. "You know good and well what I'm talking about. Taking advantage of that poor boy's feelings the way you were."

"That poor boy can speak up if something's bothering him, can't he? He doesn't seem to have any trouble talking about other things. In fact, he goes on and on more than anybody I ever saw."

"Conrad *is* a mite fond of the sound of his own voice," Frank admitted, "but when it comes to what he's feeling, he's pretty close-mouthed."

"And stiff-necked."

Frank inclined his head in acknowledgment of Rebel's point.

"Anyway, how do you know I'm not just acting the way I really feel?" she went on.

"For one thing, I'm old enough to be your pa. I'm almost old enough to be your grandpa."

"But you're not either one of those."

"And I've seen the way you look at Conrad when he's not watching," Frank went on as if he hadn't heard her.

"He *is* a handsome boy," Rebel said, a touch of wistfulness in her voice.

He ought to be, Frank thought. He's my son, after all.

But he didn't say that. Conrad hadn't mentioned anything about them being father and son while Rebel was around, and Frank didn't figure it was his place to do so.

"If you're going to keep riding with us, sooner or later you're going to have to tell him how you feel," he said. "Lord knows Conrad might not ever get around to it."

"Am I going to keep riding with you?" Rebel asked. "Aren't you afraid to have me around? I might double-cross you."

"I don't think so. I'm a pretty good judge of character, if I do say so myself."

Rebel's face grew more solemn as she said,

"Ed won't give up, and he'll drag Tom and Bob along with him."

"That's another reason to have you around," Frank pointed out. "As long as you're with us, they'll be less likely to bushwhack us. Your brothers may let Ed boss them around, but I reckon they wouldn't want a bunch of lead to start flying around if you were where some of it might hit you."

"So you want to take me along as a shield."

"Your words, not mine."

A tense silence fell between them for several moments. Then Rebel said, "You still haven't told me where you're going."

"A place called Ophir. A mining boomtown north of here, in the mountains."

"Why?"

Frank hesitated, but only for a second. He wasn't going to drag Rebel along with him and Conrad by force, even though what he had said about the advantages of having her with them was true. If she didn't want to go, that would be the end of it.

But if she was going to accompany them, she deserved to know what she was getting into. There might be danger along the way. Frank considered it more likely than not that there would be.

"Conrad's building a spur line up there,

and the construction has run into trouble."

"A spur line?" Rebel repeated with a frown. "You mean like a railroad?"

"That's exactly what I mean."

"He owns a *railroad*?"

Frank nodded.

"Wait a minute," Rebel went on. "He said that you own part of the business too."

"That's right."

"So you're really a railroad magnate, not a gunfighter?"

Frank chuckled. "I wouldn't call myself a railroad magnate, not by a long shot. The percentage I own is pretty small compared to Conrad's."

"Do you own other businesses, you and Conrad? Besides the railroad?"

"To tell you the truth, I don't know what all we own. There are some mines, I know that, and Lord knows what else."

She let out an unladylike whistle. "I never knew I'd been riding the trail with a couple of rich men."

"Money never meant that much to me," Frank said. "As long as I've got enough for food and ammunition, that's all I need."

"You don't have a big fancy house somewhere?"

Frank shook his head. "Nope. A hotel like this is about as fancy as I ever get. A lot of nights I sleep out under the stars."

"I can't imagine being rich and not living like it."

Frank leaned forward slightly and clasped his hands together on the table. "What would you do if you had a lot of money?" he asked.

"I'd go back to Texas and get our ranch back," Rebel answered without hesitation.

"And then?"

"Why, I reckon Tom and Bob and I would run it like we always have. . . ." She nodded slowly as she began to understand. "Oh. I reckon I see what you're getting at, Frank."

"I lived a long time before I ever had much money," he said, without offering any explanation of how he had come to own a small part of the vast Browning business empire. "By the time I did, I didn't have any interest in changing the way I live. So I've just gone on my way and let Conrad and the lawyers I hired do all the worrying." He smiled. "I'd say I got the best end of the deal."

"I think maybe you did." She paused for a moment and then said, "Tell me about the trouble Conrad's having with this railroad of his."

"I don't know a lot about it myself just yet, only what he told me when he asked me for help. Evidently, there have been some instances of sabotage, and a payroll got stolen. Things like that. Plus the Apaches have been raising Ned too."

"You mean raising hell," Rebel said with a smile. "No need to pretty it up for me."

"Conrad met me in El Paso and told me what was going on, asked me if I'd come out here and give him a hand. I felt like I ought to pitch in, especially since I do have a financial interest in the spur line and in some of the mines up around Ophir." He didn't say anything about forcing Conrad to pay him for that help. Frank had already started to think that maybe he had been a mite too petty about that.

"Have you two known each other for long?"

"A few years," Frank answered vaguely.

"I can see why he'd want you to act as a troubleshooter, the reputation you've got and all. And now you've got to worry about Ed and those danged brothers of mine, along with the railroad's problems."

Frank shrugged. "Life doesn't always wait for you to get finished with one challenge before it drops another one right on your plate."

"No, I reckon not."

The waiter came over and asked if they wanted more coffee. Frank looked quizzically at Rebel. She shook her head, and Frank told the man, "No, I reckon we're done. Everything was fine."

"Thank you, Mr. Morgan," the man said. He knew who Frank was. By morning, the whole town probably would.

Frank stood up and put his hat on, then went around the table to hold Rebel's chair for her. "Now that you know who we are and where we're headed, do you still want to ride along with us?"

"Do I have a choice?" she asked.

"Yes. You do."

"I'll go along," she said. "I don't want anything to happen to you or Conrad, and I don't want to see Tom and Bob get hurt either. Best chance I have to stopping that is to stick close to you two and hope that the boys give me a chance to talk some sense into them."

"I was hoping that's what you'd say. I appreciate it, Rebel."

As they were on their way up the stairs to the second floor, Frank added, "I'd be obliged too if you'd remember what I said about Conrad."

"About telling him how I feel?" Rebel laughed. "I know you want to help him, Frank, but some things he's just got to figure out on his own."

Frank nodded, but at the same time he

144

hoped he wouldn't have to knock the young-ster in the head with a two-by-four just to get him to pay attention. Sometimes that worked with mules, but he wasn't sure about mule-headed young men.

Frank was up early the next morning, and had already bought the supplies and had them loaded on the packhorse before he joined Conrad and Rebel for breakfast in the hotel dining room. They looked up at him as he came to the table and sat down, hanging his hat on the back of his chair. Judging by the tense expressions on their faces, they weren't getting along any better than they had been before.

Conrad said, "I was just telling Rebel that if she'd like, I'm willing to pay for a train ticket so she can go back to El Paso."

"And I was just telling Conrad that I don't need anybody taking care of me like I'm a newborn baby calf," Rebel said. "If I wanted to go back to El Paso, I wouldn't ask for his permission or his help. But as it so happens, I don't want to go back."

"Where are you going then?" he asked.

Frank said, "With us."

Conrad's eyes narrowed as he looked across the table. "What do you mean? We haven't discussed this—"

"Rebel and I hashed it out last night," Frank said. "She wants to trail along with us, and I think it's a good idea."

"Hardly!" Conrad burst out. "It's a terrible idea, and no one consulted with me about it—"

"That's because I don't need you telling me where I can and can't go," Rebel broke in.

Conrad looked daggers at Frank. "Am I to assume that my opinion means nothing in this matter?"

Frank signaled to the waiter for another cup. There was already a pot of coffee on the table. He said, "Rebel and I figured that if she's along, the rest of the Callahans will be less likely to jump us. And she wants a chance to talk to her brothers before there's any more trouble."

"What about the question of the whole arrangement being improper? Downright scandalous even?"

"I don't care about that," Rebel said. "So there's no reason for you to care either, Conrad."

"Fine," he muttered. "Let the whole world think you're a trollop."

Her eyes narrowed and her mouth tightened. "The whole world can go to hell, and so can—"

"I think I'll have some flapjacks," Frank interrupted. "And maybe a thick slice of ham and some fried potatoes and some biscuits and gravy. It's liable to be a long day. Eat hearty, children."

"I'm not a child," Conrad snapped.

"Then don't act like one," Rebel said.

"Me? You're the one who—"

Frank sighed. It was going to be a long trail to Ophir.

Chapter 12

The sun had been up for an hour when they rode out of Lordsburg. Under normal circumstances, Frank would have considered that a late start to the day, but where Conrad was concerned it was actually pretty early. So the time of their departure was a compromise, Frank supposed.

Judging by the stiff backs of Conrad and Rebel, compromise was something that was going to be in short supply on this trip.

Dog was certainly in good spirits, though, ranging far ahead of the horses most of the time. That was fine with Frank. There was no better advance scout than the big cur. If there was trouble waiting for them, Dog would let him know.

Rebel wore jeans and rode astride; no sidesaddle for her. She rolled up the sleeves of her man's checked shirt so that her tanned forearms were visible. Her hair was tucked up in her brown hat. The most colorful thing about her was the blue bandanna she wore knotted around her neck.

Frank had bought another Winchester in Lordsburg — or rather, Conrad had, since he paid for it. The rifle now rode in a sheath strapped to the saddle under Rebel's right leg. It was possible she might get separated from them, and now that he had decided to trust her, at least to an extent, Frank didn't want her to be unarmed in case she had to defend herself.

The Mogollons rose to their right and in front of them, looking deceptively close in the thin air, but for the time being the trail still crossed a long, flat stretch of territory. They followed the rails already laid down by the work crew of the New Mexico, Rio Grande, and Oriental. Conrad said, "The work went well on this part. The trouble didn't really start until construction reached the mountains."

"I'm not surprised," Frank said. "Hard to sneak up on anybody out here on these flats. There are a lot more places to hide in the mountains."

Conrad hadn't been happy when he found out that Frank had told Rebel about the problems that were taking them to Ophir, but he hadn't acted any surlier over that than over the simple fact that she was accompanying them. By now he seemed to have gotten over some of his resentment. He and Rebel were talking together with grudging civility.

"It should take us about three days to reach Ophir," Conrad said, "but we ought to catch up to the construction crew sometime tomorrow."

"You sound like you've made this trip before," Frank commented.

"I have. I've been to Ophir several times over the past year, checking on our mining operations. In fact, it was making the long journey by buggy that gave me the idea a rail line was needed."

A frown creased Frank's forehead. "You didn't tell me you'd been up here."

"I didn't see that it made any difference."

"Well, maybe it doesn't. But it's nice to know that if I need information about the lay of the land, I can pick your brain."

"You'd be better off picking someone else's brain. I always hired drivers and guards, and I didn't pay much attention to where we were going, as long as we got there safely."

Frank suppressed the urge to shake his head. He couldn't imagine traveling somewhere and not paying attention to the surroundings. Studying the terrain, taking note of landmarks — that sort of thing was second nature to him. That was why he seldom got lost in country that he had visited before. Everything he had seen on previous visits was still stored away in his brain, ready for him to use when he needed it.

They made camp that night in the foothills of the Mogollons. Frank had kept a close eye on their back trail all day and hadn't seen any signs of anyone following them. Nor had he spotted any Apaches watching them from the hills. Of course, that didn't really mean anything. If the Apaches didn't want to be seen, then nobody was likely to spot them. Frank's instincts hadn't felt any watching eyes, though.

He and Conrad took turns standing guard that night anyway. Rebel offered to take a turn, but Frank told her to go ahead and get a full night's sleep. As much as he was convinced that Rebel no longer wanted to see the two of them dead, he wasn't ready to put them both completely at her mercy.

Rolling up in his blankets, he was soon sleeping soundly.

They had camped next to a clump of boulders that had a stairstep shape. Conrad climbed a couple of the rocks to one that was formed like a bench and sat down there with his rifle, ready to keep watch for four hours or so. He could see Frank and Rebel below him, both of them snug in their bedrolls against the chill of night. Dog lay stretched out next to Frank. Faithful companion, Conrad thought.

He'd had dogs before, but never one as loyal as the big cur. Dog was a steadfast friend to Frank, and Conrad wondered what that would be like. Not to have a faithful pet necessarily, but just to have a friend.

His mother was the closest thing to a real friend he'd ever had, and that didn't really count. She had to be fond of him; he was her child. Thinking back over his life, especially the past few years, he couldn't recall anyone who had been particularly close to him. There were the women who had thrown themselves at him, and the men who had chummed around with him at Harvard, but none of those were real friends either. They had been drawn to him because of his money. That was the only reason they had spent time with him. He was convinced of it.

Conrad's gaze lingered on Frank. He could never think of the gunfighter as his father. Too much time had gone by when neither of them was even aware of the other's existence. The bond that should have been there between father and son simply wasn't there and couldn't be forced, no matter how hard Frank tried with his paternalistic advice.

But perhaps someday they could be friends, could feel a mutual respect for each other.

Not likely, Conrad told himself bitterly, since Frank had no respect for him. In the eyes of Frank Morgan, he was just a helpless tenderfoot, a greenhorn, a damned Easterner. And all that was true. Conrad was not a frontiersman, and doubted that he had the ability to ever fit that description. The fact that he was a canny businessman meant nothing to Frank, who judged men solely by how they handled horses and guns and things like that.

No, Conrad thought with a sigh, he and Frank would never be like a typical father and son, and they would never be friends either. Hoping otherwise was just a waste of time.

And where, he asked himself as he suddenly stiffened, had Rebel gotten off to?

Because her bedroll was empty, the blankets thrown back.

He hadn't even noticed her leaving.

Alarmed, Conrad started to his feet. He froze as he heard a sound near him, the scraping of a foot on the rock. He turned quickly toward it, bringing up the rifle in his hands. If she thought she could ambush him—

"Conrad, wait!" Rebel's familiar voice hissed. "Don't shoot. It's just me."

She pulled herself up on the rock next to him. "What are you doing here?" he asked in an angry whisper as he settled back where he had been sitting. "You're supposed to be sleeping."

"I know. I couldn't go to sleep. So I thought I'd come up here and talk to you for a little while."

"Really? I was under the impression that you didn't care for talking to me."

"What gives you that idea?" Rebel asked as she sat down beside him. Her hip was close to his, but not quite touching.

Butter wouldn't melt in that one's mouth. She would say anything, do anything, to get what she wanted, Conrad warned himself. He had to be careful—

"If you don't want me up here, I'll go back down," Rebel said when Conrad didn't answer. "I don't want to annoy you."

There was something in her voice, a hint of hurt feelings, and for some reason that bothered him. He said quickly, "I didn't say that you annoy me."

154

"You sort of act like it. Not only right now, but all the time."

"You've misinterpreted my attitude," Conrad said stiffly. "I have nothing against you. Well, other than that business of trying to kill us, of course."

"I've said I was sorry for that. Didn't you ever make a mistake, Conrad? Didn't you ever do something and wish later that you could take it back, make things like it had never happened?"

"That's impossible," he said.

"I know that. But it's not impossible to forgive somebody."

He frowned. "Is that what you're doing? Asking for forgiveness?"

With an exasperated sigh, Rebel threw her hands in the air. "What do you think I've been doing for the past couple of days? Don't you pay *any* attention to what's going on around you? Or do you just live in a world of your own all the time?"

Wounded, he said, "I'm sure I don't know what you mean."

"All right," she grated. "If you don't notice what people say, maybe you'll notice this."

She turned toward him, moving quickly so that he didn't quite know what was happening, and put a hand on either side of his face.

Leaning in, she pressed her mouth hard against his.

The kiss took him by surprise. His eyes widened. And then, as if of their own accord, they closed. He gave himself over to the sensation of Rebel's hot, sweet, moist lips moving against his. Instinctively, he returned the pressure.

Conrad couldn't have said how long the kiss went on. Long enough so that when Rebel finally pulled her head back, he was breathless and his heart pounded heavily in his chest and he could feel the blood racing through his veins like a mountain stream cascading down from the high country.

"Oh, my," he said.

"Damn right," she said. And then she kissed him again.

This one didn't last as long, but it was almost as potent. When they broke apart, he felt as if he might never be able to breathe correctly again. She had permanently impaired him with her passion. A voice in the back of his brain shouted madly for him not to trust her. She was a seductress, a jezebel, a . . . a . . .

"If that doesn't convince you I'm sorry, I don't know what will," she said. "But that's darned well as far as I'm gonna go just to say I'm sorry."

"Was that . . . the only reason you kissed me . . . to say you were sorry?"

"Why else?"

"Well, I thought perhaps . . . I'm unsure how you feel toward me, Rebel. I don't know if you actually, well, *like* me, or if you just, uh, enjoy, uh . . ."

"I don't go around kissing fellas just for the fun of it," she said solemnly, "if that's what you're getting at."

"Yes, I . . . I suppose I was."

"And as for whether or not I like you . . . you're not the most likable sort in the world, Conrad Browning. You don't go out of your way to get anybody to like you. You just go your own way, and if anybody doesn't care for it, then to hell with them."

"I'm accustomed to having a great deal of responsibility in the business world. I have to make important decisions and see that they're implemented properly."

"You didn't decide I was going to kiss you," Rebel pointed out. "That just sort of happened."

"Yes," Conrad said softly, "it did."

"And it didn't kill you either."

"No. It most certainly didn't."

"You see what I'm saying, Conrad? Just let things happen. You don't have to be in complete control all the time. Then folks might

157

see you a little different."

"You really think so?"

"I kissed you, didn't I?" Rebel stood up and brushed off the seat of her trousers. "Reckon I'll go back down there and try to get some sleep. Morning comes early in these parts."

"You're leaving?" he said, trying not to sound overly alarmed by the prospect — when in truth he didn't want her to go.

"Why not? You have anything else you want to say — or do?"

Conrad took a deep breath. "Uh . . . no. No, I don't suppose I do. Good night, Rebel. I hope you get to sleep all right this time."

"Thanks. Good night, Conrad."

Did she sound a little disappointed that he hadn't asked her to stay up here with him? He wasn't sure. He started to call to her as she began to climb down the rocks, started to ask her to come back. But he didn't, and a moment later she was gone. He watched as she crawled back into her bedroll, pulled the blankets tight around her, and lay still. He couldn't tell for sure from where he was, of course, but he thought she went to sleep fairly quickly.

At least he didn't have to worry about dozing off while he was on guard duty. After the things she had said — and done — he had a feeling that he wasn't going to be sleeping any time soon.

After a peaceful night and a good breakfast the next morning, they followed the spur line northward, climbing into the mountains through a long pass. Frank knew that even with a good crew, building a rail line through mountains was a slow, back-breaking process. Often the rail bed had to be blasted out of the sides of the peaks with dynamite. There were tunnels to be dug, trestles to be constructed, and steep grades to be somehow tamed. More than twenty years earlier, as the great drive to complete the transcontinental railroad was under way, the Union Pacific had fairly raced westward across the Great Plains while the Central Pacific, building east from the West Coast, had been forced to grind its way foot by foot through California's Sierra Nevadas and then into the mighty Rockies themselves. A lot of laborers, coolies imported from China, had died before the two lines finally linked up at Promontory Point, Utah. Of course, plenty of Irish workers on the Union Pacific had been killed in construction accidents too. All in all, building railroads was just a mighty dangerous business under the best of circumstances.

The men working for Conrad didn't need any extra dangers holding them back. That was why The Drifter was here.

Conrad and Rebel were unusually quiet today. They weren't sniping at each other as they often did. The night before, not long after Frank had turned in, he had roused from sleep enough to think that maybe he heard a pair of voices talking softly. Dog had been sleeping peacefully beside him, so he knew the conversation, if he was really hearing one, didn't represent a threat. He had gone back to sleep.

Now he wondered if Conrad and Rebel had had a talk of some sort while Conrad was standing guard. Maybe they had worked things out between them. Frank hoped that was the case.

As they climbed higher, there were places where they had to ride on the roadbed itself, letting the horses pick their way along between the cross-ties. The ledges on which the tracks were laid were too narrow to proceed any other way. They were on one such ledge that curved around the side of a mountain when a booming noise sounded. Frank was in the lead. He reined in, forcing Conrad and Rebel to do likewise.

"Hear that?" he asked.

"It would be difficult to miss such a

160

sound," Conrad said. "It was an explosion of some sort, wasn't it?"

Frank nodded and said, "Yeah, we must be getting close to the railhead. That blast wasn't too far away. They're probably blasting out a tunnel or leveling a slope."

He had just hitched Stormy into a walk again when another explosion sounded. This one was much larger and seemed to shake the very mountain.

"Frank!" Conrad said. "That didn't sound right!"

"Yeah, it was too big for a normal blast," Frank said with a frown. "Maybe somebody used too much dynamite."

Worried now, Frank got the big Appaloosa moving again. They had gone only a short distance when he heard the sudden popping of gunshots up ahead. Something was definitely wrong. He couldn't gallop up this ledge, though, not without risking a fall. There was about a forty-foot drop-off to his left, not tremendously high, but steep enough so that a tumble down it would probably be fatal. As guns continued to bark, Frank rode forward slowly, his face grim as the delay chafed at him.

Then, with a pounding of hoofbeats, a rider came into view about a hundred yards ahead of them, swinging around the curve of the mountainside. The man was running his horse recklessly. As he spotted the riders on the tracks ahead of him, he jerked up the gun in his hand and began to fire, flame spouting from the muzzle of the revolver.

Chapter 13

Frank whipped out his Colt as a slug sizzled past his head, close enough so that he felt the wind-rip of its passage as well as heard it. Another bullet struck a cross-tie in front of Stormy and kicked up splinters. The big Appaloosa stood steady, though, not spooked by the shots.

The gun in Frank's hand came level, but before he could pull the trigger, the horse charging down the ledge suddenly faltered. Frank figured one of the animal's hooves had hit one of the cross-ties wrong, throwing it off stride. The horse nickered frantically as it tried to regain its balance.

The rider yelled a curse and tried to bail out of the saddle to his left, away from the drop-off. He was too late. The out-of-control horse plunged over the edge, taking the rider with it. The man screamed as he found nothing but empty air beneath him and his mount.

He was still in the saddle when the two of them struck the rocky slope about thirty feet down from the ledge. The impact separated them. Man and horse bounced off and fell the remaining ten feet, landing on the rocks, among which flowed a tiny creek.

Frank had had the best view of the accident because he was in the lead, but Conrad and Rebel saw the fall too. Rebel cried out in horror, and Conrad exclaimed, "Good Lord!"

Grimly, Frank holstered his gun, knowing he wouldn't need it again, at least not right away. He hitched Stormy into a slow, careful walk and rode forward until he reached the spot where the man and horse had gone off the ledge. He dismounted and looked down at the broken, motionless bodies below.

"Are they dead?" Conrad asked.

Frank was about to say yes when the horse abruptly tried to rear up, whinnying in pain. At least two of the animal's legs were broken. Frank didn't hesitate. He turned to Stormy, pulled his Winchester from its saddle sheath, and drew a quick bead. The rifle cracked, and the injured horse fell silent. Rebel turned her face toward the rock wall for a moment even though Frank knew she understood. She had been raised on a ranch, and she would be all too aware that sometimes a quick end was the greatest mercy.

The man hadn't moved, and from the way his head was canted at an odd angle on his shoulders, Frank didn't expect him to. Conrad dismounted, walked up alongside Frank, and asked, "Who in blazes was he, and why was he shooting at us?"

"I don't know, but I've got a hunch he was mixed up somehow with that last big blast we heard." Frank turned to Stormy, replaced the Winchester, and took his rope off the saddle. He tied one end of it to the saddle horn.

"What are you doing?" Conrad asked.

"Got to go down there and make sure he's dead."

"Can't you tell that from here?"

"I'm pretty certain, but that's not good enough," Frank explained. "Not when you're talking about a man's life."

Rebel had dismounted too. She came up to them and asked, "You want me to hold Stormy's reins, Frank?"

"That's not necessary. He won't go anywhere."

Frank tossed the rest of the rope over the edge and then put on a pair of gloves he took from his saddlebags. Grasping the rope tightly, he stepped down off the ledge and began lowering himself, bracing his feet against the rocky slope as he let himself down. It didn't take long for him to reach the bottom.

When he got there, he stepped past the body of the horse with its bullet-shattered skull and went to the rider, who had landed a little farther out from the base of the wall. The man wore high-topped boots, buckskin trousers with fringe down the outside of the legs, and a faded blue bib-front shirt. His hat, a high-crowned black Stetson, had come off during the fall and lay several yards away. The man had a close-cropped beard and thinning dark hair. His nose had been broken at least once in the past, and a knife scar slanted from his jawline across his left cheek. Although the physical details were always somewhat different, he might have been any of a thousand hardcases and gunmen Frank had encountered over the past three decades.

And he was definitely dead, as a check for a pulse in his broken neck quickly told Frank. Other than a few scrapes, that was his only injury.

Of course, if he had kept charging toward Frank, Conrad, and Rebel, shooting as he came, he would have been dead a few seconds later. Dead from the bullet that Frank would have put through him.

A search of the man's pockets turned up nothing except a double eagle and a few smaller coins. Then the sound of hoofbeats made Frank look up. Conrad called, "Frank, somebody else is coming!"

Several somebodies, from the sound of it, and they were in a hurry too. Frank took hold of the rope again and began walking up the steep slope.

By the time he got to the top, a group of about a dozen riders had come around the shoulder of the mountain. They weren't galloping along the ledge the way the fleeing man had been before he and his horse fell, but they were moving at a fast clip anyway. They slowed as they came in sight of Frank and his companions. Riding two abreast, they came on down the slightly slanting ledge.

As the men came closer, Frank saw that they were fairly bristling with weapons. He saw several rifles and shotguns, and nearly all of the men wore holstered revolvers. One of the pair in the front had the look of a leader about him. He was big and brawny, with wide shoulders and a blunt, sunburned face. Like the others, he wore canvas trousers, a flannel shirt, and lace-up work boots rather than the higher-heeled riding boots such as Frank's. A fedora was jammed down on his thatch of rusty hair instead of the wide-brimmed Stetson that would have been more common in this part of the country.

The man reined in and rested the rifle he carried across the pommel of his saddle. Leaning to the side, he peered down at the bodies of the man and the horse lying at the bottom of the slope and then straightened to ask, "What happened? Did they fall off?"

"That's right," Frank said as he coiled his rope and replaced it on the saddle. "The hombre took a couple of shots at us first, but his horse lost its balance and went over before we had a chance to do anything."

The big man grunted. "Good riddance. Might have been helpful if we'd gotten our hands on him before he died, though, so we could ask him who hired him to blow up our dynamite shed."

"We heard the blast," Frank said with a nod. "It sounded like a whole shed full of dynamite going up, all right."

"Who are you folks?" the man asked, but before Frank could answer, Conrad stepped past him and lifted a hand in greeting.

"Sam!" he called. "It's me, Conrad Browning."

"It sure is," the man called Sam said with a grin. "Didn't recognize you at first, Mr.

Browning, in that cowboy getup. Don't suppose I ever saw you before except in a suit."

He swung down from his saddle and strode forward to shake hands with Conrad. Turning to Frank, Conrad said, "This is Sam Brant, my construction superintendent. Sam, meet Frank Morgan."

"The Drifter, eh?" Brant gave Frank a hard, calloused hand and a firm grip. "When Mr. Browning said he knew you and thought he could get you up here to give us a hand, I didn't know whether to believe him or not."

"You can see for yourself that I was right," Conrad said. He nodded toward the dead man below. "You say he blew up our supply of dynamite?"

"All that was in the shed," Brant replied. "We still have part of a case that we were using."

Brant's accent told Frank that the man wasn't a Westerner. He probably came from Ohio or Pennsylvania or some place like that. From the looks of him, and judging by the fact that he was ramrodding the construction of this spur line, he was an experienced railroad man. Even though their backgrounds were completely different, Frank felt an instinctive liking for him.

"One of our boys saw him skulking around the shed," Brant went on, "and raised a yell, but it was too late. The shed blew, and that gent jumped on a horse he had hidden in the brush and took off. I grabbed some of the men and came after him."

"Ever seen him before?" Frank asked.

Brant cuffed his fedora back and hunkered on his heels at the edge of the roadbed to look down at the corpse. After a moment of intent study, the construction boss shook his head. "No, if I ever saw him, I don't recall it. Looks like a bad sort, though, from what I can tell."

"That was my impression too," Frank agreed. "Like you said, it would have been nice to be able to question him."

Brant straightened. "Well, we won't have that chance, but it's just a matter of time until some other spalpeen tries something. We'll catch the next one and hold his feet to the fire."

"You mean that metaphorically, of course," Conrad put in.

Brant just grunted. He turned his attention to Rebel and took his hat off, holding it over his heart as he said, "I'm sorry, miss, I didn't mean to be ignoring you until now. Sam Brant is the name, and I'm at your service."

"Uh, this is Miss Callahan," Conrad said quickly. "She's traveling with us."

"Escorting the lady to Ophir, eh? That's gentlemanly of you lads."

Brant didn't press for an explanation of who Rebel really was or why she was with Frank and Conrad, and they didn't offer one. The members of the railroad construction crew who had given chase to the now-deceased intruder turned their horses around and started back to camp on Brant's orders. "I'll be along shortly, with Mr. Browning and his friends," Brant told them.

Then he turned back to Frank and the two young people and went on. "You are heading for our camp, aren't you?"

"That's right," Frank said. "Seems like the best place to start, since you're obviously still having trouble."

"Aye, that's for sure," Brant agreed with a disgusted scowl. "This business today, blowing up the dynamite shed, I mean, is the first time anybody has tried anything in several days, but there have been problems off and on ever since the last time Mr. Browning was here. Why, it was only a week ago that somebody took potshots at one of my crews as they chopped wood for our cookstoves."

"Have you seen any sign of the Indians?" Conrad asked.

Brant shook his head. "The savages themselves, no. But we've seen their handiwork."

The grim tone of the man's voice told Frank what to expect, but he asked the question anyway. "What do you mean by that?"

"I mean," Brant said, "that three of our boys went out to hunt fresh meat a while back, and when they never came back to camp we sent out a big, well-armed search party. Found their bodies about a mile up a canyon, stuck full of arrows. Their scalps were gone too."

"We ran into Indian trouble too," Conrad said.

Brant balled one hand into a big fist and smacked it into the palm of the other hand. "I don't know why the Army doesn't come in here and clean out those red heathens!"

"That's easier said than done," Frank pointed out. "Fifteen years ago, Victorio and his braves led the Army a merry chase through these very mountains. The soldiers never did catch him. He wound up being trapped and killed by the Mexican Army, down south of the border. In more recent times, it was Geronimo who had the soldier boys running around in circles, mostly over in Arizona Territory. But it's not as simple as just sending in the Army."

"No, I suppose not," Brant said. "Still, it's their job to pacify the savages, and I don't know why they're not at least trying to do it."

Conrad said, "I've spoken to some of the politicians in Washington, Sam, and they promised me that troops will be dispatched to this region as soon as they're available. Until that time comes, though . . ." Conrad shrugged. "We're on our own."

"Not entirely." Brant nodded toward Frank. "We've got Frank Morgan to help us now."

"I'll try not to let you down," Frank said wryly.

Brant grasped the reins of his horse. "Well, come on, folks. I'll take you on up to the camp."

They mounted and rode along the ledge. Conrad asked, "Will you be able to go ahead with construction without your supply of dynamite?"

"Well, like I said, we've got part of a case left, so we can carry on for a little while. We've rigged a temporary telegraph line between the camp and Lordsburg, so I'll wire down there and have several more cases of the stuff put on the next work train that comes up the line. It'll be here in a few days. So blowing up the shed shouldn't slow us down much. It'll just cost you some extra money to replace that lost dynamite, Mr. Browning."

"I don't care about that," Conrad said. "I

can stand some added expenses, as long as construction carries on."

"It'll do that," Brant vowed. "If you plan to stay around for a few days, you'll see for yourself."

"I haven't decided yet what I'm going to do. I thought I might go on to Ophir and leave Frank at the camp to investigate." Conrad paused. "I'm afraid I wouldn't be much help at work like that."

Frank said, "Whatever you think is best." He had thought that Conrad might want to remain at the camp, but it didn't surprise him that the young man was leaning toward going on to Ophir. Even though the settlement was a mining boomtown, it would offer more in the way of comfort and civilized amenities than a railroad construction camp.

The roadbed continued its long curve around the side of the mountain, reaching a peak and then gradually sloping down until it finally reached a valley that was several miles wide. The tracks had crossed part of the valley, stopping at a wide gorge where a foaming, fast-flowing river brawled along at the bottom. The little creek that paralleled the tracks flowed into that stream just west of a partially completed trestle.

"We were blasting out some holes for the support pillars," Brant explained as the group rode toward the sprawling cluster of tents that marked the location of the construction camp. There were also several freight and passenger cars parked along the tracks, as well as flatcars piled high with wooden cross-ties and steel rails. Building a railroad took a lot of men, equipment, and material.

Frank looked at the spidery framework of the trestle, which spanned about three fourths of the width of the gorge. It always amazed him that such fragile-looking structures could support the enormous weight of a locomotive and a whole train of cars.

"You'll want to spend the night here at least before you start on to Ophir," Brant said to Conrad as they all dismounted. "There's room for you in one of the cars where the foremen and I sleep. As for the lady . . ."

"Anywhere's fine with me," Rebel said, "as long as I've got room to spread my bedroll."

"Uh, I was about to say we can fix up a private compartment for you, ma'am," Brant went on.

"I don't want you going to any trouble, Mr. Brant."

"No trouble at all, ma'am."

Frank could tell that Rebel didn't cotton much to being called ma'am, but she didn't say anything except to thank the construction boss graciously for his hospitality. It occurred to Frank to wonder: If Conrad did go on to Ophir, would Rebel stay here at the camp . . . or would she go with him?

That question could wait. For now, Frank had a job of his own to do. He was going to find out who was behind these attacks on the New Mexico, Rio Grande, and Oriental, and put a stop to them so that the rails could go on safely through the mountains. With any luck, maybe nobody else would have to die to make that dream a reality.

Chapter 14

The men who had returned to the camp ahead of Frank and the others had already reported that the saboteur was dead. They had also spread the word that Frank Morgan, the famous gunfighter known as The Drifter, would be riding into camp soon, so quite a few of the workers were on hand to greet the little group and to stare curiously at Frank. He was used to being gawked at, and while he didn't like it very much, he didn't allow it to bother him either.

Brant introduced Frank to his assistants, the men who served as foremen of the various work gangs, and to Nathan Buckhalter, a surveyor and topographical engineer. Buckhalter had been in charge of the initial survey carried out long before construction even began, and he was the one who had determined the best route for the line to follow. If unforeseen difficulties forced any deviation from that route, Buckhalter was on hand to determine which way the railroad should go.

Conrad took Rebel into the car that provided living quarters for Brant, Buckhalter, and the other bosses of the project. The workers slept in the scores of tents pitched around the railhead.

Once Frank had met everyone, Brant led him over to a blackened pit in the ground a couple of hundred yards from the camp. A few wisps of smoke still drifted up from the ugly crater.

"That used to be our dynamite shed," Brant explained. "You can see for yourself what happened when all the explosives stored there went up."

Frank looked at the distance between the camp and the place where the dynamite had been stored. "Good idea keeping the stuff this far away."

"Yeah, that's just common sense around a construction area," Brant said with a nod. "And it's lucky we are that none of the men were close enough to get caught in the blast. Nobody was killed or even hurt."

"How was the explosion set off?"

Brant took off his fedora and ran his fingers through his bristly reddish hair. "You know, in all the confusion I never did find out the details. Let's go talk to Hank Willard. He's the one who first saw that skunk who wound up falling off the ledge."

Willard was a short man with unusually muscular arms and shoulders. They had gotten that way from spending hours every day swinging the heavy maul that drove in the spikes fastening the rails to the cross-ties. He shook hands with Frank when Brant introduced them and said, "Beggin' your pardon, Mr. Morgan, but I've read a plenty o' them dime novels about you. Never thought I'd actually get to meet anybody so famous."

"Well, you have to remember that all those stories are just made up," Frank said with a smile.

"You don't say! You mean you never met the Steam Man of the Prairie or tangled with Count Marzeppi or shot it out with five hundred badmen at once?"

Frank had to laugh. "I don't reckon I'd still be here if any of that was true."

"Well, they was good stories anyway."

"Tell Mr. Morgan about what happened earlier, Hank," Sam Brant prompted.

"It was like this," the spiker said. "I been helpin' out with the trestle, since we ain't actually layin' any track right now, and one o' the bosses sent me back to the tool car to fetch a saw blade to replace one that busted.

But when I got there I seen somebody skulkin' around the dynamite shed, and I knew he hadn't ought to been there because we already had a case o' the stuff down in the gorge. I seen him go in, and I waited until he come out again, and when I got a better look at the way he was dressed, I knew he weren't no railroad man. Looked more like a cowboy." The word dripped scorn, and Willard added hastily, "No offense, Mr. Morgan."

"None taken," Frank assured him. "What did you do then?"

"Well, I figured I better see what the fella was up to, so I started over toward the shed. He saw me comin' and acted spooked, so I yelled at him to stay where he was. He didn't do it, though. He run off into the bushes. So I run after him."

"And he had a horse hidden in the brush?"

"That's right. He jumped on the horse and took off, and I was a-yellin' at him, and about that time I noticed some sparks and seen a fuse leadin' into the shed, a-burnin' to beat the band. I thought for a second I could run over there and stomp it out, and I even started in that direction, but then I seen the sparks goin' right into the shed and knew I had best put some distance 'tween me and it. Good thing I did too, because a couple o' seconds later the whole shebang went up. Knocked me right off my feet, it did. When I got up, I seen Mr. Brant and some o' the boys runnin' to find out what had happened, so I yelled to 'em about the fella who got away, and they took off after him." Willard paused and rasped his fingers over his beard-stubbled jaw. "I hear the gent's dead."

Frank nodded. "Yes, he is."

"I ain't sorry to hear it. I come near to gettin' blowed up, and it ain't a feelin' that I like."

"You just saw the one man?"

Willard nodded solemnly. "Yeah, I'm pretty sure he was alone."

Frank turned to Brant. "There wasn't a guard on the dynamite shed?"

"There will be from now on, once we get a new one built," Brant said grimly. "But before this . . . no, we didn't have one. Didn't think it was necessary. Nobody figured one of the bastards would sneak up so close to camp like that to carry out his deviltry."

"The shed being set off by itself made it a little easier for him," Frank mused. "And I suppose that during the day there wouldn't be that many people around who might spot him. Everybody was working."

"That's right," Willard said. "'Twas just luck I was in the right place at the right time to see him sneakin' off after he'd laid that fuse."

Frank walked back over to the smoking crater that was all that was left of the shed. A look at the ground told him there wouldn't be any point in trying to backtrack the saboteur and find out where he had come from. The ground was too stony for his horse to have left prints. And the fact that he had fled along the already completed part of the line didn't mean anything. The man had just been trying to get away from his pursuers and probably hadn't paid that much attention to where he was going; otherwise, he wouldn't have chosen such a perilous path.

"Any ideas?" Brant asked hopefully.

Frank hated to let the construction boss down, but he shook his head. "This sabotage today is a dead end. I'll figure out a schedule of guard duty for the camp so it'll make it more difficult for anybody who doesn't belong here to come around, and I'll be scouting the area for any signs of the gang that's doing this. Also, I think you should send out some men to bring in that body, and Conrad can take it with him to Ophir and try to find out if anybody there knows the man."

Brant frowned. "Reckon we should have

brought him back with us while we were out there."

"Probably, but I didn't think of it at the time."

"And I was so damned mad, I was happy to leave him for the buzzards," Brant said. "But I'll tend to having him fetched in, Mr. Morgan."

"That's another thing," Frank said. "If we're going to be working together, you might as well call me Frank."

"All right," Brant agreed with a grin, "and I'm Sam."

They shook on it, and then Brant said, "Let's get on back. Supper will be ready soon, and our cooks turn out a pretty good venison stew."

As they walked away from the crater, Frank glanced back at the spot where the dynamite shed had stood. A thought had occurred to him, and he wondered how long that saboteur had been at work before Willard spotted him.

Specifically, he wondered if the man might have stolen a case or two of the explosives before setting his fuse and blowing up the rest of the supply. The man hadn't had any dynamite with him when he took that fatal tumble off the ledge, but that didn't mean he couldn't have cached it somewhere before setting the fuse.

Frank hoped that wasn't the case. The thought of a couple of cases of dynamite in the hands of men who wanted to stop the railroad put a cold feeling in the pit of his stomach.

In the car that served as living quarters, Conrad supervised as a couple of the men rigged blankets across one end of the car to close it off and give Rebel some privacy. She protested, saying, "There's no need to go to so much trouble just for me."

"Nonsense," Conrad said briskly. "A lady needs her privacy."

Rebel laughed. "That's something nobody's accused me of very often. Being a lady, I mean."

"Well, we're going to see to it that you're properly taken care of, so you might as well get used to it."

"I reckon I might as well," Rebel agreed with a shrug. "Anyway, it might be nice to have folks fussing over me for a change. Lord knows my brothers never did. They just thought of me as another one of the boys." She added, "Just don't get in the habit of trying to spoil me, Conrad. Wherever I am and whatever I'm doing, I pull my weight."

"Fine. And speaking of that . . . what are

you going to do now? Are you going on to Ophir with me, or staying here at the camp with Frank?"

She looked at him and said bluntly, "I figured on going with you. Frank can take care of himself."

Conrad felt his face reddening. "Are you implying that I need someone to take care of me?"

"Well, you *are* a greenhorn out here . . ."

"I'll have you know I shot a man once," he declared stiffly.

She looked surprised by that. "Really? Did you kill him?"

"Well . . . no. But he was wounded rather severely."

Conrad didn't like to think about that incident, since he had gotten sick after taking part in the flurry of violence that had seen him use a gun against another man for the first time in his life. But even though he had reacted strongly afterward, he thought he had handled himself well enough during the fight itself. That was the way he remembered it, at least. He certainly didn't need a *girl*, even a frontier girl like Rebel, to protect him from badmen.

On the other hand, the prospect of her accompanying him to Ophir was rather appealing in some ways. He hadn't forgotten those kisses. . . .

But as that thought went through his head, he recalled what was waiting for him in the boomtown, and realized that it might not be a good idea for her to go along.

Perhaps it was too late for such a discussion. Rebel said in a tone that brooked no argument, "I'm going with you anyway. *You* can protect *me* if you're so good with a gun."

"It's my hope that neither one of us will need any protecting."

"Yeah, that'd be downright lucky, wouldn't it?"

"All right," Conrad said with a sigh. "We'll ride on in the morning, and I hope we can reach Ophir by tomorrow evening."

"You know how to get there?"

"Yes, I've followed the route several times. It won't be a problem."

"It's settled then. We'll get started in the morning. In the meantime, you think there's anything to eat around here? I'm getting mighty hungry."

One of the other cars was fitted out as a combination kitchen and dining car. The workmen lined up outside to get their bowls and plates filled, but Brant, Buckhalter, and the other supervisors took their meals inside. Brant and Frank returned to the car about the same time as Conrad and Rebel walked over to it, and the four of them went inside together to sample the stew prepared by the railroad's cooks.

"Were you able to find any clues in what was left of that dynamite shed?" Conrad asked as they sat down at a cloth-covered table with bowls of stew already on it. There were glasses of wine for them as well, a welcome touch of civilization as far as Conrad was concerned.

Frank shook his head. "There wasn't anything left of it except a hole in the ground. And the ground's too hard to take prints, so I can't backtrack the hombre who set off the explosion. I hate to say it, but we may have to wait for the varmints to try something else and hope we can get a line on them then."

Conrad frowned and said, "We can't afford too much more sabotage, or the project will grind to a complete halt."

"I'm afraid you may be right about that, Mr. Browning," Brant put in. "The men are already spooked, and having that shed blow up today isn't going to help matters any. A railroader knows when he signs up for a job that there's going to be dangers along the way; that just goes with the territory. But having to worry about being gunned down by snipers or riddled with arrows by Indians are added problems, and our boys don't like it."

"I don't blame them," Frank said. "You can spread the word if you want that I'm going to do my best to put a stop to all that."

Brant nodded and said, "That sure might help, Frank. Everybody knows your reputation."

"Which is none too good in certain circles," Conrad put in.

Frank shot him a narrow-eyed glance, and Conrad knew he had gone too far. "I've done plenty of things I'm not proud of," Frank said, "but I never rode the owlhoot trail, and folks know that about me too."

"I'm sure you won't let us down," Brant said in an attempt to smooth over the friction. "I reckon before you know it, the New Mexico, Rio Grande, and Oriental will be steaming right into Ophir!"

Conrad hoped that was the case. Otherwise, before this was all over he might be ruined. Frank could afford the losses, because Frank . . . well, because he just didn't care.

But this project was the first big one Conrad had attempted on his own. It meant a great deal to him. So much, in fact, that he had been willing to go begging his father for help. He picked up his glass of wine, raised it, and said, "To Ophir."

To his ears, the words sounded as much like a prayer as they did a toast.

Chapter 15

The next morning, Frank wasn't surprised when Rebel announced her intention of traveling on to Ophir with Conrad. She told him while they were alone briefly after breakfast, outside the dining car.

"I hope that's all right with you, Frank," she said with a worried frown. "I know one reason I was traveling with you was so that I could try to talk some sense into Ed and Tom and Bob when they show up again. If I'm not here, I can't do that."

"You talk like there's no doubt they'll try to kill me again," Frank commented.

"There's not any doubt in my mind," Rebel said grimly. "I know Ed, and I know my brothers. Ed won't rest until he's avenged Simon and Jud, and he'll be able to talk Tom and Bob into going along with whatever he wants."

"I don't think they'll bother me while I'm

here in this camp. Too many people around for that. And to tell you the truth, I'm more worried about Conrad than I am about myself, so I'm sort of glad you want to go with him."

A smile curved Rebel's lips. "Don't let him hear you say that. He gets a burr under his saddle whenever he thinks somebody is saying he can't take care of himself."

"He's a prideful fella," Frank said with a nod. "Always has been, I suspect."

"How long have you known him?"

"Only a few years," Frank said, but if Rebel heard the regret in his voice, she gave no sign of it.

Conrad came out of the railroad car then, so nothing more was said about the past, or about Conrad's ability to take care of himself. He said, "Rebel has decided to accompany me to Ophir, Frank. I hope that's all right."

"Fine by me," Frank told him. "You mind taking the body of the hombre who blew up the shed into the settlement with you? You can turn him over to the local law and see if anybody recognizes him."

Sam Brant walked up in time to hear what Frank was saying. With a frown on his face, he said, "Sorry, Frank, but I've got bad news about that. The men I sent out to bring in that corpse told me that when they got there, the body was gone."

"Gone?" Frank repeated, his eyebrows rising in surprise.

"Yeah, I'm afraid so. That polecat's partners must have shown up and taken his body away so that nobody could identify him. We should have brought him in when we had the chance."

Frank rubbed at his jaw in thought for a second and then said, "Yes, you're right. That's a possible lead we overlooked. But there's nothing we can do about it now."

"Except keep a closer eye out for trouble, since we know for sure now that there are more of those scoundrels lurking up here in these mountains."

Frank had been pretty sure of that already, because he didn't think one man could have raised as much hell as Conrad and Brant had described to him, but he didn't say anything.

"Miss Callahan and I are riding on into Ophir, Sam," Conrad said.

Brant's frown deepened. "Are you sure that's a good idea, Mr. Browning? What with all the trouble going on around here, I mean."

"We'll be perfectly fine," Conrad responded immediately. Frank recognized the tone of voice. The quickest way to get Conrad to do something was to tell him that he shouldn't.

"Sam, could you spare a few men to ride into town?" Frank asked the construction boss.

"That's not necessary—" Conrad began stubbornly.

"I'll go you one better," Brant said. "I actually need to send a couple of men to Ophir to bring back some supplies. That'll be quicker than wiring Lordsburg and having 'em sent up on the work train."

"You're just sending them along as caretakers," Conrad accused.

Brant shook his head. "No, sir, it's as legitimate as it can be. I was planning on doing that in the next day or two even before you arrived."

"You're sure about that?"

"Positive."

"Well, all right," Conrad said grudgingly. "I suppose under the circumstances it would be best for us to all travel together. I wouldn't want anything to happen to Miss Callahan."

In a tart voice, Rebel said, "Miss Callahan can take care of herself. Anyway, I told you I don't like being called that."

"Let's just get the horses ready," Conrad said.

They were ready to leave a short time later. Frank shook hands with Conrad and on an impulse hugged Rebel. It seemed hard to believe that less than a week earlier, she had been trying to kill them. Frank wondered fleetingly if he had been too quick to accept her change of heart. He didn't think so. He was willing to place a lot of faith in his ability to judge someone's character. That ability had helped to keep him alive for quite a few danger-filled years. Sometimes, he thought that being able to look in a person's eyes and get an inkling of their heart and soul was more important than being fast on the draw. . . .

Brant sent two tough railroaders with Conrad and Rebel. The men were well armed, each of them carrying a pistol and a rifle. Rebel had her Winchester and could handle herself in a fight. As for Conrad . . . well, he could make a lot of noise with that Colt Lightning of his anyway. He might scare somebody off with it.

Once they were gone, Frank spent a few minutes talking with Brant about the posting of guards around the camp, and then went to saddle up Stormy. Brant followed him and asked, "What are you planning to do today, Frank?"

"Take a look around, get to know the lay

of the land," Frank replied. "I want to see if I can find any signs of a camp. Those saboteurs have to be staying somewhere when they're not causing trouble for the railroad."

"Keep your eyes open," Brant said with a frown. "There are those Apaches to consider too, and those red devils can hide in places where you wouldn't think that a flea could hide."

Frank nodded as he tightened the cinches on the Appaloosa's saddle. "I know. Dog's pretty good at sniffing them out, though."

A few minutes later, he was ready to ride. He swung up and gave Brant a wave as he heeled Stormy into a trot that carried him away from the camp. Dog ran out ahead of horse and rider with boundless canine enthusiasm, ranging back and forth.

They followed a trail down into the wide gorge. The partially completed trestle rose on their left. Men were already at work on it today, strengthening the existing structure with support beams and crosspieces, while another crew was busy with picks and shovels hacking out the holes in the floor of the gorge where the giant legs of the trestle that hadn't been erected yet would sit. If they came to a particularly rocky spot, they would have to use some of the now-limited supply of dynamite to blast out a socket.

The river itself was a typical fast-flowing mountain stream, fed by snowmelt from the peaks above as well as by springs. Frank knew that if he dipped his hand in it, the water would be icy cold. A temporary pontoon bridge had been laid across it, so that the workers and their carts full of supplies could get back and forth from one side to the other. Stormy's hooves clattered on the planks as Frank rode across that temporary span. The trestle loomed high above him, reaching at least a hundred feet into the air.

Once he was across the river, Frank followed the trail up the far side of the gorge. The timbered slope was steeper on this side, and the path that had been hacked out zigzagged to the top. When he reached it, Frank reined in, turned Stormy, and looked back at the gorge and the construction camp on the far side. It was a bustling place, emblematic of the progress that was making its way into these mountains, fighting every step of the way. Once the air here had been full of nothing but the songs of birds and the chuckling of the river. Now it was noisy with the shouts of men and the clatter of donkey engines and the ringing clangor of picks and shovels. Before the day was over, a dynamite blast or two would probably punctuate that racket.

There was a trace of sadness in Frank's

smile as he turned Stormy to the north. If he had it in his power to do so, he would not turn back the clock on the West to an earlier, simpler time. The world had to go forward. But for every gain there was a loss, and no triumph was without a touch of the bittersweet. That was the way of life.

"Too much philosophizing, Stormy," he said, and the Appaloosa gave a toss of his head as if he had been reading Frank's thoughts. "Let's go see if we can find those bastards who want to stop this railroad. Come on, Dog!"

Frank spent the morning riding in everwidening circles around the construction camp, crossing and recrossing the river several times. On more than one occasion, it took him a while to find a ford where he could get across the stream, but that just gave him the chance to look over still more of the countryside. It was a rugged but beautiful land, full of contrasts — lush green pastures and towering pine trees in one place, and a mile away nothing but bare, sunblasted rock. He came across a wide stretch of lava that had flowed down from one of the now-dormant volcanoes that had formed the mountains in aeons past. Over the years the lava had hardened into a black, razor-edged hell that had to be ridden around.

Nowhere did Frank find the remains of a campfire or anything else to tell him that the gang of saboteurs had holed up there. He was frustrated, but tried not to let it bother him. There were countless places in these mountains where a group of men could hide. It would take a lone rider weeks, maybe even months, to search them all out. It would have been unreasonable to expect that he would find what he was looking for right away.

He had brought food with him, and ate his lunch sitting on a log at a spot that overlooked a sweeping vista of spectacular scenery. A little brook trickled out of the side of the hill nearby. Frank, Stormy, and Dog all drank from it, and the water was as cold and clear and good-tasting as Frank knew it would be. Then he resumed his search.

The afternoon was just as futile as the morning had been. He saw plenty of pretty sights, like a waterfall that plummeted a good fifty feet straight down a rock wall to form a foaming, churning pool at the base, but he didn't find the badmen he was looking for. Late in the day, wondering if Conrad and Rebel had reached Ophir by now, he turned back toward the camp, guided by his frontiersman's instincts.

Arriving a short time before dusk, he could tell from the atmosphere of the camp that there hadn't been any trouble during the day. A few men were still working, finishing up some final tasks before calling it a day, but most of the crew had already put away their tools, gone back to their tents to wash up, and then converged on the kitchen car to get their supper. Frank saw quite a few men lined up there with their plates and bowls.

He unsaddled and rubbed Stormy down, then put the big Appaloosa in the makeshift corral with the other horses that were kept at the camp. With Dog trailing along behind him, Frank walked over to the car that served as the office and living quarters for the bosses. Not surprisingly, he found Sam Brant inside, going over some maps with Nathan Buckhalter and a couple of the other supervisors. Frank noticed that the blankets that had given Rebel some privacy the night before had been taken down.

Brant looked up from the maps and greeted him with a smile. "Glad to see you're back, Frank," he said. "Did you find anything?"

Frank shook his head regretfully. "I'm afraid not. But I'll keep looking. From the way it seems around here, I assume nothing happened today?"

"Nothing but a heap of hard work. We were just figuring out how we're going to tie the trestle into the other side of the gorge. The approach isn't quite as easy over there as it is on this side, and we'll be reaching it in another few days. Once the structure's all in place, we can lay the track itself. That part won't take long." Brant sighed. "I'll be glad to get it done too. It's taken us a while to make it this far."

Buckhalter said, "This gorge is the last remaining major physical obstacle between here and Ophir. We'll have to build a couple more small trestles, but nothing like this."

"I admire you fellas," Frank said. "I couldn't even design a railroad, much less build one."

"It's important work," Brant said proudly. "The rails have opened up the whole country to development. Without them, the United States wouldn't be near the nation that it is."

"Well, keep up the good work, and I'll try to do my part. Right now, I reckon I'll go get some supper, though."

Brant stood up. "We'll join you. Come on, boys. We can get back to wracking our brains later."

The group of men walked along the tracks to the kitchen car and went inside to eat in the small dining area. Frank noticed that the stew had a lot less meat in it tonight, and when he commented on that, Brant said, "We're running low on fresh meat. Ever since the Apaches ambushed that hunting party, nobody wants to go out and look for deer."

"I saw a few today," Frank said, "but I didn't think about you needing fresh meat. Tell you what, tomorrow when I go out scouting, I'll take my packhorse along with me. If I can down a buck, I'll load the carcass on the horse and bring it back with me."

"That sounds just fine, Frank," Brant said. "We'd be much obliged, that's for sure."

Night had fallen completely by the time they finished eating. As the men left the car, Brant and Buckhalter and the others turned back toward the office car. Frank said, "I think I'll take a walk around the camp, maybe check on the guards."

"Good idea," Brant said. "We won't be turning in for a while anyway."

With a wave, Frank set off on his stroll. Dog padded along beside him. Men with rifles had been stationed every hundred yards around the perimeter of the camp, standing guard duty in four-hour shifts. Frank spoke to several of them, and they all assured him that no one had tried to sneak in while they were watching.

He found himself at the edge of the gorge, west of the trestle at the spot where the little creek flowed into the river. The slope below him was steep and choked with brush. Frank didn't think anybody would try to make their way through that thicket, but nothing was impossible, he supposed. He walked along the edge toward the trestle. It loomed like a giant black spiderweb in the darkness.

Dog suddenly stiffened and growled. Frank stopped and reached down to feel the bristling fur around Dog's neck. The big cur had heard or smelled something that bothered him. He stared intently toward the trestle.

Frank looked the same direction, narrowing his eyes as he searched the shadows. After a moment, he caught his breath as he glimpsed movement on the framework of the giant bridge, far out from the edge of the gorge and almost at the top of the trestle. As hard as it was to believe, someone was climbing up the trestle from the bottom of the gorge.

Frank realized that he had overlooked that possibility. He had made sure that a guard was posted at this end of the trestle, so that no one could get to it from the camp, but he hadn't thought that anyone would climb up from the bottom of the gorge. He broke into a run along the rimrock with Dog bounding along beside him.

The guard at the end of the trestle heard somebody coming and challenged him. "Who's there?" the railroader called.

"Frank Morgan. Somebody's out there on the trestle."

"Can't be!" the guard exclaimed. "Nobody came past me."

"They climbed up from the bottom," Frank said as he stepped past the rifle-wielding sentry. "Come with me. Dog, stay here!"

Obediently, Dog sat down, but he was still growling and clearly didn't like being left behind.

Frank and the guard started out onto the trestle. Their footsteps rang on the planks that made up the floor of the bridge, undoubtedly carrying a warning to whoever was skulking around out there, but there was nothing they could do about that.

The gorge was about five hundred feet wide, and the trestle already spanned more than half that width. Frank and the guard passed over the river, boiling and foaming along a hundred feet below them. As they approached the end of the trestle, a dark shape suddenly rolled onto it from the side, pulling itself up and over the edge. "Look out!" Frank barked as he lifted his Peacemaker.

Colt flame erupted from the black shape that crouched at the end of the trestle, blooming like a deadly crimson flower in the night.

Chapter 16

Earlier in the day, on the road to Ophir, Conrad and Rebel rode side by side, trailed by the two railroad workers who hung back about fifty yards. From time to time Conrad heard them laughing. He figured they were lagging behind so that they could talk about him. Or else they were making crude comments about Rebel. Or both.

He found himself wishing he was alone out here with her.

That would have been quite pleasant, riding along under the vast blue dome of the Western sky with spectacularly beautiful mountain scenery all around them, accompanied only by this beautiful, independent, self-reliant young woman.

Instead, Frank and Sam Brant had sent along a couple of rough-hewn nursemaids. Conrad was still angry about it, but he realized it was a reasonable precaution, what with all the trouble that had been going on in the area.

"What sort of place is Ophir?" Rebel asked him.

"It's a typical mining boomtown, I suppose."

"That's just it. I've never been to a mining boomtown. Our ranch was about halfway between Fort Davis and Marfa, and those are just little cow towns. El Paso is the biggest city I've ever seen."

"Ophir is nowhere near as big as El Paso," Conrad said. "It's becoming a respectable-sized town, though. At first there were only tents and a few rough shacks there — at least so I've been told, because I never visited the place while it was like that — but in recent months people have begun to put up more substantial buildings. There are even a couple of brick buildings in town now. Ophir has three hotels and a newspaper and a number of stores and restaurants."

"What about saloons?" Rebel asked with a smile.

Conrad sighed. "Yes, there are plenty of saloons, unfortunately. I suppose they're a necessary evil anyplace where you have a lot of men working as you do in the mines. They certainly pander to a rough element, though, and they contribute nearly all of the crime and the disturbances of the peace in the settlement."

"What about whorehouses?" Rebel asked mischievously. "Are there whorehouses in Ophir?"

Stiffly, and without looking at her, Conrad replied, "I'm sure I wouldn't know." He felt his face growing warm.

"Well, maybe not from experience, but you're bound to have heard about them if they're there."

"Of course there's talk. . . . I suppose there are places where a man can . . . can relieve himself of his more unnatural urges . . ."

"You think it's unnatural? I grew up on a ranch, and it seems like the most natural thing in the world to me."

"It's not the same," Conrad insisted. "A cow doesn't have to pay another cow to . . . to . . ."

"That's true," Rebel agreed. "I never saw any money change hands . . . or hooves."

This was the most absurd conversation. Conrad wished Rebel would change the subject. If she wouldn't, then he'd be forced to.

"I reckon it's different where men and women are concerned," she went on.

"Of course it is. There has to be a certain amount of decorum involved. Without that, humans would find themselves descending to the same level as animals."

"We wouldn't want that," Rebel said with mock seriousness.

"No, we wouldn't," Conrad insisted. "It's our sense of right and wrong that sets us apart from the animals, and when we lose that, we've lost everything."

"I don't know that I'd go so far as to say that. Animals may not know much about right and wrong, but they have a certain innocence about them, I reckon. They live their lives and take their pleasure where they find it, and they don't waste even a second worrying about what's proper or not or what tomorrow's going to bring." A wistful note crept into Rebel's voice as she added, "I think it would be nice if human folks could live like that for a while, every now and then."

"You're talking about anarchy," Conrad said.

"I'm talking about doing what *feels* right, not what some set of rules allows or what some sour-faced preacher or politician says is right."

Conrad shook his head. "I'm sorry. I just can't imagine living that way, even for a short period of time."

"Well, that's all right, Conrad. Not all of us are as stiff-necked as you are."

He glanced over at her. The smile on her face took most of the sting out of her words. Most, but not all.

He asked himself why her disapproval mattered one little bit to him. She was nothing more than a somewhat attractive annoyance. Well, more than somewhat attractive, he supposed, but still a definite annoyance. And not that long ago she had been even worse than that. She had been an active danger to him and Frank.

Could a leopard change its spots? Could a wild frontier girl with a grudge put all that behind her? Rebel claimed that she had, and Conrad's instincts told him he could believe her. The problem was, he didn't fully trust his instincts. Was he letting her beauty blind him to the facts?

The questions went around and around in his head, but there were no answers for them. For the past few days, Rebel had certainly seemed trustworthy enough. But it would take only one moment of betrayal to change everything.

They had brought food with them, and stopped for lunch next to a little pond formed by a spring that trickled out of a rugged rock wall. Conrad thought it was a pretty spot, but he didn't really pay that much attention to it. He talked to the two railroaders as he ate, asking them questions about the work on the spur line. The men seemed a little uncomfortable chewing the fat with the big boss, the owner of the line, so Conrad didn't press them on anything. He knew they would have a certain loyalty to Sam Brant, and he didn't want to challenge that.

He noticed after a while that Rebel had wandered off to the other side of the pond, which was about a hundred feet across. She was standing there tossing rocks into it. Conrad walked around to join her while the other two men took advantage of the opportunity to smoke for a few minutes. One took out a pipe and filled it with tobacco from a canvas pouch, while the other rolled a quirly.

"What are you doing over here by yourself?" Conrad asked as he came up to Rebel.

"I didn't want to intrude on the conversation between you railroad men." She picked up a rock and threw it a little harder than she had before. It skipped across the surface of the water.

"It wouldn't have been an intrusion," Conrad told her. "I was just passing the time of day with those men."

"Well, I didn't want to interrupt."

A frown creased his forehead. "Are you feeling like I neglected you? My God, you can't be upset because I talked to them instead of you!"

"Ha! Don't flatter yourself, Mr. Browning."

"I thought you were calling me Conrad."

She picked up another rock. He wondered for a second if she was going to throw it at *him*. But then she lobbed it into the water and said, "Right now Mr. Browning seems more like it."

"Suit yourself," he said with a shrug. He felt confident that he could plumb the minds of the young women he met back in Boston, since most of them were interested primarily in prestige and money. He had no real idea what a girl like Rebel might value. Livestock perhaps. Or a good saddle.

"You know what I'd like to do?" she asked.

"I have no earthly idea," he replied honestly.

"I'd like to take all my clothes off and go swimming in this pond."

"Good Lord!" Conrad exclaimed without stopping to think about it. "Have you felt that water? It's ice-cold. You'd freeze to death."

"I don't reckon I would. I've gone swimming without a stitch lots of times, even when it was cold. Once you jump in, you get used to it."

He shook his head. "I don't think so."

"You never did that? Took off all your clothes and . . . jumped in?"

He couldn't answer. An unwanted image appeared in his brain. He seemed to see Rebel standing there at the brink of the water, poised to dive in, divested of all her garments so that she was nude. He could imagine the sunlight playing on the thick blond hair tumbling around her shoulders and striking highlights off her smooth, bare skin. In his mind's eye he saw her arrow sleekly into the water, and as she came up her hair would have darkened from being wet and the cold would cause her nipples to grow hard and erect, turning into pebbled buds of brown flesh. . . .

He turned away abruptly, jerking around with a sharply indrawn breath. "Conrad?" Rebel said anxiously. "What's wrong?"

"Nothing," he said hastily. "Not a thing. Everything's fine." Without turning around, he stalked off toward some nearby trees.

He wasn't sure, but he thought he heard her laughing softly to herself as he strode away.

After a while, he was fit to ride again, and the group continued on toward Ophir. Rebel didn't say anything about the conversation they'd had beside the pond, and Conrad was

211

grateful for that. He was convinced that she had known exactly what she was doing. She was upset with him because he had ignored her, and so she had punished him by planting that tantalizing but utterly improper image in his mind.

It wasn't that he was a puritan — though he had some in his family tree — or that he was unversed in the ways of the world. But Rebel had a boldness about her that was shocking. He put it down to the way she had been raised on the frontier without a proper grounding in the proprieties. Even if certain things were *done,* they certainly were not *talked* about.

He hoped to reach Ophir by nightfall, but as the sun continued its westward journey, it became obvious that wasn't going to be the case. In the late afternoon one of the railroaders asked, "You want to make camp, Mr. Browning, or would you rather push on after dark?"

Conrad thought about it for a moment and then said, "The trail is easy enough to follow, and I don't think it will take us more than another hour or so to reach Ophir. It makes more sense to push on."

"Whatever you say, Boss."

They rode on, and once again the two men from the construction camp fell back a good ways. Conrad kept stealing glances at Rebel and wondering whether or not she was still upset with him. She hadn't been very talkative this afternoon. That was all right with him. He was still thinking about the things she had said earlier, even though he didn't really want to dwell on them. His mind wouldn't let him forget the pictures it had conjured up.

Still, he wasn't so distracted that he didn't hear the gunshot, or see the sudden spurt of dirt and rocks ahead of his horse as a bullet plowed into the ground.

Conrad yanked back instinctively on the reins, causing El Diablo to rear and paw at the air. Almost unseated, Conrad grabbed the saddle horn desperately and clung to it as another shot rang out. He didn't see where this bullet went.

El Diablo's front legs came back down on the ground with a jarring impact that went all through Conrad. He looked over at Rebel and saw that she had whipped her Winchester out of its sheath and was looking around for some sign of the bushwhackers. Another shot blasted, and the slug clipped a branch in a nearby tree.

"Come on!" Conrad called. "Let's get out of here!"

The two railroad men were already fleeing, galloping toward Conrad and Rebel as fast as they could ride. Conrad jabbed his heels into El Diablo's flanks and sent the big black horse lunging forward. Rebel was right behind him on her chestnut gelding. She still hung onto her rifle in case she needed it.

Conrad thought it was much better to run than to fight. He leaned forward over his mount's neck, making himself a smaller target. A glance over his shoulder told him that Rebel was doing likewise. Her hat had come off and hung by its neck strap behind her head. Loose now, her blond hair streamed out behind her. Conrad paid no heed to it at the moment, but he would remember later how lovely she looked like that.

Right now he was more concerned with staying alive. He didn't hear any more shots, but he wasn't sure if he would be able to over the rolling thunder of hoofbeats. Gradually, he became aware that he had pulled well ahead of the others. El Diablo was running with efficient, powerful strides, carrying Conrad along faster than he had ever ridden before. He might have been frightened by that if he hadn't been so worried that he was about to be shot out of the saddle. He was worried about Rebel too. He didn't want to run off and leave her to the mercy of the bushwhackers. He began to pull back on the reins, trying to slow El Diablo.

The big black didn't respond, but kept running as swiftly as ever. What was wrong with the horse? Hadn't the little Mexican liveryman back in El Paso told Frank that El Diablo was a terrible racehorse despite his speed and strength? According to Pablo Gomez, El Diablo was content to run behind the other horses. Well, not today! Today the horse seemed determined to outrun everything else on the face of the earth.

Conrad looked back again and saw that Rebel was a good fifty yards behind him. Sawing viciously at the bit, Conrad tried again to slow El Diablo. Finally, the horse began to ease his pace. He was still running fast, but he was no longer pulling away from the others. They began to catch up.

"Conrad, slow down!" Rebel yelled when she came within earshot. "The shooting stopped!"

"I'm trying to!" he shouted back. El Diablo fought him every step of the way, but gradually he managed to pull the horse down to a trot.

Rebel spurred up alongside him. The two railroaders were a short distance behind them. Rebel said, "We got away from those damn drygulchers! I saw them up on a ridge back there a ways!"

"I'm surprised you didn't shoot at them!"

"I thought about it," she said grimly. "I was afraid you were going to fall off that black devil and break your fool neck, though, so I came after you instead."

They slowed their horses to a walk, although El Diablo tossed his head in irritation and impatience. "Lord, that big fella of yours can run!" Rebel went on. "Those bushwhackers never had a chance to draw a bead on you."

"Are you all right?" Conrad asked anxiously. "You weren't hit?"

"No, I'm fine."

He turned in his saddle and called back to the railroaders. "Are either of you men wounded?"

"We're all right, Boss," one of them answered. "Just a mite spooked."

The other man said, "That's the sort of thing that's been happenin' all the time lately. No wonder all the boys are scared."

"Frank Morgan will find out who's responsible for this trouble and put a stop to it," Conrad declared. "That's why he came up here."

"I sure hope you're right, Boss."

Conrad's pulse was still pounding, but he wasn't as breathless now as he had been a few minutes earlier. That wild ride on El Diablo's back had literally stolen his breath away. As he got himself under control again, he said, "We're still going on to Ophir. Now that we know some of the miscreants are around, it's more important than ever that we reach the settlement."

"I'd like to line up one or two of them miscreants in the sights of my rifle," Rebel said savagely.

"With luck it won't come to that."

"You've got your kind of luck and I've got mine," Rebel snapped.

That was all too true. Everything was different about them, Conrad told himself. It seemed unlikely there could ever be a true meeting of the minds between them, no matter how physically attractive he found her.

They rode on, bunched together more closely now. Conrad didn't know if that was a good idea strategically, but it was certainly more comforting that way. Night fell, but they kept moving. As darkness cloaked them, Conrad relaxed a little. Ambushing them would be more difficult now.

Ophir was set in a valley between two peaks in the Mimbres Range. About an hour after dark, the four riders topped a ridge and were able to look down into the valley where they saw the lights of the boomtown glittering invitingly. Conrad heaved a sigh of relief.

"There it is," he said. "We'll be there shortly."

The trail followed an easy slope down from the ridge. Less than fifteen minutes later, they reached the southern end of Gold Street, Ophir's main thoroughfare. The business district stretched for five blocks in front of them. The side streets were lined with tents, shacks, and in a few cases more permanent dwellings that were so freshly built they still smelled of raw lumber. Lights burned in most of the buildings along Gold Street, and plenty of horses and wagon teams were tied up at the hitch racks. The boardwalks were crowded with men. It hadn't rained for a while, so the street, which was often a muddy morass, had dried out and was now dusty instead.

Music and revelry came from the saloons. Conrad was more interested in reaching the Holloway Hotel, where he always stayed when he was in Ophir. He was tired and covered with trail dust and wanted a hot bath and then a hot meal. He hoped there would be a room at the hotel for Rebel too. He didn't care where the two railroaders spent the night. They would probably find some squalid saloon or brothel to occupy their time, and that was all right with Conrad as long as they protected the company funds

Sam Brant had given them to use for the supplies.

"Looks like a mighty lively place," Rebel commented as they passed the Big Nugget Saloon. Raucous whoops came from inside the place, and Conrad didn't even want to think about what might have prompted them.

"Yes, it's far from genteel," he began, but then he stopped as they passed one of the mercantile stores and he heard his name called. He reined in and turned El Diablo toward the boardwalk. A young woman with brown hair stepped up to the railing and waved.

Conrad swung down from the saddle and stepped up to the boardwalk, holding onto his horse's reins. With a happy squeal, the young woman threw her arms around him and kissed him hard on the mouth. Instinctively, Conrad embraced her as well.

"Well," Rebel said coldly from the back of her horse, "the gals sure know how to welcome a fella in this town. That a friend of yours, Conrad?"

Carefully, Conrad broke the kiss and disengaged himself from the pretty brunette's arms. He looked around at Rebel. Her face was set in taut lines. He said, "Uh, yes, I suppose you could say that. Rebel, allow me to present Miss Pamela Tarleton . . . my fiancée."

Chapter 17

Frank felt as well as heard the sizzle of the bullet through the air as it passed within inches of his cheek. He heard the guard behind him cry out in pain as the slug thudded into flesh, but there was no time to turn around and check on him. The Peacemaker in Frank's hand bucked and roared as he squeezed off a couple of shots.

The man crouched at the end of the trestle rocked backward as the bullets struck him, but he didn't fall. He managed to stand upright and fired again. This shot was wilder than the first, whining several feet over Frank's head. Frank triggered again, and this time the bullet burrowed deeply into the would-be killer's belly, doubling him over. He swayed back and forth for a second, and then toppled off the side of the trestle, pitching out into the empty air above the gorge. Even though he was already mortally wounded, he managed to utter a short scream as he plummeted through the darkness. That cry was cut short as he slammed into the rocky ground below.

Frank whirled toward the guard who had accompanied him. The man lay on his back with arms outflung where he had fallen when the first shot struck him. Frank grimaced as he saw that the bullet, riding on an upward angle, had caught the guard just under the left eye and bored on through his brain before exploding out the back of his skull. The guard was dead, a pool of blood staining the timbers of the trestle under his shattered head.

Frank knew that could have just as easily been him. The bullet that had killed this man had missed him by bare inches. Grimly, Frank turned back toward the end of the trestle. The man who had climbed up from the bottom of the gorge had been up to something, and Frank figured it couldn't have been anything good. He hurried toward the end of the trestle.

As the echoes of the shots died away and Frank approached the point where the partially completed trestle stopped, he heard a hissing and sputtering sound. Dropping to a knee at the edge of the structure, he leaned out to peer down into the forest of support beams and crosspieces below him. The thick shadows under the trestle made the flaring sparks of a burning fuse all the more visible as they raced toward a wooden crate that had been wedged between a couple of crosspieces about fifteen feet below the top of the structure.

Frank went cold inside. He didn't have to see the writing on the crate to know that he was looking at a boxful of dynamite — and there was no time to climb down and put out that fuse.

Instinctively, he lunged upright, whirled around, and broke into a run, trying to get off the trestle before the dynamite exploded. He hated to leave the guard's body behind, but the man was already dead and there was nothing Frank could do for him. He dashed past the corpse.

The shots had roused the camp, and Frank saw some of the railroad workers hurrying toward the trestle, carrying lanterns that made bobbing points of light in the darkness. "Get back!" he shouted at them. "Dynamite! Get back!"

Dog knew that something was wrong. The big cur stood at the end of the trestle and barked furiously, almost as if he were encouraging Frank to run faster. Frank was already legging it for safety as fast as he could.

One of the men from the camp must have heard his warning shouts. A new cry went up: "Fire in the hole!" The railroaders who had been approaching the trestle turned around and headed back the way they had come, fleeing frantically.

It seemed to Frank that it had been an hour since he had spotted that sputtering fuse, rather than mere seconds. He had been running forever, and the end of the trestle still loomed in front of him, seeming to retreat instead of drawing closer. He knew it couldn't be much longer before the sparks reached the dynamite. . . .

With a huge thunderclap of sound, the night seemed to split in two behind him. The darkness was ripped apart by the sudden hellish flare of the blast. The roar pounded Frank's ears like giant fists, and another one slammed into his back, lifting him and throwing him forward. For a second he felt like he was flying, but then he slammed into something hard and unyielding and tumbled over and over. Somewhere in the dim recesses of his stunned brain, he was still thinking clearly enough to realize that the explosion had thrown him the rest of the way off the trestle and he had landed on the ground at the edge of the gorge.

He came to a stop sprawled on his stomach. For a moment or two, all he could do was lie there and try to catch his breath. A terrible ringing filled his ears.

Something wet touched his face. He jerked his head up. His ears might not be working that well, but he could still see all right. In a reddish, flickering light, he saw Dog's face close to his. The big cur was standing over him. That had been Dog's tongue Frank felt on his face.

He reached up shakily and grabbed hold of the thick fur around Dog's neck. Using Dog to support him, Frank pulled himself into a sitting position. Dog crowded against him, licking him again, and Frank said, "It's all right, Dog. It's all right, old boy."

At least, that was what he was trying to say. He couldn't even hear his own voice over the strident ringing that filled his skull. A cold feeling of horror struck him. Was he deaf? Was his hearing gone forever?

If that was the case, there was nothing he could do about it. He told himself to concentrate on more pressing problems. Climbing unsteadily to his feet, he swung around so that he could look toward the trestle.

Or what was left of the trestle, to be precise, and that wasn't much. The explosion had torn a lot of it apart, and more of it had collapsed following the blast. What was left was on fire.

Something crashed down right beside Frank, and he had jumped aside before he realized that he had heard the impact. The ringing was beginning to subside. Something else slammed to the ground not far away. Frank jerked his head in that direction and saw a big piece of one of the support beams. The explosion had thrown debris high in the air — and now it was coming down.

"Come on, Dog!" he called. "Let's get out of here!"

This time he heard the words he spoke, although they still sounded muffled and distorted. In a stumbling run, he moved back away from the edge of the gorge, heading for the construction camp itself. Smaller pieces of wreckage continued to rain down around him and Dog, and several of them stung as they hit him.

One of the lantern-wielding men suddenly loomed up in front of Frank. Grabbing his arm, the man yelled, "Frank! You all right?"

The words sounded like they came from far away, but Frank understood them. He nodded as he recognized the strained face of Sam Brant. The construction boss's normally ruddy features were drained of color as he stared past Frank at the destroyed trestle.

"What the hell happened?"

"Dynamite," Frank said. "A whole case of it jammed between a couple of support beams. There was nothing I could do . . . to stop it."

"Who would do such a thing? How'd he get out on the trestle? We had a man standing guard!"

Frank had to draw a couple of breaths before he could speak. "Somebody climbed up . . . from the bottom of the gorge. Never thought about anybody . . . trying that."

Brant cursed fervently for several seconds before he got control of himself and asked, "Did the bastard get away?"

"No, I got him. He fell off the far end of the trestle with a couple of my bullets in him. I spotted him climbing up and the guard and I went out there to see what was going on, but he opened fire on us before we got to the far end."

"Walt Desmond was standing guard," Brant said. "What happened to him?"

"Sorry, Sam."

"Good Lord! He was caught in the blast?"

Frank shook his head. "No, the first shot the saboteur took at us hit Desmond and killed him. There was nothing I could do for him. Then I saw the fuse burning and got off of there as fast as I could. I'm sorry I had to leave Desmond's body out there."

Brant shook his head. "We'll be hard put to find enough left of him to bury, but we'll try." The hand that wasn't holding the lantern balled into a fist. "But the son of a bitch who planted the dynamite, you said you shot him and he fell off the far end?"

"That's right."

"Then his body should be somewhere down below in the gorge. We'll have to find it and see if anybody recognizes him."

"Yes, and we'll do that tonight," Frank agreed. "This one won't get away from us after he's dead."

Frank stayed where he was for a few minutes, catching his breath and letting his hearing get back to normal while Brant hurried off to supervise the effort to keep the fire from spreading to the vegetation on the edge of the gorge. The trestle itself was probably going to be a total loss, but the destruction would be even worse if the fire spread to the camp.

As the men worked to contain the flames, Frank reloaded the chambers in his Colt that he had emptied during the brief gunfight. Then he holstered the weapon and went over to rejoin Brant. "I'm going down there to take a look," he told the construction boss.

"I'll come with you," Brant said. "Things are going to be all right up here, I think. The fire's not spreading."

He called to a couple of the railroaders and told them to come with him and Frank. It was a grim-faced group of men that followed the trail down into the gorge with Brant's lantern lighting the way. They trooped across the temporary pontoon bridge, past the spot where the trestle had ended before the explosion, and then spread out a little to look for the body of the man who had planted the dynamite.

Frank knew about where the saboteur had fallen, so it didn't take long to find him. "Over here," he called to the others, and a moment later the yellow glow from Brant's lantern washed over the bloody, crumpled body as it lay on the rocky ground about fifty feet from the edge of the river.

Frank rolled the man onto his back. The beard-stubbled features were contorted in a grimace of death, but one of the railroaders Brant had brought with him exclaimed, "Say! That's Mike Lovejoy!"

"You know him?" Frank asked Brant.

The construction boss nodded. "Yeah, he worked for the line a while back, when we first started building the spur north out of Lordsburg. He was a gandy dancer, but I fired him when he wouldn't do his job. Damn loafer."

"Looks like he decided to get back at you and hooked up somehow with the gang that's trying to stop the spur line," Frank mused. "Had he worked on trestles before?"

Brant shrugged. "Yeah, he'd been in the railroad business for a while, so I reckon he must have helped to build trestles before. It would take an experienced man to climb up there in the dark, especially carrying a case of dynamite. He had to know where to put it to do the most damage too."

"I was thinking the same thing, so I'm not surprised he used to work for you." Frank rubbed his jaw in thought. "Was he close friends with anybody else who's still part of the crew?"

"I don't really remem—" Brant stopped short and exclaimed, "Hey! Are you thinking that there might be other members of the bunch still working against us from the inside?"

"It's a possibility," Frank said.

The man who had recognized the saboteur spoke up again, saying, "I don't remember Lovejoy havin' any friends, let alone close ones. He was a prickly son of a bitch.

Good worker, though . . . but only when he wanted to be."

"The fact that he wasn't close to anyone doesn't mean there are no men in the crew who are really working for whoever's trying to stop us," Frank pointed out.

"Yeah, that's right," Brant said glumly. "As if we didn't have enough to worry about already, now we've got to be looking over our own shoulders all the time, wondering if the fella behind us is really working for the enemy."

That suspicion would damage morale, Frank knew, but Brant was right — if a former member of the crew could be working against them, there was nothing to prevent someone who was still in camp from turning traitor too.

Frank turned his head and looked up at the wreckage of the trestle. Small fires still burned here and there, but most of the flames were out. A few of the pillars were still in place, but they went up only so far and then ended jaggedly where the explosion had ripped the rest of them away.

"How long is this going to set you back?" he asked Brant.

"No telling," Brant said with a shake of his head. "Several weeks at least. Maybe a month or more."

"But you can rebuild the trestle?"

"Sure." Brant gave a hollow laugh. "It'll just cost time and money and a heap of sweat, that's all."

The railroad could afford the time; there was no real hurry about getting the spur line to Ophir, although the sooner it was completed the better. Frank thought that Conrad could probably afford the cost of rebuilding the trestle too.

But it was one more expense, one more disaster pushing the New Mexico, Rio Grande, and Oriental that much closer to the edge of ruin. Conrad had asked him to come here so that he could stop that from happening.

But so far, Frank thought bitterly, he wasn't one step closer to accomplishing that goal. Men had died and havoc had been wreaked, and somewhere the mastermind behind all of it was laughing. . . .

Chapter 18

"Fiancée?" Rebel echoed as she looked at Conrad and Pamela Tarleton standing there on the boardwalk beside Gold Street in Ophir.

"That's right," Pamela said a smug smile. "And who is this . . . person, Conrad?"

"This person is sitting right here," Rebel snapped, "and she can speak for herself. My name is Rebel Callahan."

"Rebel?" Pamela's smile became less smug and more scornful. "One of those dreadful unreconstructed Confederates, I suppose."

"I wasn't born until after the War of Northern Aggression, but I carry the name proudly," Rebel said. "Proudly enough to get down off this horse and—"

"Ladies, please," Conrad said nervously as he moved to put himself between Rebel and Pamela. Rebel had started to swing down from the saddle, and Conrad wouldn't put it past her to step up onto the boardwalk and start a physical altercation with Pamela. That was just the sort of untamed frontier girl she was.

She had Pamela beat where looks were concerned, though. He had to admit that.

But not by much. Even here in a mining boomtown in the middle of the Mimbres Mountains in New Mexico Territory, Pamela Tarleton managed to dress in an elegant, stylish manner. Her dark green gown was cut low enough in front to reveal the top of the valley between her rather large breasts, and it hugged her slender waist tightly before flaring out over her hips and thighs. Her brown hair fell below her shoulders in the sort of thick curls that made a man want to plunge his hands into it and run his fingers through the silken tresses. The hair framed a lovely face highlighted by a pair of compelling green eyes. Back in Philadelphia, where she came from, she was widely acclaimed as a beauty and deserved every bit of the reputation. Now that he looked back and forth between them, Conrad wasn't sure if Rebel was prettier or not. It would have been a damned close contest.

Pamela put a hand on his arm and said, "Conrad, dear, you should have told me that you were coming. The prospect of seeing you again would have brightened considerably the dreary days I've been forced to spend here."

"I didn't know exactly when I'd arrive. Besides, I wasn't sure you'd be here either."

"Where else would I be? My father insists on dragging me along with him, although why he thinks I need to come on these business trips, I'll never know!"

"I'm sure he just wants to show off his beautiful daughter," Conrad said. Flattery was usually effective with Pamela, and he wanted to distract her from Rebel — and from asking questions about Rebel.

But the tactic didn't work, because Rebel said, "I reckon you forgot to tell me that you're engaged to be married . . . Conrad, dear."

Good Lord! Could she have *said* anything worse?

Pamela stiffened. "What does this . . . this woman mean by that?" she demanded. The way she said "woman" made it sound almost as insulting as if she had called Rebel a whore.

"She doesn't mean anything," Conrad said hastily. "She's merely speaking facetiously. Making a joke, if you will." He managed to put a weak smile on his face, but he didn't know if it would fool anyone.

Pamela wasn't fooled. She said, "Are the two of you . . . traveling together?" Again, her tone of voice made the innocuous words sound much worse than they really were.

"We rode up together from Lordsburg," Conrad was forced to admit. He knew from experience that it was difficult for him to lie to Pamela. She saw right through him.

"That's right, lady," Rebel put in. "We spent a lot of days — and nights — together on the trail, didn't we, Conrad?"

"We weren't *alone*—" he began to explain. Suddenly, anger at being trapped between them like this flared up inside him. He said, "Perhaps we should start over with some proper introductions."

Pamela sniffed. "I don't need to be introduced to—"

"Miss Callahan, this is Miss Tarleton," Conrad went on stubbornly, determined to defuse this situation. "Miss Tarleton, this is Miss Callahan." He turned back to Rebel. "Miss Tarleton is one of the Philadelphia Tarletons, and the daughter of Mr. Clark Tarleton, the noted financier and industrialist." Switching his attention back to Pamela, he continued. "Miss Callahan is from Texas and is the former owner of a cattle ranch there. She had business dealings with an acquaintance of mine, Mr. Frank Morgan, and accompanied Mr. Morgan and myself here to New Mexico Territory. Everything was completely proper and aboveboard, Pamela, I assure you."

"She came along with you and this fellow Morgan unchaperoned?"

"Well, yes. You have to understand, darling, the West is a somewhat less formal place than what you're used to."

"I should say so! Where I come from, proper young women do not travel unattended with gentlemen who are not related to them."

Rebel said, "Then maybe you better get it through your head that you ain't back where you came from anymore."

"Trust me, Miss Callahan," Pamela said coldly. "I am well aware of that."

Rebel sat on her horse and glared. Pamela turned her head away and ignored the other girl. But at least they didn't look like they were ready to start swinging punches at each other, and Conrad was grateful for that. Not that Pamela would have ever thrown a punch, he amended mentally. She was much too genteel for that. Rebel, on the other hand . . .

"Is your father here?" Conrad asked Pamela, hoping that a change of subject would be in order.

"Yes, he's inside this store, talking to the merchant," she replied, gesturing vaguely toward the front door of the building. Conrad glanced up at the sign over the door. It read KANDINSKY'S GENERAL MERCANTILE.

Pamela went on. "He's making some sort of arrangement with the man to supply provisions for the workers at the mine."

Conrad nodded. "I see."

She tugged on his arm, urging him toward the door. "Come inside with me, dear. I'm sure Father will be glad to see you. He's always been fond of you."

Conrad hesitated and glanced at Rebel. She said scathingly, "Go ahead. Don't mind me. I'll just take your horse and go on down to the livery stable with him."

"Thank you, Rebel," he said, ignoring the little frown that Pamela gave him when he used the other girl's name. "That's very kind of you."

"*De nada,*" Rebel said as she took hold of El Diablo's reins and turned her chestnut away from the boardwalk. Leading the black horse, she rode on down the street toward a livery barn with its big double doors open so that light spilled out into the street.

Conrad couldn't help but notice how stiff her back was. He knew he had offended her, and he was sorry about that. He probably

237

should have told her that he was engaged to be married, but he truly hadn't known that Pamela would be here in Ophir. He had known that she might be, in fact probably would be, but it had been easier not to say anything about that to Rebel, and before that, not to say anything to Frank. . . .

"Come along," Pamela said again.

"Of course, dear." Conrad allowed her to lead him into the store.

Clark Tarleton stood at the counter at the rear of the emporium, talking to the proprietor. He was around fifty, a tall, broad-shouldered, beefy man who despite his expensive clothes and well-barbered appearance still bore traces of the steel-mill laborer he had been in his youth, before he had raised himself by hard work and sheer willpower from that position to become one of the leading industrialists in the East. He had added mining to his business interests several years earlier, and now owned several mines in this southwestern corner of New Mexico Territory. Conrad supposed that technically Tarleton was one of Browning Mines and Manufacturing's rivals, but that wouldn't be the case for much longer. Once he and Pamela were wed, like the merger of two royal families in Europe by marriage, everything would be all in the family.

And as the head of that family, Conrad would one day be mentioned in the same breath as Vanderbilt, Carnegie, Gould, Rockefeller, and all the rest. It was a dream of his, a dream that someday soon he would grasp. All he had to do was bring that spur line in successfully, expand his power in the railroad business as he also built up the mining operation, and marry the beautiful daughter of one of the richest men in the country. That was all.

"Father," Pamela said, "look who's here."

Tarleton swung around, and a smile creased his rugged face when he saw Conrad. "Browning!" he said as he stepped toward them and extended his hand. "Good to see you again, young man. How are you?"

Conrad grasped his future father-in-law's hand firmly. "I'm just fine, sir. It's good to see you too. How are things in Philadelphia?"

Tarleton chuckled. "I wouldn't know. I'm never there long enough to find out. Always traveling, you know. My interests are so widespread they keep me busy all the time."

"I can certainly imagine."

"Luckily, I have Pamela to keep me company," Tarleton said as he put an arm around his daughter's shoulders for a moment. "But not for much longer, if you succeed in stealing her away from me."

"I suppose she'll be traveling with me then."

"For a while maybe," Tarleton said, "but then you'll have her at home, no doubt, giving birth to all the Browning heirs."

Pretending to be scandalized, Pamela said, "Father! How you do go on!"

Conrad just smiled, too uncomfortable with the subject to get into any discussion of heirs and how they came about.

Pamela gave him a veiled look and went on. "Anyway, I'm not sure whether Conrad still intends to marry me or not. He's taken up with a frontier woman, a wild creature who rides astride and carries a rifle."

Tarleton frowned. "What's that?"

"It's nothing, I assure you, sir," Conrad said quickly. "While I was traveling up here to Ophir with an associate, we escorted a lady who was also heading in this direction." That was a considerable distortion of the facts, but Conrad didn't care. He just wished Pamela and her father would drop the entire subject of Rebel. "The situation was totally innocent."

His brain picked that precise moment to remind him of the way Rebel had kissed him and the wanton images that had filled his head when she talked about taking off all her clothes and jumping into that pond. He felt his face warming at those memories and coughed uncomfortably into his hand.

"Well, I suppose we can't blame you for trying to be a gentleman," Tarleton said. He added to Pamela, "Isn't that right, darling?"

"I suppose," she agreed, but she didn't sound like she was convinced.

"How's your mining operation going, sir?" Conrad asked in an attempt to steer the conversation into safer waters.

"Quite well. Lucky for us, there's plenty of gold and silver to go around, eh, or you and I might be at each other's throats. Figuratively speaking, of course."

"Of course." Conrad was glad that wasn't the case. Having Clark Tarleton as a friendly rival and potential partner was one thing; having a man like him as an enemy was something totally different.

"What about that railroad of yours?" Tarleton asked. "Is everything on schedule there? The sooner we have reliable rail service in and out of this place, the sooner we'll all be that much richer, eh?"

"It's coming along just fine," Conrad lied. "The line should be completed soon."

"Really?" Tarleton slipped a cigar from his vest pocket and began to peel the wrapper from it. "I've heard rumors that there have been problems with the construction. Indian trouble, among other things."

"Well . . . it's true that there seems to be a band of renegade Apaches loose in the mountains, and while their presence has made the workers a bit nervous, construction is continuing on a steady pace."

"What about the accidents I've heard talked about?"

"Any project as large as the building of a railroad will have problems—"

Tarleton bit off the end of the cigar. "I've been told that it's deliberate sabotage."

"The situation is being taken care of even as we speak," Conrad told him, anxious for Tarleton not to see him as weak. "That business associate I spoke of is out at the construction camp right now, getting to the bottom of the problems and putting an end to them."

Tarleton narrowed his eyes and asked, "Who might that be?"

Conrad had hoped to avoid bringing Frank's name into the discussion, but he didn't have much choice. "Frank Morgan," he said. He didn't know if Tarleton would recognize the name or not.

"The infamous gunman?" Tarleton's eyebrows arched. "I saw a traveling stage play about him once. Terribly violent. They say he's killed hundreds of men. Good Lord, son, how do you know a man like Frank Morgan?"

Conrad thought quickly, trying to come up with an answer that would avoid the full truth. "We met several years ago. He . . . was an old friend of my late mother's."

"I see," Tarleton said. He didn't, not really, though, and Conrad was glad of that. "Well, Conrad, I hope this doesn't backfire on you. I know you're anxious to solve the problems plaguing your railroad, but having a man like Frank Morgan working for you may present you with even more problems."

"I have every confidence in him, sir. He's never let me down."

And with a shock, Conrad realized that was true. Both times he had been kidnapped, Frank had rescued him. Of course, he might not have ever been in danger to start with if it hadn't been for the grudge those outlaws held against Frank.

"I hope you're right," Tarleton said, and then he took Pamela's arm. "We're on our way back to the hotel. Would you like to join us for a late supper?"

Conrad looked down at his clothes, which were covered with trail dust. "I'm hardly presentable. . . ."

"That's not a problem. We'll give you time to clean up. You can meet us in the hotel dining room in, say, an hour?"

Conrad felt himself nodding. "That's fine. Thank you, sir."

"Not at all. I'm looking forward to spending more time with you, and I know Pamela is too."

"Of course I am," she murmured. She leaned forward to kiss Conrad discreetly on the cheek. "We'll see you later, darling."

They strolled out of the store, leaving Conrad there. He was rather dizzy and upset from the whole encounter. He had known that Pamela and her father were likely to be here in Ophir, but he had been hoping that he wouldn't run into them right away. He liked to plan out such things in advance. That hadn't happened tonight, and he had been forced to improvise. But he hadn't done too badly, he told himself. The whole thing with Rebel was embarrassing, of course, but Pamela seemed to be willing to forget about it.

The problem, he suddenly realized, was that he didn't know if he could forget about Rebel. . . .

"So, young man," the proprietor of the store said from behind him, "did you want something?"

"Yes," Conrad said. "But I'm not sure what."

Chapter 19

Rebel was seething inside as she rode down to the livery stable. She was mad at Conrad, of course, but she was also angry with herself. She should have known better than to let herself become interested in some damn Eastern dude who acted most of the time like he had a corncob shoved up his butt.

If he hadn't been such a handsome man . . . and if he hadn't jumped on her to shield her with his own body like he had during that fight with the Apaches . . . she probably never would have done more than casually despise him. The fact that he was rich didn't mean anything to her. The fact that he was intelligent, and that he obviously had at least some measure of courage, those things were more important. After traveling for a day or two with Conrad Browning and Frank Morgan, she had realized quite honestly that her cousin Ed and her brothers were in the wrong in this vendetta they had against Morgan. He was a good man, and he never would have killed her other cousins if they hadn't forced him into it. The best thing for the Callahan boys to do would be to forget about Frank Morgan.

But they wouldn't. Rebel knew that in her heart. It was only a matter of time before they showed up and tried to kill Frank again.

The thought that Conrad might be hurt or killed when that happened made a pang of fear go through Rebel, despite her current irritation with him. He could be damned annoying, but she had come to care for him anyway.

And that was what made her the most upset.

She wasn't worried about Pamela Tarleton. Rebel was confident that if she wanted to, she could take Conrad away from some pale, skinny little simp from Philadelphia. The question was whether she really wanted Conrad or just had a crush on him.

Damn a problem you couldn't shoot or whip into submission anyway, she thought as she dismounted and led the horses into the stable.

Making arrangements with the elderly

proprietor to care for them didn't take long. Then she asked, "What's the best hotel in town?"

"That'd be the Holloway House, miss," the old-timer told her. He pointed to an impressive two-story structure on the other side of the street in the next block. "Right over yonder. You can't miss it."

"Thanks." Rebel left the saddles at the stable but took her saddlebags and rifle with her, along with Conrad's Winchester. If the Holloway House was the best hotel in Ophir, she was confident that he would be staying there as well. Nothing but the best for the great Conrad Browning. She would find out his room number and give him the Winchester. Dumb greenhorn would forget his head if it wasn't screwed on.

As she approached the hotel, she saw Pamela Tarleton going into the place with an older man who had to be the father she and Conrad had mentioned. Clark Tarleton, that was his name, Rebel recalled. He was an impressive-looking gent, for an Easterner. Unlike most of them, he appeared to have done at least a little honest work at some time in his life.

Rebel hung back, giving the Tarletons time to get inside the hotel and go up to their rooms or into the dining room or wherever they were going. All she knew was that she didn't want to run into Pamela again — especially not while she was holding a gun. The temptation might be too great to plant a few shots around that hussy's feet and make her dance.

When Rebel went into the hotel lobby a few minutes later, she didn't see any sign of Pamela or Tarleton. She walked up to the desk, noticing the way the clerk's eyes widened at the sight of the two rifles she was carrying.

"I'd like a room," she said.

"Ah . . . yes, ma'am. Just for yourself?"

"I ain't got a husband, and I ain't expecting any gentlemen callers," she snapped. "So, yeah, just for me."

"Of course." The clerk turned the registration book around. "If you'll just sign in . . ."

Rebel looked around for someplace to put the Winchesters, and wound up laying them on the desk. She scratched her name in the book and put "Fort Davis, Texas" in the place for her home address, since that was the closest settlement to the ranch she and her brothers had owned. As it was now, she didn't really have a home. She didn't know where she would go or what she would wind up doing. All she was sure of was that she intended to stick close to Conrad until she was sure her brothers and cousin no longer represented a threat to him. She had decided to come with him because she knew that Frank Morgan could take care of himself. Conrad likely couldn't.

"The rate is one dollar a night," the clerk said as Rebel shoved the book back over to him.

"You got a mighty high opinion of your rooms, don't you?"

"I don't set the prices, ma'am," the clerk said with a shrug. "Ophir *is* a boomtown, after all. Everything costs more here."

"I reckon if you charge that much, the hotel ought to provide a hot bath too," she said, suddenly wanting to get some of the trail dust off and change into clean clothes.

The clerk smiled. "Actually, we do have a bathhouse just out back, and I believe there's a fresh tub of hot water that's been recently drawn. There should be an attendant back there to help you."

"Much obliged." Rebel picked up the key the clerk put on the counter. "Reckon I'll clean up first, then go upstairs."

"As you wish, ma'am."

"I wish you'd quit calling me ma'am. Never did like the sound of it."

Without any more conversation, she picked up the rifles and headed down a hallway toward the rear door of the hotel, looking for that bathhouse.

She found the windowless building just outside the hotel's back door. There were two zinc-plated tubs with a canvas partition between them. Canvas curtains could be pulled across in front of each tub to give the bathers some privacy. A heavyset Mexican woman perched on a stool just inside the bathhouse door greeted Rebel with a smile.

"The señorita wishes to bathe?"

"Darned right I do," Rebel said.

The woman pointed to the tub on the right. "That water is freshly drawn and is still hot."

"Sounds mighty fine." As Rebel approached the tub, she saw little wisps of steam rising from the surface of the clean water. The sight made her realize just how badly she wanted to sink down into it and soak away some of the aches and pains of the past week, not to mention all the trail dust.

She pulled the curtain, placed the rifles and her saddlebags next to the tub on a chair that had a towel draped over its back, and started taking her clothes off. Within minutes, she was nude. She lifted a leg and poised it over the water, then lowered it slowly, adjusting to the heat. She stepped in with her other leg and sank slowly into the tub, sighing in pleasure as she did so. She leaned back and closed her eyes. The hot water felt wonderful.

She was going to just sit here and soak and not even think about Conrad Browning, she told herself. Wherever he was, whatever he was doing, he was on his own.

Conrad was about to leave the emporium when the two men Sam Brant had sent with him and Rebel came in to give the order for supplies to the proprietor. Since he was already there, Conrad waited until the transaction was complete, satisfying himself that the men had carried out Brant's orders as they should. Then one of the men asked, "Anything else you want us to do, Mr. Browning?"

"No, that's fine," Conrad told them. "Have a good time the rest of the evening. Just be ready to start back to camp first thing in the morning with those supplies."

"Yes, sir, we sure will." Grinning, the men headed down the street, bound no doubt for an evening of drinking, gambling, and whoring. In a way, Conrad envied them their simple pleasures, even though he could never lead such a life himself.

Following that brief delay, he walked over to the Holloway House. The clerk greeted him with a smile, remembering him from previous visits.

"No need for you to sign in, Mr. Browning," he said as he reached for a key on the board behind him. "I'll take care of that for you. You want your usual room?"

"Yes, please, George, if it's available."

The clerk slid the key across the desk. "Yes, sir, here you go. Got any bags you need help with?"

"No, not this time." Conrad frowned as he realized he had left his saddlebags on El Diablo. He hoped that they were over at the stable. Wherever Rebel had gone, surely she wouldn't have taken them with her. He said to the clerk, "I'll be right back."

It took only a few minutes to walk over to the livery stable and reclaim his saddlebags from the elderly owner. The old-timer said, "The gal who brought them horses in took both rifles with her, but I ain't sure where she went."

"That's fine," Conrad said with a distracted nod. He was glad she hadn't taken his saddlebags with her, because he wanted to wash up and put on some clean clothes before he had dinner with Pamela and her father.

The clerk wasn't behind the desk when Conrad came back into the hotel. He started to go upstairs, but then changed his mind. He knew from experience that there was a bathhouse right behind the hotel. He had intended to wash up with the water in the basin in his room, but perhaps he had time for an actual bath. The hotel kept hot water available for its guests most of the time.

He walked down the hall and through the rear door. The bathhouse door was open. He stepped inside and saw that the Mexican woman who usually worked there was gone. Were all the hotel employees shirking their duty at the moment?

The curtain on the right was pulled, meaning that someone was using that tub. Conrad went into the compartment on the left and reached down to test the temperature of the water. It was only warm, not hot, and it looked like it had been used by a previous bather, but probably only once. That wasn't too bad for a frontier town, although it would be totally unacceptable in any fine hotel back East, of course. With a sigh, he set his saddlebags aside and began to get undressed. As he did, he heard a faint splash from the other tub as whoever was in it moved around.

When he was naked, Conrad put one foot in the tub, still wishing the water was warmer. He lifted his other leg and lowered that foot into the water. As he did so, he heard more splashing from the other side of the canvas partition. It sounded like the other bather was standing up to get out of the tub.

That was when Conrad's foot came down on the bar of soap left in the tub by whoever had used it before. The soap had sunk to the bottom, and he never saw it.

He certainly felt it, though, when it squirted out from under him and threw him completely off balance. He realized he was falling, and with a startled yell he reached out to grab something and try to stop himself.

What he got hold of was the canvas partition. It slowed his fall so that he merely splashed down in the tub without injuring himself, although a lot of the water sloshed over the sides. But the canvas tore all along the top where it was nailed to the ceiling, and it fell too, so there was no longer any barrier between the two tubs.

Conrad sprawled there in the water, half-stunned, staring at the nude body of Rebel Callahan as she stood upright in the other tub, the towel she had just picked up from the chair next to it clutched in her hands but not yet concealing any of her bare loveliness.

All the mental images that Conrad's

fevered brain had conjured up when Rebel talked about swimming nude in the pond flashed into his mind so that he could compare them with the reality. As exciting as those images had been, Conrad now knew they couldn't hold a candle to the real thing. Rebel was a vision, her smooth pink skin glowing and glistening damply, the curves of her body sweeping in and out in a sensuous rhythm as pleasing to the eye as the notes of a brilliant concerto were to the ear. Conrad was so overwhelmed that he couldn't do anything except lie there and stare at her, enthralled by her beauty.

Instead of trying to cover herself, she dropped the towel, surprising him even more.

Then she snatched up one of the rifles lying next to the tub and yelled, "You son of a bitch!" She jerked the Winchester's lever as she swung the barrel toward him.

Conrad realized his danger at the last second and gulped down a breath of air just before he ducked under the surface of the water that remained in the tub. The rifle blasted, the sound deafening in these close quarters even though his ears were underwater and the report was somewhat muffled. Knowing that the outraged young woman would have to work the rifle's lever again before she could fire a second shot, he stuck his head up and said urgently, "Rebel, no! Don't—"

Then he was diving for cover again as another shot roared.

As he huddled there holding his breath, wondering if he was going to die in this tub, the thought occurred to him that the only way this situation could get worse would be if Pamela Tarleton chanced to step into the bathhouse at this very moment. Perhaps it would be better if Rebel just went ahead and shot him before that could happen. . . .

Chapter 20

"Dios mio!" the Mexican woman shrieked as she hurried into the bathhouse and saw the naked blond woman standing in one tub and pointing a rifle at the other tub. A wisp of smoke still curled from the barrel of the Winchester. "Señorita, no! Do not kill him!"

"If I wanted to kill him, he'd already be dead," Rebel grated. "I just want him to think twice before he pokes his head up again like a turtle." She set the rifle aside and picked up her towel again, wrapping it around herself as she stepped out of the tub.

A long half minute went by before Conrad Browning's head popped out of the water again. He gasped for air after holding his breath longer than he was used to. Wide-eyed, he looked around frantically, evidently intending to duck for cover again if he needed to.

"Take it easy," Rebel told him scathingly.

"I'm not going to plug you — even though I ought to, you . . . you damned sneak."

"You can't believe that . . . that I did that on purpose!" he yelped. "It was an accident!"

"Sure it was," she snapped. "Just like you accidentally forgot to tell me you had a fiancée waiting for you when we got here!"

"I . . . I wasn't certain she would be here—"

"Save your breath, Conrad. I'm not interested anymore."

The Mexican woman edged forward hesitantly and said, "Señorita . . . you will not shoot that man?"

"No," Rebel said. "I'm not going to have anything more to do with that man."

The attendant crossed herself and muttered a prayer of thanks in Spanish, obviously glad that she wouldn't have to deal with having a dead man in one of the bathtubs.

"I don't know how you got in here, Conrad, or what you hoped to accomplish," Rebel went on, "but the least you can do is be a gentleman and turn around while I get dressed."

"Yes, of course," he said, twisting in the other tub so that he faced away from her. Without looking at her, he said, "Rebel, I really am so sorry—"

258

"I don't want to hear it," she interrupted him coldly. To the Mexican woman, she said, "Guard that door."

"*Sí, señorita!*"

With the attendant's formidable figure standing there to keep anyone from coming in, Rebel quickly began pulling on some clean clothes from her saddlebags. Footsteps sounded outside, and the doorknob rattled as someone grasped it. The Mexican woman held it on the inside so that it wouldn't turn.

"*No entrada!*" she called through the door.

"What's going on in there?" The shouted question came from the desk clerk. "We heard gunshots—"

"Everything is all right," the attendant replied. "An accident only, nothing to worry about."

"Are you sure, Luz?" the clerk asked. "No one's forcing you to say that?"

Conrad spoke up. "This is Mr. Browning, Bennett. Everything is fine, I assure you." He sounded more calm and collected than he looked, huddled there in a tub now less than half full of water, trying to keep the more important parts of his anatomy under the surface. If Rebel hadn't been so mad at him, she would have had to laugh, he looked so ludicrous.

But she was still too upset with him for

that, so she just finished buttoning her shirt instead and then sat down in the chair to pull on a pair of socks and shove her feet into her boots. She slung the saddlebags over her shoulder and picked up her rifle.

"I'll leave your Winchester here," she told Conrad.

"Thank you," he said in a weak voice. "Can I turn around now?"

"You could, but I'd rather you didn't. I might see something I don't want to see."

Lord, he was blushing all over, Rebel noted. That was good. He deserved to be embarrassed, sneaking in here that way and pulling down the partition just so he could get a look at her in the altogether. Hell, it wasn't like she wouldn't have considered giving him a look, if he had asked nice enough. . . .

But that was before they had arrived in Ophir and she'd found out that he was engaged to be married to that Pamela Tarleton. That had pretty much changed everything.

She put her hat on without bothering to tuck her hair up into it. With the Winchester under her arm, she went to the door and nodded to the attendant. The Mexican woman let go of the knob and stepped back. With all the dignity she could muster, Rebel opened the door and stepped out. The desk clerk and several other men stood there, still curious about the shots they had heard. Without looking at them, Rebel walked past them and into the hotel through the rear door. She had thought earlier about getting something to eat in the dining room, but under the circumstances, she decided that she wasn't hungry anymore.

By the time she got up to her room, her anger had subsided a little. She was still mad, but when she thought about how miserable Conrad had looked in that tub, it was hard for her not to laugh. And when she thought about the way he had stared at her, his eyes drinking in every facet of her nudity, she felt something else, a little fluttering inside that was damned disturbing. She didn't want to feel that way just because he had seen her without her clothes on.

Maybe it *had* been an accident, she told herself. He had looked plenty shocked when she first saw him, that was for sure. And he *had* fallen in the tub. She knew that because she had heard the splash and seen all the water that had sloshed out onto the floor. But maybe he was capable of pretending to fall just so he could pull that curtain down and take a gander at her. It seemed far-fetched, but she wouldn't put anything past a fella from Boston.

She flung herself down on the bed with a sigh. She had told Conrad that she was through with him, and yet ever since she had come up here to her room, she had done nothing but think about him.

She had only enough money to stay here for a few days, and then she would have some decisions to make. The problem was that she didn't have any idea what she wanted to do.

Life sure had been a whole heap simpler before she met Conrad Browning.

Right offhand, he couldn't remember a time when he had felt more humiliated. He was sure there had been occasions that were more embarrassing, but he couldn't recall them. The only thing he had to be thankful for was that Pamela didn't know about the incident — yet. She might still hear some of the gossip that was bound to circulate about it, though. The spectacle of a naked man cowering in a bathtub while a naked woman shot at him with a Winchester had to be talked about, especially in a relatively small settlement like Ophir.

Since he was in no mood to finish his bath, Conrad had asked the Mexican woman to step outside while he got dressed. Then he went into the hotel, doing his best to ignore the curious stares of the bystanders who still lingered outside the bathhouse. When he reached the lobby, he went over to the desk and said quietly to the clerk, "I need you to do me a favor, Bennett."

"Of course, Mr. Browning."

"Miss Tarleton and her father are waiting for me in the dining room. Could you go in there and tell them that I'm not feeling well and that I've retired for the evening?"

"Certainly. Is there any other message you'd like me to give them?"

Conrad shook his head glumly. "Just convey my apologies."

He went upstairs to his usual room, unlocked the door, and went inside. After turning on the gas lamp set in a wall sconce, he dropped his saddlebags and rifle on the bed and then stood there, unsure what to do next. He hadn't eaten supper, but he wasn't really hungry either. He didn't want to see anyone in the hotel, didn't want to endure the stares and the snickers. It might take him a long time to live down this fiasco.

Surely Rebel didn't think that he had pulled down that partition on purpose. That was insane. She must know that it had been an accident. He'd had no idea that she was on the other side of that flimsy wall.

Where was she right now? he wondered.

He had intended to see to it that she had a room here at the Holloway House for as long as she wanted to stay in Ophir. After all, she had come along with him to make sure that her murderous cousin and her brothers didn't do anything to threaten him, and he could certainly afford to pay for her accommodations.

But then he'd run into Pamela before he had a chance to explain the situation to Rebel, and after that everything had gone to hell.

Actually, he reminded himself, he'd had plenty of chances to tell Rebel that he was engaged. He simply hadn't done it. Was that because he enjoyed the attention from her and didn't want to jeopardize it? He was human, after all, and he had known that she was interested in him. What normal man wouldn't enjoy the company of a woman as beautiful as her?

Well, it was too late now. Rebel must hate him, and he couldn't blame her for that. He'd led her on, and then he had embarrassed her, not once but twice tonight. He deserved her scorn.

What he needed, he told himself suddenly, was a drink.

But not in the hotel bar. That would be just asking to be made fun of. Ophir had plenty of saloons, though, and he was willing to bet that he could slip into one of them, keep his head down and not call attention to himself, and not be recognized while he had a drink — or two. Especially since he was still wearing his dusty clothes. He hadn't put on clean ones after hurriedly drying off in the bathhouse.

The more he thought about it, the better the idea sounded. He left the room and used the hotel's rear staircase, so that he could leave the building without going through the lobby.

When he stepped out through the rear door, he saw that the bathhouse was closed. The partition between the tubs would have to be replaced. Walking quickly, Conrad navigated his way through a couple of shadowy alleys until he reached Gold Street. Then he tugged down his Stetson to make it harder for anyone to recognize him as he stepped out onto the boardwalk.

He headed for the saloon he had seen earlier as they rode into town, the Big Nugget. It was one of the largest drinking establishments in Ophir and there was always a good crowd on hand. The more people there were around, the easier it would be for him to blend in unrecognized, he reasoned.

As he approached the batwinged entrance,

he heard the same sort of raucous hilarity that had been coming from the place earlier. Taking a deep breath, Conrad pushed through the batwings and walked toward the bar, which was on his right. To the left were tables crowded with men who were drinking and gambling. Saloon girls in short, spangled dresses circulated among the tables, delivering drinks and laughing as the customers pawed them. Four more girls wearing even scantier outfits danced on a small raised stage at the rear of the room while a slick-haired professor pounded on a piano and a bearded old-timer sawed away at a fiddle. The air in the place was thick with tobacco smoke and the rank smells of whiskey, beer, and unwashed flesh. All in all, it was crude, loud, and squalid.

It was also exactly what Conrad wanted at the moment.

He worked his way through the crowd to the bar and ordered a beer. A heavyset bartender brought it to him and expertly scooped up the coin Conrad dropped on the hardwood. Spotting an empty table in a corner, Conrad carried his beer over to it and sat down. He knew he had been lucky to find a place to sit. Every other table in the Big Nugget was occupied.

He wasn't by himself for long, though.

One of the saloon girls appeared beside the table almost as if by magic and said, "Hello, honey. You don't want to drink alone, do you?"

Actually, that *was* what he wanted to do, but before he could say anything the girl had sat down beside him without being invited. She was tall and rather slender, with straight red hair. Her blue dress was scandalously short and cut low enough in the front so that he could see fully half of her breasts. She grinned at him, exposing teeth that were a little crooked. Young enough so that there was still some freshness about her, she was probably prettier than most of the females in the Big Nugget tonight.

But compared to either Rebel or Pamela, she was undeniably plain, and Conrad wasn't attracted to her at all. As she edged her chair nearer and leaned toward him so that her breasts were even more visible, he felt only a vague revulsion at the very idea of taking her to bed, which was probably what she wanted.

"Buy me a drink, sugar plum?" she asked.

"Of course," he said. "In fact . . ." He took a coin from his pocket and slid it toward her on the table. "I'll pay you to go drink with someone else."

She frowned as she tried to comprehend

what he was saying. "You don't want me to drink with you?"

"That's right." He smiled, not wanting to hurt her feelings even though she was only a soiled dove. "It's nothing against you, miss. I just don't desire any company at the moment except this fine product of the brewer's art." He lifted the half-empty mug of beer.

"Lawsy, you talk funny," she said as she made the coin he had offered her disappear. "You ain't from around these parts, are you?"

"No, I come from a place far, far away."

"Albuquerque? No, lemme guess. Santa Fe?"

Conrad shook his head. "Farther than that."

"Denver!"

Conrad was about to disabuse her of that notion when a man stepped up beside the table and said, "Honey, you run along now and bother some other cowboy."

"I wasn't botherin' him none," the girl said with a pout. "Was I, mister?"

"No, you were fine," Conrad told her. "But I'd just as soon be alone."

"You heard the man," the stranger said. He was well dressed in a brown tweed suit and had sleek dark hair. Something about him was vaguely familiar, but Conrad couldn't place him.

Still pouting, the girl got up and left the table. The stranger took her place in the chair.

"Perhaps you didn't hear me," Conrad said. "I'd prefer to be alone right now."

"Oh, I heard you," the man said, "but I reckon you better listen to me. My name's Jonas Wade. I saw you back in El Paso with Frank Morgan, as I was leaving that hotel where Morgan saved my life." He swept a well-manicured hand at their surroundings. "I own this place now, thanks to three queens and a pair of jacks that showed up in my hand at just the right time."

"You won it in a poker game?"

"That's right. Luckiest day of my life, I guess — except for the day I met Frank Morgan."

Conrad nodded slowly. "I remember you now. We weren't introduced, but I saw you with Frank. My name is Conrad Browning."

Wade's eyebrows rose in surprise. "The mine owner? The fella who's building a spur line up here from Lordsburg?" He held out a hand. "I've heard of you, and I'm mighty pleased to meet you, Mr. Browning. Is Frank with you?"

"Not at the moment, no. He's still down at

the railroad construction camp."

"That's good," Wade said with a nod. "If he was here in town, I wanted to warn him."

"Warn him about what?"

"There are three men in town — I think they're relatives of that hombre Frank had to kill back in El Paso — and they say that as soon as they see The Drifter again, they're going to kill him."

Chapter 21

The mood in the camp was still somber the next morning after the explosion that had destroyed the trestle. No one would soon forget the guard who had been killed or the destruction that had been caused.

After breakfast, Frank and Sam Brant stood outside the railroad car where the construction boss and his foremen had their office and living quarters. Each held a cup of coffee. Frank said, "What are your plans for today, Sam?"

Brant heaved a sigh. "We'll get started rebuilding that trestle, I suppose. There's really nothing else we can do. The line can't go anywhere until it gets across this gorge."

Frank rubbed his jaw in thought for a moment and then said, "I don't know much about building a railroad, but hasn't the roadbed already been graded between here and Ophir?"

"Yeah, you can follow it all the way on to the settlement without any trouble. You thinking of leaving?"

"Not at all. The reason I asked was because I wondered if you could somehow get rails and cross-ties across to the other side and have some of the men laying them while the rest of the crew was working on the trestle."

Brant's forehead creased in a frown. "I guess you could load ties on a cart and trundle it down the trail on this side of the gorge, across the pontoon bridge, and then up the trail on the other side. Only way to get rails across, though, would be to have a gang of men carry them one at a time the same way. It'd be slow as hell."

"But you'd be making at least a little progress that way," Frank pointed out. "Or do you need the whole crew working on the trestle?"

"No, I've really got more men than I need for that," Brant said slowly. "You see, normally what you do is you send a crew on ahead of you to build the trestles and have them ready when the rails reach them. That way it doesn't take long to lay the rails across the trestle and then you just go right on once you're on the other side. The men working on this one ran into problems, though, and it's a damn big project. We caught up to them before they finished. And now we're stuck here."

"Unless you put as many men on the trestle as are practical to work on it, and have the others carry ties and rails across and start putting down track. Even if they only get a mile done in the time it takes to rebuild and finish the trestle, that's that much you won't have to build once you're across. You could consider it a running start."

"Well, it might work," Brant allowed, but he still sounded a little dubious. "Only a fella who'd never built a railroad would have come up with an idea like that, though."

Frank grinned. "Sometimes a fresh pair of eyes comes in handy. Helps you see things differently."

"I'll talk to the boys about it and see what they think," Brant said with a nod. "In the meantime, what do you figure on being up to today?"

Frank's expression grew more serious. "I'm still convinced that the gang causing you so much trouble is holed up somewhere around here. I'm going to keep looking for them."

"Well, good luck to you. If you find them, though, don't try to tackle them alone. Come on back here and tell me. I've got plenty of men just itching for a crack at those bastards."

Frank nodded, but he was thinking that the railroaders might not be much of a match for the gang. Based on the two encounters so far, he suspected the troublemakers were hired guns, at least for the most part. They would be experienced killers, and pitting even tough railroaders against them might not be enough.

He would deal with that problem, though, when he found the gang's hideout. He finished his coffee and then went to get Stormy ready to ride.

A short time later, he rode out of camp with Dog padding along beside him. The day before, although he had ridden all around the camp, he had concentrated his search in the area north of the railhead, across the river. Today he decided to turn his efforts more to the south. It was possible the gang was trailing the railroad, rather than staying out ahead of it.

Frank followed the rails back toward the pass where he and Conrad and Rebel had run into the man who had blown up the dynamite shed. As he rode, he wondered about the two young people. By now they ought to be in Ophir.

He knew good and well that Conrad and

Rebel were interested in each other; it didn't take a genius to see that. Conrad was so blasted stuffy, though, that he might not do anything about it, thinking that Rebel was somehow not good enough for him. That was a foolish notion, of course. Rebel was a fine-looking young woman, and she could ride and shoot. As far as Frank was concerned, that put her well ahead of any girls Conrad might have known back East. Conrad, of course, would probably see it differently. He tended to see most things differently than Frank.

For the time being, Frank contented himself with hoping that Conrad and Rebel had made it to Ophir without running into trouble. If there were any personal matters between them, they would have to hash those out for themselves.

It was a pretty morning, but there were thunderheads building up over the mountains. There might be a shower later, or even a storm. Frank hoped that wouldn't be the case, but he had a slicker rolled up behind his saddle in case the skies opened up.

Before he reached the pass, he veered off onto a likely-looking trail that led up higher into the mountains. This was a game trail, he decided as it switched back and forth and climbed steadily. At one point he was able to rein in, twist around in the saddle, and look back down the mountain toward the river gorge. He saw the construction camp at least a mile away and hundreds of feet below him. From this distance he could make out the railroad cars and the tents, but he couldn't see any people, even though he knew that Sam Brant's crew would be scurrying around down there, busily working as they rebuilt the destroyed trestle.

He faced forward again, and was about to hitch Stormy into motion when a flash from the slopes above him suddenly caught his eye. The reflection was only there for a second, but Frank knew he hadn't imagined it. He stiffened in the saddle.

Somebody was up there, and the flash might have been a reflection off a gun barrel, or more likely, a pair of field glasses. Out here in the middle of nowhere, there was only one thing for somebody to be keeping an eye on — the construction camp.

Frank had a hunch that whoever that watcher was, he was up to no good.

"Stay close, Dog," he ordered the big cur as he began to ride higher along the trail. After a few minutes, he reined Stormy to a halt again and swung down from the saddle. Sound carried well in this thin air, and if he rode any closer, he chanced that the watcher would hear the clink of the Appaloosa's shoes against the rocky ground. Frank estimated that the flash he had seen was now about five hundred yards above him on the side of the mountain. He would have to go the rest of the way on foot.

In some places, the climb was fairly easy; in others, he had to lean forward and hang ono the slope with both hands as he slowly made his way upward. He stopped often and checked to see where he was in relation to the spot where he had seen the reflection. He was circling it gradually, getting above that point.

Of course, if the watcher wasn't there anymore by the time Frank got in position, then he would have had this climb for nothing. He didn't let himself dwell on that possibility.

The day was warm enough and the climb difficult enough so that by the time Frank reached his objective, his faded blue shirt was stained with sweat. He paused, took his hat off, and sleeved beads of moisture from his forehead. Then he put the Stetson back on and crawled forward on hands and knees, up a slanted rock that overlooked a broad ledge about ten feet below it. When Frank came to the edge of the rock, he saw that the ledge was littered with boulders.

And sure enough, a man was crouched among those boulders. He had a rifle, a canteen, and a canvas pouch. A pair of field glasses hung around his neck on a strap. As Frank looked on, the man leaned forward, lifted the glasses to his eyes, and trained them on the railroad construction camp, which was visible far below.

After a few minutes, the man lowered the glasses and let them hang from their strap as he settled back into a more relaxed position. He opened the canvas pouch and took out a biscuit. He began to eat it, washing it down with sips of water from the canteen.

The man's hat was lying on the ground at his side, so Frank had a good view of his head, but couldn't see much of his face from this angle. He was stockily built, with thick dark hair, and from what Frank could see of his face, it was rather red. Frank didn't know if that was from the sun or if the man was naturally florid. The man turned his head a little and Frank saw part of a thick dark mustache. The watcher wore black trousers, a brown leather vest, and a gray shirt. He didn't appear to be armed except for the rifle that lay on the ledge beside him.

Now that he had his quarry in sight, Frank could afford to be patient. He took a long look around at the rugged mountainside. He wasn't sure how the watcher had gotten up here, unless there was a trail at the other end of the ledge. Frank could see this end, where the ledge petered out among the cluster of boulders, and he knew there was no way up or down there.

With a frown, Frank pondered his next move. He could jump this hombre here and now and try to get some information from him, such as who he was and why he was keeping such a close eye on the camp, or he could try to follow the man and hope that he would lead him back to the rest of the gang causing trouble for the New Mexico, Rio Grande, and Oriental.

Frank hadn't decided on a course of action when the problem was solved for him. The rock on which he lay suddenly shifted. It hadn't been as firmly lodged in the side of the mountain as he'd thought. The rock didn't go very far, only a couple of inches, but that was enough to cause a noise and make the watcher spring to his feet and twist around to peer upward in surprise. When he saw Frank, he started to reach down and grab for his rifle.

Might as well make his move now, Frank thought as he launched himself into the air, dropping swiftly toward the man on the ledge.

The man had his rifle in his hands, but hadn't had time to lift it and turn when Frank crashed into him in a clean tackle. The impact knocked the watcher off his feet and drove him to the rocky surface of the ledge. He cried out in pain as Frank's weight came down on top of him. The rifle slipped out of his grasp and clattered away. Frank got his left hand on the ground, pushed himself up, and drove his right fist into the man's face. That stunned the watcher. He went limp, all the fight knocked out of him.

Frank came to his feet and drew his Colt as he stood over the man. His hat had fallen off when he leaped from the rock, but he didn't bother to pick it up just yet. Keeping the man covered, he said in a flinty voice, "Don't try anything funny, partner. I don't want to kill you, but I'll put a bullet through your knee if I have to."

The man just blinked groggily, and Frank didn't know if he understood or not. After a moment, though, the man rolled onto his side and let out a groan. He said in a thick voice, "Don't . . . don't shoot . . . mister."

Frank backed up a couple of steps and rested a hip against one of the boulders. He said, "Who are you?"

The man lifted his head and shook it, obviously trying to clear away some of the cobwebs from his brain. He managed to sit up. Looking owlishly at Frank, he asked, "Who are you?"

"I just asked you the same question," Frank pointed out. "You first."

"My name . . . my name is Walt Scheer." He reached up and rubbed his jaw, wincing a little as he encountered a painful spot that ached from being slugged by Frank's fist.

"Why are you keeping an eye on that railroad camp, Scheer? Planning to cause some more trouble for those men down there?"

"What?" Scheer frowned in what appeared to be genuine confusion. "I haven't caused any trouble for them."

"No? You didn't have anything to do with that trestle blowing up last night?"

"Is that what happened? I could tell there had been a fire, but I wasn't sure about an explosion."

"Quit trying to pull the wool over my eyes," Frank snapped. "Are you trying to tell me you don't work for the gang that's been causing so much trouble?"

Scheer looked up at him, meeting The Drifter's gaze squarely. "I work for the Southwestern and Pacific Railroad. I'm a construction engineer."

That answer took Frank by surprise. He was expecting Scheer to lie, of course, but he hadn't expected the sort of claim that the man had just made.

"What have you got to do with that spur line going from Lordsburg to Ophir?"

"Nothing," Scheer said. "Yet. But when the NM, RG, and O fails to finish the line, the SW and P plans to step in and take over the job. I'm up here studying the route so that we can do it better."

A frown creased Frank's forehead. "That doesn't sound too likely to me. You were watching the camp."

"You can see the camp from here, sure," Scheer said. "But take another look. There's also a good view of the gorge, and you can see for at least three miles on the other side of it." He warmed to his subject, turning and pointing. "There's the roadbed that's been graded. But look over yonder." Scheer began to seem excited as he pointed in a different direction and went on, "The trestle is in the right spot, but if you curve the line to the west a little once you reach the top of that slope, your roadbed will go over more level terrain. There's already a natural cut through that ridge too, so you could use that instead of having to blast out one of your own."

Frank's curiosity got the better of him. He had to turn and look where Scheer was pointing. There were several feet between him and the so-called engineer, though. If Scheer tried to jump him, Frank would have plenty of time to deal with that threat.

After studying the landscape on the far side of the gorge for a few moments, Frank had to admit that Scheer might be right about the alternate route he suggested being easier. Frank said, "Nathan Buckhalter was in charge of the survey that laid out the route—"

Scheer snorted in contempt. "Nathan Buckhalter is a poor excuse for a surveyor and an engineer. He wouldn't know the best way for the line to go if it came up and bit him."

"Professional jealousy?"

"There's nothing to be jealous of." Scheer folded his arms across his chest. "I'm twice as good at my job as he is at his."

That display of puffed-up pride did as much as anything to convince Frank that Walt Scheer was telling the truth. The man was what he seemed to be. He was spying on Conrad's railroad not because he wanted to sabotage it, but because the company he worked for wanted the job of building the spur line for itself. Of course, before they could do that, the New Mexico, Rio Grande, and Oriental would have to fail. . . .

"How do you know the railroad's not

going to reach Ophir?" Frank asked sharply. "Even if you're telling me the truth, Scheer, how do I know that other hombres working for your bosses aren't trying to stop that railroad?"

With a shake of his head, Scheer said, "I wouldn't know anything about that. I was just sent up here to study the route and figure out if there were ways we could improve upon it. There are, and that's what I intend to report to my bosses — unless you're planning on killing me."

Frank lowered the Peacemaker and slipped it back into its holster. "Not unless you give me more cause than you have so far," he said.

"As for how I know the NM, RG, and O is going to fail . . . I don't. But with men like Nathan Buckhalter working for it, I don't see how the line's ever going to succeed."

Frank wasn't convinced that Buckhalter was as bad at his job as Scheer made him out to be. At the moment, that wasn't really important, though. He said, "Somebody has been causing trouble for the line and trying to make sure it never gets through to Ophir. You got any ideas about that?"

"Not really." Scheer paused and then added, "Unless those men who are camped over that way about a mile have something to do with it." He pointed to the east, over a series of rugged ridges.

Frank's interest quickened. "There's a camp over there?"

Scheer shrugged and said, "There was yesterday when I saw it. I couldn't say if the men are still there or not."

"You can find the place again?"

"Of course." Scheer sounded a little offended. "I'm an expert at terrain and topography. I don't get lost."

"Grab your hat and prove it."

"What do you mean by that?"

"You're going to show me where this camp is."

"Why should I do that? And by the way, you never told me who you are."

"My name is Frank Morgan. Some folks call me The Drifter."

Scheer's eyes widened. "I've heard that name. You're some sort of . . . of gunfighter."

"When I have to be. Right now, though, I'm the fella you're going to take to that camp you saw yesterday — and you'd better hope that you've been telling me the truth."

Chapter 22

As Frank had suspected, there was a trail leading down from the other end of the ledge, which was about a quarter of a mile away. That was how Scheer had gotten up here. The trail led down to a little canyon with a tiny creek running through it. A few trees and some sparse grass lined the stream. Scheer's horse was picketed there, cropping at the grass.

Scheer led the animal while he and Frank walked, as they made their way back to the spot where Frank had left Stormy and Dog. The Appaloosa tossed his head when the two men came into view, and Dog bounded forward, stopping to growl at Scheer when he came closer.

"Easy, Dog," Frank told him. He wasn't ready to declare Scheer a friend yet, so he didn't give the command that would have told Dog it was all right to trust the stranger.

Dog kept a wary eye on Scheer.

"Is that a wolf?" the engineer asked nervously.

"Not full-blooded. He might have a little wolf in him, though. I'm not all that sure about his ancestry."

Scheer watched Dog as warily as Dog watched him. "He looks like he wants to tear my throat out."

"He won't, though — not unless you do something he thinks is a threat to me."

"What if he's wrong?"

"That would be a shame," Frank said dryly.

He had been carrying Scheer's rifle. Now he put it back in the saddle boot on the man's horse, telling Scheer to keep his hands away from it unless they were attacked. Scheer promised him hastily that he would do so.

They mounted up, and Frank said, "All right, take me to that other camp you were talking about."

Scheer led the way. They rode through canyons and along ridges and past towering spires of rock. Sometimes, they passed through narrow defiles where they had to ride one behind the other and the sky was nothing but a narrow blue band between dizzyingly high walls of stone. Finally, they came to the top of a slope that was thickly covered with pine and juniper trees. "Down there," Scheer said in a half whisper. "There's a little valley, and that's where the camp is."

Frank hadn't come anywhere near this place during his search the day before, and it might have been weeks before he came across it without Scheer to lead him here. He couldn't see anything because of the trees, but as he leaned forward in the saddle and sniffed, he smelled wood smoke in the air. Just a faint tang, but it was there, an unmistakable indication that there was a campfire somewhere close by.

"Get off your horse," Frank said quietly to Scheer. He swung down from his own saddle.

"What are you going to do?" Scheer asked as he dismounted.

"Go down there and take a look around. You're coming with me."

Scheer held up his hands. "Listen, I'm not a gunfighter. I'm not any kind of a fighter. I'm just an engineer. I draw up plans. I can barely shoot a rifle."

"I don't plan on doing any fighting. I just want to get a look at the place and see what I'm up against."

Scheer's face was beaded with nervous sweat. "I probably ought to stay here and hold the horses."

Even though Frank had just about decided that Scheer was telling the truth, he didn't want the man at his back while he was trying to sneak up on the place where the saboteurs were camped. He said, "We'll tie the horses so they can't wander off. You're coming with me." He pulled the rifle from its sheath and pressed it into Scheer's hands. "Here. You shouldn't need it, but just in case you do."

Scheer was pale, and his hands trembled a little as he took the rifle. "You're going to get me killed."

"I'll do my best not to," Frank said. If Scheer was putting on an act, he was damned good at it.

They started moving down the slope through the trees. Frank gave Scheer whispered instructions on where and how to place his feet so that their progress would be as quiet as possible. Scheer nodded, and his nerves seemed to relax a little. The prospect of sneaking up on the camp had scared him, but now that he was actually doing something, he wasn't quite as nervous.

After about a hundred yards, the trees started to thin out some. Frank slowed down even more until he and Scheer were barely creeping forward, using every bit of cover they could find. Scheer wasn't doing too badly for a man who was clearly not accustomed to the wilderness. As Frank heard voices, he dropped into a crouch behind some undergrowth and motioned for Scheer to do likewise. Carefully, Frank parted the brush and peered through the little gap he had made in the branches.

They were almost at the bottom of the slope. The ground leveled out into a small, grassy park. On the other side of that clearing, about a quarter of a mile away, a cliff rose some two hundred feet into the air. The rock face bulged out, creating a cavelike space at the base of it. That was where the men were camped. The overhang broke up the smoke from their fire, dispersing it so that it wouldn't be visible from a distance. They were also protected from the rain there, and that was going to come in handy because the clouds Frank had seen earlier in the day had finally concentrated enough to form a mountain shower. A drop of rain hit the back of Frank's hand as he and Scheer crouched there looking toward the cliff. Thunder rumbled quietly in the distance.

"What do we do now?" Scheer asked in a whisper as more drops of rain pattered down around them.

"We get to the construction camp as fast as we can and pick up some reinforcements there. Then we'll come back and have it out with those saboteurs."

"How do you know they're to blame for what's been happening to the railroad?"

"I don't, not for sure, but if they have a reasonable explanation for being camped out here like this, they'll have to convince those railroaders."

"I don't like this," Scheer said. "Things could get out of hand, especially if those men are innocent."

"I don't much cotton to it either. But I'll see to it that the railroad men don't turn into a lynch mob," Frank assured him.

They started backtracking up the slope. The sky grew darker and the wind picked up, although the rain was still sporadic. They were almost at the top when Frank suddenly heard voices over the soughing of the wind in the trees. A second later, Stormy gave an angry nicker, and Dog began to growl. Somebody was up there where Frank and Scheer had left the horses.

"Careful, Royal!" a man called out. "That varmint looks like a wolf. He's liable to come after you."

"If he moves, shoot him," another voice growled.

Frank's heart took an angry leap in his chest as he heard Dog being threatened. He abandoned stealth and burst through the undergrowth with a crackling of brush. Behind him, Scheer did his best to keep up.

The Peacemaker was already in Frank's hand as he emerged from the trees and brush into the open. His keen, experienced eyes took in the scene in an instant. Four armed men stood there while a fifth hung back about a hundred yards holding their horses. The men had spotted Stormy, Dog, and Scheer's horse and had snuck up here to see who the animals belonged to.

Frank didn't recognize any of the roughly dressed hombres, but the same wasn't true for them. One of the men yelled, "It's Morgan! Gun him!"

The pistols in their hands jerked up and spouted flame. "Get back!" Frank shouted to Scheer as he triggered a return shot that smashed the shoulder of one of the men. He backed away, still firing, hoping that the trees would give him and the engineer some cover.

But Scheer, backing up hastily, tripped over a rock and fell backward with a startled yell. The rifle flew out of his hands as he toppled down the slope. Frank knew he couldn't expect any help from Scheer in this fight.

Dog and Stormy were pitching in, though.

As Stormy lunged forward, rearing up on his hind legs and slashing the air with his deadly iron-shod hooves, Dog launched himself in an attack as well. The big cur slammed into one of the gunmen and took him down, tearing at the screaming man with his teeth. Another man left his feet in a frantic dive to avoid Stormy's rush. The big Appaloosa was an awesome sight as lightning flickered in the sky above him.

That left only one of the four hardcases who wasn't either wounded or under attack by Stormy and Dog. That man emptied his Colt in Frank's direction, forcing The Drifter to throw himself to the ground and roll behind a tree for cover. The last couple of bullets slammed into the trunk above his head.

Before Frank could bring his Colt to bear, the gunman yanked a second revolver from a cross-draw holster on his left hip and bounded forward. Scheer's out-of-control tumble had come to an end when the engineer crashed into a tree trunk. The gunman dropped into a crouch beside the stunned Scheer and jammed the barrel of his pistol against Scheer's head.

"Morgan!" the gunman bellowed. "Give it up or I'll blow his brains out!"

Lying about twenty feet away along the

slope, Frank had no trouble seeing that the man's thumb looped over the hammer of the gun was all that was holding it back. Even if Frank shot him and killed him instantly, his thumb would slip off the hammer and the gun would go off, putting a bullet through Scheer's skull. For a second, Frank considered trying a shot at the gun itself, in hopes of knocking it away from the engineer's head before it could fire, but he knew that was hopeless. He had promised Scheer he would do his best not to get him killed, so there was only one thing he could do now, even though it went against the grain for him.

"Take it easy!" Frank called to the gunman. "I'm coming out!"

"Come with them meat hooks held high, or I'll kill him!" the man threatened.

Frank climbed to his feet and came forward slowly, his hands lifted slightly above his head. The Colt was still in his right hand, but he had flipped it around so that he held it by the cylinder. As he came closer, the gunman ordered, "All right, put that smokepole on the ground and step away from it."

After placing the Peacemaker on the ground, Frank moved away from it. Lightning flashed and thunder boomed. The rain began to fall a little harder.

"Call off your dog and your horse, damn it!"

"Dog!" Frank said. "Dog, come here! Stormy!" He whistled. "Back off, Stormy!"

Dog obeyed the command reluctantly, but after a second he left his victim moaning on the ground and trotted over to Frank. Stormy stopped rearing up and stood where he was, fiercely blowing air out through his distended nostrils.

The hardcase, who seemed to be the boss of the bunch, straightened to his feet and pulled Scheer upright with him. The engineer had recovered somewhat from crashing into the tree, but now he was pale and terrified from being threatened with the gun. The man kept the pistol barrel pressed against Scheer's skull as he jerked his head toward the top of the slope and barked at Frank, "Get movin'."

Frank trudged up the slope. The gunman yelled, "Brady, get over here!" and the man holding the horses hurried forward. The boss continued. "Get Morgan's gun and the rifle this bastard dropped, and then tend to Slovack and Dennehy."

The man pushed Scheer toward Frank, and then stepped back to cover both of them as the engineer stumbled forward. Frank caught hold of Scheer's arm to steady him.

There was no doubt now that Scheer had been telling the truth about not working with the saboteurs. Nor did Frank wonder any longer if these men were part of the gang trying to stop the spur line from getting through to Ophir. The fact that they had recognized him and immediately tried to kill him was proof enough of that.

It proved something else too, but Frank put that aside for the moment. He had more pressing worries, such as staying alive and trying to see to it that Walt Scheer did too.

The man called Brady went first to the hombre Frank had shot and tore strips of cloth off the wounded man's shirt to use as bandages. He tied them tightly around the bullet-shattered shoulder, ignoring the shrieks of pain that his rough ministrations brought. "Gotta get the bleedin' stopped," he muttered, as much to himself as to the patient.

Then he moved over to the other injured man and began binding up those wounds as best he could too. Glancing up at the boss, he said, "I don't know if Dennehy's gonna make it, Royal. Damn dog like to gnawed his arm right off."

"Do what you can for him," Royal said. To the other man, the one who'd had to jump for his life when Stormy came after him,

Royal snapped, "Thad, don't let them horses wander off while Brady's busy."

"Sure thing, Royal." Thad gathered up the reins and held them tightly.

"While you're at it, get the Winchester off Morgan's saddle."

Thad swallowed. "I, uh, I ain't sure about gettin' that close to that big spotted horse, Royal. He don't like me."

Royal grunted a curse. "Somebody's got to, blast it. Now do what I told you. Morgan, you keep that horse calmed down, or I'll kill the son of a bitch."

"Easy, Stormy," Frank said in a strong, calm voice. "Easy, boy." He looked at Thad. "You can get the rifle now. Just don't make any sudden moves while you're doing it."

Stormy looked like he could barely keep from unleashing his fury as Thad came up and slid the rifle out of the saddle boot. The young gunman backed off in a hurry once he had the Winchester.

The rain was coming down steadily now. The wind had turned raw and chilly. Scheer said to Royal, "Mister, can I get my hat?" He pointed to where his hat had landed when it came off during the unexpected fall.

"Go ahead," Royal said. "Brady, you about finished with Dennehy?"

Brady came to his feet. "I've done all I can

for him. Once we get back to camp, maybe I can patch him up a little better."

"All right. You and Thad get him on his horse. Slovack, stop your whimperin'. Get up and get mounted."

The man Frank had shot said, "I . . . I don't know if I can, Royal. My shoulder really hurts."

"I got a cure for it," Royal grated. "It's called a bullet through the head. Your shoulder won't hurt a damn bit after that."

Muttering curses, Slovack climbed slowly to his feet and staggered over to his horse.

Royal waggled the barrel of his gun at Frank and Scheer. "Mount up, you two. Morgan, you go right ahead and try something if you're of a mind to. It'd give me great pleasure to ventilate you."

"You're the boss right now, Royal," Frank said.

The man uttered a humorless chuckle. "Meanin' it ain't always gonna be that way? I don't think so, Morgan. Now that we've got our hands on you, we ain't lettin' go. I'm tempted to just go ahead and kill you here an' now, but I'm gonna hold off for a while and think it over. Might be some way we can make even better use of you."

Frank wasn't sure what Royal meant by that. He would never cooperate with the gang, that was for sure. But the important thing was that he and Scheer hadn't been executed out of hand, and as long as they were still alive, there was a chance they could do something to turn the tables on their captors. Frank was going to hold onto that hope for as long as possible.

Once everyone was mounted up and Thad was leading the horse on which the half-conscious Dennehy rode, Royal said, "All right, let's go." The group moved out, riding along the top of the slope until they came to a trail that led down to the little valley where the camp was located. They turned and rode downhill, and the rain slashed at them, hard and cold and merciless.

Chapter 23

Frank was soaked to the skin by the time they reached the cavelike area underneath the overhanging cliff. So were the other members of the group. Frank had a slicker in his gear, but he hadn't asked if he could put it on, figuring that Royal would say no. None of the hardcases seemed to have slickers with them, and they were in a mighty foul mood the wetter they got.

The men who were already in camp must have built up the fire when the wind grew colder, because it was burning brighter now and giving off welcome heat. Several of them picked up rifles when they noticed that the newcomers had a couple of prisoners with them. One of them called out, "Royal, we heard shots up on the ridge. Who the hell's that you got with you?"

"This one's Frank Morgan," Royal replied as he pointed the barrel of his revolver at Frank. "I don't know who the other bastard is."

"Morgan! The Drifter hisownself, you mean?"

"That's right." Royal said to Frank and Scheer, "You two get down off your horses. Brady, you and Thad see to Dennehy."

Royal didn't dismount until after Frank and Walt Scheer had swung down from their saddles. Slovack complained until a couple of the other men helped him from his horse. Several more gathered around the injured Dennehy as Brady and Thad placed him on a blanket spread on the sandy ground that formed the floor of the cave.

In the light from the fire, Frank glanced up at the rock wall looming above his head and saw images painted there, crude representations of men and animals and geographical features like mountains and rivers. The images had faded with time and been dulled by the smoke from countless fires, but they were still visible, mute testimony to the fact that men had been using the place for shelter for a long time, maybe as long as hundreds of years. Frank had seen such ancient pictures before and knew that Indians had daubed them on the rock, using paints and dyes made from berries and other plants. Standing in the presence of such an-

301

tiquities was always impressive, and it was so even now, although at the moment Frank had plenty of other things on his mind.

Still holding a gun, Royal came over and glared at Frank and Scheer. He was a burly man with slightly stooped shoulders and a rugged face dominated by a big nose that had been broken at least once. In his rasping voice, he asked Scheer, "Just who in hell are you, mister? You workin' with Morgan?"

The engineer licked his lips. "My name is Walt Scheer. I work for the Southwestern and Pacific Railroad. I'm a surveyor and construction engineer." He glanced over at Frank. "I never saw this man before today. I don't know who he is or what he's doing up here."

Royal grunted. "Is that so? Looked to me like the two of you were pards when you came runnin' out of those trees."

"He forced me to go with him," Scheer said with a note of desperation in his voice. "Think about it. I never shot at you or put up any kind of a fight."

"No, you didn't put up a fight, that's for damned sure," Royal said scornfully. "You were too busy fallin' down that hill."

"Leave him alone," Frank said. "He's telling you the truth. He doesn't know anything about what's going on. I ran into him

302

earlier today and made him come with me because I thought he might be part of your bunch. Now I know he's not."

"I don't give a damn about that," Royal said. "He knows where our camp is, so he's a threat to us."

Scheer took half a step forward. "No, I'm not," he said anxiously. "I swear I'm not. Let me go and I won't tell anybody where you are or what you're doing."

"What *are* we doing?" Royal asked.

If Frank had had a chance, he would have told Scheer to plead ignorance. As it was, he gave the engineer a warning look, but Scheer either didn't see it or ignored it. Eager to co-operate, Scheer said, "You're trying to wreck the spur line that the New Mexico, Rio Grande, and Oriental Railroad is building and keep it from getting to Ophir. Right?"

"Yeah," Royal said heavily. "That's right. And since you know about that . . ."

The gun in his hand came up.

"Wait a minute," Scheer babbled, backing up now. "I'm not going to say anything. I don't care what you're doing. I don't want the spur line to go through either. Once it fails, the company I work for will come in and take over." His voice rose as Royal eared back the revolver's hammer. "We're on the same side!"

Frank suddenly lunged toward Scheer, slamming into him and knocking him down just as Royal's gun crashed, driving him out of the way of the bullet that Royal had aimed at his head. Howling in fear, Scheer cowered on the ground as Frank knelt beside him and looked up at Royal. Fingers of lightning clawed at the sky and lit up the gunman's face with an electric glare.

"Get out of the way, Morgan," Royal grated. "We don't need this snivelin' son of a bitch no more."

"You might as well kill us both then," Frank said, "because I'll never cooperate with you."

"No, I told you I'm keepin' you alive. Might be able to use you against young Browning." An ugly grin pulled at Royal's wide mouth. "After all, what boy wouldn't want to keep his ol' pappy safe?"

A breath hissed between Frank's tightly clenched teeth. Royal knew that Conrad was his son! How the hell was that possible? Conrad certainly hadn't told anyone. It had been obvious that he wanted to keep their relationship as much of a secret as possible. But Royal and these other hired killers who were trying to wreck the spur line knew.

Confusion reigned in Frank's head for a few seconds until he pushed it all aside. He said, "You don't have to worry about Scheer. He's no threat. You can see that for yourself."

Scheer was still crying and had his arms over his head, even though he had to know that wouldn't protect him from a bullet. The gesture was just instinct, pure self-preservation, even though it was futile.

Royal glowered down at them for a long moment before finally lowering his gun. As he slid the weapon back in its holster, he said, "All right. He lives . . . for now. But if either of you tries anything, he'll die mighty quicklike."

Frank nodded. To Scheer, he said in a low, urgent voice, "Take it easy. Pull yourself together, man. You're all right now."

Royal motioned some of his men forward. "Put 'em over there against the cliff and tie 'em up," he ordered. "As long as they stay quiet, you don't have to gag them. In fact, if they start to raise a ruckus, just bend a gun barrel over their heads. Don't kill Morgan, though."

"What are you going to do?" Frank asked as several of the hardcases grabbed him and Scheer and shoved them toward the base of the cliff.

"I got to think," Royal said. "Luck's dropped you in my lap, Morgan, and now I got to figure out what to do with you."

By the time a few more minutes had passed, Frank and Scheer were sitting with their backs pressed against the rock, their arms pulled behind their backs and tied there uncomfortably. Their legs were still loose, though, so Frank was grateful for that small favor.

Right now, he would take any break he could get, no matter how slight.

The day passed slowly, and it seemed even longer than it was due to their captivity, their uncomfortable position, and the pouring rain that continued to fall for hours. The time gave Frank a chance to study their captors, though. The men all wore range clothes and were heavily armed. Their coarse-featured, beard-stubbled faces were typical of drifting hardcases, the sort of gunmen for hire who would do anything as long as the money was good enough. A couple of them, including Thad, were younger than the others and probably hadn't been riding the owlhoot trail for as long, but that didn't mean they were any less dangerous. Their leader, Royal, seemed to be more intelligent than the others, but it was an animal cunning, mixed with ruthlessness. Any man who rose to the leadership of a gang of killers such as this was likely the most dangerous of them all.

The rain finally stopped in the late afternoon. The clouds broke as the sun was going down, which allowed a red glare to fall over the landscape for a few minutes before the shadows of dusk began to gather. It looked to Frank almost like the door into Hell had been opened briefly, and he had to wonder just what sort of gibbering demons had crawled out and loosed themselves on the earth during that time.

He didn't have to wait long to find out.

Royal and several more of the men had been talking among themselves for a while, occasionally casting veiled glances toward Frank and Scheer. Frank didn't like the looks of the discussion, but he couldn't hear what they were saying. Beside him, Scheer talked a lot, complaining about everything under the sun, especially the fact that their captors hadn't fed them anything during the long day. Frank's stomach was empty too, but he didn't see how it was going to do any good to bitch about it.

As it began to grow dark, Royal and a couple of the men stood up and walked toward them. Scheer fell silent, perhaps sensing that something bad was about to happen. Royal and the others stopped in front of the prisoners, and the boss of the gang hooked his thumbs in his gun belt and said, "I'm glad you talked me outta killin' this fella, Morgan. Turns out we've got a use for him after all."

"Anything," Scheer said quickly. "I'll help you any way I can."

"Better not be so quick to volunteer," Frank advised him quietly.

Royal laughed. "Hell, it don't matter whether he volunteers or not. We're gonna do the same thing either way." He motioned toward Scheer. "Take him, boys."

"Wait! What are you — don't—" Scheer let out a yell as the two men picked him up by the shoulders and feet and started to carry him toward the fire.

Royal stayed where he was and said to Frank, "You know how the Apaches have been givin' trouble around here, Morgan? How a band o' renegade bucks has been raisin' hell?"

"I've heard about it," Frank said, not mentioning anything about the encounter he and Conrad had had with the Indians on their way to Lordsburg.

"Well, what do you think a bunch o' savages like that would do if they was to catch a lone white man out by himself?" Without waiting for Frank to answer, Royal went on. "I'll tell you what they'd do — they'd grab him and have themselves some fun with him, that's what."

Over by the fire, Scheer writhed in the grip of the hardcases and cried, "Put me down! Let me go! Please!"

They paid no attention to his begging.

Frank felt a cold ball of horror form in his guts as Royal went on. "You know how Apaches have fun, don't you, Morgan? Ain't nothin' those red heathens like better than torturing a white man. Seems to me that if a bunch of Apaches got hold of ol' Walt over there, they might just take his hide off him, one strip at a time."

Scheer heard the words and screamed. The sound was cut off abruptly as the men carrying him dropped him by the fire. The impact of his landing on the hard-packed ground knocked the breath out of him.

"And just to make it more interestin'," Royal went on, "maybe the knives they'd use to take his hide off would be heated up in the fire beforehand, so they could cook him a little at the same time they were skinnin' him."

A bitter taste rose in Frank's throat. At the same time, his brain was working rapidly, so he swallowed the bile and said, "Are you telling me that the Indian raids on the railroad weren't really the work of the Apaches at all?"

"Now, wouldn't that be a neat trick?" Royal asked with an ugly grin. "Fact of the matter is, there are some Apaches up here in these mountains, and they don't like us pale-faces. But as to whether or not they've really done everything they've been blamed for . . . well, that's a good question. But when the folks down at that railroad camp find Scheer's body in the mornin', all skinned and scorched, don't you reckon the Apaches will get the blame again?"

That was exactly what would happen, Frank knew. By the time Royal and his henchmen got through torturing Scheer, it would probably be impossible to identify him. But the railroaders would be able to tell he had been a white man, and when they saw what had been done to him, they would be certain the Apaches had done it. The grue-some discovery would damage morale in the camp that much more.

"I can't believe you'd do such a thing," Frank said coldly.

"Believe it," Royal said. "We're gettin' paid a heap to make it harder for those boys to finish that railroad. And I don't give a damn who gets hurt along the way."

Scheer had gotten his breath back. He began to scream again. Royal jerked his head around and snapped, "Shut that son of a bitch up!"

A gun rose and fell, the barrel thudding

against Scheer's skull as the engineer arched his back up off the ground. He slumped down limply as the blow fell, out cold now.

That was probably the most merciful thing that could happen to him, Frank thought bleakly. He was tied up and outnumbered twenty to one, and there was nothing he could do to stop the hired killers from carrying out their grisly scheme.

Royal swung back toward the fire and ordered, "Get on with it."

Frank wanted to close his eyes or look away, but he forced himself not to. He had promised Scheer that he would try to keep him safe, and he had failed in that promise. The man was going to die in a drawn-out, agonizing fashion. Frank hoped the pain wouldn't make Scheer regain consciousness, but he was afraid that wouldn't be the case.

One of the men hunkered by the fire, holding the tip of a razor-sharp bowie knife in the flames until it glowed red-hot. While he was doing that, several of the men ripped Scheer's shirt open and then pulled it off him. They left his trousers on. It would take a while to get to that part of his body with their torture.

The man with the knife turned toward the helpless victim. "Hold him down, boys," he said with a grin. "Even out cold, he's liable to jump around a mite once he feels this hot blade peelin' his skin off."

Several men grasped Scheer by the shoulders and legs, clamping tight grips on him. The knife-wielder leaned over him. Scheer's body jerked wildly, even though he was still unconscious, when the blade came in contact with his skin.

"Look at him jump!" one of the men said with a laugh as the man with the knife made a long, shallow cut across Scheer's chest.

Frank's jaw clenched so tight he thought his teeth might start to shatter. Despite his reputation as a gunfighter, he had never been a bloodthirsty man, never believed in senseless violence.

At this moment, however, he gladly would have put a bullet through the brain of every man gathered around the helpless engineer. And he never would have lost a second's sleep over the killings.

The man with the bowie knife lifted the blade. Crimson droplets clung to it. They sizzled as he thrust the knife back into the flames. "We'll just heat this up a little more," he said. "Then a cut down each side and we'll start to peel the hide back, just like one o' them damned Apaches was doin' it."

He was too impatient in his cruelty to wait for long, though. After only a few moments, he took the blade out of the fire and turned back toward Scheer.

Then he toppled forward, dropping the knife, and landed in a limp sprawl across Scheer's bleeding body. It took everyone under the overhang of the cliff, including Frank, a second or two to realize that the thing sticking straight up from the fallen man's back was the shaft of an arrow.

Chapter 24

Conrad looked around warily as he entered the hotel dining room. He had a multitude of worries this morning. Pamela and her father were staying at the Holloway House, so they might have come down for breakfast. Likewise, Rebel could be in the dining room.

And then there was the matter of Rebel's cousin Ed and her brothers Tom and Bob. From the descriptions Jonas Wade had given him the night before, Conrad knew the Callahan boys were in Ophir, and they were still looking for Frank Morgan, still bent on avenging the deaths of Simon and Jud Callahan back in El Paso. If the Callahans saw Conrad, undoubtedly they would recognize him from the fight at Mimbres Tank. Whether or not they would try to kill him outright, Conrad didn't know. He didn't want to risk it, though.

Thankfully, he didn't see any familiar

faces in the dining room except for the waiter. The hour was early. Pamela and her father were probably still asleep. Rebel was an early riser, but she wasn't here and Conrad wasn't going to look that gift horse in the mouth. As for her brothers and cousin, they were probably sleeping off a drunk in some squalid saloon or whorehouse. Also, they had no way of knowing that he was staying at the Holloway House, other than the fact that it was the best hotel in town and obviously he would prefer quality lodgings.

Conrad felt a few eyes following him as he went to an empty table and sat down. He was expecting that interest. By now, the story of how he had wrecked the bathhouse and exposed Rebel would have gone around among the hotel staff, which meant that some of the guests probably had heard it too. A rumor was a pernicious thing, fast on its feet and exceedingly difficult to kill. With all the dignity he could muster, he sat down at the table, and as the waiter approached, Conrad said, "Good morning, George. I'll start off with coffee."

"Yes, sir, Mr. Browning," the man said without hesitation. No matter how many embarrassing things happened to him, Conrad Browning had a great deal of money, and no one in Ophir was likely to forget that.

Wealth was the great ameliorator.

Conrad gazed straight ahead while he waited for his coffee. The waiter returned with cup and saucer a few minutes later and placed them in front of Conrad, who said, "Thank you, George. I'll have hotcakes, a slice of ham, and fried eggs."

"Yes, sir!"

The man's eagerness to please made Conrad feel better. All might not be right with the world, but at least there were signs that eventually normalcy would return.

That comforting thought was going through his head when the voice said behind him, "Well, if it ain't the peeper."

Conrad closed his eyes for a second and took a deep breath as he recognized Rebel's voice. Control, he told himself. Calmness and dignity. They would see him through any ordeal. He picked up his napkin from his lap, where he had carefully arranged it, and set it on the table. Then he rose, not being hasty about it, and turned to face her. He was smiling as he said, "Good morning, Miss Callahan. Would you care to join me for breakfast?"

The invitation clearly took Rebel by surprise. She frowned and said, "What?"

Conrad motioned elegantly toward the empty chair next to his. He was determined

316

to act as if nothing had happened. If he carried himself in that manner, perhaps other people would then act like nothing had happened too. "Please, join me. You look lovely this morning."

That was true. As she had in Lordsburg, she wore a dress instead of her usual range garb, a simple light blue gown that clung to the lines of her body. As she hesitated, Conrad pulled out the chair, and after a second Rebel said under her breath, "Why the hell not?" She sat down.

As Conrad took his seat, he lifted a hand and signaled to the waiter. "George, another cup of coffee, please."

"Coming right up, Mr. Browning!" When he brought the coffee, he asked, "Would the young lady like breakfast too, sir?"

"She would," Conrad said without waiting for Rebel to make any comment. "Bring her the same thing I ordered."

"Yes, sir."

"That's mighty high-handed of you," Rebel said after George had scurried off to the kitchen. "How do you know I want to eat with you?"

"I don't," Conrad replied. "But *I* want to eat with *you,* so I saw no reason not to go ahead and order for you."

"You didn't, eh? What are you going to do

317

if Miss Fancy Pants and her daddy come in and see me sitting here with you? Miss Fancy Pants don't like me, not even a little bit."

"I assume your whimsical sobriquet is in reference to Pamela," Conrad said smoothly. "If she and Mr. Tarleton come in, I intend to ask them to join us as well." Bravado, that was the key. "Nothing like an early morning gustatorial assemblage to clear the air, eh?"

"I get it now," Rebel said. "You figure nobody can be mad at you if they don't know what the hell you're talking about, right?"

"I assure you—"

"No, let *me* assure *you*," Rebel said as she leaned forward. "I ain't forgotten about anything that you did, from kissing me under false pretenses to lying about that woman you plan on marrying to yanking down that partition while I didn't have no clothes on. I ain't forgotten, and I sure as hell ain't forgiven."

Conrad tried not to gulp in the face of her wrath. "Really, Rebel," he said, not quite as smoothly as before, "I thought since you agreed to have breakfast with me—"

"I'm hungry. That's all it amounts to. It don't mean nothing else."

"All right." Conrad tried to regroup. "That's a start at least—"

"No, it ain't. You and me are still finished."

He wanted to explain to her that he understood that. Whatever had passed between them on the trail was over and done with. He was going to marry Pamela, and his life was going to proceed on the course he had laid out for himself before Rebel Callahan had ever inserted her frequently annoying but equally beguiling presence into his existence.

But for some reason, those words didn't want to come out of his mouth. He looked at Rebel and they froze in his throat. If he told her they were through, that bridge was burned. There would be no rebuilding it.

And Lord help him, he just wasn't ready to take that step.

Before he could say anything, some instinct made him glance toward the arched entrance between the dining room and the lobby. Clark Tarleton stood there regarding Conrad with a cool stare. Pamela wasn't with him.

Conrad shot to his feet as Tarleton started to turn away. "Clark!" he called. "Come join us."

Stick to the plan, such as it was, he told himself. Act like everything is normal.

Rather than make a scene, Tarleton came forward slowly into the dining room, but he came grudgingly, with a look of annoyance and embarrassment on his rough-hewn face. He ignored the hand that Conrad thrust out toward him and gave the young man a curt nod instead. "Conrad," he said.

"Please, come sit down and have some breakfast," Conrad said, taking Tarleton's arm and guiding him toward the table where Rebel sat. "I feel like I owe you a meal, since I had to ask you to forgive me for that missed dinner engagement last night."

"I'm sure you didn't feel like dining," Tarleton said, pausing for a second before he added, "especially after everything that happened."

That threw Conrad for an instant. He had hoped against hope that Tarleton was somehow ignorant of the previous night's events. Obviously, that wasn't the case.

"I can explain everything—" he began.

"I'm sure you can," Tarleton cut in. "You've always been a very glib young man."

"Please, sir . . ." For the moment, Conrad forgot that he and Tarleton were business rivals and regarded the older man simply as a prospective father-in-law. He had to make things right somehow.

Tarleton interrupted him again, though, and said to Rebel, "Miss Callahan, isn't it? You're the young lady I've heard so much about."

She met his gaze squarely and answered, "I reckon I am." A faint flush tinged her face with red, however. Chances were that anybody who had heard the story would imagine her without her clothes when looking at her, even if only for a second. It was just human nature to do so.

Conrad knew that he certainly couldn't get that image out of his brain. He might succeed in forcing her out of his thoughts for a short time, but then when he relaxed his vigilance even for a moment, up she popped again, all wet and sleek and shining. . . .

Tarleton took Rebel's hand. "It's a pleasure to meet you, Miss Callahan. My name is Clark Tarleton."

"Miss Fancy Pants's daddy?"

Conrad waited for the explosion, but none came. Instead, Tarleton chuckled and said, "I take it you're referring to my daughter Pamela. I should be offended, I suppose, but even a father has to be honest. At times, Pamela's behavior deserves having such a name pinned on her."

"Oh." His graciousness put Rebel off stride, Conrad saw. She said, "I didn't really mean to insult her."

"I know that. It's just that the two of you are from vastly different worlds. Pamela has been pampered and spoiled her whole life.

321

She has much more in common with young Browning here."

"She can have him," Rebel said with a smile. "I don't want him."

Tarleton sat down in the chair Conrad had occupied, forcing the younger man to go around the table and take another chair. Tarleton still had hold of Rebel's hand too. Conrad frowned. What in blazes was going on here?

"As for myself," Tarleton went on, "even though I lead a life of relative luxury now, I've done plenty of hard work in my life."

Rebel nodded. "I can tell that."

"Once you've lived a hardscrabble existence, you never forget it, no matter how much fortune smiles on you. You always remember the struggle, and how you had to be tough to survive."

"Damn right," Rebel said with another nod, more emphatic this time. "Sounds like you and me think a lot alike, Mr. Tarleton, in spite of our differences."

"Call me Clark," Tarleton said with a smile.

Conrad had to make an effort to keep his jaw from hanging open. The two of them were . . . were flirting with each other! That was insane. Tarleton was old enough to be Rebel's father. More than old enough.

322

"Is your wife back East somewhere?" Rebel asked.

"My wife passed away many years ago," Tarleton said with a solemn shake of his head. "I'm a widower."

"I'm sorry to hear that."

"The pain has pretty much gone away, leaving just the good memories. I will admit, however, that it was a challenge raising Pamela mostly by myself."

"Awww," Rebel said. "I bet it was."

This was getting more ludicrous by the second. Conrad happened to know that after Pamela's mother had died, Pamela had been raised by a series of governesses, tutors, and household servants. Tarleton had spent nearly all of his time in his office or traveling across the country to check on his widespread business interests. The man was a blatant liar.

But Rebel was smiling now and so was Tarleton, and neither of them was paying any attention to Conrad. In an effort to nip this disturbing trend in the bud, he said, "How is Pamela feeling this morning? Is she going to come down for breakfast?"

Tarleton glared at him, obviously not pleased with the interruption. "She doesn't feel well. She's just going to take coffee in our suite."

"Well, I . . . I hope she feels better later," Conrad said.

"I wouldn't count on it anytime soon."

The waiter came up and asked, "You'll be having breakfast, Mr. Tarleton?"

"Yes, of course." Tarleton looked at Rebel. "That is, if the lady will be."

"It's already been ordered," she assured him, not mentioning the fact that Conrad had ordered it for her.

"Well, then, bring me my usual, George," Tarleton told the waiter.

"Yes, sir, right away."

Conrad sighed. His plan to hold on to his dignity and self-control had worked, he supposed. He wasn't the object of ridicule now. In fact, no one was paying any attention to him at all. He was no longer worthy of notice.

And to his great surprise, he found that that was even worse.

Chapter 25

It was a miserable morning for Conrad. Tarleton offered to show Rebel around Ophir, and to Conrad's great vexation, she agreed immediately. He supposed they were going to continue their ridiculous flirtation. They were just doing it to spite him, he told himself. Rebel was angry with him over everything that had happened, and Tarleton felt that Conrad had not been properly respectful to Pamela. So they were working out their grudge against him by pretending to be interested in each other. It wasn't going to work, he vowed.

But despite his best intentions, he found himself wandering around Ophir, trailing them at a distance, keeping an eye on them instead of going on about his own business. It was maddening.

The two men Brant had sent into the settlement found Conrad around mid-morning and reported that they had loaded on the packhorses all the supplies they had purchased. "We'll be gettin' on back to the camp now," one of them said.

Conrad knew they should have been on their way earlier. Probably, they had been sleeping off a night of carousing. However, he couldn't summon up the mental energy to reprimand them. He simply nodded and said, "From the looks of those clouds over the mountains, there may be a storm brewing. Be careful."

"We sure will, Mr. Browning. Anything you want us to tell Mr. Brant or Mr. Morgan?"

Conrad couldn't think of any message he wanted to convey. He shook his head wordlessly.

Tarleton and Rebel had lunch together in the hotel dining room. Conrad watched them go in, and decided he couldn't stomach sharing another meal with them. He walked down the block to a Chinese restaurant instead.

But before he could go in, he heard his name called and turned around to see a woman coming toward him on the boardwalk. She was around thirty years old and had bright red hair and a very erect carriage. Conrad recognized her immediately. He lifted a hand to the brim of his hat and nodded politely as he said, "Good morning, Mrs. McShane. It's good to see you again."

"Hello, Mr. Browning," Allison McShane said. "I heard you were back in town. Do you have any comment for the *Ledger* about the railroad line? A tentative date perhaps for its arrival?"

Mrs. Allison McShane was the editor and publisher of the Ophir *Ledger*, the settlement's only newspaper. It was unusual for a woman to occupy such a position, but her husband Evan was the one who had started the paper, bringing his wife and young daughter and son to New Mexico Territory a year earlier when Ophir was nothing but a raw, wide-open tent city. Evan McShane had gotten the paper started, and then promptly fallen ill of a particularly virulent fever and died, leaving his wife and children to make their own way in the world. Everyone in town had suspected that Mrs. McShane would take the young'uns and go back to wherever they'd come from, but instead she had decided to keep the newspaper going. As the town had grown and become more respectable, the *Ledger* had become more successful. Mrs. McShane was well thought of. She was soft-spoken and had impeccable manners. She also had a canny business sense and the nose of a bloodhound when it came to tracking down news. Conrad had no doubt that she knew all about the incident at the bathhouse, even though she wouldn't write anything about it in the paper. She had more decorum than that. At least he hoped so.

Now he shook his head in reply to her question and said, "No, I'm afraid not. Construction is progressing as fast as possible, but it's still too early to say when the railroad will arrive."

"Surely you could hazard a guess."

"I'd rather not."

Mrs. McShane smiled. "That's fine. Thank you anyway." She started to turn away, then stopped. "By the way, Mr. Browning, I've heard rumors that there have been quite a few problems during the construction. Sabotage, Indian attacks, things like that."

Conrad would have preferred to keep that quiet, but he knew better than to try to keep secrets from Mrs. McShane. Chances were she already knew what was going on, and if he lied about it that would only make things look worse.

"There have been problems," he admitted gravely, "but steps are being taken to correct them."

"What sort of steps?"

I brought in my father, who happens to be a notorious gunman with the blood of scores of men on his hands. The thought went through Conrad's mind, but of course there was no way he could say it. Instead, he just smiled and said, "I'd rather not comment on that right now. Discretion, you know."

"Of course." She smiled. "But would this have anything to do with a man named Frank Morgan?"

Conrad liked to think he had a good poker face, but he knew his features revealed his surprise at that moment. "Who told you—" he began, then stopped short as he realized she might be trying to trick him into an admission.

"Frank Morgan is a famous man, Mr. Browning," Mrs. McShane said. "I would imagine that it's difficult for him to go anywhere or do anything without word of his actions getting around. What exactly is your connection with him?"

Conrad took a breath and gathered his thoughts. "He's an old friend of the family. He also owns stock in the New Mexico, Rio Grande, and Oriental."

"So he's an investor?"

"You could say that."

"A drifting gunman owns part of a railroad? A man who some say is a hired killer?"

"He's used his gun for money," Conrad snapped, "but he's never been a hired killer. He fought only for causes he believed in." He wasn't sure why he was defending Frank, but the words came out before he could stop them.

"So you're saying he's an altruistic gunfighter?"

"I . . . I just think his reputation has been somewhat overblown. I've always found him to be a . . . a gentleman."

"A gentleman and a scholar?" There was a mocking tone in the woman's voice as she asked the question.

"As a matter of fact," Conrad said, "I've never known him to be without a book or two in his saddlebags. He's quite well read."

"He sounds like a fascinating man. Will he be coming to Ophir? I'd like to interview him."

"He may be here at some time. . . . I don't really know what his plans are."

Allison McShane smiled and nodded. "Well, be sure to introduce him to me if he does come to town. Thank you, Mr. Browning. I'll let you go on about your business now."

Conrad tugged on his hat brim again. "Always a pleasure, Mrs. McShane," he said, even though in this case it certainly hadn't been.

He ate lunch, and by the time he came out of the restaurant, the clouds to the south were thick and dark and thunder rumbled in the distance. It was raining down there, Conrad thought, but up here in Ophir the sun was still shining.

His mood wasn't very sunny, though. He saw Rebel and Tarleton on the opposite boardwalk, strolling arm in arm.

To hell with them, he told himself. His frown was as dark as those thunderheads. He had business to conduct, by God, and he wasn't going to let himself be distracted from it any longer by an old fool and a young hellion.

The railroad was going to need a depot when it arrived in Ophir. Conrad had his eye on a piece of land on the southern outskirts of the settlement that he thought would be a perfect location. He spent the afternoon talking to a local attorney who represented the owner of the property. Conrad knew he would have to pay a pretty penny for the land, probably more than it was actually worth, but he believed in getting what he wanted, no matter what the cost. He also had some discussions with carpenters and stone-masons, since someone would have to build the depot. By the end of the day, nothing had been settled, but Conrad felt that genuine progress had been made. He was in a better mood when he returned to the hotel.

Pamela Tarleton was waiting for him in the lobby. She stood up from the overstuffed chair where she had been sitting and came toward him. It was too late to back out the door and pretend he hadn't been coming in, Conrad decided. But Pamela was smiling and didn't look upset with him, so perhaps everything was all right after all.

"Conrad, darling," she said as she took his hand. "I've been waiting for you all day."

"I'm sorry, Pamela. Your father said you didn't feel well this morning, so I spent the day conducting business. I didn't mean to ignore you."

"Don't be silly," she said as she linked her arm with his. "I know you have to take care of these things."

"Then you're not angry with me?"

"Not at all."

He never had learned when to leave well enough alone. "Not about . . . anything?"

"Conrad . . ." Her hand tightened on his arm. "I heard about what happened, of course, and I forgive you. I suppose it's only natural that a man would be tempted by such a brazen hussy. Once we're married, I know you'll never stray."

"I haven't strayed," he said stiffly. "And Miss Callahan is not a hussy."

"But . . . parading around . . ." Her voice dropped to a whisper. *"Naked!"*

"She wasn't parading around," Conrad insisted. Just as he had done earlier when Allison McShane was asking him about Frank, he found himself defending Rebel without really knowing why. "She was totally innocent, and I was completely to blame for the unfortunate incident. I just hope that someday she can forgive me for the embarrassment I caused her."

"Why would you care whether she forgives you or not?" Pamela demanded. "She's only a frontier trollop — and she's trying to get her hooks into my father!"

So that was it. Pamela was jealous of all the attention Tarleton had paid to Rebel today. Conrad had to suppress the urge to laugh. At the same time, he didn't like the way she was talking about Rebel.

"Despite what you may think, Miss Callahan is a lady," he said.

"Really? Have you heard the way she speaks? Heavens, Conrad, she sounds like an uneducated bumpkin!"

"Can you ride a horse all day or throw a lasso or brand a steer?"

"What? Of course not! Why would I want to do any of those things?"

"What would you do if someone took a shot at you? Would you keep your head, or would you scream and collapse in a dead faint?"

Pamela's eyes narrowed as she looked up at him. "I don't care for the turn this conversation has taken, Conrad. I think we had better change the subject."

"Just don't call Rebel a trollop or any other names," he snapped. "She doesn't deserve them."

Pamela glared at him for a moment, and then she said, "My God, despite everything that's happened, you're still infatuated with her!"

"What? Don't be ridiculous!"

"I'm not. I offered to forgive you for your utterly boorish behavior, and yet you still leap to her defense!" She pulled away from him, and when he reached for her, she pulled back even more. "I think you should just leave me alone, Conrad," she said coldly. "Leave me alone, and go somewhere and think about the things you've said and done."

"All right," he said. "I will."

Her chin lifted defiantly. "And when you're ready to come back to me and beg for my forgiveness — again — I'll think about it."

"You do that, Pamela," he said curtly. He turned and stalked out of the Holloway House, well aware that some of the people in the lobby had probably witnessed and perhaps overhead part of that scene. More grist for the rumor mill, he told himself. And he realized with a surge of anger that he didn't really give a damn either.

He was glad that he didn't run into Tarleton and Rebel on his way out of the hotel. As upset as he was, he might have given them a piece of his mind. Without him really thinking about what he was doing, his steps turned toward the Big Nugget. He wanted a drink.

He didn't see Jonas Wade when he came into the saloon, but that was no surprise. It was a little early yet. The saloon keeper was also a gambler — which was how he'd gotten the Big Nugget in the first place, of course — and he would probably have a game going later. Conrad thought that he might sit in on it. He had never been much of a poker player, but he needed something to distract him from the troubles with the railroad and the confused mess that his personal life had become.

Getting a beer at the bar, Conrad carried it over to a table and sat down. He nursed the drink for quite a while as the saloon began to fill up with customers. There were a few townsmen, but most of the men wore the rough garb of miners. A dozen or more mines were located in the mountains not far from Ophir, so Conrad wasn't surprised by the miners' presence. Without the business that the miners brought in, this settlement probably wouldn't exist.

The saloon girls in their spangled dresses began to circulate through the crowd. One of them paused by Conrad's table and looked down at him. "Hello, honey," she said with a crooked-toothed smile. "Remember me?"

"Of course I do," Conrad said. "We spoke last night. You're . . . you're . . . You know, I don't believe I ever heard your name."

She laughed. "No, I don't reckon you did. It's Abby."

"Well, then, good evening, Abby. It's good to see you again."

She motioned toward the empty glass in Conrad's hand. "You want another of those?"

"You know, I believe I do." He hadn't had any supper and he wasn't that used to drinking, but if the first beer had made him feel good, it stood to reason that another one would make him feel even better.

Abby went to the bar, and was back in just a few minutes with another full mug of beer. As she bent to set it on the table in front of Conrad, one of the miners at the next table suddenly leaned over and slapped her sharply on the rump. He said, "Hey, now, that's one hell of a nice ass you got there, gal!"

Abby jerked forward at the unexpected slap, and the mug slipped out of her hand. It hit the table and overturned, dumping all its contents right in Conrad's lap. He scraped his chair back and jumped up, furious and mortified at the same time.

He wasn't the only one who was mad. Abby turned around and confronted the man who had slapped her. "Keep your damn hands to yourself, mister!" she flared at him.

The miner was big and brawny and drunk. "Spitfire, eh?" he rumbled as he came to his feet. "Well, c'mere, Red." He reached for her. "I wanna take you upstairs. I bet a redhead like you's got freckles all over."

His thick fingers clamped around her arm. She pounded a fist against his chest and said, "Let go of me, you bastard!"

The miner just grinned. "Yeah, you're full o' fight, all right. Just the way I like my gals. Ain't nothin' more fun than tamin' one like you."

Conrad stepped around Abby and poked a finger against the miner's broad chest. "The lady asked you to let her go."

The man glared at him and said, "What the hell? I don't see no lady here, just a saloon whore!"

"Let go of her," Conrad grated.

The miner looked down at Conrad's beer-soaked trousers and laughed. "And why do you reckon I should listen to somebody who can't even keep from pissin' all over hisself?"

That was the last straw. Conrad had long since stopped thinking about what he was doing. It just felt so damned good to be confronting a simple problem directly, with no negotiation, no glib talk, no highfalutin Eastern airs.

Instead he said, "I'll piss on you, you son of a bitch!" and slugged the miner in the jaw as hard as he could.

Chapter 26

The blow landed cleanly and took the miner by surprise. Conrad had always been rather muscular, and the punch packed enough power so that the miner was thrown backward and lifted completely off his feet. He came crashing down on the table where he and several of his friends had been sitting. The table legs broke and the whole thing collapsed. The stunned miner landed on the floor in the middle of the wreckage as his friends jumped back, yelling in anger.

That anger was directed immediately at Conrad. "Get that bastard!" one of the men shouted as he lunged forward, swinging a malletlike fist.

Abby stuck a leg out and tripped him before he could reach Conrad. She snatched up a drink tray from another table and swung it over her head, then brought it down on the man's skull with a ringing impact.

The man sprawled out, knocked senseless.

But there were still several of his companions bent on handing Conrad a thrashing. As they came at him, he knew he should be scared, but for some reason he wasn't. His blood sang in his veins. He had once heard Frank comment that barbarism was the natural state of mankind. There must have been some truth to that, because he certainly felt barbaric right now.

Ducking under a roundhouse blow, he stepped closer to the man who had thrown it and hooked a punch into the man's midsection. Breath laden with whiskey fumes exploded from the man's mouth as Conrad's fist sunk almost wrist-deep in his guts. Acting quickly, Conrad brought up a sharp left that clicked the man's teeth together and glazed his eyes.

A fist belonging to someone else struck Conrad a glancing blow on the side of the head. The punch landed hard enough to stagger him. He caught his balance and jabbed a right into the face of the man who had hit him. Someone else grabbed him, jerked him around, and struck him in the chest. His enemies were all around him, so he began to flail wildly at them, knowing that whoever he hit had it coming.

He was only vaguely aware of hearing

someone shout, "Hey! It's the boss! All you Browning men, come on!"

As more miners threw themselves into the fracas, it quickly went from a small, isolated fight to a full-fledged brawl that threatened to engulf the entire saloon. Conrad was in the middle of it, swinging punches right and left, absorbing the punishment being dealt out to him. He tasted the salty tang of blood in his mouth and didn't care. His elegant, oh-so-genteel friends back in Boston would probably raise their eyebrows superciliously if they could see him engaged in such pugilistic excesses. He didn't give a damn. He just wanted to hit somebody.

When someone bumped into his back, he twisted around and started to throw a punch, but the man shouted, "Hold it, Mr. Browning! It's me, Bob Elkins!"

Conrad held back his fist. He recognized the man as one of the workers from the mine his company owned up in the mountains. "Elkins!" he exclaimed. "Is the whole crew here?"

"Damn near," Elkins said with a grin stretched from ear to ear across his rugged, blood-smeared face. The battle ebbed and flowed around him and Conrad, but they were able to snatch a few seconds for a shouted conversation. "They're givin' hell to those Tarleton men too!"

"Tarleton!"

"Yeah. Didn't you know? That first fella you laid out was Ned Cameron, the foreman up at Tarleton's mine!"

So this combat was primarily between Browning men and Tarleton men, eh? Conrad liked the sound of that, and he liked the way his employees had jumped into the middle of the fight on his behalf. That was loyalty for you, by God! He wouldn't let them down.

"Let's clean up those bastards," he growled.

Elkins let out a whoop. "I'm with you, Boss!"

They stood back to back, the wealthy young man from Boston who owned the mine and the brawny miner who toiled there, and their fists wreaked bruising, bloody havoc around them. Men popped up in front of Conrad and he knocked them down again. Exhaustion began to creep over him, but he ignored it. The area around his left eye began to swell, making it hard to see. He didn't care as long as his vision was still good enough to let him land his punches. Blood flowed like the finest claret, and Conrad Browning was drunk on it. It was the most exhilarating feeling he had ever experienced.

Eventually, though, someone grabbed him from behind, pinning his arms. He thrashed and cursed for a moment before he realized that it was Bob Elkins holding him. "Take it easy, Boss!" the miner said. "We've done whipped 'em all!"

Conrad's hair had fallen in his eyes. He tossed his head to get it out of the way and looked around him. The saloon looked like a tornado had struck it. Busted-up tables and chairs were scattered around the room. The bloodied and battered forms of men lay sprawled in the wreckage, moaning softly in their pain. Half-a-dozen miners were still on their feet, and although they looked to be on the verge of collapse, they still had the strength to grin at each other triumphantly. Conrad recognized all of them. They were his men. His warriors.

The saloon girls and the customers who hadn't taken part in the epic combat stood around the edges of the room, looking on with expressions of awe. The bartenders peeked over the hardwood, coming out now that the fight was over. Conrad felt a pang of regret as he saw Jonas Wade stepping tentatively through the debris, a devastated look on his face. "My saloon," the gambler said in a hollow voice. "My beautiful saloon."

Conrad shook loose from Elkins's grip. His reason had returned to him, and even though he had enjoyed the brawl, he felt bad now for the damage it had done to the Big Nugget. Jonas Wade had been friendly to both him and Frank, and Conrad knew he had to make this right.

"Jonas," he said as he stepped forward and extended a hand toward the saloon owner, "don't worry, I'll pay for all the damages—"

"Conrad!" Wade exclaimed in surprise. "You were part of this?"

"Part of it? He started it!" Bob Elkins said proudly. "Decked that son of a bitch Ned Cameron just as pretty as you please!"

Abby stepped up and said to Wade, "Don't blame Mr. Browning, Boss. Cameron was being a jackass, as usual, and wouldn't let go of me. That was after he made me drop a full mug of beer on Mr. Browning."

For a moment more, Wade just looked around and shook his head. Then he sighed and took Conrad's hand. "It's mighty kind of you to offer to pay for all this—"

"I insist," Conrad said.

Wade shook his head again. "If you were defending one of my girls, then you're not to blame even if you threw the first punch. Getting your place busted up is just one of the problems of running a saloon, I reckon."

"How about this?" Conrad proposed. "Make all of Tarleton's men pony up for their share, and then I'll make up the difference in whatever it takes to put this place back right."

"Well . . ." Wade rubbed his jaw. "That's still mighty generous of you. But I might just take you up on it. I haven't owned the Big Nugget for long, and I don't have a lot of operating capital."

Conrad shook Wade's hand again and said, "Then it's a deal."

Abby rested a hand on Conrad's shoulder and said, "Your mouth's bleedin', Mr. Browning, and you really ought to get a wet rag on that eye of yours before it swells up anymore. I'd be mighty pleased to take care of you, if you'll let me."

Conrad thought there was more to her words than an offer of nursing care, but if so, he wasn't going to take her up on it. He would allow her to tend to his injuries, but that was all.

The fight had knocked all the cobwebs out of his brain. He was thinking clearly now for what seemed like the first time in ages. He knew what he had to do.

He didn't know where his father was at this moment, but he hoped Frank was having as good a night as he was.

Frank reacted before anyone else as more arrows began to fly out of the darkness beyond the reach of the firelight. Even with his hands tied behind his back, his finely honed muscles and reflexes enabled him to surge up from the ground and lunge toward the fire. A couple of bounding steps brought him close, and then as an arrow whispered past his ear, he threw himself forward in a rolling dive that landed him beside the unconscious Scheer and the dead torturer.

One of the hardcases gave a gurgling scream as he pawed at the arrow that had gone through his neck. A sheet of blood flooded down his chest. He fell to the ground, flopping grotesquely as he died.

Another man spun off his feet as an arrow ripped through his thigh. As he sprawled on the ground, he clawed out his revolver and emptied it blindly into the night as he screamed curses. Another arrow came out of the darkness and thudded into his chest, toppling him over backward.

Shots roared, the reports echoing off the looming cliff as the gang of saboteurs fought back. By the fire, Frank twisted around and got his hands on the knife that the first man to die had dropped. Working by feel and trying to ignore the chaos around him, he turned the bowie around so that the blade rested against the ropes holding his wrists together. He began to saw desperately on the bonds, knowing that he was running the risk of cutting his wrists so deeply that he could bleed to death. But he knew he would die anyway if he just waited helplessly with his hands tied behind his back.

There were enough large rocks scattered around the cavelike area under the cliff so that the hardcases were able to take cover behind them and burn a lot of powder shooting at their unseen adversaries. The problem was that they were firing blind, and there was no way to know if they were hitting any of the Apaches or not. It seemed to Frank when he glanced up that there were fewer arrows flying out of the shadows now, but he couldn't be sure about that.

At least the members of the gang weren't paying any attention to him at the moment. One of the ropes suddenly parted, and after a couple of minutes that seemed much longer, the other bonds fell away too. Frank's hands were free. He stuck the bowie knife behind his belt and rapidly flexed his fingers, trying to get full feeling back into them as quickly as he could. When he was confident that he could use them normally, he crawled over to Scheer and the dead hardcase. The

347

butt of a gun stood up from the dead man's holster. Frank snagged the Colt and slid it into his empty holster. Then he rolled the man off Scheer and grabbed the unconscious engineer. One of the dead man's arms fell in the fire, and the stench of burning flesh filled the air. Frank didn't take the time to pull the man out of the flames. He started dragging Scheer toward the edge of the camp instead.

Even though it was dangerous, he thought they had a better chance with the Apaches than with the killers working against the railroad. Scheer would be terribly mutilated by now if not for the timely interruption. For the second time in recent weeks, Frank was in the unusual position of being thankful for an Indian attack.

"Damn it, Morgan's gettin' away!"

That shout came from Royal as Frank knelt to get his hands under Scheer's arms and pull the engineer upright. A bullet ripped past Frank's head as he straightened with Scheer. Letting the unconscious man sag against him and holding him up with his left arm, Frank reached down with his right hand and palmed out the Colt he had lifted from the dead torturer's holster. He snapped a shot at Royal and made the boss owlhoot dive for cover again behind a boulder.

Then, half-carrying and half-dragging Scheer, Frank staggered away from the cliff and into the darkness. He didn't know what they would run into out there, but he was willing to take the chance.

The battle continued behind them, the hardcases yelling curses and shooting their guns, while the Indians were content to fight in silence and send arrows flying into the camp. Frank kept moving until he and Scheer were at least fifty yards away from the base of the cliff. Manhandling the engineer's deadweight like that was exhausting, but Frank had made the man a promise and couldn't abandon him. He stopped and leaned against the trunk of a tree, letting Scheer slide to the ground.

As Frank watched, he saw that the arrows weren't having much effect now. The hired killers were all crouched behind rocks. Three of them had been killed, but that still left well over a dozen of them, and they were well armed. They could wait out the attack if they chose to.

Several of them panicked, though, and made a break for their horses, which were kept in a rope corral on the other side of the camp. That started a stampede of men, and Royal must have been smart enough to see that he couldn't stop it. He bellowed, "Let's get out of here!" and headed for the horses with the others, firing as he ran.

Giving up good cover was usually a foolish tactic, and a couple of the men paid the price for that rashness, going down as arrows skewered them. The rest of the gang reached the already saddled horses, though, and leaped onto the animals. With a swift rata-plan of hoofbeats, they fled into the night, a couple of arrows winging after them to speed them on their way.

That left Frank and Scheer on their own, in the dark, with a pack of hostile Apaches practically in their laps.

Frank knew Stormy was somewhere close by, along with Dog. All he had to do was whistle and the Appaloosa and the big cur would make it to his side if they had to charge through hell to do so. But if he called the animals, that would draw attention to him and Scheer. He was sure the Apaches had seen the two of them fleeing, but the Indians might not know exactly where they were now.

Scheer let out a groan at Frank's feet. Frank dropped into a crouch and clapped a hand over Scheer's mouth. The man tried to struggle, but he was only half-conscious. Frank put his lips close to Scheer's ear and hissed, "Take it easy! It's me — Morgan!"

Scheer stopped fighting, and after a moment Frank took his hand away from the man's mouth. "Wh-where are we?" Scheer whispered.

"Stay quiet," Frank whispered back as he used the bowie to cut the bonds on Scheer's wrists. "There are Apaches close by."

They stayed where they were beside the tree as Frank listened intently. He didn't hear anything moving in the darkness, but he knew that didn't mean a thing. The Apaches were out there.

The hoofbeats of the retreating horses had faded to nothing. Frank's hope was that the Apaches would go after the members of the gang, but he didn't really expect that to happen. Their habit was to strike quickly and then fade away themselves, disappearing so that they could come back and fight again some other day. Even if they didn't pursue Royal and the others, they might leave, heading back to wherever they were holed up in the mountains. Then Frank and Scheer could get out of here too. The engineer wasn't hurt all that bad, but he probably needed some medical attention anyway.

They waited for at least half an hour before Frank deemed it safe for them to move. Then he helped Scheer to his feet and said, "We still need to be quiet and careful. We'll stay away from that fire, just in case any of the Indians are still around. Once we've put some distance behind us, I'll whistle up my horse. Maybe yours will come along with him."

"I hope so," Scheer said. "I don't know how far I can walk. I hurt like hell."

"That's a good thing," Frank told him. "At least you're alive to hurt."

Scheer grunted. "Yeah. I guess you're right."

They started off, moving cautiously through the shadows, but they hadn't gone twenty feet when a handful of dark shapes suddenly loomed around them, appearing so unexpectedly that it was like they had shot up out of the ground. A guttural voice said in Spanish-accented English, "Do not move, gringos, or you die!"

Chapter 27

Frank had known that their chances of getting away were slim. He stood there calmly, not wanting to spook the Indians who surrounded them. Scheer didn't take it so well. He let out a yelp of alarm and quailed back against Frank.

"Steady," Frank said. He put his left hand on Scheer's shoulder and squeezed. "Don't give them any excuse for killing us."

"They . . . they don't need an excuse!" Scheer panted. "They're savages!"

An explosive grunt came from the Apache who stood right in front of them. It took Frank a second to realize that the man had just laughed.

"You are the men who were tied," the Apache said, in English again. Frank knew that many of the Apaches, especially the leaders, spoke three tongues — their own, Spanish, and English.

"We were prisoners," Frank agreed. "The men who held us captive were evil men."

"We saw them cut this one," the spokesman said as he gestured at Scheer. "Why should we fight the white men? They kill each other."

One of the other warriors said, "We fight them because of what they did to our people. To our women and children."

"I know this," the leader said, a note of tolerance in his voice as if he were explaining something to someone who didn't understand. "And we will continue to fight until all who died are avenged many times over. But our loss will be no less for all that."

Frank found the conversation interesting — he sensed there was more going on underneath the surface than what he knew about — but at that moment Scheer groaned again and swayed a little as if he were about to pass out. Frank tightened his grip on the engineer and said to the leader of the Apaches, "We are not your enemies. Your enemies are our enemies, so you are our friends. This man is hurt and needs help."

For a long moment, the leader didn't respond. Then he grunted again and said, "Bring him."

One of the other men said something in Apache, the words coming out hard and angry. The leader replied in a tone equally sharp. To Frank he commented, "I told my warriors we are not going to kill you . . . yet."

"Fair enough," Frank said with a nod as he got an arm around Scheer's waist. "Come on."

The leader of the war party turned and stalked off through the darkness. Frank followed, helping Scheer along. The rest of the Apaches continued to surround them. They hadn't disarmed Frank, but clearly they didn't consider him much of a threat. Outnumbered as he was, they could cut him down any time they wanted.

He would take a few of them with him if it came to that, though.

The group plunged into a thick stand of pines, and when they emerged from the other side of it they found a couple of young men holding the reins of a dozen horses. The young men spoke in rapid Apache. Frank had a feeling they were asking how the fight against the white men had gone. When they saw the two prisoners, they reached for the knives at their waists, obviously wanting to fall on Frank and Scheer and cut them to pieces. The leader spoke to them sharply, and they relaxed a little. Their gazes were still hostile as they stared at the two white men.

Frank said to the leader, "I have a horse nearby. Will you let me call him?"

The Apache nodded solemnly. "Go ahead."

Frank put a couple of fingers in his mouth and gave a shrill whistle. If Stormy and Dog were in earshot, that would bring them.

A few minutes later, Frank heard hoofbeats in the darkness. The Appaloosa loomed up out of the shadows, his dappled coat making him hard to see in the shifting patterns of light and dark. Dog walked stiffly beside him. The hair on the big cur's back bristled, and a growl sounded deep in his throat.

"Easy, Dog," Frank said. "Easy." The Apaches liked dogs — especially boiled.

One of the Indians reached for Stormy's reins. If he intended to claim the horse for his own, he was in for a disappointment. He had to jerk his hand back quickly to keep from losing a couple of fingers as Stormy bit at him. The Apache exclaimed angrily in his own tongue.

"This is a horse that belongs to only one man," the leader said.

Frank nodded. "That's right. But he'll leave folks alone, as long as they don't bother him."

"Mount up," the Apache said. "Your

friend can ride with you."

Frank had already noticed that Scheer's horse hadn't trailed along with Stormy. There was no telling where the animal was, and the Apaches didn't seem disposed to look for him. As a people, they didn't value horseflesh the same way many other tribes did. The Sioux and their allies always fought on horseback, and the Comanche at the height of their power probably had been the finest light cavalry in the history of the world, equaled perhaps only by the Russian Cossacks. The Apaches, though, usually regarded a horse as a potential meal as much as they did as transportation. They wouldn't go out of their way just to capture another horse.

"Come on," Frank said to Scheer. "Can you climb up into the saddle?"

"I . . . I'll try," the engineer replied. With Frank's voice steadying Stormy, Scheer got a foot in the stirrup and pulled himself up while Frank boosted him at the same time. When Scheer was straddling the hull, Frank used the same stirrup and swung up behind the engineer. He reached around Scheer to get hold of the Appaloosa's reins.

The Apaches mounted up too, and the leader set off with his horse at a walk. He seemed to know where he was going, even though the night was fairly dark. The Apaches probably knew just about every foot of these mountains, Frank told himself.

The route they followed was a twisting one that curved in and out of arroyos, along ridges, and around upthrusts of rock. Frank had no idea how far they were from the railroad construction camp, and he wasn't sure he would be able to find his way back there, if he ever got the opportunity. He wondered if he could convince the Apaches to let them go. It seemed unlikely, but the fact that they were still alive gave him reason to hope.

On the other hand, maybe the Indians were just taking him and Scheer back to their camp so that they could torture the two white men to death in familiar surroundings.

It was far into the night before the leader called a halt in a small box canyon with a few trees and a tiny spring at its end. Even though horses could never make it up the rock wall that closed off the canyon, Frank figured the Apaches could climb it and would be out of there on foot in a hurry if they were ever trapped here. Any mounted pursuit wouldn't be able to follow them, so the canyon wasn't as much of a box as it appeared to be.

Once they were inside, the warriors stacked brush across the narrow opening.

With that side closed off and cliffs around the other three sides, they could light a fire here without having to worry about it being seen. As a hideout, it was primitive but effective.

Frank slid down from Stormy's back and then helped Scheer to the ground. A couple of the Indians got a fire started while some of the others tended to the horses. The leader and a couple of warriors came over to stand in front of Frank and Scheer. As the flames of the fire grew brighter, Frank got his first good look at their captors. All of them had the typical squatty build of the Apaches and wore leggings, breechcloths, and long-sleeved shirts, mostly blue. The leader was a little taller than the others. A band of red cloth held back his thick, graying hair. His face showed the lines of both age and hardship.

"I am Mano Rojo," he announced. "In your gringo tongue, Red Hand. My father rode with Mangas Coloradas and Delgadito. I rode with Loco and Geronimo. Now I lead this band. We are the last Apaches to fight against the white men. We fight because our hearts are heavy with grief and because our bellies burn with anger. The white men have taken everything from us except our lives. To take those, many of them must die first. What do you say to this?"

Frank's hopes rose even more. The fact that this Apache chief was talking to him was encouraging. He said, "I am Frank Morgan. I have heard many stories of the bravery of Mangas Coloradas and Delgadito, of Loco and Geronimo. The Apaches are not my enemies."

"Yet you have fought against them," Mano Rojo said sharply.

"When I was attacked, I have fought," Frank replied, meeting the chief's gaze squarely. "Never have I sought out the Apaches to do them harm."

Mano Rojo nodded slowly. "Your name is familiar. I have heard it in these mountains, and even below the border in Mexico. You have another name."

"Some call me The Drifter," Frank acknowledged.

Again a grunt of laughter came from the Apache. "You have the red hand too, Frank Morgan."

It was Frank's turn to nod. "I would live in peace, but that is a hard thing to do."

"Hard for the Apaches too."

"Loco has gone in," Frank pointed out. "So has Geronimo. They live now on reservations, at peace with the white man."

Mano Rojo's face darkened. "This is what we would have done as well. When word

360

came to us in Mexico that Loco had gone in, we rode north to do the same, bringing our families with us. But before we could travel to the place where the Army is and say to the leaders of the whites that we wished to live in peace, we were set upon. Our camp was attacked. Our women and children were killed, except for a few young men. Our warriors barely escaped with their lives. Some died. It was a mistake for those who attacked us to allow any of us to get away."

The words were flat, almost expressionless. Scheer, who was leaning against a rock, asked, "What's he babbling about, Morgan?"

"He's explaining why they're still at war with the whites," Frank said. "Pay attention and you might learn something." He turned back to Mano Rojo. "This is a bad thing. A tragedy. Do you know who was responsible for it?"

"White men," the Apache chief said. "Now all white men must pay."

The wheels of Frank's brain turned over as quickly as those of a racing wagon. He understood a lot more now. These warriors had been on their way to surrender to the Army when a force of unknown white men had attacked their camp and slaughtered their families. No wonder they were raiding in the area. They were mad with grief and had a blood debt to settle.

But they couldn't settle it by attacking innocent people, no matter what they thought. Frank said, "The men who build the railroad through the mountains are my friends. They are not the ones who attacked your camp and killed your loved ones."

"How can you know this?" Mano Rojo demanded.

"Because I know them and know they would not do such a thing. They are interested only in building the railroad. Besides, they are workers, laborers, not gunmen. They would not be able to fight the Apaches and win." An idea was beginning to form in Frank's head. He had no way of knowing if it was correct, but at least it was a possibility.

Mano Rojo said, "My warriors want to kill the two of you. Mostly the young ones feel this way, but some of the older men want to kill you too. You are still alive only because you puzzle me. The other white men, the ones who held you prisoner, seem more evil than you. Why do they hate you?"

"Because they want to stop the railroad, and we want to stop them." That wasn't true of Scheer, but Frank was willing to stretch a point. He just hoped that the engineer had sense enough to keep his mouth shut. He pressed on. "They planned to torture my friend and leave him for the men with the railroad to find, so that they would think the Apaches had done this thing. I believe they have done other evil things and made it look like you and your men were to blame, Mano Rojo."

The chief frowned. "This is true?"

"You have my word on it. Their leader told me as much himself."

"Then they want the whites to hate us even more."

Frank nodded. "That's right. They want you and the men from the railroad to kill each other."

Mano Rojo might not have any formal education other than what he had gotten from the priests at the missions when he was a boy — his Spanish was proof of that — but his brain was quick and cunning anyway. He said, "Such men would not turn away from killing women and children."

"That's exactly what I was thinking," Frank said. What better way to cause trouble for the railroad than to stir up the Apaches, and what better way to do that than by attacking them while they had their families with them, on their way to a peaceful surrender when they weren't expecting trouble.

It all fit, Frank told himself. But he had

no proof of any of it.

"I will make a bargain with you, Mano Rojo," he went on. "If you allow my friend and me to leave here in peace, we will tell the leaders of the whites that you and your warriors were going to come in, as Loco and Geronimo did. We will tell them of the evil thing that was done to your people. And this I swear. . . . I will find the men who did this thing and see to it that they are punished for it. Then you and your men can live in peace."

Mano Rojo didn't say anything. He just stared at Frank as the seconds dragged by and turned into minutes. At least he was thinking about it, Frank told himself. Finally, Mano Rojo turned to the two men with him and spoke to them in their native tongue. All Frank had to go by was the tone of the conversation. He thought that the other two Apaches were rejecting his proposal, and he hoped that Mano Rojo was arguing in favor of it.

The talk went on for several minutes. At last, Mano Rojo turned back to Frank and said, "We will allow you to leave in peace."

Scheer started to heave a sigh of relief.

"But not this one," Mano Rojo went on, pointing at the engineer.

"What!" Scheer exclaimed. He stood up from the rock where he had been resting.

Frank held out a hand to stop the engineer from saying or doing anything else. His sudden move had made the other two Apaches finger their knives.

"You should let both of us go," Frank said. "My friend needs medical attention."

"We will tend to his wound," Mano Rojo said calmly. "He will be safe here. And when we know that you have done as you say you will do, Frank Morgan, then he will be freed."

"They want to keep me as a hostage?" Scheer asked. "Morgan, you can't let them do that!"

"I don't reckon I've got a whole lot of choice in the matter, if they've got their hearts set on it," Frank said.

"But . . . but they're savages! You can't trust them!"

Frank fixed the engineer with a flinty stare. "I think I can trust Mano Rojo . . . if he gives me his word."

The chief nodded gravely and said, "As you have given me yours."

Frank took a deep breath. The situation wasn't perfect, far from it, in fact, but he figured it was the best he could do under the circumstances.

"Then we are agreed," he said. A faint smile touched his lips. "As the white men would put it, we've got a deal, Mano Rojo."

Chapter 28

Since Conrad had never before taken part in a brawl such as the one that had erupted in the Big Nugget, he wasn't quite sure what to expect the next morning. What he got were stiff and aching muscles, bruises so sore that they made him wince when he touched them gingerly, and a shiner to be proud of. His left eye was ringed with a large circle of black and blue and purple. The swelling around the eye had gone down enough so that he could see better, but it was still puffy.

He looked at himself in the mirror over the dressing table in his hotel room and shook his head. The excitement and exhilaration of battle had kept him from realizing just how much damage he was absorbing. Now there was no doubt. He clenched his jaw to keep from groaning as he pulled on his clothes.

Despite the pain, his head was still clear and he felt surprisingly good. The more he moved around, the less his muscles hurt. As he went downstairs, he realized that he was ravenously hungry.

More than anything else, he simply felt *alive* to a greater extent than he could remember feeling, perhaps ever.

Glancing around the dining room as he came in, he didn't see Rebel, Pamela, or Tarleton. The waiter was familiar, though, and as he came up to the table where Conrad sat down, he shook his head and said, "I'm sorry, Mr. Browning. I heard that you were involved in a disturbance. That eye must hurt like the dickens."

Conrad grinned. "It does smart a mite," he said.

"What can I bring you?"

"A pot of coffee. Strong and black. Flapjacks. Then a steak and some potatoes."

The waiter bobbed his head. "Yes, sir."

"By the way, George . . ."

"Yes, sir?"

"Have you see Mr. Tarleton or Miss Pamela this morning?"

George shook his head. "No, sir, I'm afraid not. They haven't come down yet."

"What about Miss Rebel Callahan?"

"No, sir, not her either."

"All right, thank you. Bring that coffee now."

"Right away, sir!"

Conrad leaned back in his chair and rubbed his jaw as the waiter hurried away. He wasn't sure who he wanted to see first. That was out of his hands, he supposed. He would play the cards as they were dealt.

As it turned out, Pamela entered the dining room first, while Conrad was halfway through his first cup of coffee and still waiting for his food. The coffee had already helped him recover a bit more of his strength. He was sitting where he could keep an eye on the entrance, so he saw Pamela come in. He came to his feet and stood there until he caught her eye. She hesitated, but then walked toward him.

"Conrad, darling, you look so . . . so battered," she said. "I want to give you a big hug, but I'm afraid I might hurt you."

"I doubt that you would, but perhaps we'd better not take the chance," he said dryly. "Sit down, Pamela. Join me. We have things to talk about."

"We do?" she asked, arching her eyebrows quizzically.

"That's right." He held out a hand toward the empty chair on the other side of the table. "Please?"

"All right." She waited until he came around the table to hold her chair for her, and then sat down. "You look like a positive ruffian! It's scandalous. I hear that you were attacked in one of the drinking establishments."

"The Big Nugget Saloon," he said as he settled back in his own chair. "But I wasn't exactly attacked. I threw the first punch."

"Really? I must say, Conrad, you surprise me. You sound almost proud that you initiated the fisticuffs."

"I am. The varmint had it coming, and I let him have a good one."

"The . . . varmint?"

"I could call him some other names," Conrad said casually, "but it wouldn't be polite to use such language in the presence of a lady."

"Well, I'm glad to see that you haven't totally lost the qualities of a gentleman. The way you're dressed and your general demeanor had me worried that you were turning into one of these horrid . . ." She lowered her voice as she looked around the room. *"Westerners!"*

"Thank you," Conrad said simply.

"For what?"

"For comparing me to Western men. It's about time I evoked such a comparison, I think, since many of my business interests are located out here and I plan to spend much more time west of the Mississippi than I have in the past."

Pamela frowned prettily. "I suppose that's all right for now, but after we're married, surely you plan to spend most of your time in Boston."

Slowly, Conrad said, "That's another thing. . . ."

Pamela stared across the table at him, not saying anything as understanding soaked in on her. Her eyes gradually widened, and she said in a whisper, "No, you can't possibly . . . Conrad, you don't mean . . . I know there have been problems, but you can't just—"

"I'm sorry, Pamela," he said. "I know it's a dastardly thing to do, but I simply don't think it's meant to be. You and I aren't right for each other, and you know it."

"I know no such thing! My God, Conrad, we've made so many plans—"

"*You* made plans," Conrad said. "I just went along with them."

The expression on her face was turning from shock to anger. "You went along with them, all right," she said. "You led me to believe that you wanted this marriage as much as I did."

"At the time, that was true. But it's not any longer, and I think it's much better to cause a bit of pain now than a great deal of pain later."

Pamela's face began to flush with rage. "This is because of that little blond slut, isn't it?" she hissed.

"I'll thank you not to talk about Rebel that way," he said tightly, a little angry now himself.

She leaned forward, keeping her voice low so that there wouldn't be a scene. "You fool! Don't you know that she's forgotten you and set her sights on my father now?"

"She's just trying to make me jealous," Conrad said, shaking his head.

"Don't make me laugh. She's decided that Clark Tarleton is the better catch. And she's right. My father is a *man*." Pamela's mouth twisted in a contemptuous sneer. "You're just a little boy."

Conrad kept a tight rein on his temper. "I'm sorry I've hurt you, Pamela," he said. "As I've indicated, I think this is the best thing in the long run."

She shook her head, glared at him, and probably would have had more to say if her father hadn't entered the dining room at that moment. Clark Tarleton spotted his daughter and Conrad sitting at the table and strode quickly across the room, a scowl on his face. Ignoring Pamela for the moment, he snapped, "I hope you're pleased with yourself, Browning. Because of that brawl you and your men started last night, half of my best men are laid up and won't be able to work for several days. Some of them even have broken bones. It'll be weeks before they can go back to work!"

Coolly, Conrad said, "While it's true that I threw the first punch, Tarleton, it was your foreman, Ned Cameron, who really caused the fight by acting like a boor. He's the one you should be blaming for any inconvenience, not me."

"Well, I do blame you—" Tarleton stopped short as he glanced down at his daughter and saw how ashen and upset she looked. "Pamela?" he said. "My God, what's wrong?"

"Conrad has done more than cause trouble for you at the mine, Father," she said. Her voice shook a little. "He's just broken our engagement."

"What!" Tarleton roared, and any hope of getting out of here without a scene was gone. "How dare you!"

"And do you know *why* he doesn't want to marry me anymore?" Pamela went on. "It's because of that Callahan woman!"

"Rebel? Good Lord!"

Conrad stood up, well aware that everyone

else in the dining room was watching now. Let them, he thought. He didn't care anymore.

"That's not the entire reason," he said. "I've been trying to explain to Pamela that she and I just aren't suited to be married to each other. I've decided—"

"That's just it!" Pamela broke in. Her voice quavered, and tears rolled down her cheeks. "*You* decided! You didn't ask me. You just made up your mind, and that was it! The engagement was off."

Conrad took a deep breath. "I'm sorry, but . . . yes, that's the way it is. The way it has to be."

"You . . ." Tarleton grated. "You damned insolent pup!"

He brought his fist up and swung it, aiming right at Conrad's head.

Conrad knew that Tarleton was still a strong man despite his years. He couldn't afford to underestimate him. Ducking under the blow, he stepped in and swiftly got hold of Tarleton's arm. He twisted it and brought it around behind Tarleton's back, forcing the older man to turn.

"Clark, don't do this," he said, hoping to head off any further trouble. "I'm sure it'll be best for everyone—"

"Let go of me!" Tarleton bellowed. He

drove the elbow of his other arm back into Conrad's belly, striking hard with it. Conrad coughed and started to double over, breathless for the moment. Tarleton twisted free of his grip.

Conrad expected Tarleton to try to hit him again, and he set himself and brought up his arms to block any blows. Instead, Tarleton straightened his coat, took Pamela's arm, and helped her up from her chair.

"Come along, my dear," he said. "This man isn't worth brawling with. You're better off without him."

Pamela was still crying, but she sniffed and tried to put on a brave face. "You're right, Father," she said as she lifted her chin and stared defiantly at Conrad. "He's not good enough to be a member of our family."

They turned to leave. Conrad was sorry the situation had deteriorated so badly and turned out in such an embarrassing manner, but at the same time he was glad to see them go. The idea of not having to marry Pamela was like a huge weight off his shoulders. He had never realized just how heavy it was until it was gone.

He hadn't been watching the dining room entrance after Tarleton came in, so now as he watched the two of them leave and looked in that direction, he was surprised to see Rebel standing there. She was dressed in range clothes again, boots and jeans and a man's shirt, and Conrad wondered how long she had been there. Had she witnessed all of the embarrassing scene with the Tarletons, or just part of it?

More importantly, what did she think of the whole thing?

She stepped aside as Tarleton and Pamela walked past her. Tarleton glanced at her, but didn't stop or say anything. Rebel didn't come any farther into the dining room, which meant Conrad had to go to her. He was acutely conscious of eyes following him as he walked across the room.

"Rebel," he said as he came up to her, "I'm glad you're here."

"You are?" she said, and she sounded genuinely surprised. "You're glad I got to see you wrestling with a man more than twice your age?"

"You don't understand," he said quickly. "I didn't want to hurt Mr. Tarleton. He was just upset because of the fight in the Big Nugget last night—"

"I heard about that," Rebel cut in. "Regular saloon tough, ain't you?"

"No, not at all. I was just defending a lady—"

"A saloon girl, was the way I heard it."

Conrad took a deep breath and forged ahead. "At any rate, I'm not ashamed of what happened last night. I am, however, sorry that I upset Pamela this morning."

"What did you do?" Rebel asked.

"I told her that our engagement is off," Conrad said proudly. "I explained that we weren't suited for each other and that it would be much better for both of us if we did not get married."

Rebel's eyes widened. "You broke it off with her, just like that?"

"Swift and merciful," Conrad said decisively.

"I wondered why she was cryin'. Now I reckon I know." For a moment, Rebel didn't say anything else. She just looked at Conrad and shook her head solemnly and a little bit sadly. It didn't take long for him to grow uncomfortable as she looked at him with a mixture of anger and pity.

"Rebel, I thought you would be pleased," he said. "I don't understand—"

"No," she cut in. "You sure as hell don't."

And with that, she turned and walked away, not looking back at him.

Conrad watched her go, flabbergasted by her reaction. Didn't she know that he had ended things with Pamela because he wanted to be with her? Surely she could see that!

But he hadn't told her, he reminded himself. For a second he thought about running after her and trying once again to explain, but then he decided he couldn't do that. He was too proud. If she wanted to jump to conclusions about him, then so be it.

Slowly, he went back to his table and sat down. George stood nearby, a tray of food in his hands, a worried look on his face. He said, "Uh . . . Mr. Browning . . . you still want your breakfast?"

Conrad summoned up a faint smile and shook his head. "I'm sorry, George," he said. "I seem to have lost my appetite."

Chapter 29

Mano Rojo had given Frank his word that he and Scheer would not be harmed, but while Frank believed the chief, he wasn't completely convinced that the rest of the Apaches would live up to the bargain. They were independent cusses, and they had good reason to hate all white men.

So Frank slept lightly that night, counting on his own senses as well as those of Stormy and Dog to warn him if any of the warriors came creeping close with murder on their minds. He was awake quite a bit, and during those times he thought about everything that had happened. The more he mulled it over, the more he was convinced that Royal and the rest of the gang of saboteurs were the most likely culprits when it came to the attack that wiped out the families of these Apaches.

Royal and the others were working for

somebody, though. They were strictly hired guns, and they would have nothing to gain by stopping the spur line other than a payoff.

The question was who would profit if Conrad's venture failed.

The next morning, Frank shook Walt Scheer awake and asked him, "Who owns the Southwestern and Pacific?"

Scheer blinked sleepily and then rubbed his eyes. Since he didn't have a shirt, he had begged a blanket from the Apaches. One of the Indians had also given him some sort of foul-smelling medicinal ointment to rub on the long cut on his chest. The wound was caked over with dried blood and medicine, but at least the flesh around it wasn't inflamed. It might heal without infection setting in. Scheer would have an ugly scar, but that was a hell of a lot better than being dead.

He pulled the blanket tighter around his bare shoulders, yawned, and said, "What?"

"I asked who owns the Southwestern and Pacific," Frank repeated, keeping the impatience he felt under control.

"I don't really know," Scheer said with a shake of his head. "Some sort of syndicate back East, I believe. The line has offices in Philadelphia and Boston."

"You said the SW and P plans to take over

the spur line if Conrad Browning fails to get it through?"

Scheer nodded. "That's right. It should be quite a lucrative enterprise. The mines around Ophir produce a great deal of ore. There are also successful ranches in the area. The spur line will have plenty of business once it's completed."

"So to some people, there's enough at stake to justify murder."

Scheer's eyes widened. "I didn't say that," he replied quickly. "I don't know anything about murder, or sabotage, or the attack on those savages."

"Would be mighty ironic, though, if Royal and his friends work for the same fellas you do. It's like the old saying about one hand not knowing what the other hand is doing. They would have tortured you to death without ever knowing that all of you have the same boss."

A shudder went through Scheer at the mention of the fate he had so narrowly avoided. "I suppose it's possible," he said as he looked down at the ground. "I don't know anything about it, though."

Frank nodded. He believed the engineer. Scheer had no reason to lie.

The Apaches didn't have much to eat, just some dried venison and berries, but they shared with Frank and Scheer. Mano Rojo saw to that. Frank still had the impression that the rest of the band would have gladly killed the two white men, but no one was willing to stand up to Mano Rojo and insist on it.

When they had finished eating their meager breakfast, Mano Rojo brought one of the other Apaches over to Frank. "This is Maldito," he said. "The Little Evil One."

Maldito lived up to his name. He was even shorter and more stockily built than the other warriors. During some battle in the past, he had lost an eye. A white scar slanted across the empty socket where his left eye should have been. He squinted balefully at Frank with his right eye and fingered the hilt of the knife at his waist.

"Maldito will take you to where you can find the white man's town," Mano Rojo went on.

"So he's to be my guide?" Frank said.

Mano Rojo nodded. "That is right."

"He looks more like he'd rather skin me alive or stake me out on an anthill."

Maldito muttered something in the Apache tongue. Mano Rojo spoke sharply to him.

"He understands enough of your tongue to know what you said," the chief told Frank.

"He says that he will not dishonor his mouth by using white man's words, but he agrees with you. He would like to kill you. But he will not. Maldito has ridden with me for more than twenty summers. He will do as I have told him."

Frank hoped Mano Rojo was right about that. He wasn't afraid of Maldito, but he would hate to have to kill the ugly little man.

Scheer spoke up, asking, "Do you still want to keep me here?"

Mano Rojo nodded. "You will stay with us. You will not be mistreated. You have my word on that."

Scheer was smart enough not to voice any doubts he might have felt on that score. He just nodded and said, "Thank you, Mano Rojo."

"Do not thank me," the Apache snapped. "Your life is truly in the hands of Frank Morgan. If he does not find the men responsible for the attack on our people and see to it that they are punished properly, your life will be forfeited."

Scheer looked at Frank. "Don't let me down, Morgan," he said.

"I won't," Frank promised. More than Scheer's life was riding on this vow. If there was going to be peace in this region, he had to satisfy the Apaches. Otherwise, they would continue to attack white men wherever they found them. Eventually, they would all be hunted down and killed, but there would be plenty of other deaths too before that happened.

Frank could prevent any more needless killing by finding whoever was responsible for the massacre. He wouldn't rest until he had done so.

He got Stormy ready to ride while Maldito threw a blanket on the back of one of the scrubby ponies the Apaches rode. When they were both mounted, Maldito pointed to the west. This was going to be a mighty quiet trip, since the Apache wouldn't speak English and Frank knew only a few words of Maldito's language. Maybe it wouldn't take too long to get where they were going. Frank hoped that proved to be the case.

He gave Scheer a friendly wave and said encouragingly, "Don't worry. I'll be back to get you as soon as I can."

"I'll be here," Scheer replied with a dispirited sigh.

Frank and Maldito rode out, heading west. Even though it was daylight now and he could see where they were going, Frank was still lost in a matter of minutes because the trail twisted and turned so much as it wound its way through the rugged mountains. Most of the time, even with the sun overhead, he wasn't completely sure which direction they were going. Finding his way back to the Apache camp would have been impossible. Which was exactly what the Indians had intended by hiding out in such a remote location, of course. Frank had no doubt that Maldito could get back there without any trouble.

After a while, they came to a fast-moving but shallow stream and forded it where the bottom was firm with gravel. Frank wondered if this was the same river that cut the gorge through the mountains so that it intersected the railroad. He thought about asking Maldito, but decided it probably wouldn't do any good.

They descended into a winding gully and stayed in it for a long time as it snaked across the landscape. When they finally came out, they rode up a hill, and Maldito reined in as they reached the top. He lifted an arm and pointed.

Frank brought Stormy to a stop and looked down the slope on the far side of the hill. At the bottom of it he saw the roadbed that had been graded for the spur line. With it and the sun to orient himself, he suddenly knew where he was again, and that was a good feeling.

He looked over at Maldito and said slowly, "I know you understand most of what I'm saying. Thank you for bringing me here."

Maldito surprised Frank by speaking in English. He pointed to the spot where they had stopped the horses and grunted, "Here. One week."

"You want to meet back here in one week?" Frank asked. He had to make sure he understood correctly. Scheer's life might depend on it.

"Here. One week," Maldito said again. "Bad men punished, or white man die."

"You're saying that I have one week to find out who attacked your people, or my friend will be killed?"

Maldito smiled, but it didn't make him any less ugly. Frank took the expression as a sign of agreement.

He hadn't known that Mano Rojo was giving him a time limit, but there was nothing he could do about it now. He nodded and said, "One week. Bring my friend with you. I will meet you and tell you the truth."

Maldito took out his knife, ran his thumb along the keen edge, and smiled again. Frank thought he was looking forward to that meeting in a week's time. But was he hoping that Frank would be successful — or that he would have two more white men to kill?

Without saying anything else, Maldito slid his knife back into its sheath, turned his pony, and rode away. He went back into the gully and disappeared in a matter of moments. Frank waited until the Apache was gone and then rode down the hill toward the graded trail. Dog trotted along beside him.

When they reached the roadbed, Frank reined in again and looked both ways along the route. If he turned south it would take him back to the construction camp. The workers would still be rebuilding the destroyed trestle; that chore would take them quite a while. If he headed north instead, Frank told himself, he would wind up in Ophir, where Conrad and Rebel had gone.

It would be nice to see his son again and be sure that Conrad had made it safely to the boomtown, but there was another reason for riding on to Ophir. If he went back to the construction camp, he might be able to forestall any more incidents of sabotage, but that was just fighting a holding action. It wouldn't put him any closer to the brains behind the effort to ruin Conrad's plans. With the deadline that Mano Rojo had given him, he didn't have time to waste. He had to uncover the mastermind as quickly as possible.

There was no guarantee that mastermind was in Ophir, but it was certainly possible. A man who would hire a gang of killers to blow up trestles and murder railroad workers might want to be somewhere close at hand, so that he could move quickly should the opportunity arise to seize control of the spur line. Also, if Frank went to Ophir, he might be able to get on the trail of whoever owned the Southwestern and Pacific Railroad. Unless and until he found out something to convince him otherwise, he regarded the boss of the SW and P as the man with the most to gain if Conrad failed.

Frank didn't spend a lot of time mulling it over. He made his decision and turned Stormy north toward Ophir.

The ride took most of the day, but the sun was still above the mountains when he rode into the settlement. It was a bustling place. Ophir wasn't the first boomtown Frank had visited, so he wasn't surprised by the number of horses and wagons on the street or the people hurrying along the boardwalks, going about their business. He wasn't sure where he would find Conrad, but he knew his son well enough to figure that he would be staying at the best hotel in town. Veering Stormy toward the side of the main street, Frank hailed one of the townsmen passing by on the boardwalk.

"Say, friend, what's the best place to stay

around here?" Frank asked.

The man pointed up the street. "The Holloway House is the fanciest hotel in town," he said. "It ain't cheap, though."

Frank knew what the man was implying. His clothes were covered with trail dust and several days' worth of beard stubble darkened his face. He looked like a saddle tramp, not the sort of gent who would stay in a place like the Holloway House.

He wasn't going to take the time to explain that that wasn't really the case. Instead, he just nodded, said, "Much obliged," and heeled Stormy into a walk again. They headed up the street toward the hotel.

When he saw the Holloway House with its whitewashed walls and its big front window and its real second story instead of open air behind a false front, he knew this was where Conrad would stay. It was one of the most impressive structures in Ophir. He brought Stormy to a halt, swung down from the saddle, and looped the Appaloosa's reins over the hitch rack in front of the hotel. "Stay here," he told Dog as he stepped up onto the boardwalk.

Before he could reach the double doors at the hotel entrance, one of them opened, and sure enough, Conrad Browning himself stepped out onto the walk. Conrad stopped short at the sight of the lean, muscular figure striding toward him. A grin creased Frank's face as he raised a hand in greeting to his son.

Then he saw Conrad glance over his shoulder, looking past Frank at something — or somebody — coming up behind him. Conrad's eyes widened with alarm, and Frank wasn't a bit surprised when he heard the harsh voice call out, "Morgan! It's time!"

Chapter 30

Although he was upset over everything that had happened that morning, first with Pamela and then her father and finally Rebel, Conrad knew he couldn't sit around moping all day. There was still work to do, so he resumed his efforts of the day before, trying to get all the details of the depot's construction smoothed out so that the building would be ready when the railroad arrived.

He didn't see Pamela or Tarleton as the day went by, but once he spotted Rebel on the boardwalk on the opposite side of the street. She was talking to two men. Conrad recognized them as her brothers Tom and Bob. He had known from his conversation a few nights earlier with Jonas Wade that the Callahan boys were in town, but he hadn't run into them so far. Obviously, Rebel had, and he hoped she was trying to talk some sense into them. Continuing with their quest to kill Frank would bring them nothing but trouble.

It occurred to Conrad to wonder if the Callahans wanted *him* dead too. They had certainly been willing to kill him when he was traveling with Frank, but would they come after him simply because he was acquainted with the object of their thirst for revenge? They didn't know he was Frank Morgan's son. They had no real reason to want him dead.

And if Tom and Bob Callahan were over there talking to Rebel, where was their cousin Ed? He was the driving force behind the vendetta. Conrad looked around nervously, half afraid that Ed Callahan might be somewhere nearby, drawing a bead on him.

He didn't see Ed anywhere. Across the street, Rebel was still talking to her brothers. Without drawing attention to himself, Conrad walked down the block and turned in at the Big Nugget, pushing through the batwings and walking into the saloon.

Repairs were already under way as men worked to put right the damage that had been done during the brawl the previous night. The chairs and tables that had been broken beyond fixing had been hauled out and replaced. A makeshift workshop had been set up in one corner of the big room where carpenters fastened new legs to some of the tables. A couple of women knelt on the floor with brushes and buckets of soapy water, trying to scrub up as many of the bloodstains as they could. Not all of the dark stains would come up, though. They would be visible permanently on the floorboards.

Even with the work going on, the Big Nugget was open for business. Conrad saw Jonas Wade behind the bar and went over to say hello to the gambler.

When they had exchanged greetings, Conrad said, "Whatever the total of the damages turns out to be, let me know the difference between that and the amount you collected from Tarleton's men, and I'll see to it that you're paid."

Wade nodded. "I still say that's mighty generous of you."

"Think nothing of it. It's only fair. Besides, I intend to be doing business for a long time in Ophir, and I want to get off on the right foot."

Wade leaned an elbow on the bar. "Listen, I heard that you're not planning to marry the Tarleton girl anymore."

"Word's gotten around that quickly, has it?"

"Well, you weren't exactly discreet about breaking off the engagement with her in the middle of the Holloway House dining room."

Conrad winced and said, "Yes, that's certainly true. I might do things differently if I had the chance to try again."

"You're not saying you'd still want to marry her?"

"Not at all."

"That might just be a good thing," Wade said slowly.

It surprised Conrad somewhat that the saloon owner would offer a comment on his personal life like that. With a frown, he asked, "What do you mean by that?"

"Well, it's none of my business. . . ." Wade hesitated, looking like he wasn't sure if he wanted to continue this conversation or not. Then he shrugged and said, "I'm not sure you can trust her father."

"Clark Tarleton? He's a very respected businessman." And a man Conrad had considered a friend until today.

"Maybe so, but when you're around a saloon all the time, you hear things. Hardcases drift in and out, and in the past few days I've overheard some of them mention Tarleton."

"They weren't planning to rob him or anything like that, were they?" Conrad asked, a little alarmed. Despite everything that had happened between him and Pamela, he didn't want to see anything bad happen to her or her father.

Wade grunted. "Not hardly. From what I heard, it sounded more like those hombres were *working* for Tarleton."

"At his mine, you mean?"

Wade shook his head. "These weren't miners. Hired guns were more like it. I never saw them before, but I know the type. I don't know how long they've been here in Ophir either, since I haven't been around that long myself."

Conrad rested his hands on the bar. His frown deepened. This was certainly puzzling. "Do you know what happened to these men? Are they still around town?"

"I haven't seen them for a day or two," Wade said. "Could be they drifted on." His voice hardened. "Either that, or they're off somewhere up to no good."

Conrad didn't know what to make of it. Under the circumstances, he couldn't very well ask Tarleton about it either. They weren't that friendly at the moment.

A wild thought popped into his head. He and Tarleton were business rivals. Was it possible that Tarleton had some connection with the sabotage that had plagued the construction of the spur line?

Almost as fast as that idea occurred to

Conrad, he discarded it. Tarleton might be his rival when it came to mining, but the man had no connection with railroading. The failure of the spur line would actually hurt Tarleton's business interests, because it would be to his advantage to have rail service to Ophir.

"I'm not sure what this is about," he said to Wade, "but it doesn't have anything to do with me."

"Just thought you might want to know. But you're right. Since you're not engaged to Miss Tarleton anymore, I reckon it's none of your business — or mine."

"I appreciate the concern regardless." Conrad shook hands with the saloon keeper again. "Remember, let me know about the damages."

"I'll do that."

When Conrad stepped out of the Big Nugget, he glanced across the street and saw that Rebel and her brothers weren't standing there anymore. A check along the boardwalks on both sides of the street didn't reveal them or their cousin. Feeling relatively safe, Conrad started back toward the Holloway House.

Rebel was waiting for him in the lobby.

If he'd had time, he would have backed out before she saw him. She was too alert, though, and quickly stood up from the chair where she'd been sitting. "Conrad," she said as she came toward him.

He wasn't sure what she was going to say or do. With Rebel, it was always a mystery until it happened. He was ready to duck, though, in case she took a swing at him.

"Hello, Rebel." Perhaps he could mend some fences with her. "About this morning—"

"Never mind that," she cut in. "I felt a mite sorry for Pamela, believe it or not, but she really is a prissy little thing and you'll be better off without her."

"Does Clark know you feel that way about his daughter?"

"Why should I care what Clark Tarleton thinks?"

"Why, I was under the impression that you were quite taken with him."

"Oh, hell, I was just — never mind."

Conrad forced himself not to smile, but he felt his heart leap inside his chest. Rebel had been about to say that she didn't really care about Tarleton. She had just been using him to make Conrad jealous. Conrad had told himself all along that was the case, but as much as he wanted to, he couldn't fully believe it. Now he was sure, despite the fact that Rebel hadn't come right out and said so.

He put a hand on her arm and drew her off to a corner of the lobby where they would have more privacy.

"Rebel, I really think that we should talk —" he began.

"That's what I'm trying to do, you jughead!" she burst out. "I'm trying to tell you that my brothers and my cousin are in town, and they're still gunning for you."

Conrad nodded. "I know."

"You know?"

"Well, I knew they had come to Ophir," he clarified. "I wasn't sure whether or not they were still carrying a grudge against me."

"Ed damn sure is. He wants you dead almost as much as he wants to kill Frank. Tom and Bob . . . well, they're not so sure, but they're so used to going along with whatever Ed wants that I'm afraid they're liable to come after you too."

"I've been keeping my eye open for them. In fact, I saw you talking to your brothers a while ago. That's the first time I've seen them since we arrived in Ophir. I haven't seen Ed at all."

"That's because he's been denned up in a whorehouse, staying drunk and working up his meanness. But Tom says he's sober now, and he's ready to start looking for you and Frank."

"There's really no reason for them to be angry with me," Conrad pointed out. "I had nothing to do with the deaths of your other cousins."

"They say you kidnapped me."

Conrad's eyebrows shot up. "What? I did nothing of the sort!"

"Well . . . actually, you kind of did. I didn't want to go along with you and Frank at first. But that was before I got to know the two of you."

Conrad took off his hat and rubbed his temples wearily. "This is insane," he said. "Didn't you tell them that they were wrong about what happened?"

"Yeah, and I did my best to convince them to stop letting Ed lead them around by the nose." She shook her head. "I don't know if I did any good, though."

"Perhaps if I had a word with them . . ."

"Have you gone completely loco? You need to stay away from them if you can."

Conrad nodded. "Yes, that makes sense. I'll do my best. I won't go hunting trouble." He dropped his hand to the butt of the Colt Lightning on his hip. "But if it comes to me, I suppose I'll have no choice but to deal with it."

Rebel laughed, but there was no humor in the sound. "Hell, Conrad, you're no gunfighter. You may be Frank Morgan's son, but you didn't inherit his skill with a Colt."

Conrad stiffened as he stared at her. "What . . . what makes you think—"

"That you're Frank's son? Anybody who's around the two of you for very long could see that. You don't look that much alike except at certain times, but then suddenly the resemblance is there and you can't miss it. And there are other little things that you both do . . . the way you hold your head when you're interested in something, the way your eyes squint a little when you laugh, things like that."

Conrad shook his head. "That makes no sense. Why, until I was nearly grown I never even knew that—" He stopped short as he realized what he was about to admit.

"You never knew that Frank was your father?" Rebel finished for him. "It doesn't matter all that much whether you were raised around him or not. The things that tie a father and son together are in the blood. Bonds like that can't be broken, no matter what."

Conrad's pulse hammered in his head. Memories came flooding back, most of them bad. "You don't understand," he heard himself saying to Rebel. "He . . . he's completely different from me. He's a gunman, little better than an outlaw."

"I've been around Frank Morgan enough to know that's not true. He's no owlhoot. Never has been."

"He caused my mother a great deal of pain," Conrad grated. "He left her to raise me alone."

"You said you didn't know about him. Maybe he didn't know about you."

"No. He didn't know about me," Conrad admitted. "But he never tried to find out either. And then, when he came back into my mother's life after all those years, it was her involvement with him that led to her death."

Even as he spoke the words, Conrad knew they were not completely true. The person really responsible for Vivian Browning's death had been a lawyer named Charles Dutton, a man who had pretended to be Vivien's friend while really betraying her and trying to steal her company. Outlaws hired by Dutton, the gang led by Ned Pine and Victor Vanbergen, had been the ones to gun Vivian down. Frank's presence might have spooked Dutton into acting more hastily than he would have otherwise, but when you got right down to it, Frank wasn't to blame. And if not for Frank, Conrad would have been murdered too, and Vivian's death would have gone unavenged.

Conrad had told himself that he was

thinking more clearly now, but it wasn't true. He still had blinders on when it came to Frank Morgan. The resentment he felt toward his father had clung stubbornly. He'd been unable to put it aside, even though Frank had never been anything but friendly toward him. Frank had come here to New Mexico Territory and put his life on the line for no other reason than to help his son.

My God, Conrad thought. He might even love me. . . .

Suddenly he couldn't breathe, almost like he had been punched in the gut. His vision blurred. He couldn't see Rebel clearly. Blinking, he swung away from her. She caught at his sleeve and said, "Conrad? Conrad, what's wrong?"

He shook free of her and walked toward the hotel entrance, trying not to stumble. He pawed at his eyes with the back of his hand and his chest rose and fell rapidly as he tried to catch his breath. Unfamiliar emotions ran riot inside him. He had never been one to admit easily that he was wrong.

But when it came to Frank Morgan, he had been wrong for years. Conrad could see that now. With Rebel trailing him with a worried look on her face, he pushed open one of the hotel's double doors and stepped out onto the boardwalk. He needed air. Some instinct made him turn to his right. . . .

Utter shock went through him, freezing him as he saw the very man who had just been in his thoughts walking toward him. Frank Morgan was here in Ophir, on the same boardwalk as Conrad, and as Frank saw his son, he smiled and raised a hand.

Behind him, Ed Callahan came out of the mouth of an alley and stepped up onto the boardwalk. "Morgan!" Ed yelled. "It's time!"

His hand was poised over the butt of the gun on his hip, ready to hook and draw.

Chapter 31

Frank reacted to the challenge without missing a beat, stopping and turning smoothly, not hurrying but not wasting any time either. As he faced Ed Callahan, Rebel's brothers Tom and Bob stepped out of the alley where Ed had been waiting and backed up their cousin, spreading out to either side of him.

As it always did at moments such as this, time seemed to slow down slightly for Frank Morgan. The world around him receded. All the unimportant details of his surroundings faded away. His attention was centered on the man who wanted to kill him. Every little thing, every blink of the eyes, every tensing of the muscles, became vitally important. Frank took note of them all, knowing that watchfulness was as important as speed when it came to surviving a gunfight.

"You don't have to do this, Callahan," Frank said.

"The hell I don't! You killed my brothers!"

"Only because they forced me to. I wasn't going to just stand there and let them kill me."

"Those weren't fair fights," Ed said. "Simon and Jud weren't gunslingers. They didn't have a chance against you." He flexed his fingers slightly. "I do. I'm a heap faster than they were."

Suddenly Rebel's voice rang out along the boardwalk. Frank hadn't known she was there. She must have come out of the hotel behind Conrad. She said, "Tom, Bob, please! Don't do this. Just step away."

Tom Callahan said, "Damn it, Rebel, Ed's our cousin! He's family. Family's got to stand with family."

"Go back inside, Rebel," Bob added. "This don't concern you no more."

"The hell it doesn't!" Rebel pushed past Frank and ran toward her brothers. That put her between Frank and Ed.

Ed's hand dipped toward his gun, moving with blinding speed.

Frank bit back a curse. He reached for his Colt as he realized what Ed was trying to do. The son of a bitch was using Rebel as a distraction and a shield. Frank's only chance was to fire past her before Ed could get off a shot and risk hitting her.

Conrad slammed into Frank's shoulder, though, as he leaped forward and shouted, "Rebel, no!" The impact knocked Frank a step to the right. Conrad lunged after her in a diving tackle. His arms wrapped around her waist and brought her down.

At the same instant, Ed got off the first shot. Flame licked from the barrel of his Colt. Frank heard the slug sizzle past his ear.

The Peacemaker in his hand bucked twice as he triggered a pair of shots. Both bullets thudded into Ed Callahan's chest and drove him backward. Instinctively, his cousin Bob grabbed him and kept him from falling. But then, as blood welled out over Bob's fingers from the wounds in Ed's chest, a horrified expression appeared on Bob's face and he let Ed's limp form slide on down to the boardwalk.

Conrad and Rebel had landed on the edge of the boardwalk. They rolled off, falling the couple of feet to the street. Frank stayed where he was and held the Colt steady. A dozen feet away, Tom and Bob stood frozen. Tom's hand was on the butt of his gun, but he hadn't drawn the weapon. Bob stared down at the blood on his hands as Ed lay huddled at his feet.

"It's up to you, boys," Frank said softly to the Callahan brothers. "You've got it to do, if you still want to."

"No!" Rebel cried from the street. She twisted out of Conrad's grip and pushed herself up on her knees. Grasping the edge of the boardwalk with both hands, she leaned forward and pleaded, "Let it go! Didn't you see what just happened here? Ed was willing to shoot *me* if he had to! He didn't care about me or either of you. He was just using you to help him get Morgan!"

Slowly, the fingers of Tom's gun hand straightened out. He lifted the hand away from the gun. "Rebel's right," he said in a choked voice. "Ed didn't give a damn about us."

"If family didn't mean nothin' to him," Bob said, sounding equally shaken, "then it don't have to mean anything to us either."

"*I'm* your family!" Rebel said. "Let that mean something for a change."

Tom nodded. "She's right." He looked squarely at Frank and said, "It's over, Morgan. Ed didn't give you a choice any more than Simon and Jud did. But it's over now, and it'll stay that way."

Frank nodded and lowered his Colt. He opened the cylinder, thumbed out the empty shells, and replaced them with fresh cartridges from the loops on his gunbelt. Then he slid the iron back into leather.

"No hard feelin's, Morgan?" Bob asked.

"No," Frank said. "Just regrets that Ed pushed it so far."

The shoot-out had drawn a lot of attention. People converged on the spot as Conrad helped Rebel to her feet. She went to her brothers and hugged them each in turn, not caring when some of the blood on Bob's hands got on her shirt.

The town marshal came hurrying up with a shotgun clutched in his hands. Frank explained what had happened, and since there were plenty of witnesses to back up his story, including Conrad Browning, the lawman nodded in acceptance.

"Don't know if there'll be an inquest or not," he said. "That'll be up to the county sheriff and the coroner. Will you be around for a while just in case there's a hearing, Mr. Morgan?"

"I may not be in town, but I'm not planning on leaving the area any time soon," Frank replied.

"That's good enough for me." The grizzled old star-packer shook his head as he looked down at Ed Callahan's sprawled body. "Too bad it had to come to this. I seen too much o' dyin' in the years I been wearin' a badge."

"We've all seen too much of dying," Frank said.

He waited until the crowd broke up and Ed Callahan's body had been carted off in the undertaker's wagon. Rebel was still talking to her brothers, so Frank took advantage of the opportunity to grasp Conrad's arm and draw him aside.

"You could have gotten killed, jumping into the middle of things like that," Frank said quietly.

"I'm sorry. I know I could have gotten *you* killed. But when I saw that Rebel was in danger, I . . . I just didn't stop to think. I had to save her."

"Does she know how you feel about her?"

"Well, I've wanted to tell her . . . but it's complicated. There was all that business with Pamela—"

"Who?"

Conrad sighed. "That's right, you don't even know about her — or her father."

"Nope," Frank said with a shake of his head. "I reckon I'm lost."

"It's a long story." Conrad glanced at Rebel. "It looks like Rebel's going to be busy with her brothers for a while, so why don't we go over to the Big Nugget and have a drink? I can tell you all about it there, and I'm sure Jonas Wade would like to say hello to you."

"Jonas Wade?" Frank repeated with a puzzled frown. "The gambler I ran into back in El Paso?"

"That's right. He owns the Big Nugget Saloon now."

Frank grunted. "Sounds like everybody's been mighty busy while I was poking around the mountains and getting captured by saboteurs and Apaches."

"What?" Conrad asked, his eyes widening.

"Come on," Frank said with a grin. "Let's get that drink, and we can tell each other all about it."

By the time an hour had passed, both Frank and Conrad had been brought up to date on each other's activities while they were apart. They sat at a table in a corner of the Big Nugget with Jonas Wade, nursing mugs of beer as they filled each other in. As Conrad had predicted, Wade was glad to see Frank.

"A man gets tired of moving around," Wade said after he explained about winning the saloon in a poker game. "Ophir's a mighty nice place. I aim to settle here."

Frank nodded. "I can understand that. They may call me The Drifter, but that doesn't mean I haven't thought about settling down too."

Wade leaned forward in his chair. "Why

don't you?" he asked. "Marshal Everett's getting on in years and will probably retire soon. I know the town council would be thrilled to give you the job."

Frank shook his head. "I've worn a badge before. It's not something I'd care to do again."

"So do something else," Wade urged. "Buy a ranch, maybe raise some horses."

"Someday," Frank said, even though he knew perfectly well that day would probably never come. "Someday I might just do that." He took another sip of his beer. "Right now, though, I'm more interested in this fella Tarleton. Are you sure those gunslicks you overheard were talking about him?"

Wade nodded. "I'm certain. I was surprised to hear hombres like that talking about a man like Tarleton, so I paid particular attention. It sure sounded to me like they were working for him."

"That makes no sense," Conrad put in. "I know what you're thinking, Frank. But Clark Tarleton owns a mine near here. The railroad coming to Ophir will benefit him too. He wouldn't be interested in stopping my spur line from getting through."

"Unless he's a member of the syndicate that owns the Southwestern and Pacific," Frank said. "You said yourself he has a lot of different business interests, and he's from Philadelphia. That fella Scheer told me the syndicate has offices in Philadelphia and Boston."

"I have offices in Boston," Conrad pointed out. "That doesn't make me one of the syndicate."

"No, but I don't think we can rule out Tarleton's involvement. After all, he's right here in Ophir where Royal and those other gunmen could report to him on the sly."

Conrad shook his head. "It's just difficult for me to believe, that's all. But I suppose you're right. We have to consider the possibility. What's our next move?"

"Scheer's life is in my hands," Frank said grimly. "I'm convinced the attack on Mano Rojo's people was carried out by Royal and his bunch. If they're working for Tarleton, we've got to spook them into coming out in the open somehow, so that the connection will be exposed."

"How do we do that?" Conrad asked, keeping his voice low so that the conversation wouldn't be overheard.

An idea had occurred to Frank as he thought back on the things that Scheer had told him. "If you can figure out some way to talk to Tarleton again, tell him that the spur line's route is going to be changed. Tell him

411

it's going to angle to the west after it crosses the gorge and go through the natural cut in the ridge."

"How's that going to do us any good?" Conrad asked with a frown.

"I got a pretty good look at that ridge while I was with Scheer," Frank explained. "The cut in it is a deep one, and the wall on the east side bulges out quite a bit."

Conrad nodded. "Yes, that's why Nathan decided not to route the tracks through there. Too much danger of rock slides, or of that whole side of the cut collapsing one of these days. We wouldn't want it to fall on one of our trains."

"Of course not. But if you told that to Tarleton, and then something was to happen . . . like an explosion that blew down the wall of that cut, say . . . then we'd know it had to be Tarleton who gave Royal the orders."

Conrad's hand clenched into a fist. "By God, you're right! I hate to think that he's capable of such a thing, but we have to find out."

"And if nothing happens, we've cleared Tarleton as a suspect," Frank pointed out.

Conrad nodded decisively. "All right. I'll do it. I'm not sure how I'll manage to have the conversation with him, since we're on the outs at the moment, but I'll think of something."

"Don't waste any time," Frank urged. "I just have a week to uncover the ringleader before those Apaches kill Scheer."

"You're hoping that once we have the goods on Tarleton — if he's guilty — he'll confess to being behind the attack on the Apaches too?"

"If he's guilty, he'll tell us the truth about all of it," Frank said grimly. "One way or the other."

The discussion might have continued, but at that moment Jonas Wade said, "Good Lord! What's a lady like her doing in here?"

Frank and Conrad looked toward the entrance of the Big Nugget, as Wade was doing, and Frank saw why the saloon keeper was surprised. A very attractive redheaded woman about thirty years old had just pushed through the batwings and now paused there, looking around. She wore a high-necked, long-sleeved dress that was positively prim next to the spangled getups sported by the saloon girls. As the old saying went, she was as out of place as teats on a boar hog.

But when her gaze lit on Frank, Conrad, and Jonas Wade, she smiled and started straight across the room toward them.

Chapter 32

Conrad stood up and went to meet the woman, saying, "Mrs. McShane, it's good to see you again. Were you looking for me?"

"For your friend Mr. Morgan actually," the redhead replied. She didn't slow down as Conrad fell in step beside her. She marched up to the table and said to Frank, "Are you Frank Morgan, sir?"

He came to his feet and took his hat off. "Yes, ma'am, I am."

"Allison McShane," she said, introducing herself, sticking her hand out like a man. "I'm the editor and publisher of the Ophir *Ledger*."

Frank shook hands with her. "Glad to meet you, Mrs. McShane."

"I heard about the unfortunate incident in front of the hotel," Allison said. "Would you care to comment on it?"

Frank shook his head. "No, I don't believe

I would. It's over, and I'd like to leave it that way."

"Then perhaps you'd consent to a more wide-ranging interview. I'd like to inform the readers of the *Ledger* that a famous man is in our midst."

Frank hesitated. He had been interviewed by journalists many times, but seldom by one as pretty as this Allison McShane. Never, come to think of it. But he didn't care for publicity. Newspaper stories and dime novels had already done enough to inflate his reputation almost beyond believability.

"I appreciate it, but I don't reckon that would be a good idea."

"I disagree," she said crisply. "I think the readers would be very interested."

Frank shook his head. "Sorry, no."

"Well, I tried," Allison said. Something about her made Frank think that she wasn't giving up so easily, though. She would bide her time and try again. But now she just looked around the Big Nugget and said, "So this is what a saloon looks like."

"Yes, ma'am," Wade said. "You've never been in one before?"

She smiled reprovingly at him. "Do I look like the sort of woman who would frequent saloons?"

"No, ma'am, you don't. I meant no offense."

"None taken." Allison lowered her voice a little. "Why are so many people staring at me?"

It was true. Quite a few of the miners and townsmen in the saloon were looking at her. Frank said, "I reckon it's because they're not used to seeing a lady of your quality in here, Mrs. McShane. I'm not sure Mr. McShane would be happy about it either."

"There is no Mr. McShane. I'm a widow."

"Oh. Sorry to hear that."

"No apology necessary. You couldn't have known." She paused and then asked Frank, "Are you certain you won't reconsider about that interview?"

"I'm sure."

"Ah, well, that's journalism's loss, I suppose." She smiled at the three of them. "Good day, Mr. Morgan. Mr. Browning. And Mr. . . . ?"

"Jonas Wade, ma'am." The saloon keeper stepped forward eagerly. "Let me see you out."

"Thank you. You're a gentleman despite your profession."

"Yes, ma'am."

Frank chuckled as he and Conrad sat down again while Wade escorted Mrs. Mc-

Shane out of the saloon. "Jonas needs to put his eyes back in his head," Frank commented. "Can't really blame him for being impressed, though. Mrs. McShane is a mighty pretty woman."

"And a persistent one," Conrad said. "She'll ask you for that interview again."

"I figured as much. I might give one to her if we can get this business with the railroad cleared up first."

"I'll talk to Tarleton," Conrad said again.

"And I'll go tend to Stormy and see about leaving Dog at the livery stable too."

Wade came back to the table as Frank and Conrad got up. "I'd seen Mrs. McShane around town," he said, "but I'm glad I got the chance to meet her."

Frank smiled. "She's quite a lady."

"Yeah." Wade rubbed his jaw. "Too good for a ne'er-do-well like me," he said musingly.

"Oh, I don't know. Looks to me like you're putting down roots. You're going to be a successful businessman."

"Yeah — in the saloon business."

Frank clapped a hand on Wade's shoulder. "No point in giving up before you even get started. Why don't you just wait and see what happens?"

"Yeah. Yeah, I might do that. Wonder if

Mrs. McShane would like to go to supper some night."

Frank and Conrad left him mulling that over and went on about their own errands.

The owner of the local livery stable was impressed with Stormy, and was happy to let Dog stay there too while Frank was in town. "I'll take good care of those critters of yours, Mr. Morgan," he promised.

"I don't think of them as my critters so much as I do my friends," Frank said.

"Well, either way they'll be just fine here."

Frank shook hands with the man and left. Night had fallen, and while some of the buildings in Ophir had grown dark, most still showed lights in their windows. The street and the boardwalks were still busy too.

Frank headed for the hotel, intending to get some supper in the dining room. As he came into the lobby, though, he saw Conrad coming toward him. The younger man's face lit up in a grin as he saw Frank.

"I did it," he said. "I talked to Tarleton."

"That was fast. How did you work it?"

"I approached him as a businessman and told him that we could still help each other make money, despite the fact that I'm no longer going to marry his daughter. I talked to him about freight rates once the spur line reaches Ophir."

Frank nodded. "Pretty smart. It sounds reasonable enough, and it gave you an excuse to mention the change in the route, I reckon."

"Exactly." Conrad looked pleased with himself, and as far as Frank was concerned, he had a reason to be.

"First thing in the morning I'll ride back out to the construction camp," Frank said. "Sam Brant needs to be told what's going on. Then we just have to wait and see what happens."

A worried frown suddenly creased Conrad's forehead. "What if Tarleton doesn't do anything right away? It'll still take time to finish that trestle, so he may not think he needs to take action yet."

"Before I left the camp, I talked to Brant about getting started on the tracks on this side of the gorge, while the trestle work was still going on. If Tarleton's men see that and report it to him, he may decide to go ahead and have that cut blown up now."

"You sound more convinced than ever that Tarleton's behind everything," Conrad commented.

"It makes sense," Frank said. "The simplest answer is always the one that's most likely to be true."

"Well, I hope you're right. I'm ready to see an end to this trouble."

"So am I," Frank said.

He left early the next morning, riding south toward the construction camp. Stormy was glad for the chance to really stretch his legs, and they made good time, arriving at the camp in the middle of the afternoon. On the way in, Frank saw that Sam Brant had adopted his suggestion and had men carry rails and cross-ties across the river and start laying them on the roadbed to the north of the gorge. It was slow work, though, and only a hundred yards or so of track had been laid. If Nathan Buckhalter began surveying a route that curved from the present one and went through the cut in the ridge, it would certainly look like the railroad was about to swing in that direction too. All it would take would be to stake out the route and perhaps start grading another roadbed. The effort had to look convincing, but that was all.

Sam Brant was halfway up on the trestle as Frank rode by. The damaged sections had been cleared away, and work was well under way to replace them. Brant spotted Frank and waved at him. The construction boss began climbing down the spidery framework.

Frank reined in and waited for Brant. When the superintendent reached the bottom of the trestle, he dropped off a support beam and said, "Welcome back, Frank! The boys had just about given up on you, but I figured you were still around somewhere."

"I've been a far piece, all right," Frank agreed. "Around in the mountains and all the way to Ophir and back. Has there been any trouble while I was gone?"

Brant shook his head. "Not a bit. You must've scared those bastards off."

"It would be nice to think so, but I know that's not the case." Frank inclined his head toward the railroad cars. "Let's go where we can talk in private. I've got a lot to tell you."

That put a worried frown on Brant's rugged face. He stalked up the path to the top of the gorge. Frank swung down from the saddle and walked with him, leading Stormy.

Once they were inside the superintendent's car, Frank explained everything that had happened since he rode out a few days earlier. Brant's expression grew more worried the longer Frank talked.

"I know that fella Scheer," Brant said when Frank was finished. "I know of him, I suppose I should say. Never actually met him. I don't think you should trust anything that somebody who works for the SW and P tells you."

"He didn't have any reason to lie about anything. And there was certainly nothing fake about what that bunch of hired killers was doing to him."

"Yeah, I guess you're right about that," Brant said grudgingly.

"What about Tarleton? Have you ever heard any rumors connecting him to the rival railroad?"

"No, I can't say as I have. That doesn't necessarily mean anything, though. I work out in the field, not in the offices. Always have."

Frank nodded. "Can you get Nathan Buckhalter to cooperate and make it look like you're changing the route?"

"Sure, Nathan'll do whatever I tell him to. He was right about the route in the first place, though. That cut's just too dangerous. The fact that Scheer thinks the tracks should go through there is typical of the way the SW and P cuts corners to save a little money."

"Don't worry, you won't have to really lay tracks through there. I think Tarleton will act before it ever gets to that point."

"You're right. Some more of that stolen dynamite in the right place, and that whole wall of rock would come down and close off the cut for good."

Brant called in Nathan Buckhalter and explained everything to him. The surveyor nodded in understanding. "I'll make it look good," he told Frank. "Give me a day or two and I'll have plenty of stakes driven."

"I hope that'll be enough," Frank said. His head lifted as he heard a whistle. "What's that?"

Brant grinned. "Supply train comin' in from Lordsburg, with a whole new shipment of dynamite to replace the stuff those sons o' bitches stole and blew up. We've been waiting on the stuff. Now we can pick up the pace a little."

Frank nodded, remembering what Brant had said about having more explosives sent up from Lordsburg.

"First thing in the morning, we'll move it well away from the camp and cache it," Brant went on. "And this time it'll be well guarded around the clock."

"Good idea," Frank told him.

Brant went out to greet the engineer of the supply train. Frank followed him. The train consisted of a couple of flatcars piled high with more rails and ties, and an enclosed freight car. That would be where the shipment of dynamite was. Since there was no way for the locomotive to turn around, the cars were run onto a temporary siding and then unhooked so that the locomotive and tender could travel back to Lordsburg in reverse the next day. There would be a round-house in Ophir where locomotives could turn around when the spur line was complete.

An hour later, dusk was settling down and the work had just about come to a halt for the day. Frank knew from his conversation with Brant that men were still standing guard all night. He stood on the platform at the front of the car and looked out at the gathering shadows, hoping that Walt Scheer was all right. He didn't particularly like the man, but he felt some responsibility for his well-being.

He wondered as well how things were going with Conrad and Rebel. Rebel would be good for Conrad, Frank thought, and the boy finally seemed to realize that. The two of them still had some kinks to iron out in their relationship, but Frank was willing to bet they could do it.

And one of these days, if all went well, he would be a grandfather. That was enough to put a smile on a man's face.

If nobody killed him first . . .

Chapter 33

Since the gunfight in front of the Holloway House had been a rather harrowing experience, Conrad figured that Rebel might need a little time to get over it. He didn't approach her until late the following afternoon, when he went to her room in the hotel and knocked on the door. When she opened it, he thought he saw pleasure in her eyes for a second, but then it was replaced by a look of wariness.

"What do you want?" she asked.

"I think we need to clear the air between us," Conrad declared.

A man's voice came from inside the room. "Clear the air about what?"

Conrad looked past Rebel and saw her brothers. Tom sat in an armchair while Bob perched on the edge of the bed. "Oh," he said. "Your brothers are here."

"Where else would they be?" Rebel asked.

"I assumed they had rooms in one of the other hotels or boardinghouses in town."

"As a matter of fact, we do," Bob said. "But we came over to talk to Rebel about what we're goin' to do next."

"That's right," Tom put in. "We ain't got a ranch to go back to no more, so we got to figure out where we want to go."

"Or if we want to stay here," Bob went on. "We're good hands, and there are several growing ranches hereabouts. With all the miners that need feedin', there's a good beef market."

Conrad nodded. "That's true." He looked at Rebel. "But what would you do?"

"I can make a hand too," she said with a touch of defiance in her voice. "Bound to be some rancher who'll hire me."

"Maybe you could stay here in town," Tom said with a sly smile. "I reckon Mr. Browning here would like that."

"Yeah, since he wants to court you and all," Bob put in.

Rebel blushed and whirled on him. "You hush that up! Nobody's said anything about courtin'!"

"Well, he'd better," Tom said, inclining his head toward Conrad, "or else we're liable to get a mite suspicious of his intentions. And seein' as how we're your brothers, we might

426

just have to give him a whippin' if he don't mean to do right by you."

Conrad felt his face warming. He put a hand on Rebel's arm and asked, "Is there someplace we could go and talk privately?"

"I sure hope so," she said fervently. "Let's get away from these two. They've gone plumb loco."

"It's almost supper time," Conrad said as Rebel stepped out into the hall and pulled the door closed behind her. She was wearing a dress again, and he thought she looked lovely. "There's a restaurant in the next block. Why don't we try it instead of the hotel dining room for a change?"

"Sounds good to me," Rebel agreed.

As they left the hotel and started down the boardwalk, Conrad took a chance and linked his arm with hers. She didn't pull away, and he took that as an encouraging sign.

"You know, you could stay here in Ophir," he said. "I'm sure you could get a job."

"Doin' what? Being a maid or a cook in the hotel? Clerkin' in some store?" She shook her head. "That's not the sort of thing I want to spend my life doin'."

"Actually, I was thinking that perhaps you could work for me," Conrad said. "Once the railroad goes through, I'll be spending a lot of time here, and I'll need a capable assistant."

Rebel laughed. "Work for you? I don't think so."

Conrad wasn't sure if he should feel offended by her reaction or not. "You wouldn't even consider it?"

"That just wouldn't work out, Conrad. Trust me on that."

"All right," he said grudgingly. "But I'm sure we can come up with something."

"I'll think on it," she promised.

Before they reached the restaurant, Conrad heard his name called. He and Rebel stopped and turned. Allison McShane was coming up behind them on the boardwalk. "Good evening, Mr. Browning," she said. She gave Rebel a friendly smile and a nod. "Miss Callahan."

"What can we do for you, Mrs. McShane?" Conrad asked. Night had fallen, and he was eager to sit down to supper with Rebel.

"I've been looking for Mr. Morgan," Allison said. "I'd still like to persuade him to let me conduct an interview with him. But I can't seem to find him anywhere in town."

"He rode out early this morning," Conrad explained.

"On business?"

Conrad hesitated. He didn't want to go into detail about what Frank was doing or where he had gone. But for all her gentility,

Allison McShane was like a bulldog once she got her jaws locked on something.

As it turned out, Conrad didn't have to come up with an answer. Three dark shapes moved out of an alley mouth behind her, and a voice said, "Hold it, Browning! Don't move!"

Conrad's hand dropped toward the butt of the Colt Lightning on his hip. He didn't know if these men intended to rob him or kidnap him, but since Rebel and Mrs. McShane were with him, he had to protect them. It was an instinctive reaction.

He didn't get a chance to draw the gun. With a rush of footsteps from the other direction, two men jumped him. A six-gun rose and fell, thudding against Conrad's skull. Brilliant lights exploded inside his brain like Fourth of July rockets, followed by a sweeping tide of blackness.

But just before he sank into that stygian abyss, Conrad heard something that chilled him to the core of his being. One of the men who had attacked him ordered in a harsh whisper, "Grab the women too! We'll take them with us!"

Then Conrad knew nothing more.

Frank was restless that night as he slept in Brant's railroad car. Some instinct had him on edge, and even though he couldn't explain it, he knew better than to ignore it. When he came awake, far into the night, he sat up in the bunk he was using and looked around in the darkness. Snoring came from several of the other bunks.

Then he heard again what must have woken him. Through the open window beside him came the sound of growling. Dog was supposed to be sleeping outside the car, but something was bothering the big cur.

Frank trusted Dog's instincts and senses as much as he trusted his own. He swung his legs off the bunk, pushed his feet down into his boots, and stood up. Quickly, he buckled on his gunbelt. Thinking that he ought to wake Sam Brant in case there really was some threat to the camp, he stepped across the aisle and reached down to give the superintendent's shoulder a shake.

But Brant wasn't there. The construction boss's bunk was empty.

Frank's forehead creased in the darkness. Maybe Brant had woken up and sensed there was trouble too. He might already be out there, taking a look around the camp. Frank walked quietly to the back of the car, eased the door open, and stepped out onto the platform. He dropped lithely to the ground.

Dog came padding over to him and nuzzled his hand. "What's wrong, old boy?" Frank asked in a whisper. Dog looked toward the siding where the freight car and the flatcars were parked, and a whine came from deep in his throat. "Quiet," Frank told him, and then both of them started toward the siding, moving soundlessly through the shadows. Frank's jeans and dark blue shirt made it more difficult to see him in the darkness, and he was grateful for that.

Before he reached the siding, he heard something else that surprised him: a low, rumbling sound from the tracks beyond the cars. The locomotive that had brought the supplies was getting up steam again.

Frank glanced at the sky. The stars told him it was well after midnight, but it wouldn't be dawn for a couple of hours yet. If the locomotive was pulling out for Lordsburg, it was getting a mighty early start. But he supposed that was possible, and it might explain why Sam Brant wasn't in his bunk as well. The construction boss might have gone to talk to the train crew before the locomotive pulled out. Frank relaxed slightly, thinking that maybe he had been too suspicious.

Then the next moment he tensed again as he heard voices and realized that he hadn't been suspicious enough.

"Damn it, why'd you bring them out here? Why didn't you just kill them in town?"

"Because that's not what the boss ordered us to do. And since he's your boss too, you can take it up with him, I reckon."

Frank stood there breathing shallowly as his brain tried to digest what he had just heard. The first voice belonged unmistakably to Sam Brant. The second one was less familiar, but the circumstances under which Frank had heard it before meant that he was unlikely to forget it. The second man was Royal, the leader of the gang that had been carrying out the sabotage.

But not the mastermind, though. Royal was just working for somebody else, as was Sam Brant. Hadn't Royal just said that they had the same boss?

Brant was a traitor, working against Conrad and the railroad. That was hard to believe. Frank had liked and trusted the man, and he had always been a good judge of character.

Everyone made mistakes sometimes, though, even The Drifter. The important thing was that it wasn't too late to rectify this one. Frank eased his gun out of its holster and slid through the shadows, moving closer to the car that held the dynamite shipment. He saw several dark shapes standing there, shapes that were men.

"Who's that woman anyway?" Brant asked.

"Hell if I know," Royal replied. "She was with the Browning kid when we grabbed him, along with that girl. Tarleton told us to bring all of 'em out here and turn them over to you. He said you could get rid of 'em so that nobody would ever know what happened to them."

Frank froze again. Royal and some of his men had kidnapped Conrad in Ophir, that much was obvious. From the sound of it, Rebel had been with him and was a prisoner too. That didn't come as a real surprise. Who was the other woman Royal had mentioned? Frank had no idea, unless it was Allison McShane. She was the only other woman in Ophir Conrad was acquainted with, as far as Frank knew.

Now he had to be more careful than ever. Not only did he have to worry about starting a gunfight around that dynamite, but he also had to think about the safety of the prisoners.

"Yeah, I know what to do with them," Brant said. "Open the door of that freight car and toss them inside. There's enough dynamite in there to blow practically this whole camp to Kingdom Come, and if they're on top of it when it goes off, there won't be enough of them left for anybody to ever find. Nobody can prove we had a thing to do with their disappearance."

Frank's blood felt like ice water in his veins as he listened to Brant. The traitor planned to set off a third explosion, the biggest blast of them all. From the sound of what Brant had in mind, the explosion would kill most of the workers and destroy all the supplies. It would be a setback that the New Mexico, Rio Grande, and Oriental couldn't overcome, especially if its principal owner, Conrad Browning, was also dead. Brant — and Tarleton — would win. Frank had no doubt now that Tarleton was connected to the rival railroad. With his mining interests, if he was able to take over the building of the spur line as well, Clark Tarleton would soon be the most powerful man in the territory.

And all it would take to accomplish that goal was hundreds of deaths.

Carefully, so that it wouldn't make too much noise, one of the hired killers slid back the door of the freight car. "Damn," he said. "How many crates o' dynamite you got in here?"

"Enough," Brant said. "Enough to do the job. I made sure that extra cases were sent up from Lordsburg."

Frank wasn't sure how Brant intended to explain how he survived the blast. Then the answer came to him. The locomotive. Brant was going to take the engine and pull it back out of range of the giant explosion. He could claim that he was going back to Lordsburg on the railroad's business, and no one would be alive to deny the story. The locomotive had only an engineer and a fireman on it, and Brant could pay them off, if he hadn't already, or even kill them to keep them quiet.

One by one, three bodies were lifted from the ground and heaved into the freight car with the dynamite. Brant himself closed the door except for a small gap and said, "All right, get the hell out of here. I'll give you time to get away and then light the fuse. Steam's up in the engine, so it won't take me long to pull out either."

"All right, Brant. Tell Tarleton we'll be waitin' in the usual place for the rest of our money," Royal said.

"I'll tell him."

Royal and the half-dozen men with him began to drift away into the night. Frank waited for them to leave. A pitched gun battle was the last thing he wanted right now. Stray bullets might penetrate the walls of that freight car and strike Conrad or one of the women. Or worse, hit some of that dynamite and set it off. Frank couldn't take that chance. Royal and his men could be rounded up later.

Brant had left the freight car door open about a foot. Frank guessed that the fuse leading to the dynamite came out through that gap. When Royal and his men were gone, Brant fished out a lucifer and snapped it to life on his thumbnail. The sudden flare of the match lit up his face for a second.

That was when Frank stepped up behind him, gun leveled, and said, "Drop the match, Sam."

Brant stiffened. "Morgan!" he breathed.

"That's right, Sam, and I heard enough to know what you've been up to — and what you're about to do."

"Better back off, gunfighter," Brant warned. "All I have to do is touch this match to the fuse, and the whole place blows up."

"Not quite. I imagine that's a pretty slow-burning fuse. Go ahead and light it. I'll have plenty of time to kill you and then come put it out."

"Maybe . . . if I light the end of it."

Brant did something then that Frank didn't expect. He flipped the burning lucifer through the gap, into the freight car. At the same instant, his other hand came up, gripped the door, and slammed it shut, so that Frank couldn't see if the match landed on the fuse inside the car or not. Brant lunged to the side, twisting and clawing a gun out of his pocket.

Frank fired, but Brant was moving, and while the bullet clipped him and made him stagger, it didn't bring him down. Colt flame bloomed in the darkness as Brant returned the fire. Bullets whistled past Frank's head as he was forced to dive behind a nearby stack of cross-ties for cover.

Then Brant was off and running toward the engine, while Frank had no idea whether the fuse was burning, or if it was, how close it was to the dynamite.

They might be minutes — or even bare seconds — away from a blast that would be like the end of the world for anyone unlucky enough to be caught in it.

Chapter 34

Frank had no choice. He jammed his Colt back in its holster, scrambled over the pile of ties, and sprinted toward the freight car. He shouted, "Dog! Get him!" as he ran. Dog took off after Brant.

With his heart slugging in his chest, Frank reached up, grabbed the door of the freight car, and pulled. The door slid on its tracks, banging back against the stops. Sparks lit up the inside of the car as they crawled along the fuse toward the stacked crates of explosives. Frank was barely aware of Conrad, Rebel Callahan, and Allison McShane lying there unconscious, unaware of the razor-thin margin that stood between them and death.

Brant's toss had been a good one. The lucifer had landed on the fuse only a couple of feet from where it was attached to a box of blasting powder. The small explosion that would result from that would set off a much larger one as it spread to the crates of dynamite. The fuse burned about a foot per minute, and more than half of it was already gone.

Frank grasped the floor of the freight car and levered himself up and in. On his knees, he lunged across the intervening space and reached desperately for the fuse. His hand closed around the burning end, smothering the sparks with his bare flesh. His lips pulled back from his teeth at the burning pain, but it was as nothing compared to the relief that flooded through him as the fuse went out. Just to make sure, he yanked it loose from the box of blasting powder and threw what was left of it aside.

Still on his knees, he turned to Conrad, Rebel, and Allison. A quick check told him that they were all alive and seemed to be all right except for being knocked out and tied up. Leaving them where they were, he slid out of the car and dropped to the ground beside the tracks.

The locomotive was gone, backing away from the camp with a chugging and puffing of its engine. Brant was getting away.

Frank ran toward the makeshift corral where the horses were kept. A whistle alerted Stormy that he was on his way, and the big Appaloosa was ready, tossing his head in anticipation. Frank threw the gate open, ran inside, and swung up bareback. There was no time for a saddle and tack. Stormy didn't mind, though. He burst out of the corral and launched into a gallop, obeying the commands that Frank communicated with his knees and heels. Frank grabbed the Appaloosa's mane and held on.

Men were already coming out of their tents and yelling questions in response to the shots that had been fired a couple of minutes earlier. They would see the door of the freight car standing open and would find Conrad and the women. Meanwhile, Frank sent Stormy racing along beside the railroad tracks as the locomotive continued to back away. It was picking up speed now, even going backward.

Frank and Stormy passed Dog, who was bounding along barking. Frank knew from that that the big cur had been unable to catch Brant before the man reached the locomotive. Brant was trying to escape even though he had to realize by now that his plan to blow up the camp was ruined. He had run a big risk — if the dynamite in the freight car had exploded, the locomotive might not have been far enough away to escape the blast — but since Frank had had the drop on him, he hadn't had any choice but to chance it.

Sparks cascaded upward from the diamond stack of the big Baldwin locomotive. As Frank drew closer, he saw spurts of orange flame from the cab. Brant must have spotted him giving chase and was firing at him. Frank leaned forward over Stormy's neck, making himself a smaller target. He urged the Appaloosa on. He had to catch up soon, or the train would pick up so much speed that it would outdistance him.

Stormy stretched his legs, pouring every bit of his speed and stamina into the pursuit. The gap between horse and locomotive dwindled, then began to grow larger again. Frank could almost feel Stormy reach down inside himself and bring up one last burst of speed.

They passed the cowcatcher and were alongside the engine. Brant triggered more shots from the cab. Frank returned the fire and saw sparks fly as his bullets spanged off the metal sides of the cab. Brant was leaning out to the side, trying to get a better shot, but he jerked back as Frank's bullets came too close.

Stormy drew even with the cab. Frank holstered his Colt, reached out for the nearest grab-iron, and swung himself off Stormy's back and into the cab. His boots had barely touched the floor of it when Brant lunged at him, swinging the fireman's shovel. Frank ducked under it. The shovel hit the brake lever and knocked it forward. With a shriek of metal against metal, the speeding locomotive began to slow.

Frank saw a couple of still, huddled shapes on the floor of the cab, and realized that they belonged to the engineer and fireman. They must not have been working with Brant after all. He had shot them both once the locomotive was under way. Frank lunged at Brant while the man was off balance from the missed blow with the shovel, but his foot slipped in the pool of blood that had spread around the engineer's body. Frank tackled Brant, but awkwardly, and Brant didn't go down. He smacked the handle of the shovel against Frank's head.

Dizzy from the blow, Frank fell to the floor of the cab. He rolled to the side as Brant tried again to bash his brains out with the shovel. Lifting his leg, Frank kicked Brant in the hip, knocking him toward the controls at the front of the cab as the train finally lurched to a stop.

Brant hit the throttle and knocked it wide open. The train began to lumber forward as Brant slashed back and forth with the shovel, aiming the blows at Frank's head. Frank barely avoided them, and finally managed to reach out and grab Brant's ankle. He heaved as hard as he could.

Brant went over backward and landed hard on the floor of the cab. Frank came up on his knees and reached for his Colt, but it was gone. It had slipped out of the holster sometime during the fight. He lunged at Brant instead, swinging his fist. The punch landed solidly as Brant tried to get up. Both men sprawled across the cab. Frank almost fell out, but he grabbed the side at the last second and stopped himself.

They surged to their feet at the same time and stood there slugging away at each other. From the corner of his eye, Frank saw that the locomotive was barreling through the construction camp. The siding where the freight car full of dynamite was parked flashed past. Men ran along the tracks, waving their arms and yelling, although Frank couldn't hear them over the rumble of the engine.

Brant landed a punch that slammed Frank back against the coal tender. He bent and snatched a gun from the floor. Frank knew it was the one that had fallen from his holster. Brant thrust the revolver at him and shouted, "You've ruined everything, Morgan, but at least you'll die!"

"Brant!" Frank shouted back, pointing

ahead of them. "The trestle!"

Brant's eyes widened with terror as he realized what was about to happen. He dropped the gun, then spun around and lunged toward the controls. At the same moment, Frank leaped from the cab, sailing out into the air, taking his chances this way. He had a last glimpse of Brant inside the cab, leaning against the brake lever. Sparks shot from the drivers as a metallic scream like the unholy wail of a banshee filled the air.

But it was too late. The locomotive reached the end of the tracks and plunged out onto the unfinished trestle, which buckled under the huge weight. For an instant, the locomotive seemed to leap out into the yawning emptiness of the gorge. . . .

Then it plunged down, taking Sam Brant with it.

The crash was awesome. Frank saw it from the bush at the edge of the gorge where he hung with his feet dangling. He had been able to grab the bush as he fell after his leap from the cab of the runaway locomotive. A ball of fire blossomed in the rocks along the river as the locomotive and the tender slammed into them. Frank looked down and thought that while the explosion was only a fraction of the size of the one that Brant had planned, it was still a fitting end for the traitor. Frank turned his head away as some of the sizzling debris pelted down around him.

Then he started to climb, pulling himself up from the edge of the gorge. He wasn't to the top yet when a hand reached down from above and clamped strongly around his wrist.

"Let me help you . . . Dad," Conrad said.

Clark Tarleton was seated in the lobby of the Holloway House when Frank walked into the hotel the next afternoon. The industrialist and mining magnate was reading a copy of the Ophir *Ledger*, and he didn't seem to notice Frank at first. Finally, though, Tarleton lowered the paper and looked over it at the man standing in front of him, and his eyes grew wide with shock.

"Thought I was dead, didn't you, Tarleton," Frank said. "I'm not. Neither are Conrad, Rebel, or Mrs. McShane. But Sam Brant is, and so is Royal. Brant died last night out at the construction camp, and Royal went down this morning when him and his gang were paid a visit by a posse that Marshal Everett put together on the quiet, so you wouldn't hear about it and take off for the tall and uncut. I wanted at least one more witness who would testify against you, and we got more than that. Royal's bunch

445

put up a fight, but several of them surrendered when they figured out they were trapped. They talked, Tarleton. They talked a lot. Told us all about how you had men posted at heliograph stations between here and the camp so you and Brant could talk to each other by flashing Morse code from one station to the next. That's how you gave Brant his orders. Pretty slick setup. In the end, though, it wasn't enough."

Tarleton's face had hardened as Frank talked. As Frank fell silent, Tarleton blustered, "You're insane, sir. I don't even know you."

"I think you do. I'm Frank Morgan."

Tarleton rattled his newspaper. "You're a madman as far as I'm concerned."

"Bluff all you want," Frank said. "I heard Brant and Royal admit last night that they were working for you. I reckon when the authorities here get in touch with the ones back East, they'll find out pretty quicklike that you own part of the Southwestern and Pacific Railroad. You may own all of it through some dummy companies, for all I know. You had plenty of reason for wanting Conrad's spur line to fail, so your railroad could take it over. That motive, and the testimony of the men who are in custody, will be enough to put you behind bars for a long time, Tarleton."

Tarleton folded the paper and slapped it against his thigh. His eyes cut first one way, then the other.

Frank smiled. "Thinking about making a run for it? I wouldn't advise it."

"I . . . I know who you are," Tarleton said. His carefully controlled façade was slipping. "You're a gunfighter. I'd have no chance against you. I won't fight you."

Frank held up his right hand. There was a burn on the palm. "I can still draw, but I'd rather not until this heals up. That's why I brought along some help, just in case you started a ruckus."

Conrad stepped through the door Frank had left open behind him. He said to Tarleton, "Come along, Clark. The marshal is waiting for you. You'll be spending some time in his jail, until the sheriff can get up here from Lordsburg to take custody of you."

"Conrad." Tarleton set the paper aside and stood up. "How can you do this? You can't believe this madness. You and I were friends."

Conrad shook his head. "Not really. You tried several times to have me killed."

"My God! How can you believe that? You were going to marry my daughter!"

"You never would have allowed that to

447

happen. You've had me marked for death for a long time."

The color had drained out of Tarleton's face, leaving it ashen and haggard. His hands clenched into fists. "I won't go to jail," he growled as Conrad came forward.

"You don't have any choice in the matter," Conrad said.

"The hell I don't!"

And with that, Tarleton lunged forward, swinging a fist at Conrad's head.

Conrad leaned to the side, letting the blow go harmlessly past his ear. He stepped in closer and hooked a right to Tarleton's midsection. The punch knocked the breath out of Tarleton, but he managed to grab Conrad and barreled into him, knocking him over backward. Both men crashed to the floor of the lobby.

Frank stepped back, giving them plenty of room.

Tarleton landed on top of Conrad. Clubbing his fists together, he slammed them into the younger man's jaw. Conrad was stunned, but he had the presence of mind to heave his back up off the floor, throwing Tarleton off balance. Tarleton fell to the side, still gasping for air.

Conrad rolled over and came to his feet, beating Tarleton by a couple of seconds. He could have stepped in and struck as Tarleton was struggling to his feet, but he held back, letting his opponent get upright again before he waded in. Conrad landed a couple of hard punches, but Tarleton was tough enough to absorb a considerable amount of punishment. He shrugged off the blows and threw a hard left and right of his own. The combination landed on Conrad's chest and chin and rocked him back a step. Catching his balance, Conrad set himself and drove a straight right into Tarleton's mouth as the older man bored in. Blood spurted as the punch pulped Tarleton's lips and staggered him.

Conrad didn't let up now. He came in hard and fast, sledging punches that pushed Tarleton back across the lobby. Tarleton ran into the registration desk and knocked it over on the clerk, who had taken refuge behind it. As the brutal combat surged back in the other direction, Frank stepped forward and lifted the desk, rescuing the hapless clerk.

By now, quite a crowd had begun to gather. Rebel and her brothers stood just inside the door of the hotel, along with Allison McShane, Jonas Wade, and Marshal Steve Everett. Wade was holding Allison's hand, and she didn't seem to mind. More of the townspeople pushed in to watch Conrad and Tarleton slugging away at each other.

Suddenly, a scream came from the staircase leading down to the lobby from the second floor. Conrad's head jerked around. He saw Pamela Tarleton standing there, hands pressed to her face in horror, a look of disbelief in her eyes.

The distraction gave Tarleton a chance. He smashed a right and a left into Conrad's face, knocking the younger man off his feet. Tarleton had to know by now that he had no hope of escape, but since no one was interfering, he pressed his attack, obviously intent on making Conrad pay for helping to ruin all his plans. Tarleton drew his leg back to deliver a devastating kick to his fallen opponent.

Conrad twisted out of the way, though, and reached up to grab Tarleton's leg. He heaved on the leg and brought Tarleton crashing down. Scrambling onto his knees, Conrad threw himself forward and got his hands around Tarleton's neck. He bounced Tarleton's head off the floor and then started throttling the life out of him. . . .

Frank stepped forward, got hold of his son, and pulled Conrad up and off the now-senseless Tarleton. "That's enough," Frank said. "You don't want to kill him."

"You're wrong about that," Conrad said as he lifted a trembling hand and wiped the back of it across his bloodstained mouth. "Right now I'd like very much to kill him. But I won't. We'll let the law handle him."

"Wise decision, youngster," Marshal Everett said as he came forward with a pair of handcuffs. He bent over and snapped them around Tarleton's wrists. Then he motioned to some of the townsmen and said, "Take him down to the hoosegow. I'll be along in a minute to lock him up."

Conrad turned toward the stairs, where Pamela still stood staring at him. "I'm sorry it had to be this way," he said to her. "I truly am. Hurting you was something I never wanted to do."

She wiped tears from her cheeks as her father was picked up and hustled out of the hotel. She spit, "Go to hell, Conrad Browning."

Rebel started forward, a fighting gleam in her eyes.

Frank moved to intercept her. "It's all over," he said quietly. "I reckon Conrad could use a gentle hand right about now. He won the fight, but he took quite a bit of punishment along the way."

Rebel glared at Pamela for a second longer, then turned to Conrad and smiled.

"Your pa's wrong about one thing," she said as she took his hand. "I think I'm the winner here."

Rebel and Conrad both were, Frank thought with a grin. That's what was so good about it.

Chapter 35

"You sure you want to boss this job your-self?" Frank asked.

"I can handle it," Conrad said confidently. "At least until my new construction superintendent can get here."

Frank held out his hand. "Well, good luck."

Conrad gripped Frank's hand firmly. "Thank you. Thank you for everything." He started to turn toward the street, where El Diablo waited and where Rebel was already mounted on her chestnut. Then he paused and said, "Frank . . . Dad . . . did I do all right?"

"You did fine, son," Frank said. "You did just fine."

Conrad nodded, mounted up, and turned his horse toward the south. Rebel was right beside him as the two of them rode away.

Damned dusty road, Frank thought as he

wiped away the little bit of moisture that had sprung up in his eyes.

A week had passed since the pair of showdowns, first with Sam Brant and then with Clark Tarleton. It had been a busy time too. Tarleton had been taken to Lordsburg, where he was now in jail awaiting trial on a multitude of charges. Frank had ridden out to visit with the Apaches, reclaiming Walt Scheer from them and explaining to Mano Rojo that justice had been done. Royal and quite a few other members of the gang were dead, and the rest were behind bars. So was Tarleton, who had been the driving force behind the whole thing, including the attack on Mano Rojo's people. Mano Rojo had agreed that he and the other warriors would follow Geronimo's example and turn themselves in to the Army, with a promise that they would fight no more. Frank was glad to hear that. He wasn't going to excuse the past behavior of the Apaches, but there weren't that many of them left. In the end, if they kept fighting, they would be hunted down and exterminated. A proud people deserved better than that, and Mano Rojo and his men had suffered enough tragedy already.

During the week, he had also sat down with Allison McShane for that interview she wanted, but in the course of their talk Frank had asked a couple of subtle questions of his own, finding out enough to know that Allison wasn't opposed to Jonas Wade courting her. Frank didn't know how things would work out between them — that was up to them — but he was glad that Jonas would at least have a chance with her.

Pamela Tarleton was on her way back to Philadelphia, might even be there by now. Conrad had seen to that, paying all the expenses of her trip home. Pamela had accepted his help. Not particularly graciously, but she was accustomed to being taken care of, and her father couldn't do that anymore. Rebel was of the opinion that Conrad ought to just leave Pamela to fend for herself, but of course he wasn't going to do that. He was too much the gentleman to abandon a lady in distress, even one who now hated him.

Other than that minor disagreement, Conrad and Rebel had come to a pretty good understanding. Frank figured there would be wedding bells for those two sooner or later. He hoped Conrad would invite him to the ceremony. That seemed likely, since he and his son were closer now than they had ever been. Of course, that didn't take much, but still, it was a good start.

Conrad was on his way out to take over the construction of the spur line and supervise it personally, at least for a while. Tom and Bob Callahan were already down there, working as hunters to provide fresh meat for the railroad workers.

Frank leaned on the railing along the boardwalk in front of the hotel and watched the dwindling figures of Conrad and Rebel as they rode out of Ophir. Lifting his right hand, Frank looked at the palm. The burn he had gotten when he snuffed out that fuse was almost healed now. Another few days and he would be able to draw a gun as well as ever.

But he hoped he would never have to. The past few weeks had been packed full of excitement and danger, but he was getting too old for these rowdy-dows. Seeing Conrad and Rebel together made him think again about grandchildren. The time was coming for him to settle down. . . .

A man riding past the hotel caught Frank's attention. The man was roughly dressed and had a lean, wolflike quality about him. He wore a gun strapped low on his thigh. He was looking at Frank with mean, narrowed eyes, eyes that glittered with recognition. The man paused his horse for a second, but then rode on, turning in at a saloon down the street.

Later today or tomorrow at the latest,

Frank thought with a sigh. The challenge would come then. That stranger fancied himself good with a gun, and the thoughts that had gone through his head as he recognized Frank were plain to read on his face. He figured he was going to be the man who finally outdrew and gunned down The Drifter.

What was that old saying? The more things changed, the more they stayed the same? Frank drew in a deep breath. The mountain air was crisp and clean.

But he thought he smelled a faint hint of gun smoke in it . . . before he realized that the scent clung to him.

In Lordsburg's jail that night, Clark Tarleton lay on a hard, uncomfortable bunk and wondered just how everything had gone wrong, as he had wondered every night for the past week. Luck had always been with him, but now it seemed to have deserted him.

He would get it back. He would win in the end, he told himself. He always had. He had plenty of money to hire the best lawyers in the country. No prosecutor in some backwater territory would put him behind bars permanently. Besides, he had friends, powerful friends, who would come to his aid. They couldn't afford to do otherwise, because he knew as much incriminating information about them as they knew about him. It was only a matter of time before he was free.

Footsteps sounded in the corridor that ran through the center of the cell block. Other than that, the place was quiet. There were only a few other prisoners, and they were all asleep.

The footsteps came to a stop outside the door of Tarleton's cell. One of the guards checking on him? Tarleton swung his legs off the bunk and stood up, seeing the dark bulk of the man through the bars. The only light in the cell block was all the way down at the other end of the corridor, so the visitor's face was in shadow.

After a moment of silence, Tarleton demanded impatiently, "Well? What is it?"

"Tarleton?" the man asked in a whisper.

"Yes. Damn it, man, speak up."

"I've got a message for you from a friend. A friend back in Boston."

Tarleton stepped closer to the bars. "It's damned well about time."

The stranger's hand came up from his side, and for a second Tarleton couldn't comprehend that the man held a knife. Then, as understanding dawned on him, he opened his mouth and tried to shout in

458

alarm. Before any sound could come out, however, the man's hand shot between the bars, grabbed Tarleton's shirt, and yanked him forward. The razor-sharp blade sank easily into Tarleton's throat, cutting off any outcry. The stranger yanked the knife to the side, opening a huge wound. He stepped back quickly as blood spurted. Tarleton fell to his knees, clawing at the bars as he went down. His mouth opened and closed, but no sound came out except a little gurgle that couldn't have been heard more than a few feet away. Tarleton's grip on the bars slipped and he fell over backward. A dark pool formed and widened around his head as he twitched a few times and then lay still.

The stranger squatted and reached through the bars one more time, wiped the blade clean on one leg of Tarleton's trousers, and then walked quietly out of the cell block without looking back.

The next day, in an office in Boston, a door opened and a clerk came in. He laid a telegram on the desk belonging to the man whose office this was. The man picked up the telegram, read the words printed on it, and nodded. "Thank you, Harding," he said. The clerk left.

The man at the desk leaned back in his

chair and steepled his fingers in front of him. It would have been better, of course, if everything had worked out and Tarleton had handled his part of the plan successfully. But he hadn't, and at least Tarleton was dead now, so that he could never reveal the name of his partner in the scheme. All the tracks were covered, so to speak. No one would ever be able to connect the man at the desk with Clark Tarleton or the Southwestern and Pacific Railroad.

A shame about the spur line, but he hadn't been all that interested in that part of the plan in the first place. As far as he was concerned, the idea was to cause enough trouble for Conrad Browning so that Conrad would turn to his father for help. That was exactly what had happened. Frank Morgan had come galloping to the rescue, as the man at the desk had known he would, and time and again, Morgan had been a hairbreadth away from death.

But somehow he had always dodged it. Morgan was the luckiest man on the face of the earth. Either that, or the very best at what he did . . .

The man at the desk sighed. He was tired of living in fear. For five years now, ever since the death of Vivian Browning, he had expected to look up and see Frank Morgan in front of him, ready to claim his vengeance. Well, no more. No more! This gambit might have failed, but it was only the first move in the game. The man's right hand clenched into a fist and slammed down on the desk.

Inside the quiet, elegant office with its dark walls and shelves of law books, Charles Dutton trembled with anger — and not a little fear — and said hoarsely, "Frank Morgan, it's time for you to die."

Afterword

Notes from the Old West

In the small town where I grew up, there were two movie theaters. The Pavilion was one of those old-timey movie show palaces, built in the heyday of Mary Pickford and Charlie Chaplin — the silent era of the 1920s. By the 1950s, when I was a kid, the Pavilion was a little worn around the edges, but it was still the premier theater in town. They played all those big Technicolor biblical Cecil B. DeMille epics and corny MGM musicals. In Cinemascope, of course.

On the other side of town was the Gem, a somewhat shabby and run-down grind house with sticky floors and torn seats. Admission was a quarter. The Gem booked low-budget "B" pictures (remember the Bowery Boys?), war movies, horror flicks, and Westerns. I liked the Westerns best. I could usually be found every Saturday at the Gem, along with my best friend, New-

462

ton Trout, watching Westerns from 10 A.M. until my father came looking for me around suppertime. (Sometimes Newton's dad was dispatched to come fetch us.) One time, my dad came to get me right in the middle of *Abilene Trail*, which featured the now-forgotten Whip Wilson. My father became so engrossed in the action he sat down and watched the rest of it with us. We didn't get home until after dark, and my mother's meat loaf was a pan of gray ashes by the time we did. Though my father and I were both in the doghouse the next day, this remains one of my fondest childhood memories. There was Wild Bill Elliot, and Gene Autry, and Roy Rogers, and Tim Holt, and, a little later, Rod Cameron and Audie Murphy. Of these newcomers, I never missed an Audie Murphy Western, because Audie was sort of an antihero. Sure, he stood for law and order and was an honest man, but sometimes he had to go around the law to uphold it. If he didn't play fair, it was only because he felt hamstrung by the laws of the land. Whatever it took to get the bad guys, Audie did it. There were no finer points of law, no splitting of legal hairs. It was instant justice, devoid of long-winded lawyers, bored or biased jurors, or black-robed, often corrupt judges.

Steal a man's horse and you were the guest of honor at a necktie party.

Molest a good woman and you got a bullet in the heart or a rope around the gullet. Or at the very least, got the crap beat out of you. Rob a bank and face a hail of bullets or the hangman's noose.

Saved a lot of time and money, did frontier justice.

That's all gone now, I'm sad to say. Now you hear, "Oh, but he had a bad childhood" or "His mother didn't give him enough love" or "The homecoming queen wouldn't give him a second look and he has an inferiority complex." Or "cultural rage," as the politically correct bright boys refer to it. How many times have you heard some self-important defense attorney moan, "The poor kids were only venting their hostilities toward an uncaring society?"

Mule fritters, I say. Nowadays, you can't even call a punk a punk anymore. But don't get me started.

It was, "Howdy, ma'am" time too. The good guys, antihero or not, were always respectful to the ladies. They might shoot a bad guy five seconds after tipping their hat to a woman, but the code of the West demanded you be respectful to a lady.

Lots of things have changed since the heyday of the Wild West, haven't they? Some for the good, some for the bad.

I didn't have any idea at the time that I would someday write about the West. I just knew that I was captivated by the Old West.

When I first got the itch to write, back in the early 1970s, I didn't write Westerns. I started by writing horror and action adventure novels. After more than two dozen novels, I began thinking about developing a Western character. From those initial musings came the novel *The Last Mountain Man: Smoke Jensen.* That was followed by *Preacher: The First Mountain Man.* A few years later, I began developing the Last Gunfighter series. Frank Morgan is a legend in his own time, the fastest gun west of the Mississippi . . . a title and a reputation he never wanted, but can't get rid of.

The Gunfighter series is set in the waning days of the Wild West. Frank Morgan is out of time and place, but still, he is pursued by men who want to earn a reputation as the man who killed the legendary gunfighter. All Frank wants to do is live in peace. But he knows in his heart that dream will always be just that: a dream, fog and smoke and mirrors, something elusive that will never really come to fruition. He will be forced to wander the West, alone, until one day his luck runs out.

For me, and for thousands — probably millions — of other people (although many will never publicly admit it), the old Wild West will always be a magic, mysterious place: a place we love to visit through the pages of books; characters we would like to know . . . from a safe distance; events we would love to take part in, again, from a safe distance. For the old Wild West was not a place for the faint of heart. It was a hard, tough, physically demanding time. There were no police to call if one faced adversity. One faced trouble alone, and handled it alone. It was rugged individualism: something that appeals to many of us.

I am certain that is something that appeals to most readers of Westerns.

I still do on-site research (whenever possible) before starting a Western novel. I have wandered over much of the West, prowling what is left of ghost towns. Stand in the midst of the ruins of these old towns, use a little bit of imagination, and one can conjure up life as it used to be in the Wild West. The rowdy Saturday nights, the tinkling of a piano in a saloon, the laughter of cowboys and miners letting off steam after a week of hard work. Use a little more imagination and one can envision two men standing in the street, facing one another, seconds before the hook and draw of a gunfight. A moment later, one is dead and the other rides away.

The old wild untamed West.

There are still some ghost towns to visit, but they are rapidly vanishing as time and the elements take their toll. If you want to see them, make plans to do so as soon as possible, for in a few years, they will all be gone.

And so will we.

Stand in what is left of the Big Thicket country of east Texas and try to imagine how in the world the pioneers managed to get through that wild tangle. I have wondered about that many times and marveled at the courage of the men and women who slowly pushed westward, facing dangers that we can only imagine.

Let me touch briefly on a subject that is very close to me: firearms. There are some so-called historians who are now claiming that firearms played only a very insignificant part in the settlers' lives. They claim that only a few were armed. What utter, stupid nonsense! What do these so-called historians think the pioneers did for food? Do they think the early settlers rode down to the nearest supermarket and bought their meat? Or maybe they think the settlers chased down deer or buffalo on foot and beat the animals to death with a club. I have a news flash for you so-called historians: The settlers used guns to shoot their game. They used guns to defend hearth and home against Indians on the warpath. They used guns to protect themselves from outlaws. Guns are a part of Americana. And always will be.

The mountains of the West and the remains of the ghost towns that dot those areas are some of my favorite subjects to write about. I have done extensive research on the various mountain ranges of the West and go back whenever time permits. I sometimes stand surrounded by the towering mountains and wonder how in the world the pioneers ever made it through. As hard as I try and as often as I try, I simply cannot imagine the hardships those men and women endured over the hard months of their incredible journey. None of us can. It is said that on the Oregon Trail alone, there are at least two bodies in lonely, unmarked graves for every mile of that journey. Some students of the West say the number of dead is at least twice that. And nobody knows the exact number of wagons that impatiently started out alone and simply vanished on the way, along with their occupants, never to be seen or heard from again.

Just vanished.

The one-hundred-and-fifty-year-old ruts of the wagon wheels can still be seen in various places along the Oregon Trail. But if you plan to visit those places, do so quickly, for they are slowly disappearing. And when they are gone, they will be lost forever, except in the words of Western writers.

As long as I can peck away at a keyboard and find a company to publish my work, I will not let the Old West die. That I promise you.

As The Drifter in the Last Gunfighter series, Frank Morgan has struck a responsive chord among the readers of frontier fiction. Perhaps it's because he is a human man, with all of the human frailties. He is not a superhero. He likes horses and dogs and treats them well. He has feelings and isn't afraid to show them or admit that he has them. He longs for a permanent home, a place to hang his hat and sit on the porch in the late afternoon and watch the day slowly fade into night . . . and a woman to share those simple pleasures with him. But Frank also knows he can never relax his vigil and probably will never have that long-wished-for hearth and home. That is why he is called The Drifter. Frank Morgan knows there are men who will risk their lives to face him in a hook and draw, slap leather, pull that big iron, in the hopes of killing the West's most famous gunfighter, so they can claim the title of the man who killed Frank Morgan, The Drifter. Frank would gladly, willingly, give them that title, but not at the expense of his own life.

So Frank Morgan must constantly drift, staying on the lonely trails, those out-of-the-way paths through the timber, the mountains, the deserts that are sometimes called the hoot-owl trail. His companions are the sighing winds, the howling of wolves, the yapping of coyotes, and a few, very few, precious memories. And his six-gun. Always, his six-gun.

Frank is also pursued by something else: progress. The towns are connected by telegraph wires. Frank is recognized wherever he goes and can be tracked by telegraphers. There is no escape for him. Reporters for various newspapers are always on his trail, wanting to interview Frank Morgan, as are authors, wanting to do more books about the legendary gunfighter. Photographers want to take his picture, if possible with the body of a man Frank has just killed. Frank is disgusted by the whole thing and wants no part of it. There is no real rest for The Drifter. Frank travels on, always on the move. He tries to stay off the more heavily traveled roads, sticking to lesser-known trails, sometimes making his own route of travel, across the mountains or deserts.

Someday perhaps Frank will find some peace. Maybe. But if he does, that is many books from now.

The West will live on as long as there are writers willing to write about it, and publishers willing to publish it. Writing about the West is wide open, just like the old Wild West. Characters abound, as plentiful as the wide-open spaces, as colorful as a sunset on the Painted Desert, as restless as the ever-sighing winds. All one has to do is use a bit of imagination. Take a stroll through the cemetery at Tombstone, Arizona; read the inscriptions. Then walk the main street of that once-infamous town around midnight and you might catch a glimpse of the ghosts that still wander the town. They really do. Just ask anyone who lives there. But don't be afraid of the apparitions, they won't hurt you. They're just out for a quiet stroll.

The West lives on. And as long as I am alive, it always will.

William W. Johnstone